The PRINCE OF POISON

The
PRINCE
OF
POISON

A Novel

PAMELA KAUFMAN

THREE RIVERS PRESS • NEW YORK

Reader's Group Guide copyright © 2006 by
Three Rivers Press, an imprint of the Crown Publishing Group,
a division of Random House, Inc.

This is a work of fiction. Names, characters, places, and incidents either
are the product of the author's imagination or are used fictitiously.

Published in the United States by Three Rivers Press, an imprint of the
Crown Publishing Group, a division of Random House, Inc., New York.
www.crownpublishing.com

THREE RIVERS PRESS and the Tugboat design are registered trademarks of
Random House, Inc.

Library of Congress Cataloging-in-Publication Data

Kaufman, Pamela.
The prince of poison : a novel / Pamela Kaufman.—1st ed.
 1. Richard I, King of England, 1157–1199—Relations with
women—Fiction. 2. Eleanor, of Aquitaine, Queen, consort of
Henry II, King of England, 1122–1204—Fiction. 3. Great
Britain—History—John, 1199–1216—Fiction. 4. John, King of
England, 1167–1216—Fiction. 5. Illegitimate children of royalty—
Fiction. 6. Kings and rulers—Succession—Fiction. 7. British—
France—Fiction. 8. Pregnant women—Fiction. I. Title.
PS3561.A8617P75 2006   2005011226

ISBN-13: 978-1-4000-8063-2
ISBN-10: 1-4000-8063-0

Printed in the United States of America

Design by Namik Minter

10 9 8 7 6 5 4 3 2 1

First Edition

To Theo

Enoch and England

BOOK ONE

Enoch. Suddenly the very name was a sunburst in my soul. I'd dwelt so completely on the fact that his death was a lie, that Richard had lied to me, that I hadn't been fully aware till this moment of the portent of that lie. Enoch lived, that was the miracle, as remarkable as if I'd learned that my father and mother awaited me at Wanthwaite. . . . There was a long hazardous road ahead with Enoch, and I wasn't ready to ride it yet.

Meantime, it was enough to know that he breathed the same air I did, knew dawn and sunset, hope and despair. He might hate me forever, but I was still glad he lived.

Now I must face the physical dangers at my heels. I walked to Sea Mew and mounted. Hamo and Bok, dressed as gardeners, mounted as well.

Had the death knell stopped ringing, or were we beyond its reach? Above, an invisible lark trilled its song.

"Where is the closest port where we might sail with safety?" I asked Hamo.

Surprised at my purposeful tone, he thought a moment. "Bordeaux. It's the queen's favorite city, but she rarely goes there."

"Which way?"

He pointed directly toward the sun, where it already rested at a blinding angle on the topmost branches, and beyond to the long slope to the sea.

"Stay low as we cross the mead," I ordered.

Once again the world transformed itself, not from rain to tears or to diamonds, but to sunstruck sea spray.

I bent and whispered to Sea Mew. "It's time to swim the channel, darling. Hoyt!"

Ears raised with joy, he flew fast as a bird toward the radiance that was England.

FROM *Banners of Gold*

1

ENOCH AND ENGLAND.

Enoch and England.

My head nodded to the rhythm of the hooves.

You're being followed.

You're being followed.

I woke with a start. Ahead of me, Bok and Hamo were already dismounted—they'd heard it, too.

"Quick, off your horse!" Hamo grabbed my reins.

"Not here! Bordeaux!"

The hoofbeats behind us were getting closer.

Bok jerked me to the ground. "Into that oak—climb high! Quick, Lady Alix! It's your life!" He adjusted his nose-guard.

One oak among small pines. Beyond them, the sea washed a wide beach.

Hamo barked from his horse. "Take cover—we'll avoid fighting if we can!" Both had discarded their gardening tunics. "We'll guard your horse!" They rode toward the north with Sea Mew behind them.

I was alone, with only the pines, the oak, and a pile of brush on the scrubby landscape. My heart pounded like a kettle in the absolute silence—well, not absolute, angry rooks flapped from the oak and, on the far side of a line of spindly baby pines, the sea's hissing rolled and retreated. Now male voices rumbled over the sound of hooves. King John! *Deus juva me!*

I dashed to the oak, tripped on my borrowed nun's habit, and fell heavily onto my gravid stomach! When I could breathe again, I crawled toward the oak. Too late to climb—horses were here, the male voices clear—I crouched behind the thick trunk and just hoped it sufficed, barely before royal routiers pushed into sight.

One pointed to where I'd dismounted. "*Ils se sont arretées ici.*"

"*Pas pour longtemps. Tu vois les traces qui diregent vers le nord?*"

The first laughed derisively. "*C'est sans doute un ruse. Le roi dit qu'elle essayerait d'atteindre un port—Bordeaux est le plus proche.*"

Never underestimate his intelligence, I heard Richard warn. Aye, if intelligence be to seize the throne from Richard's unborn son I was now carrying, but to know I was planning to escape through Bordeaux! More than intelligent—the man was uncanny! At least his knights had been too distracted by the hoofprints to see me!

Eleven horsemen had dismounted to examine the hoofprints. Suddenly they fell to their knees—King John rode into sight. He looked much as I'd seen him not an hour ago at Fontevrault, except that he appeared even more inebriated. Dressed in the long red tunic of a Plantagenet king, he held a flask in his glove, from which he drank before he looked. He'd finished his pork rib, though a faint dribble of fat ran down his chin. When he tried to dismount, he sprawled on the ground.

"*Bitte, je suis bourré!*" He giggled helplessly. "*Je suis dans le vigne du seigneur!*"

Two knights helped him to his feet, as if accustomed to this task.

"Have you found the bitch?" the king asked thickly.

The knight on his right, a short man with a nose like a parrot's beak, pointed to the hoof marks.

"A trick, you stupid pissants!" John staggered along the tracks. "Her guards went north and she's probably hidden somewhere close." He looked up into my oak. "You find her knights—I'll take care of the slut."

The man with the parrot nose had to wear his noseguard to the side. Nevertheless, the giant formidable destriers made me fear for poor Hamo and Bok.

"So we're alone." John emptied his flask and tossed it away. "No hurry." He laughed. For the first time, I felt real fear; drunkalew he might be, but he was dangerous. "Time to fuck, time to die! After you give me the document you promised." He shook his head. "Or, promised. And I waited while you went to fetch it from the convent." He belched softly. "Do you believe the philosophers who say that love and death are connected? Mesiphisically—metaphysically—do you?"

He reached under his tunic to find his tool, then pissed into a bush. When he'd shaken himself dry, he whined, "Why didn't you give me Richard's document when I asked you at Fontevrault, eh? I asked you nicely, didn't I? That's all I want. Must I destroy both you and Richard's brat to get the will? My very first act as king and it's your fault!" He fondled himself. "But why shouldn't I? *Comus*, I'm king!" He whinnied in jubilant disbelief. "Only your silly bulge between me and security!" He guffawed louder. "As if my faggot brother could push his pathetic worm into your slit!"

He staggered closer; I could smell piss, wine, starch, and rosewater. He stroked his part. "Yet somebody made you gravid, *putaine*, and you might be clever enough to fool Richard, but not baby John."

He reached the oak. We stared at each other without speaking. He was handsome in the Angevin manner: dark blond wavy hair and beard, full firm lips, straight nose, fringed eyes like icy blue jewels, shifting triangles of sunlight. Yet his face was deadly, deadly and cruel.

"Die." His low musical voicie caressed the word. "*Oc*, die." He belched. "*Most beautiful damsel in all Europe*, Richard used to brag. He was right and—unlike him—I'm the expert." He bent close to whisper. "Is your slit beautiful? Can it compete with a boy's anus? That was Richard's taste!" His beard smelled of his pork. "Your face, like a cherub. Aye, my brother sought angelic boys to suck his limp little cock." He put a finger to my lips. "You're about to have a treat!"

He sank to the ground beside me. He reached inside his tunic and pulled out a sharp blade. "Don't be so frightened, sweet; this is merely to assure that you do my bidding." Now he fumbled for his cock again. "Treat, I'll give you a treat, and you'll give me a treat. I like your big titties—is that because you're English or because you carry a brat? French women have no tits! Curious thing, racial characteristics!" He nodded sagely. "Zample: all Normans have big horns in their crotches, like me. Richard was an Aquitanian."

He raised his hips so his tool stood upright. It was, indeed, impressive.

"Grand, isn't he?" He stroked himself. "I call him Raoul; Raoul, meet the most beautiful damsel in all Europe." He reached for my face—his blade pressed the back of my neck. "While I suck your *bloblos,* you'll enjoy Raoul, my *chauve a col roulé.* Turn around! And then . . ." His voice thickened. "Copulation, followed by death. God's feet, it's titillating, isn't it? Philosphers may be right!"

Was I really about to die? Aye, I thought I was—was there no escape? I saw only one.

"Suck my cock!"

I bit Raoul hard! Blood spurted! The dagger fell to the grass!

"Merde!" the king howled.

Where could I hide? Everything open! Then, a rock, out in the sea! I ran toward the surf!

Panting and belching, King John gained upon me. I sobbed—his hand clutched at my tunic—I wrenched away! Leaped over the pile of brush!

"Merde!"

Then suddenly everything was quiet. The rolling waves spread frothy fingers in the sand in stillness. I glanced over my shoulder—my pace slowed. Stopped. Where was the king? Was it a trick? Nothing but small pines, the oak, and the mound of branches. The king's horse munched at new grass. I glanced to the north for his knights, then moved back cautiously to the pile of branches between me and the tree. As I drew close, I heard him—sobs, curses, scratching sounds. The brush had concealed a deer trap! The king had fallen in! Aye, there was a clear hole where he'd stumbled.

"My lord king?" I called softly. What would I do if he were injured?

Cautiously, I peered over the edge. The hole was deep—

even standing, John reached hopelessly for the edge. The pit smelled strongly of rotting deer flesh and vomit from former victims.

John saw me!

"Help me, Lady Alix." The king raised his arms, sobbing. "Help your monarch! You can go free, I promise on my word as king, and I'll not chase you more. Your babe can live—you can live. Please!"

"Will you tell your knights to let my men go free?"

"Yes! 'Tis done! On the word of a king! Please, oh, please!" His voice broke. "If you just reach your hand . . ."

"It's too far—can you stand?"

"I think so!" He climbed on the pile of branches that had fallen with him, then clawed on small roots along the side to pull himself closer. "I'll never forget, Lady Alix! Never!" he grunted. "Richard said you were an angel, and you are!"

It was the wrong thing to say; I hesitated. Raoul twisted and turned his avid head like an adder. I withdrew my hand. "An angel, you say?"

"Oui, une ange!"

Now I was hedging for time. I didn't want his demise on my conscience, yet this man was an evil person, clever beyond belief, and he'd threatened me within the last hour. Yet angels don't kill. Nor do they get killed if they have any brains.

"Angels never copulate," I whispered. "The nuns at Fontevrault said this. So I couldn't be an angel, could I?" Not an angel, perhaps, but not a devil either—I couldn't leave him to die.

"An immaculate conception!" John cried. "You're another Mary!"

"Only if King Richard was God, for this is Richard's child, the rightful king of England." I heard horses—quick, where could I hide? Not in the oak! The sea? Aye, the black rock loomed just beyond the surf!

"Stop prattling like a pedant!"

"Oh, not pedantry, my lord!" I rose to my feet—I must run soon, before I was seen! I called softly, "Your knights are coming!"

"Your hand!" But I was running.

Holding my document high, I dashed into the sea—*Deo gratias* that Enoch had taught me to swim!

"Wait!" John howled. "Where are you?"

The first knight broke through the bushes as I plunged. Tide going out—half crawling and half swimming, I headed to the low rock. Like the time Enoch and I had dipped into the Mediterranean long ago, I opened my mouth to cleanse it. I grabbed at an island of floating seapods so I could be certain of John's fate. He was already out of the trap; his knights pointed back toward Fontevrault while he pointed to the sea. One voice sounded across the surf, "No maiden knows how to swim!"

"She's not a maiden, you fool! After her!" John seemed more sober and angrier after his adventure.

But the knights argued about his royal obligations. Well did I know the routine, for hadn't it been mine until he'd stolen the throne? Still, he protested—like all his family, he hated to fail. This time he had no choice: he must reach Rouen before some other usuperer claimed the crown, there to be inducted as duke of Normandy, then on to Canterbury for the crowning.

Yet he must also walk to the sea before he agreed to return. "You had your chance, bitch! I'm leaving Sir Christopher to finish you!"

The instant he disappeared into the trees, his knight rode with all haste toward Bordeaux!

Nevertheless, I was cautious. The moon rode high and still I sat on my rock waiting for Bok and Hamo. Should I leave without them? Perhaps they'd left without me. I couldn't blame them if they had; though I'd called them my "knights," neither was dubbed. And they'd volunteered only to get me to a port. Yet time was passing and I must retrieve my horse. I would give them three hundred more heartbeats.

I was beginning to tremble. The recent horrors of deception at Fontevrault—a waxy Richard on his death bier, so like life, so really dead—was etched in my rational cell forever; yet why should I tremble? King John was only a buffoon! The real person to fear was Queen Eleanor; it was her poison I dreaded the most. John, though now arrogant of his new power, had created only mischief in his talented family—albeit vicious mischief—and had failed more than he'd succeeded. He was a mosquito to be smacked, not a serpent under my pillow. Furthermore, now that he was king by royal proclamation, he had to solidify his position, then rule. For him, I *was* a mosquito.

Though I didn't covet England's crown except for my babe, I envied John's safe return to England. Whatever his problems, he wouldn't face a disenchanted spouse. I yearned for Enoch, aye, but I had to face that the feeling might not be mutual. Would he believe that I'd thought him dead? That I would never *never* have become Richard's concubine if I'd thought Enoch still lived? Or would he point out the truth that I'd been a willing—nay, eager—concubine of the seductive king? The truth was murky. I didn't deny that I'd yearned for King Richard's love when I'd been disguised as a young "boy" on crusade, but never after I'd wed Enoch. And I'd succumbed finally only because I'd been told that my husband was dead. And it was a Scot who'd told me—would Enoch see my side?

Was Bordeaux guarded? Certainly, it was now—I should confound expectation and head north. What a strange dilemma—I was free to do what? I had Bonel's gift of diamonds, but no way to turn them into livres. Yet I must purchase passage somewhere.

Enoch lived! I hugged myself, thinking of my darling Scot, the true love of my life. And Richard's babe? Enoch's babe, for he was my legal husband.

Yes, Enoch's child by law, but *mine* by feeling.

The beach appeared smaller and the sea lapped at my back after a long period of dryness. Was the tide returning? Aye, and dawn. I must go. My habit floated till and fro around my knees; I'd lost my shoes.

I washed my mouth again.

John, *ita me deus juvet.* Only a harmless boy? Was ambition harmless? Was deception? Was rape? Or murder? Questions now for some other poor wretch. Enoch had taught me that not all men were rapacious villains, but there were sufficient numbers to make a woman's life dangerous. I left the beach to walk next to the forest.

Suddenly, I saw a horseman approaching from the north. He wore the blue insignia of France. Nevertheless, I hid in the forest until he passed.

Unaccustomed to bare feet, I stumbled again and again on roots twisted across the path. Once I fell hard, panted with pain, perhaps broke my toe. Oh, where was Sea Mew? I limped on.

Finally exhausted, I realized I must hide in the forest until nightfall. Yet I hesitated—a boar bellowed his chilling roar within ten feet. I moved forward out of his range. Now I was stopped by rustlings and splashes that might be birds but were more likely snakes. I waded into the forest—a swamp of dead trees; I sank to my knees in muck. Gnats clouded my vision and filled my mouth. Would I prefer King John? His first virtue: He gave me courage.

Then suddenly I stepped onto solid ground. I'd entered a sunny cove with a black pool in its center where scarlet bleeding hearts were doubled in black water; red trumpet vines wound around beautiful and deadly sumacs. A large flat rock in the middle offered succor just before I fell with exhaustion. My eyes closed.

My free hand kneaded something sticky, an object trapped in the quicksand. Bony—a dead animal?

Bok's decapitated head!

My heart squeezed in horror, then fear—was anyone still near? Had a boar done this? I forced myself to examine the head more closely—no, a sword. Had John's men murdered him? Where was Hamo?

I heard nothing but my own shallow breath, saw nothing.

I examined the head again. Certainly some cutting weapon, and yet—this didn't look like a professional assault. In my preoccupation with King John, I'd forgotten the many outlaws hiding in the wood.

For dead Bok, it didn't matter. Sinews and bones and veins and blood everywhere. No wonder I'd seen so much red—this was a charnal chamber! Bok's horse—also decapitated! Everyone dead.

Except, again . . . Where was Hamo? Was it possible that Hamo himself had done the deed?

My horse? Was Sea Mew the reason for this?

Averting my eyes from the grinning head, I searched Bok's body, then the equipment on his horse. A dagger, a slab of wormy bacon in his saddlebag, three deniers in his right boot, his helmet, which could serve as a water bucket. I thrust one sore foot into his boot and—the biggest surprise—his boots fitted me perfectly. I'd just managed to pull both of them on when something moved in the wood ahead.

Sea Mew, my beloved horse! He dripped water on me— he'd found a fesh spring! He was an omen! He and I would survive! A pox on all outlaws, on Hamo if he was one! I filled my helmet from Sea Mew's spring, then again lay back on the rock. No point exposing myself on the road. The darkness with its own hazards was better than light.

The sun shone small as a sparrow's egg when I rose again.

I threw a few red flowers across Bok, whispered a prayer, and led Sea Mew onto the road. Once I could leave this cursed land, once I was in England, I would be safe. I'd escaped King John, hadn't I? I'd avoided the butcher in the wood, I was heading home to have my baby at Wanthwaite, and Enoch was alive! *Enoch and England.* I laughed silently.

Sardines. Sardines? Aye, frying in clear olive oil, hundreds of them. Succulent, fresh, no worms to pick out as I did with my bacon slab. Was I going totty? No, I caught a real whiff— sardines! Aye, sardines! I must be close to La Rochelle! The port Queen Eleanor had created from a tiny fishing village to export salt and wine to England.

I must cross misty salt flats, then climb a high dune before I could see La Rochelle's city wall. The chapel bell had just rung *basse prime* by the time I reached the dune; a crenellated wall made of sandstone encircled the small city; above the wall, tall masts of the sardine fleet swayed slowly as they docked with the night's catch. They were in a channel between La Rochelle and the islands of Ré and Oléron, a channel too shallow to accommodate seagoing vessels; the queen had constructed a long seawall south of the city where her fleet anchored. A tall seagoing ship lay there at this moment. My heart raced. Bok's three deniers would surely purchase the fish, and one of Bonel's diamonds might secure passage on the tall ship!

I scrambled down the cityside of the dune, then hesitated. *Be cautious.*

After I'd placed Sea Mew on the shady side of the dune where he munched on purple blooms, I climbed a spindly tree for a better view. Two young boys, yawning and pounding their hands together, took their places as guards at a double door in the wall. They wore short red tunics and high black boots, and carried swords, though they didn't appear to be knights—I doubted if they yet had beards. They marched till and fro aimlessly, stopping to chat each time they passed one another.

As the sun rose, the odor of sardines grew stronger. The silly guards slumped against the wall. One yawned and stretched. I began to descend. At the last moment, I paused; a young woman approached the city from the hills in a donkey cart loaded with grapes. I would wait for her to go first. Her cart wobbled dangerously on wheels of different sizes; a few grapes rolled off the top. What a charming lass with her wide straw hat and flaxen braids, what a bucolic sight! She made me smile—did the guards smile as well?

They apparently asked for a pass. *Deus juva me,* I had no pass. She did, though. The young guards handed it back and forth to each other at least three times—couldn't they read? They apparently asked her to step down—what was wrong with her pass? On the cobbles and upright, her scarlet tunic billowed around a bulge in her middle—she was pregnant, mayhap four months along. Like me.

The guard on the right punched her abdomen. She doubled forward, clutching herself. At the second strike, she screamed. I waddled down the dune to help her, then stopped, horrified. I was too late—she lay supine on the cobbles. Now both the guards kicked her again and again. One knelt beside her and said something to the other, who promptly pulled a stone from the wall and cracked her head open.

The guards each took a foot and dragged her inside the wall.

They were back almost at once. One picked something off the other's shoulder. Together, they examined the cart, then threw grapes into each other's mouths.

I burrowed into the sand close to Sea Mew. Could anyone see me? What a stupid ass I'd been to imagine that I'd escaped King John! *Deus juva me*, he was killing every gravid young woman in the kingdom! Or was it those close to ports? Or in red? A buffoon? The ineffective baby brother Richard had so indulged? John was a ruthless criminal! King of England— poor England! And he wanted to kill *me*, aye, kill me and my babe. How had I ever thought he was just a buffoon? The common illusion! Oh God, that poor peasant girl! I stuffed my mouth with sand and almost choked! Then I trembled so the sand cracked above me even as I let my water soak it below me. I didn't care.

Oh God! Jesus! *Deus juva me!*

The sun was high in its run when my mind turned from panic to purpose. My parents had been murdered, aye, bru- tally slain, by Lord Roland de Roncechaux. I'd flown for help then, but in the end I'd killed Lord Roland myself, hadn't I? I wouldn't be gravid forever, and after this babe was born . . .

Enoch and England, more than a sunburst, a necessity! Oh God, I must get to England!

But the ports—that dead peasant girl—think! Think! Bonel.

True, the Jew was the king's man, but he also protected people the king assaulted. And he felt for me—what? He'd kissed me once, told me . . . Aye, Bonel must protect me until my prince was born, and then . . .

Yet I cringed with shame. Hadn't Bonel warned me that King Richard had exploited me? Aye, Richard had used me, and his brother wanted to kill me. Very well, I'd been used and attacked. So be it. No point reviewing the past. Think of the future. John had knights, wealth, position, even his sex in his favor, but I would win. I didn't need to rehearse my own advantages—I knew them. King John thought he was King Herod of old, but it takes only one person, one babe, to upset such savagery.

And, admit it, I'd been stupid before. Even in Fontevrault Wood I'd thought I could escape the "silly boy" brother. No more. Confident, aye, but wary. Vengeance. For the peasant girl in red, for others I might never know, for myself. I would prefer not to kill. Enoch had studied the law in Paris, and he could guide me legally to a solution. It had to be done craftily and permanently.

But first, I must go to Bonel.

At sundown, reborn in my shallow grave, I cast a farewell glance at La Rochelle. Though the aroma of sardines still hung heavy, the peasant girl was gone.

Or was she? A pillar of fire burned where she'd stood; I waved, she waved back.

I stopped at a small swift river by the forest. Sea Mew refused to drink; then I, too, caught the stench of a tanning factory upstream. Nevertheless, I dipped my nun's habit in the river to remove the sea salt, then spread it on a bush to dry. At dawn, I slipped it over my scarlet Plantagenet tunic, fastened my white wimple firmly over my flaxen braids, and, with Bok's boots, was prepared to move again. The king had seen the habit, of course, but could he kill every nun in France?

No, but he could kill every pregnant nun in France. I studied my middle: a slight bulge, easily covered. My breasts, however, were also bulging more every day. Nevertheless, the habit was still voluminous.

When it became dark, I followed the path northward. There were no other travelers that night; at dawn, I turned into the forest to sleep. I continued this pattern until dense forests gave way to occasional fields surrounded by stone walls that enclosed dwellings. Twice I was forced to sleep behind a wall, but most times I could still find natural cover.

Even away from the sea, I caught glimpses of Plantagent red; John was still active in Aquataine.

Though I sliced Bok's bacon thinner and thinner, I finally ran out. Summer was waning—there were no birds' eggs or even birds. Weasels and badgers and squirrels followed me with interest, but evaded my hands. Berry bushes had been cleaned by the departed birds; once I made myself sick by eating all the wormy fruit on a summer apple tree. From the apples, I learned that worms gave sustenance. Earthworms squirmed in my mouth, however, and when I tried to suck them down whole, inside my stomach.

One rainy night, my way was blocked by city walls. I

smelled the tanning factory; the next day, I was able to drink from the stream and even catch a few fish.

It became more difficult to disguise my pregnancy, certainly to myself. I urinated frequently (which slowed my progress considerably); I slept even while riding at night, felt a ravenous hunger. These symptoms, while bothersome, were invisible; not so my body: my breasts seeped, and I carried a mangonel ball in my middle.

A hot mistral dried the vegetation and gave me a headache, then dizziness. The mistral foreshadowed a change of seasons; summer gave way to bitter cold and rain. The soft blue sky descended to an iron lid. Winds howled from the ocean. Sea Mew's hooves sank deep in black mud, and when I dismounted, so did my boots. I huddled under bushes for warmth.

I found a dead bird in the thorns; its flesh was filled with maggots—no matter.

That was disgusting! Give me a golden capon!

Capons are light brown, my lord, not gold! The color comes from egg yolk mixed with ginger!

Then get it for me! I'm a prince!

Aye, my lord, but I'm not a princess. You chose your mother badly.

There was a short silence. *No I did not! I will do such deeds that we can both be proud!*

I stroked my stomach. He continued:

Meantime, must we always be alone? Shouldn't we have company?

My eyes filled. *We'll never be alone—not so long as we have each other! I love you, baby!*

I love you, Mother, came the answer.

God knows, I yearned for love, so perhaps I'd imagined the exchange, but no matter. I would coat his maggots with gold if that's what he wanted, for he was *my* son—not Richard's or John's or Eleanor's or anyone's in the whole world but mine!

Cross the field—we must find shelter.

Hailstones tormented every surface! A sharp fireflash illuminated a hedged area to my right; a second revealed a house and outbuildings. It took a while to find an opening in the hedge, after which Sea Mew had to fend off two fierce dogs.

The first building was a granary, the second a cow byre. Black-and-white cows mooed a gentle welcome and continued munching. I'd just settled into a pile of straw when a brace of feathers attacked my head—a rooster! I wrung his neck, plucked his feathers, and ate him down.

My prince and I stayed in the cow byre for only a week. The mistress milked her cows at sunrise; she always left a little milk in the udders, for which I was grateful. Three hens laid two eggs a day that I ate at once. A small snake came looking for eggs and I ate him, too. I felt worse about the snake than I had the rooster; the snake was only a baby, and it hadn't attacked me. Nevertheless, its meat was sweeter than worms'.

One eve the dame's man came with her to gather eggs.

"If them biddies can't lay, they can go to the table," he growled.

"It's the time of year!" His dame shielded me with her skirt. "You remember last August, how sparse they were."

"I remember that there's a reward out for some criminal in these parts. The king's men were here not a week ago!"

I left the following night, taking only one hen with me. I had gained considerable weight during my sojourn.

I want milk!

I sucked the bones of my hen, which I'd cooked when lightning struck a bush.

Enjoy the marrow!

I need liquid! If you give me any more of that foul swamp water, I'll abort!

The demand of a prince—I knew that imperious cadence.

Holding my three deniers, I gazed down on a small country village on market day. When I descended, a woman with only one eye and a huge wen on her neck stared at my bulge. Three barefoot children clung to her skirts—she must recognize my condition despite my tying a rope as close as possible to my waist and stuffing dry leaves to create huge dangling breasts. Few nuns are pregnant, but many are fat. I waddled past the dame with my nose high.

Flies crawled on the skins of a brace of chickens hanging on a stick, meaning winter must still be far away despite the inclement weather.

"Greeting, Sister." A monk of the Benedictine order spread a gap-toothed smile.

"Greeting," I whispered, and smiled back. He gasped aloud. I'd fastened a dead snail to my upper gum like a boil.

With dirty hands curved like claws, I made the sign of the cross.

"*Domine Jesu Cristi, pace, pace, pace!*

Non sum dignus est intre sub tectum meum . . ."

He was gone.

I sidled to the next booth with cheese rounds aplenty. I showed my three deniers to the wizened dame behind the counter; she quickly selected two of her largest rounds and insisted on giving them to me free, if I would say a prayer for her son, who had the falling sickness. We argued a bit; I would pray forsooth, but I wanted to pay. By the time I left the market, I had my cheeses, a wooden bowl of curds, a sheepskin for the cold nights, and my three deniers.

From behind a bush where my prince and I enjoyed our acquisitions, I heard horses on the road. Drawing back, I watched one of the king's men in his short scarlet tunic emblazoned with the three lions en passant of the Plantagenet house; he was talking to my Benedictine monk, who now quickly threw off his habit.

"*Pas ici,*" said the monk/knight.

After they'd ridden away, I quickly drank my curds.

That's better, my prince approved.

I became more and more lethargic. Distances stretched forever; I slept on my horse. My undergarment—my Plantagenet tunic essential for warmth—had become tight in the middle. Trying to stay awake in daylight so I could see, I undid the stitches at the sides.

From a hillock, I surveyed where the road split below me, one branch leading along the sea in Brittany, one inland toward Angers; two soldiers manned a booth where all travelers had to show passes. The guards, large strapping young men, asked penetrating questions in rough Norman French. All the travelers became totty under their rough scrutiny; I was not the only person in France who feared John's punishment. An elderly merchant tried to protect a gravid young woman, possibly his daughter. Another pregnant woman with four children followed him behind the shed; I hoped they survived.

Would the booth close at sundown? Could I slip by in the dark? Difficult. There was a pile of pine torches behind the booth.

Brittany was out of the question. Anjou was also a Plantagenet stronghold, but I knew how to slip through Angers.

If I only had a pass!

Suddenly, a covey of nuns rode into sight. Talking and laughing and twittering like so many blackbirds, they all pulled passes from their sacks. I spurred Sea Mew to join them. A guard looked at the pass of the head sister only and waved us through. We took the road to Angers.

I soon wearied in the daylight hours. The nun on my right put her hand to steady me.

"*Gracias*," I whispered.

The nun on my left then asked my name in rough country argot.

"Sister Hilaria," I replied.

She seemed satisfied.

Occasional dense forests interspersed with fields. The trees, I noted, were brightly hued.

Colored leaves dropped in our laps at Haute Tierce. A nun helped me dismount, then helped me ease myself to the ground.

"*Soeur Jeanne,*" she said. She knew I was a stranger.

She patted my stomach sympathetically.

"A bollus," I explained.

We both smiled.

Three other nuns offered a crust of bread, a piece of cheese, a boiled egg. Tears rolled down my cheeks.

When we continued, moreover, the first nun sat pillion behind me so I could rest against her.

We entered Angers near dusk on the second day. Again we followed the head nun through the gate without incident. The nun who had ridden with me slipped to her own horse. King Richard had brought me to Angers to show me the great castle where his father had lived as a boy. We passed it now; the park had a herd of grazing deer; flying flags indicated that someone of the royal family was in residence. I could only pray that it wasn't King John.

We rode up a steep hill to the town center. Sister Jeanne indicated that we had reached our destination, but I didn't follow them through the gate to their abbey, a small shabby building in the distance. I spurred Sea Mew to a brisk canter past the hostel, past a large church, past another royal building, until I reached the gate on the opposite side of the city, hoping to beat its closing. A church bell tolled curfew. Behind the royal edifice, I dismounted.

Six guards passed near, talking and japing, on their way to bolt the gate. I flung a loose stone over the wall to alarm them. In an instant, they rushed through the gate to see who had passed without examination. Quickly, I led my horse behind them. Once on the other side, I sank into a cesspool. An arrow whizzed close—they shouted for help—a small army thundered past me. Within a few heartbeats, noisome but safe, I rode along an old Roman road.

The twists of the Seine doubled my distance. Though there was more cover of bush and copses, the countryside was also more populated. Royal soldiers and knights everywhere. I huddled on my sheepskin under dripping bushes by daylight, rode only at night.

When will we get to Bonel's?

The Seine was so high that it swept over Le Pont des Arches in places and completely inundated the old wooden bridge. Breathing deeply, I raised my eyes to Rouen's familiar fortifications, the wall high as six horses with huge rounded towers every few feet. The gate's iron spikes, now closed, rose when the cathedral bell rang *basse prime*. Immediately, a rush of people crowded the swaying arched bridge. Now I whiffed a charred odor emanating from the city.

I caught a farm woman's tunic as she passed. "Is there

something amiss in the city, milady? There's a peculiar odor . . ."

"Where ha'e ye been that ye doona knaw aboot the fire?"

"Fire?" My heart stopped. "Was much destroyed?"

"A good portion o' the town on this side." She crossed herself. "I'm sorry, Sister; mayhap half of Notre-Dame-de-la-Rond war burned." She hesitated. "They do say that a part of the royal castle went as well."

My heart leaped—had King John burned in Hell?

Had Bonel? The Clos des Juifs abutted the square of the burned Cathedral.

I swayed.

"Keerful!" The farm woman grabbed my arm. "Be ye sick?"

"No, I . . ." I stopped; she knew.

"The Pont des Arches be unsteady in this wind—gi'e me yer arm."

The Seine licked the underside of the bridge and twice soaked our feet; I walked at a slant, truly totty. I closed my eyes as the goodwife led me across the flood. The woman proved clever when we reached the gate as well. She screamed that her "Sister" had a fever—and the guard hastened us through. Once inside, I raised my eyes to the square towers of the Jewish synagogue, just visible. I began to weep.

My benefactress pressed a coin into my palm and disappeared into the crowd.

The sky was the hue of a dark-gray goose, the trees thrashed; flags whipped on the towers. The king was in residence. Was I mad? Too late to wonder. Avoiding an animal mess, I stumbled to the opposite side of Sea Mew.

"Sister, remain on my side, if you please!"

I pretended not to hear the guard.

"Sister, wait—you can't—stop her, Jérome!"

The sky belched three fireflashes in rapid succession; the streets became a rivers!

"Alix!"

Deus juva me, I knew the voice! Sir Alain, the wight who'd undressed me with his eyes when I'd ridden pillion behind King Richard.

"Alix, wait! I won't . . ."

The sky split! The street became a melee of animals, rolling gourds, screaming women!

What's happening? cried my prince.

I waddled toward a feeding shed for horses, where even the king occasionally stopped.

Only six steps away! I whispered.

Try seven; it's a better roll.

I grasped the trough for balance. Sea Mew pushed eagerly toward a pile of oats.

Try not to breathe, I ordered.

Now on my hands and knees, awkward, again feeling sick, I pushed at a stack of hay.

I'm corked in a bottle!

If you don't like the wine, try the water!

Then both of us fell silent. Wet black boots topped by a short red tunic stood close to my nose.

"Alix? It is Lady Alix, isn't it? I had a glimpse of your profile . . ."

"Sir Alain! Come quick! A brigade for the king is coming through!"

"I'll be back, sweetheart," Alain promised.

I burrowed deeper.

When I woke, still the storm raged. At least the dark streets had been cleared of brigands and outlaws, not to mention soldiers.

Yet the inability to see disoriented me. Hardly knowing if I walked toward or away from the Seine, I awaited another fireflash to reveal the spires of the cathedral. I would have fallen except for Sea Mew.

"Ahhh!"

I plucked at fat mushy toads on my face—only they were wet leaves. Branches rolled down the cobbles; water torrented in the gutters. Another fireflash outlined the spires of Notre-Dame-de-la-Rond, guiding me toward Bonel's house.

We'd go faster if you'd ride!

I could no longer mount my horse. Slowly, slowly, I pushed up the slope. I stopped frequently. Sweat drenched my entire body. Then I found a haven, the lee side of Notre Dame where the walls seemed intact. Feeling along the sooty stalls, I rounded the corner to be hit again by the elements. I sidled into the exposed square.

I stopped to regain my wits—and pissed! Aye, hot urine flowed down my legs into my boots.

"I'm so sorry! Sorry!" I wailed.

Deo gratias, no one had seen. Yet I couldn't go to Bonel's like this. I lifted my habit—my Plantagenet undertunic wouldn't raise over my belly—and put my hand down to cleanse myself. Oh God, dear God, help me! My urine was sticky—thick as honey. I raised my hand to my nose, then my lips. Blood! I was bleeding! My water had broken!

Clinging to Sea Mew, I sidled forward. I couldn't have much farther to go. Jews' Street ended on the square! Sea Mew tripped—ah!—three steps up above the square, yes, I remembered. I had to beg the horse to go up.

Mincing sideways, my legs close, I put my hand against a splintered post—I smelled soot—the former gate. Oh, thank you, Fire, I could enter directly into the street. But, oh God, let the houses be not burned! I touched a corner and groped—intact! Now the next, a row of connected houses. One—two—three—was it six?

I pulled a bell cord.

"Bonel!" I screamed. "It's me, Alix!"

The door gave way—pitch blackness—female arms.

A male voice: "Alix!"

2

WOMEN CUT OFF MY RED TUNIC, THEN STUDIED MY HEAVING middle under a brilliant torch. They all wore blue scarves close to intent eyes that scrutinized my body. They brought a second torch, pushed gently, and spoke to each other in their harsh Hebrew tongue.

The pain was so intense that I couldn't speak, even if I'd had anything to say. At the same time, I was surprised that it wasn't worse; I recalled my near death when I'd had a premature baby by Richard long ago. By comparison, this was nothing.

Four women remained by my side until dawn, then on through the day, at which point one said in rough French that I must walk. They pulled me upright, put cloth slippers on my feet, and held me by both arms as I attempted to obey. I smiled bitterly, as if I hadn't already walked miles. My bleeding had stopped, though I still felt a flutter that seemed to have descended. I walked in circles.

At least the exercise brought profound sleep; I wakened to the torch again just in time to see a fleshy triangle arch high above me and to hear, "What rhymes with joy?" *Boy*, I thought. I had a son! Instantly, I became weepy; I was alone, separated from him forever. *I miss you, baby*, I thought. There was no reply: I slept again.

When I woke next time, a tiny bundled mite lay beside me. With effort, he opened one slit-eye the color of lapis. I knew he couldn't see me, knew that the lapis would change to some other color in a few days, but I swear that he studied my face. Then he was taken away.

Someone had bound my seeping breasts and my abdomen—I could hardly breathe. I slept so soundly that I could hear myself snore. When was the last time I'd been in a bed?

I was awake. My room was a small airless closet. Footsteps went up and down the hall outside my door, female voices chatted and laughed; twice that day women attended me: My crotch was swathed in fresh linens three times. I smelled of soap. For the first time in months, I was clean. Where was my son?

Morning sounds, the clink of wooden bowls, the smell of fresh eggs.

"Are you hungry?" A familiar female voice—the midwife?

"Where's Bonel?"

"Are you hungry?"

I sighed. "Yes."

She left, then reappeared almost at once with a crust of brown bread, two boiled eggs, a mug of milk.

"Thank you." I watched her warily. "Have we met before?"

"I'm Viette, your midwife." She paused. "A fine boy."

Deo gratias, she spoke in Norman French, albeit with the thick tongue of a cow.

"Is my son . . .?"

"Rachel is his wet nurse."

"When . . . ?"

"Soon."

The instant she left, I fell asleep. Yet, at some level, I worried; I couldn't find the document naming my son as the next king of England. Not that I planned to execute his claim, but even so—had someone stolen it? I must fill in his name: Richard, of course, for his blood father, Enoch for his legal father, William in memory of my father, and Theodore because he was truly a gift from God. Aye, Theo. I would call him Theo.

Where was Bonel?

How could I summon a woman to help me? I needed a bucket.

A young female came at that instant for my bowl and methier; she listened to my request.

"Let me help you."

When I was finished, she cleaned me carefully, then tossed some sweet-smelling herb on the rushes.

I measured the time by the ring of the hours from the cathedral; apparently, the bell tower had not burned. In late afternoon, Viette and two other women walked me down a narrow corridor to a slightly larger closet, which had a small window covered by an oiled linen square. From street sounds, I realized we were in a basement. The wet nurse called Rachel took me to a cradleboard hanging on a wall where Theo was sleeping; another small wizened baby slept on another board. Rachel slowly unwound Theo's swaddling clothes and lifted him down for me to examine.

His face was beautiful—no other word sufficed—with smooth fat cheeks that dimpled when he yawned. He had

very little hair and perfect ears, and he sucked most prodigiously when Rachel tickled his lips. I was glad I'd seen his
single eye, however, since now he didn't wake. His poor wizened body made me weep; so tiny, so weak, so red. My diet of
worms and grubs hadn't agreed with him any more than it had
with me.

"A fine baby boy," his wet nurse said proudly.

"He's fragile."

"Needs a little fat, that's all. I give forth cream, you'll
see!"

I slept and ate, physically comfortable but more and
more anguished and tearful; I wept for the long months I'd
withheld tears.

Where was Bonel?

Then one morning, just before Prime sounded, I was
waked by a hideous scream—Theo! I rolled from my cot and
ran down the long narrow corridor in the direction of his
howls. Murdered, he was being murdered! Half-forgotten
tales of how Jews had committed ritual murders on Christian
children heated my fantastick cell. I burst into a room of men
with long beards, yarmulkas, and curls dangling down their
cheeks. One held a knife over Theo!

"No!" I screamed.

I was too late—my baby was covered with blood.

One man restrained me while another scolded me in Hebrew. The man with the knife finished with his grisly task.
Apparently, they wanted the tip of Theo's member—for
what? Another man lifted my son so I could view Theo's
penis myself, a raw little flower dripping blood. I wept uncontrollably. What a way to die! Would we'd both expired on

the road rather than this! The door opened behind me and
Rachel rushed in. As she spoke rapidly in Hebrew, Theo's
lapis eye opened. Poor mite; he knew nothing of how his life
had been destroyed.

I sobbed even harder. Then, by Rachel's gestures, I realized that she was apologizing for *me!* Not for the butchers,
for me! She swaddled Theo and placed him back on his
cradleboard, where he slept soundly. Rachel led me back to
my closet. Once I was safe on my pad, she laid Theo beside
me. Then, speaking in her mangled French, she explained that
the rabbi had circumcised Theo for his health's sake, did I understand?

Aye, they'd castrated my boy! And he a prince!

She tried again and mollified me somewhat, though I still
couldn't understand her reasoning. I had to admit, however,
that Theo seemed not to suffer. I also had to admit that what
was done was done.

My document suddenly reappeared. It had survived my tra-
vails surprising well, except for salt stains along the edge from
my dip into the sea. The scribe had etched the words deeply
into the vellum. At my request, Rachel supplied a stylus for
me to enter Theo's name. I then placed the document safely
between my legs.

In late afternoon that same day, Bonel summoned me to
his office.

Rachel helped me dress in one of her blue tunics, for my
red Plantagenet tunic was destroyed and my nun's habit had
disappeared. She did not, however, cover my hair with one of

the low turbans she and the other women wore. In fact, she unbraided my pale hair so it flowed freely down my back.

I'd been right; we were in a basement. Rachel supported me as we climbed to the ground floor, then along a narrow hallway to Bonel's office. She then left me.

I had to force myself to knock. Though I was again bathed, free of my bloody odor or other body emanations, scented with jasmine, *Deo gratias*, I was nevertheless apprehensive. For the first time since I'd met Bonel, I came without the king's protection. And Bonel represented the Jews to the king. Did that include King John?

I also felt shy because the last time I'd seen Bonel, he'd kissed me most ardently and supplied me with small diamonds for my security. Yet he'd never promised to put his entire community into jeopardy for my sake.

"Enter!" he called.

An exotic potentate inside an equally exotic tent confronted me. Oh, I could see the small windows covered with oiled linen, could see the low thatch, but what a transformation! Silk billowed above our heads, and every surface below was covered with skins of camels and leopards and lions; crocodile skins stretched over the tables. Tapestries embroidered with flowers twining among mathematical formulations concealed daub walls. Though it was broad daylight, oil lamps burned in the corners; a strong scent of cinnamon mixed with the jasmine I wore.

"Alix." Bonel rose from behind a desk in the corner.

"Bonel, greeting." Only his voice was familiar, for he was as strange as his room. He wore a saffron turban, a long, flowing tunic that changed colors as he walked, a heavy chain glittering with jewels, and long, pointed slippers with similar jewels. He stopped directly in front of me.

We studied each other a long while without speaking. He was somewhat taller than I recalled; his missing eye was covered with a jeweled patch.

"My commiseration; you've fallen on bad times, I hear," he said gently. "Tell me why you're here."

And I did, emphasizing the threat to my life from King John. "I'm grateful for your sanctuary, Bonel, but I kow full well that I may have put your commune in jeopardy. I'm truly sorry; I'll leave as soon as Theo can travel, which might be this very day."

"Why didn't you use the diamonds I gave you?"

"Do you want them back?"

He waved a dismissive hand.

"I didn't know how to barter them—I was afraid."

"Please sit down. This will take thought."

"Do you still represent the Jews to the royal court?"

"Yes."

I searched his good eye, then perched on a stool covered with a spotted fur. Before he could speak, I told him how I planned to disguise myself somehow—dye my hair, dress as a farm woman—and find my old friend Tib, who had helped me before.

His brows raised. "Why? Didn't she almost destroy you once before?"

More important, I thought, I'd almost destroyed her. My presence was poison for my friends.

He began to pace. "Did Richard make no provision for you? No residence?"

"He wrote a document naming our son as the next king of England." A worthless document, I could have added.

He bent over me. "Alix, he and the queen decided two years ago that John would be his heir. They knew his defects well enough, but the alternative—at that time meaning Count Arthur of Brittany, Richard's nephew—would be much too young to face France. The Earl of Pembroke and Archbishop Hubert Walter in England approved John." He lowered his voice. "And it keeps Queen Eleanor in power, no small consideration."

"I neither wanted the position or the settlement that you once suggested."

He went back to his desk. "Very noble, but—forgive me—shortsighted. You must have known as well as he did that Richard would die young." He rose again. "Perhaps he thought you would find a husband as a result of his attention. Concubines of kings notoriously do well on the marriage market."

"I'm already married!"

"What?" He stopped pacing.

"Richard told me just before he died. Enoch wasn't killed—he's alive! You must have known."

For the first time, he became confused. "Yes, I did. I'm sorry, Alix."

Sorry that he hadn't told me?

"And he wouldn't release me when Richard asked, even when he demanded, and offered money. So, of course, he'll be happy to see me!"

"Unless he wanted to maintain the marriage in order to have control of—what was the name of your estate?"

"Wanthwaite."

"Yes, Wanthwaite." He paused again. "Many English barons are just as fierce as the king where land is concerned."

"Enoch is Scottish, not English. And he . . . he'll be happy to see me. Land is no object between us."

"I hope so; he should be."

"And my son as well. Legally, he's Enoch's son."

"Legally? I wouldn't be too sure." His one brown eye pitied me—for my situation? My naïveté?

He put a hand on my arm. "I'm sorry, Lady Alix, truly sorry, but I must stop this interview. You are not the only one who has to deal with the new king—I'm leaving at once for Vernon. When I return, we can discuss your future at greater length."

"Is that why you're dressed so . . . ?" I stopped myself.

"Like an eastern potentate? No, I just returned from Barcelona, where I met with a merchant." He smiled. "A Muslim, in fact. Sometimes I travel as a leper."

"I'm sorry if I detained you, Bonel. I'll be gone—I promise—by the time you return. And some day I'll repay you . . ."

He walked me to the door. "You'll be exactly as you are when I come back. Must I assign guards?" He smiled again. "I'll have a plan next time we meet."

"I could sell my diamonds here in Rouen! Purchase passage to go back to Wanthwaite!"

"With an infant son? Wait for me, Alix."

He had assigned guards, though they were female. Feeling stronger every day, I led my guards on a merry chase through the basement hallways, for our house—Number 6—was joined to the other houses by dark passageways. Each house had a particular designation: mine was the delivery room and small infants; others were laundry, food preparation, hospice care, schooling—all female. Rachel informed me that the male Jews lived in similar divisions of activities above us. Most of the married females retired upstairs when darkness fell.

I also learned that everyone worked—there were servants, but very few. I'm sure there was class distinction as well—everyone looked up to Bonel—but labor seemed to be assigned to everyone. When Viette and Rachel thought me strong enough, for example, I was assigned to the laundry room! Me! Can you believe it? I fought like one of the spotted animals in Bonel's office against the hot sudsy water, the smelly garments, the garden behind the house where we stretched garments over shrubs. Was this Bonel's idea of how to treat a baroness? I would rather be delivering babies with Tib!

I found time, however, to become acquainted with my son, who changed every day. His skin, once a flayed red, turned to cream; his eyes remained a dark blue; his hair thickened into flaxen swirls. I loved his layers of fat, his sweet smell, his happy drool, for he was of sanguine disposition. Most remarkable, however, was his fantastick cell, which grew apace. Though he didn't talk, he had a large vocabulary of sounds close to speech; his eyes followed me everywhere, and I fancied he understood my cooings. Our love vow to each other on the road intensified. I was deliriously happy to be loved without ulterior motive— not for my appearance, my estate, or even the boyish look Richard had so admired. I needed and wanted nothing but my baby. Yet Bonel was right; with all his fast maturation, Theo remained helpless.

The two rows of houses, joined at every level, I learned, contained about a hundred Jews, the male half above the females in every way. Though Rachel insisted that the males worked, I don't consider reading of law and scripture real work. None fought as knights or plowed (though they owned a vast field behind the houses, given by King Henry I). I walked over the field one afternoon to check on Sea Mew, who was getting fat in a small barn.

Though the women stayed in the women's quarters downstairs much as Christian women stayed in their towers, unlike Christians, the Jewish women joined their husbands at sundown. Viette told me that all married people had their own rooms. She also claimed that there was no infidelity, which seemed passing strange after my period in Aquitaine.

The Jewish women were curious about me, some friendly, some hostile. The main issue was Bonel. He was betrothed to a small dark woman named Esther, a mercurial woman of merry disposition most of the time, though she seemed to dislike me—at least she ran in the other direction everytime I approached. Though Rachel assured me that Esther was exceptionally learned and had a small fortune as well, I was surprised that Bonel had decided to wed anyone at all, since his first fiancée had been killed in the York tower. Rachel informed me that a Jew of Bonel's high intelligence had to wed and have bairns.

When I thought about Rachel's words in the night, I was amazed. Bonel might want children for his own reasons, but I'd never heard of any Christian marrying for intelligence! The Jews shared one aspect of Christianity, however: Intelligence was the domain of men, many of them scholars, whom Viette at least thought didn't work.

Women had the same power among Jews that they did among Christians: male children. And again I was blamed for seducing Bonel away from Esther, because he doted on Theo. To be honest, I was of two minds about the obvious affection: I could see that Theo benefited from the male attention, which other babies received from their fathers; on the other hand, Enoch was Theo's father, the only father he'd ever know.

I took care not to be with Theo when Bonel visited.

Rachel informed me that there were many Jews living in other parts of Normandy. She didn't know about their communes or why they'd selected this duchy, but she had heard that at one time there'd been many more, before the First Crusade. What happened then? I asked. She knew only that—like York in England—there'd been a huge slaughter of Jews, this one by the Crusaders. It had happened in Mainz, she believed, which many denied was in Normandy. Nevertheless, Jews who were more informed than she was were wary. As for Rachel, she was happy; she trusted Bonel.

Both men and women were exceedingly clean, cleaner than anyone I'd known, even in the royal palaces. Though I found their food not to my taste—too salty and fatty—I could see that it, too, was clean. Everyone seemed devout: Prayers were said all day long, and there were many religious holidays.

Bonel had been back two weeks before he summoned me again. Now in the dark velvet trimmed with black fur he'd worn when we first met, he still seemed an Oriental potentate.

He rose when I entered. "Do you feel well enough for a stroll? I'd like to show you a bit of our public buildings."

"Aye, thank you." But I didn't move. Was it safe for me to be seen? And wasn't it still winter, though a weak sun shone?

He answered the second question by placing a fur throw over my shoulders. Soon we stood in front of Number 6, where he lived; to our right was the Cathedral Square with its magnificent edifice, to our left three great buildings belonging to the Jews. We turned toward the Jewish buildings.

How had he found Vernon? Had his transactions with the king gone well?

He smiled. "You neither want to know nor can I tell you."

He then asked how I had fared in the quarter, to which I gave perfunctory answers.

We both fell silent.

"You think it absurd for me to return to Wanthwaite, don't you?"

"Absolutely absurd!" He saw my expression. "Impossible, Alix."

"Why?"

"May I be frank? Because Enoch may not accept you. I hate to see you and Theo cast out in that northern wilderness."

"Enoch's my husband! He has to accept me!" My voice dropped. "He loves me."

"Loves you?" As if I were a warthog. And an idiot to boot. "Have you been in touch with him since the king died? Does he know you have a child by the king?"

I shook my head. "He has to accept me; it's the law."

"What law?"

I became flustered. We'd married in full sight of the village and of God; marriage could not be annulled in our religion.

He listened thoughfully. "Perhaps you're right; I'm not as conversant with Christian law. However . . ."

"However what?"

"I know Jewish law—no, don't laugh—your Messiah was a Jew, after all, and his ideas were rooted in Jewish law. By Jewish law, then, you're an adulteress, and your husband can cast you off."

"I'm not an adulteress!"

He turned to face me. "Canon law follows Jewish law in another way: Only the man can get an annulment or divorce, never a woman."

I didn't want to argue, but he'd never met Enoch.

He was a silhouette against the light. "You have a power-

ful enemy, Alix." He stepped close. "And very few friends."
He smiled mirthlessly. "You might as well be a Jew."

We came to our first great public building, the slaughter-
house.

"No point visiting here unless you enjoy kosher butcher-
ing."

I clutched his arm. Two pails of bloody entrails were
slowly freezing in the brisk air; they reminded me of Bok.
Bonel studied my face, then slipped his arm under my fur.

We did enter the school, a massive edifice built of stones
joined by cement in the Roman fashion. The bright room inside contained a long table and benches for Talmudic scholars
from our quarters and two visiting scholars from Andalusia.
Though all spoke to one another in Hebrew, Bonel told me
that the rabbis felt privileged because their visitors worked in
the Arabic tongue, a language which was noted for its great
scientific discoveries, as well as its literature.

Though I'd actually traveled to the Arabic countries on
the Crusade, I was frankly astonished.

Bonel recited a verse:

> *Arraying the heavens shines a single star*
> *With beauty and wisdom and peace;*
> *From Sinai it comes, from Ramah,*
> *To my heart's ill-ease;*
> *It heals the lonely and the blind;*
> *Honey water for my soul.*

He fell silent. "A single star," he repeated.
He pulled me toward our door.
Honey water for my soul. Like troubador poetry, I thought.

How strange that the Arabs had written such verse at the very same time that the Aquitanians had. Even stranger that Bonel, a Jew, responded with such sensitivity. I studied his profile: I was wrong; that kiss on the road had nothing to do with his position in Richard's court. A Jew he might be, an important man in his own culture, but most of all a man of deep feeling.

"Are those literature?" I pointed to thick volumes of vellum between heavy boards chained to the walls.

"No, sacred texts, mostly from the Torah."

"Torah?"

"Jewish law." As he continued to explain, it sounded like the Bible.

He pulled me outside.

"I'd like to study the law!" I cried.

He laughed. "I have other plans for you."

The synagogue was empty. Bonel pointed out a long low candelabra made of gold, then suggested we leave.

Sipping my wine in his office, I asked Bonel, "Did you meet with King John at Vernon?"

"Yes. I'm meeting with his emissaries in two weeks at Le Mans."

"So . . . you've seen him personally?"

"Yes."

"Do you find him as formidable as I do?"

"We have different interests in the new king. You compare him to King Richard; I compare him to King Philip of France." He smiled at my surprise. "King Philip and King John both claim Normandy. We Jews sit on the sidelines, waiting."

"Waiting for what?"

"To see who wins. Many Jews have holdings in both

England and Normandy; it will be difficult if they have to choose. But this problem is mine alone, not yours. May we talk about you?" He filled his glass a second time. "By the law you say you want to study, Enoch assumed your title when he married you. He paid a marriage portion for the privilege, as all lords do, but he bought Wanthwaite, not you!"

I heard Enoch's voice: *I ha'e bought the apple; I had to take the worm quhat came with it!*

"Furthermore, the man who married you would assume your title and the military obligation of your estate. I'm surprised Enoch didn't explain this himself."

"Because you're wrong. I inherited Wanthwaite," I said stubbornly.

"You became the king's marriage prize when your parents died and King Richard sold you for a goodly sum. Cling to your illusions if you must, but be aware that no one—not Enoch, not any assize court—will agree with you."

"Enoch . . ." I clamped my lips closed.

"Loves you?" He smiled piteously. "No doubt he coveted your perfection. King Richard had good taste. Now you want to return with another man's child. Be realistic, Alix."

I tried. "Tell me, Bonel, if Enoch should not accept me, is there any other way I could reclaim Wanthwaite?"

He looked at me strangely. "Very few men are as faithful as I am to a dream, Alix." His dead fiancée, yet even Bonel was getting married.

"What if Enoch should die?"

He started. "I don't understand."

"The law is based on custom. When the Duchess of Pembroke's husband died, her original estate reverted to her."

"Whereupon she became the king's marriage prize and he married her to William Marshal, the new Earl of Pembroke. Isn't that a precedent?" He grimaced. "Are you considering murdering Enoch, Alix?"

"Of course not! As I told you, I want to study law."

"Canon law is based on authority. There's really nothing to study." He bent forward. "In case no one has told you for a time, Alix, you are the most delectable creature on earth. Every person in our commune has remarked on it: ethereal, lovely, and tender beyond words. Now you tell me that beneath that delicate facade lies a cold, calculating intelligence."

"Yes."

He burst into loud guffaws. He rocked, wiped sweat from his face, gasped, wiped tears from his good eye, poured more wine.

"That's not all, Bonel. I want Theo christened. If any thing should happen to him . . ."

After much haggling, he promised to approach a priest at the cathedral who might be persuaded to come to an herb garden after sundown. Esther had met this priest, a Father Michael, several times. It would be a great risk, however, on many counts.

"Now you've seduced—induced—me into listening to your pleas, may I make my own wishes known?"

"Of course."

"What profession do you fancy? And don't say law—I mean something that would earn a living."

There was only one profession I knew to be open to women, provided they were virgins: to join a nunnery, obviously impossible for a woman with a child.

"Are you good with your hands?"

"Oh, you mean a seamstress!" I looked at my fingers, delicate but strong, long, flexible. "I daresay I could sew. Perhaps embroider."

He rose and paced. "What think you of the jewelry business?"

I knew nothing of it.

"We Jews have access to pearls of great worth and emeralds, rubies, and the like from the Orient, some stones from Russia."

He went on: I must learn two aspects to creating jewelry— cutting the gem stones and the setting. Eight men in the compound worked at nothing else and, at Bonel's order, would teach me the trade. Their representatives met with agents from all over Europe; they sold the finished product to lords who preferred to put their wealth into an investment more secure than land or money, and also more easy to transport.

Richard had had a collection of fine jewels, I knew, the royal jewels; he'd left them to his nephew, Otto, who lived in the Holy Roman Empire.

"Once you're proficient, I'll give you the names of two Jewish shops on a lane in London where you might find employment."

He didn't believe I would ever return to Wanthwaite; I felt sick. "Are you so famous, Bonel?"

He shrugged. "What say you?"

My voice trembled. "What can I say, Bonel, except thank you? You're offering me a life . . ."

"A life that I once took from you, don't forget."

I'd had too much wine, for now I wept.

He touched my shoulder awkwardly. "Don't cry. Who knows? You *might* gain wealth."

I sobbed. "I want to go home!"

"Be a good mother, Alix; learn the jewelry trade, regain your own strength. Theo needs a strong parent."

"Must I stay a whole year?"

He drew away. "Is that so terrible?"

I began my lessons in setting jewels the very next morning. I actually felt guilty, leaving my laundry duties to another, yet followed Bonel up the steps with mounting excitement. We walked through corridors on the upper story to the first house on the street. There we were admitted into a room even larger than his, with windows on two sides. It was far from luxurious, however; a pall of fine dust hung in the air above three tables pushed together. The four gem setters gazed at me from bloodshot eyes. Bonel introduced them as Yossi, Ely, Samuel, and Abraham; none of them acknowledged me. After Bonel left, however, Yossi pulled a chair to the table close to him and gestured that I should sit. Apparently, all I would do that first day would be to watch.

Yossi flipped six large pages of vellum in the center of the table, grunted, and shoved a page to a worker. Each page contained a drawing of a jewelry design, one a pendant with a double circle of gold with lion en passant in the center. Samuel had already created the gold circles, intricately joined with twists of flowers (garnets) both inside and between the circles.

"That's very pretty," I said.

Either they didn't understand or didn't care what I thought.

Ely spoke to me in French. Did I see the pile of garnets

in front of Yossi? They might appear to be facets, but they were precise slices that could be slipped into metal cells. It was an old technique, but still highly popular. They'd found the cameo of the two lions, already carved, in Italy. They made three such pendants every day because the demand was great and the work comparatively easy. Some, no doubt, would find the work tedious, and it did take great patience; I enjoyed it at once.

The second day, they worked on a brooch, again a double circle of gold only with filigree instead of garnets, an eagle instead of lions. This, too, was an old and popular design, and they'd had a special order. I preferred the cameo lion. In two weeks, I was permitted to paste topaz slivers around a field of pearls on a pendant. Ely explained that they made clasps for tunics, bracelets, rings, and even earrings, but pendants were both easier and more in demand.

Samuel interrupted in poor French: Pins were tricky because of the fastenings, and earrings were even more difficult; for both, they were forced to go back to Roman designs. Garnets were their most popular item, readily available and easy to set. There were always garnets piled before us, and it was the first stone I worked on.

One morning they placed a smooth, oval-shaped stone before me and asked me to identify it. I guessed emerald, though I knew that to be wrong: It was too blue in color and too opaque. Nor was it a sapphire. It was an Egyptian turquoise, an ancient stone that had been cut and polished centuries ago. Though I was exceedingly curious about how it had come into their possession, I knew better than to ask. With the turquoise, I learned that my teachers were more creative and had better taste than I'd first thought; they set it in a simple gold band and made a ring of it. When I complimented them in French, they both understood and were pleased.

I continued to work with garnets, topaz, aquamarine, seed pearls, amethyst chips. Jacob, our best designer, piled jewels on a plate and twisted wires around them in a crude depiction of his ideas. Ely then painstakingly polished tiny gems until they caught every light and arranged them into tighter designs. All the work took weeks of patience. We shared a form of madness that we recognized in one another. How had Bonel known that this was where I belonged?

On my last day, I worked on a rare star ruby from India. The next day, I would begin to cut gems.

The gemstone room was next to the setting room. The men—Saul, James, Judas, and Ben—all wore half-masks against the dust they created by sawing. Shelves along the wall were packed with uncut gemstones, and they spent the first day instructing me in passable French. They placed amethyst and tourmaline above a small flame to enhance the color, a technique, Ben explained, found in India centuries ago. Another Indian technique was to treat gems (appearing as quartz) with calcydrone. They produced rubies and diamonds and zircons and I know not what to prove their point. Only pearls remained free from some sort of treatment.

The brilliance of any gem—precious or semiprecious—depended on the cutting, and this was the art of these men. They held stones to the windows and argued the merits of slicing one way or another. All the stones had been analyzed many times. Then they brought forth a large diamond, the most precious gem of all. It was also the only gem that was valuable when colorless. Yet it was the most difficult stone to work on because it was so hard. And there were diamonds with color—red, blue, or green—called fancies, though they had none in the room. Yellow pigment lowered the price.

There were many types of cut stones: cabochons with smooth rounded surfaces, facets with flat surfaces, the carved cameo or relief, entaglio or the engraved. They used saws and fine chisels on all gems but the diamond, which was so hard that they used diamond dust on the saw.

My first cut, some weeks later, was on the least valuable stone (though very pretty), the topaz. All stones made me feel I held the world in my hands: India, Egypt, the Mediterranean, the Ural Mountains in Russia. Sweden, England, and Ireland also contributed, lands I would never visit, except for England. Pearls and opals were the most popular among jewelers; pearls must be found to fit the design, since they couldn't be cut. Jewelers considered opals bad luck because they broke so easily. A big favorite, of course, was the onyx, which could be made to appear a huge jewel. For the semiprecious stones, I preferred the moonstone, which I thought particularly beautiful in a silver setting. Among the precious stones, I liked lapis and pearl, since both reminded me of Theo.

I was prohibited from learning Jewish law, but the priest who christened Theo sent me a few legal texts in Latin. I had St. Jérome, St, John, and St. Augustine, all of whom attacked

women as the daughters of Eve, meaning we seduced our
Adam-men to perdition. Annulments, I learned, were granted
when a woman committed adultery (though not when a man
did the same); annulments were also granted to the man if
his wife's father had exaggerated her landholdings or her
wealth. Yet annulments were crushingly expensive. By Church
law, if a man didn't want to pay for an annulment from his
adulterous wife, he could kill her.

It was six months before I was permitted to cut a diamond.
The men deliberately chose the diamond—not their best diamond, of course, but a diamond even so. While my saw was
heating, I carried the stone to the window to study once
again its natural fractures. Back at the table, I waited for my
saw, then dipped it in diamond dust. Just as I was about to
cut, someone tapped my shoulder.

"Not now, please!"

It was Bonel. "Alix, you must come at once! Queen
Eleanor's here!"

3

I ran across a pool of blood and fell on my face! "Give me my baby!"

Queen Eleanor, with Theo in her arms, stared down on me. Bonel rushed to pick me up—I'd tripped on the queen's scarlet train!

"She'll murder him!" I screamed. "Please, oh, please!" I wrenched free—he grabbed me again.

"Theo, come to mother!"

"Alix, dear, *calme-té*, I'm here to save both of you!"

"Like you saved me at Fontevrault!" I cried. "And in the wood!"

I burst into tears—Theo pulled on my skirt and I grabbed him.

"This be my gamma!" he told me.

"Yes, Lady Alix, I am his grandmaman." The queen's eyes filled. "He's so like the Great One at his age, if you only knew."

"I know that you betrayed your precious Great One! But you'll not contaminate my son! Never!"

I shrank from her reaching arms. Her scent of rose water sickened me, *she* sickened me. She might not be King John— might not have a Raoul between her legs—but she was a killer nonetheless. And that red robe—I saw my peasant girl wave again! And this woman had produced John! Betrayed Richard!

I carried Theo to the door where Bonel stopped me.

"Listen to her, Alix!"

"You, too? Judas!"

The queen hissed directly into my ear. "Not enough time to discuss the past! This is urgent! Your presence has been exposed, Alix!"

"Is that why you're here? To arrest me?"

"Listen!" Her hand trembled as she reached—for the first time, I was aware of her age. What had happened in the brief time since I'd seen her at Fontevrault? She'd lost physical command.

"I've come to save you if I can! You and Theo! For God's sake, listen!"

Bonel eased her to a bench. "Continue, Queen Eleanor; she's listening."

I shot him a withering look.

"Someone told a priest who told me." Her face was now drenched with sweat. "I kept it secret at first, until—have you heard about Duke Arthur?"

"Who?"

"Another grandson, son of my dead son Geoffrey. Arthur also claims the throne."

Memory surfaced—a long trek through a dense wood, a small, vicious boy. "I met him once. Why *also?* Theo makes no claims!"

"Arthur led an army against me at Mirabeau; John rescued me."

"Was that why you betrayed Richard? Because John rescued you?"

Red spots appeared on her cheeks. "It happened after Richard had died. Listen! What you have to remember is that Arthur was captured by Lord William de Braose, one of King John's closest friends. It happens that William's wife, who is obviously above suspicion, is traveling to England this very night and I've persuaded her to take Theo with her!"

I hugged Theo closer.

He pushed back. "Theo go on boat!"

Bonel came close. "It's a good plan, Alix—thank the queen!"

"She doesn't have to thank me," the queen said with her old asperity. "I'm doing it for my grandson—and for Richard."

This strange lady, Lady Matilda de Braose, was leaving at night when the tides on the Seine were low, and she would carry two grandsons as well as Theo; the queen herself had booked passage to England at Calais.

"She will ride directly to London, where she will be the guest of Lord Robert fitzWalter for at least a month, at Baynard Castle, which has a dock on the Thames. You will follow the party tomorrow night and pick up Theo in London, identifying yourself as Lady Angela from the north. You will then take him to your estate—I forget the name."

"Wanthwaite."

"Yes, Wanthwaite."

By now I heard both the urgency and the fear. "Does King John know you're here?" My heart thumped so everyone could hear.

"Of course not!" She struggled to her feet. "May I hold Theo?"

He went to her arms.

"Who's paying?" Bonel asked.

The queen smiled. "I am, as usual. The cost is trivial."

"The journey, yes, but how much are you paying Lady Matilda?"

Now she laughed. "Clever Jew! A lot. Her husband, Lord William, owes the king a goodly sum; I've offered to pay half."

"When should Alix follow? A month, did you say?"

"Pay attention!" Now her hard imperial voice. "I said Lord Robert had offered Lady Matilda and her party Baynard Castle for a month! Alix should leave at once, tomorrow night! As soon as she arrives in London, she can pick up Theo. But leave now, Alix! That's an order!"

Her scarlet robe crackled; her face became young, bucolic—the peasant girl!

Bonel paled. "Did someone in the commune betray her?"

"Does King John know?" I asked at the same time. I tried to find the peasant girl again—I'd made her a promise, hadn't I?

The queen stared at Bonel. "I'll tell you when we're alone." Then she said to me, "If he doesn't, he soon will."

"And here in Rouen, I would be the victim, whereas in England . . ."

"Who betrayed me? I have a right . . ."

"You have no rights!"

Oh yes I had, the right to kill, to save myself and Theo.

"Is it a Jew?" Bonel pressed. "Is the entire commune in danger?"

"No more! We must move fast, before . . ."

Bonel pushed me. "Go to your room, Alix. Take Theo with you and open your door to no one till I get there!"

For the first time, I bowed. "Thank you, Queen Eleanor."

Our eyes held a single moment. "You're welcome. Now, do as Bonel says."

Back in my room, I quickly piled my scant furniture against my door. Theo watched from a corner.

"I love you, baby!" I kissed his damp skin.

No answer.

My room looked odd to me—was it the lack of furniture? No, it had the desolation of one of my camping spots on my travels through France. Twice someone knocked and called out, "Alix!" I put my hand across Theo's mouth.

Then it was Bonel.

"Did you find out who . . . ?"

"Yes. You're not packed yet?"

"Was it someone in the commune?" He didn't answer. "I don't leave until tomorrow, do I?"

"Pack for Theo."

"Not much to pack. Where are you going?"

"Have to arrange things for our trip; I'll be back."

I pulled Theo to my lap. *Only a few days and we'll be together always.*

Enoch and England.

Home, I was finally going home, everything was arranged. Yet someone knew I'd survived—someone had told the king. I was back in La Rochelle, running for my life.

Then I recalled the diamond—what must the gemstone cutters think? I went to the door, and hesitated.

Bonel knocked. "Is he packed?"

"I have to cut a diamond! They expect me!"

"Fine!" He pushed me back. "Let others think that's where you are."

"Is the queen still here?"

"Still in Rouen, if that's what you mean. She tells me she's returning to Fontevrault to die."

"Pity," I said in a hard tone. "We all must die, but not everyone can choose when and where." *Certainly not King John.*

"I'll take Theo to meet his carriage when it's time," he said in a calmer voice. "You can watch from my office window." He took my arms. "I don't want to frighten you unduly, but this is serious, Alix. Remember Fontevrault Wood?"

"I know the danger."

After he'd left, the two of us played games and sang songs through the afternoon. Though he had no real idea of what was happening, Theo jumped up and down with excitement. He was going with his "gamma"—he didn't understand that he was separating from me.

"Theo go to England!" His eyes shone.

"And Mother will be right behind you," I promised, hoping he would remember if he became frightened. "We're going home, Theo!"

"Home."

Home. One day Theo would be baron of Wanthwaite.

At dusk, Bonel returned for Theo's saddlebag. "Stay close. I'll lead you to my office."

His office was already dark. Twice, someone knocked. Once, a female called my name. I watched Theo being lifted into a cart covered with barrels—I didn't see any woman. Then Bonel was back.

"Was she in the cart?"

"Yes, come quickly."

He pulled me through the corridor, up the stairs—then up the stairs again, where he knocked on one of the closed doors.

Viette pulled us inside.

A shadow moved behind her—her husband, Ely, from the gemstone room. I knew him by his eyes and hair, as he'd always worn a mask over his nose and chin.

"Welcome, Alix," he said.

Bonel put a sack made of leopard skin at my feet. "Dress yourself for travel tomorrow. I'll collect you in late afternoon. Meantime, Viette will stay with you."

When he'd left, we crouched in semidarkness; Ely and Viette conversed in Hebrew. I swallowed to keep tears at bay. Then Viette said in accented French, "You sleep on the mat tonight; we have the floor."

At dawn, Ely put on his mask and left. I helped Viette pull the bed across the door. From a low cupboard in the corner, she took dry Jewish bread and a leather flask of wine. We sat in silence all day as she sewed what looked to be a tunic. In late afternoon, she gestured that I should put it on. It was in two pieces: an undergown of soft white muslin, then a cope of the Jewish blue linsey-woolsey to form an open coat connected at the top with laces.

"Is it for me?"

She nodded.

When the bell rang curfew, Bonel knocked. He glanced at the tunic in the gloom, then placed another saddlebag at my feet.

"Please put this nun's habit over your tunic and be fast!"

The habit, much finer than the one I'd received from Sister Hilaria in Fontevrault, fitted perfectly, even over my new tunic. Bonel was dressed as a priest.

"Let me take your sack." He put a small leopard sack inside my saddlebag, and picked up both his own and mine.

The Cathedral Square was crowded with priests. Workers on the cathedral shouted from a wooden platform across the entire back. Above human voices, chimes rang in a familiar melody, an Easter chant.

"What day is it?" I whispered.

"Thursday. Why?"

The next day was Good Friday. I stumbled on a loose cobble.

"Careful!" Bonel took my arm.

We took a narrow path sloping toward the river. A few men pushed us aside to get inside their houses before twilight deepened. A light rain fell—I slipped on wet mud.

Bonel steadied me.

A bridge loomed above the city wall with an unguarded gate.

"Where are we?"

"Unfinished bridge. Serves as shelter for the fishing fleet."

He flashed papers at an ancient guard asleep in his booth.

"Don't move." Bonel pushed me against a pylon. "I'll be right back."

Water with the stench of dead fish lapped at my feet. The Seine, bright in the distance, was black below the bridge. The rainfall increased, but there was no wind. I tried not to think of Theo—had their boat avoided that dangerous tide below Rouen? The strong fish smell made me sick.

Bonel took my arm. "Let me lead."

We walked under the bridge until it abruptly disappeared and the slime below it narrowed. I fell on all fours.

Bonel pulled me upright, and brushed mud off my front. "You're a brave girl—don't cry."

I wept for Theo—what would he do if I had a fatal accident? Would Enoch take him? Would Bonel? Bonel gathered me briefly into his arms, stroked my wet cheek, murmered in Hebrew. He was like my father; no, he was like Bonel.

"Are you all right?"

"Are we the only ones here?"

"Yes, we're the only passengers on a fishing boat—our safest transport, Alix. I've used these men often; trust me."

The acrid stench of fish scales replaced floating carcasses, then the creak of boards and slap of waves, men's voices speaking a Norman argot, one bawdy laugh, all in darkness.

"Go sideways; there's no gangplank, only a single board that may be slippery. I'll hold you from below."

Rough hands lifted me over a rail. Bonel took me again.

"Still sideways—there's no real deck."

Only two boards around a deep hole in the middle of the craft.

"Sit here." Bonel lowered me onto a coil of ropes in the prow of the boat. "I'll be right back."

The boat tipped as men moved.

"You said forty," a French voice growled.

"No, I did not, but I won't argue. Take five more."

"*Juif,*" muttered someone else.

Bonel was paying for this entire trip, not the queen, including the clothes on my back.

A tall shaggy fisherman stumbled on me as he crossed from one side to another.

"*Pardon!*"

Bonel sank beside me. At least the rain ceased.

"I hope you're keeping track of our expenses, Bonel, for I promise to pay you back as soon as I get to Wanthwaite."

He squeezed my hand.

Behind us the fishermen growled, grunted, tugged, farted, and lifted the anchor. Two oarsmen dipped as they sang some toneless chantey. We were in the center of the Seine, no longer bright.

"Peir!" called someone.

The boat rocked dangerously. The river hissed past us. Waves slapped the prow.

I'm coming, Theo!

"Are you all right?" Bonel whispered.

"Yes. How about you?"

He squeezed my hand again.

We were suddenly far from the shore on both sides, pulled by a strong current down the center of the Seine. The fishermen, now silent except for grunts, threw their lines. On my right, I could still distingush Rouen.

"Is the city burning again?" I pointed to a column of fire on one of the back hills.

"It's a signal for boatmen, so they'll know they're approaching a curve. You'll see many before we reach the Channel."

"I should think the current would suffice."

"The Seine snakes back on itself; fires mark the progress."

The peasant girl loomed on the hill; I waved back. *I haven't forgotten! Give me time!*

We hit a snag. "What was that?"

"I'm not certain. Nothing to worry about, though."

Bonel pulled my head to his chest. I must have slept.

"Stay here." Bonel disengagd himself.

I sat up. "Where are you going? Wait, Bonel!"

But he was gone. The boat was still stopped. Had they dropped anchor again? Was this where they fished? Had we reached the English Channel? No, we listed toward the Rouen side of the river, and there was Rouen itself, still in dim outline. And there was the fire, the peasant girl waved frantically—what was amiss? Was John following me?

Our fishermen spoke in agitated whispers. Someone produced an oil lamp. They were looking at some object on the shore side; one voice rang out followed by hushing. I started to tremble. Had the queen betrayed us?

Bonel bumped into me. "Why are you standing? Go back to sleep!"

"What's wrong?"

"One of the nets caught a snag, that's all. They have to untangle it."

"What sort of snag? Won't they need this rope?"

"I don't think so. I'll ask."

"It has something to do with Theo, hasn't it?"

"Absolutely not!" He put his arms around my trembling body. "You have my word, Alix."

My teeth chattered.

"Try to relax—I'll be right back."

The peasant girl still waved.

Another boat approached from the Rouen side; it, also, had an oil lamp.

The dark, the disembodied voices, the mystery, the girl in the fire, all made Rouen eerie.

Bonel returned. "Did you see anything?"

"Yes, those other fishermen took something from our net."

"We snagged a dead body, Alix, a suicide. A fisherman tied himself to a stone."

I trembled, an omen. "Maybe it was a murder!"

"Gaston recognized the man, a fisherman despondent because his wife betrayed him. We're turning him over to other fishermen for burial."

I shook even harder. Had Enoch committed suicide because I'd betrayed him? Or was it Theo? That peasant girl had waved . . .

"Don't protect me, Bonel. Lady Matilda did it, didn't she?"

"Who? Did what?"

"That woman the queen used, that Matilda de Braose! She killed Theo—just what the queen wanted!"

"Alix, control yourself. A fisherman tried to commit suicide . . ."

I didn't believe him. I don't always know the truth, but I know a lie when I hear it!

"You control yourself! First you say he did it, then that he *tried* to do it! Which is it? I won't be lied to!"

"I sometimes forget the brain behind that face."

"Richard once wrote a poem about me—want to hear it?

> *"Then there are those who pretend to be infants. But*
>> *"Are as smart as the lawyer Trebellius,*
>> *"Who've the verbal talents of a logician combined*
>> *"With all the good will of a wolf."*

"Enough! Are you a wolf?" He laughed sofly.

Finally, our fishing smack continued toward the Channel. In the distance, the other boat moved slowly, dragging the weight of something under the surface.

Bonel and I sank to our coil of rope again. "You must sleep. You have a long day tomorrow."

But Bonel's hands trembled—something was terribly amiss. Yet I believed him when he said it wasn't Theo, which should have been enough, but wasn't. Not Theo personally, but related somehow. Hadn't I been warned? A fire?

A brilliant sun shone directly into my eyes. I squinted, then screamed!

Our boat was being sucked toward a turbulent wall of foam! We circled like a dead leaf in the tide, round and round, down and down, pulled into a maelstrom. Our fishermen beat with their oars—I could see them now—four small dark Normans. A torn sail swung back and forth! Helpless! Helpless! Oh *Deus juva me*, what would happen to Theo? Or was he at the bottom of the sea waiting for me!

Where was Bonel?

"Here, Alix!" He must have seen me looking for him—he was beating an oar beside the other fishermen—hopeless, frail little men against nature. The water sucked and roared and—miracle of miracles—we turned slightly! Aye, we were turning! Oh God, not the water wall, not the sun, a low bank of land.

Bonel jumped into the water with a rope in his hand. He pulled with his body—once he slipped and recovered—he had a second rope. The fishermen, now standing, beat the water, then Peir jumped directly into the river to help Bonel. The two men pulled us to the muddy shore.

"Jump, Sister Marie-Claudine!" Bonel held out his arms.

I jumped.

When I turned, the boat was already bobbing in the middle of the river.

"Where are we?"

"Can you walk?"

"Of course!"

The wall of water had turned bright gold from the sun. The roar retreated. Bonel wrung water from his habit; I wrung mine as well. A cold wind from the Channel chilled both of us.

Bonel pushed me to the ground behind a low wall with flowers growing on top. "Shelter from the wind; I'll be back," he said. Then he was gone. A rooster crowed on the other side of the wall; sheep and goats bleated. The rising sun dried my habit somewhat. I checked Theo's document in my sack; the oiled silk had protected it. Bonel was back.

"I have to find another boat; yours has left."

"Left?" I tried to kill him!

He held me at arms' length. "It was that snag—all the boats have left!"

"I'm sorry, Bonel, I understand, I'm just so . . ." My teeth chattered. "You can't know."

"Can't I?"

"Not as I do." I wept so I could hardly speak. "Of course you're concerned because . . ."

"Because what? Can't say it, can you?"

"Yes, I can; I know you love Theo, too."

His good eye filled. "Yes, I love Theo, and I'm going to lose him. He's my son, too."

His son? Richard's? No, Enoch's!

"But you and Esther . . ."

"When I write my own poem, Alix, it won't be about your intelligence." He regained control.

"Where are we?" I asked humbly.

"Outskirts of Calais. Come, let me hide you better while I . . ."

This time he put me inside an empty cow byre.

He returned with a jug of milk and brown bread. We ate silently. "Alix, you can't sail from Calais."

"I know, the boats have all left."

"Today, but I mean never. The piers are closely guarded. You just can't."

"But it's the closest to England—only twenty miles!"

"A little farther, I think, but that's not the point. The king's guards are checking every passenger, especially young women with babies."

"I'm garbed as a nun and I don't have Theo! I'm not afraid!"

"I am. We should both be grateful for the queen's quick thinking. At least Theo's safe. And you will be, too—can you wait again?"

This time he returned with two mules. Silently, we mounted them.

"Stay close. I'm taking the back path to Boulogne, my favorite port when I sail."

Wissant, the port of Boulogne, was also guarded.

Bonel checked his religious papers to be sure they were in order when he had to show them at the border into Flanders. He brushed dry mud from my skirts, tucked one of my braids into my wimple, then asked me to make him presentable. We entered Flanders without incident. Though I knew it was foolish to think that the weather respected national borders, the fact was that the instant we were in Flanders we suffered a steady rainfall. Paths were inundated, cottages closed tight, people or animals nowhere to be seen. Bonel kept us inland from the Channel, where, he claimed, the weather was even nastier. At dusk, he passed up sanctuary in a church as too risky; he paid an innkeeper for places on his mat behind a tavern. I was the only woman among drunken louts; Bonel placed me against a wall and lay next to me so no one could mount me.

"If we fail at Ostend, we'll head south again," he said. "It's too early to brave the North Sea."

"Os—where?"

"A fishing village in northern Flanders, joined by a canal to Brugge, a jewel of a city. Ostend now has regular transport to England." He squeezed my arm. "And King John doesn't guard it."

"Do you smell sardines?" I asked the following morning.

"Sardines, eels, oysters, that's Ostend. I buy in Brugge. The pearls are small and they tend to be gray in color, but I've purchased a few."

"Have you ever sailed to England from here?"

"I go to England as little as possible. However, I did sail once from Ostend in the other direction, to the Jutland Peninsula. Those Viking boats can withstand any sea."

"Vikings? Vikings are long gone."

He smiled. "No one is gone if you look. Coastal shipping in the north is dominated by Vikings. They've stopped ravaging the countryside, that's all."

"What's in the Jutland Peninsula?"

"Remember those fine jewels you polished from Russia? That's where I get them."

Lapis, amber, diamonds. How little I knew Bonel.

Ostend was in a full-blown sleet storm. Nevertheless, fish stands were open on the beach, and ships for England lay at anchor. Bonel purchased fresh-fried oysters, sardines, and bits of salmon, which we ate under a shed.

"Hold these while I secure your passage."

"Surely they won't sail in such a storm, Bonel."

"You don't know these Vikings—they relish this."

Vikings had invaded England's rivers in their long blue boats, silent and deadly as snakes. Indeed, their boats often carried the sign of snakes or dragons. My father (who was descended from a Viking) claimed that our ancestors were clever people and brave as well. Mother said that be as that may, their real talent lay in their viciousness. Was I vicious? I had the silver eyes of my Viking ancestor.

Bonel returned. "I've bought you passage on the *Drage*. It doesn't sail till late afternoon."

"You mean I'll be on the water at night?"

"Better a short night and a long day tomorrow than the reverse. This way, you'll reach Dover just in time to find an inn. And we must talk." He opened his saddlebag. "The following morning you'll go overland on a donkey you'll purchase. Or, with luck, you may be able to ride on to London before dark tomorrow."

"You mean, I can pick up Theo tomorrow?"

"Even if you reach London, you'll have to stay in an inn one night before you go to Baynard Castle. Do you remember your instructions?"

"Of course, I'm Lady Angela from the north; Baynard Castle is on the Thames and has a dock. It's owned by Lord Robert fitzWalter, but I'm to ask for Lady Matilda de Braose."

"Lord Robert fitzWalter is also the head of the London Commune and . . ."

"Is he Jewish?"

"No, commune means that London is an independent city, not under John's rule."

"Good for London!"

"To ride to Wanthwaite, you'll need a horse, not a donkey. You understand?"

"Yes."

He heard my uncertainty. "You need money." He took a small heavy bag from his saddlebag. "This is coin enough for your journey, both from Dover and from London. Use only pence on the road, for the English won't give you change." He smiled. "Not even if you were king."

I opened the bag; several coppers lay on top of silver and gold. "This is too much, Bonel!"

"Pretend the queen gave it, which she did in part. She owes that much to you and Theo."

"Yes, except that you gave it, Bonel. You owe us nothing."

Two red spots burned on his cheeks. "You forget that I love Theo, too."

But Theo wasn't the only person getting the money.

"I'll pay you back."

He smiled. "You already have. I instructed Israel to sell Sea Mew."

A royal horse of great worth. I felt better.

"I have another matter to speak of, Alix. Ely tells me you're ready to go into the jewelry market."

"At Wanthwaite?"

Again the red spots glowed. "No, in London." He produced another heavy bag, this one filled with gems that I could sell in London while I sought a position. He had written the names and notes to two men who set gems on Jewelry Lane where I might use Bonel's name.

He placed his saddlebag between us. "You take this; I'll

take yours. Mine is lined with leather under oiled silk, proof against seawater."

"You think I'll get wet? You said the Vikings were . . ."

"Skilled? The very best. But yes, though the *Drage* will get you there safely, you will be heavily doused, no doubt."

He seemed to be finished.

"Bonel, I'm glad you're selling Sea Mew, but nothing can repay you for your kindness beyond money—everything." My voice was tight.

"I'm glad if I can help you, Alix." His throat beat under his jaw. "I try to follow the teachings of our great philosopher, Maimonides: 'Assist your reduced fellowman either by giving considerable gifts or sums of money or by teaching him a trade, or putting him in way of business, so that he might at least earn a livelihood.'"

"He sounds Christian."

He laughed. "Not the kind of Christian I've known. They've not been *Christian* to Jews."

"Bonel, what I'm about to say isn't much, except it may relieve you about your commune, about the Jews there. I know who betrayed me. A Christian."

He jumped slightly.

"I told you I was intelligent, though in this case I admit I may have been a little slow. A guard recognized me when I entered Rouen. I thought I'd evaded him, but apparently I hadn't."

He was silent a long time. "His name?"

"Sir Alain, a guard at the arched bridge. He's King John's man and he . . ."

"Wanted you?"

"Perhaps. I think so. King Richard used that bridge often and Sir Alain . . ."

"I'll look into it."

There was another long silence. I was getting nervous. "When are you and Esther getting married?"

He raised his eyes. "Did she speak to you about it?"

"No."

"Then I won't either." He reached for my hands. "You still have Enoch to care for you."

"Yes."

"A mirage, but you'll find out yourself."

"He's my husband. You don't know what . . ."

"I know men; I know the law."

"And I know human feeling. It doesn't change."

He laughed. "God, you're naive! You note that I didn't say stupid! You're right, I haven't met Enoch, and maybe he's different from all other mankind."

"Enoch loves me."

"*Loved.* Enoch loved you."

"You're cruel!"

"Just trying to make you face reality. Didn't you tell me that Enoch fought with France just so he could get a good shot at you?"

"Yes, but . . ."

"No buts, Alix. Just remember that you have jewels." He stood. "And remember that being intelligent begins with being realistic. Forget wishes, accept what you actually find. Time to go."

I stood.

His face changed. "Maybe . . ."

I didn't want to argue in the few heartbeats we had left.

"You say you owe me something for my care. Would it be too much to ask for a farewell kiss?"

I offered my face.

"Not out in the open like this. This is no kiss between a priest and a nun."

And it wasn't.

"This isn't goodbye, Alix. You'll see."

4

THE *DRAGE* LURCHED SO VIOLENTLY THAT I FELL TWICE BEFORE I could reach the only other female passenger, who gestured frantically that she was saving my place. When I finally stumbled to the prow, she pulled me to a "seat" before a huge projecting pole with a dragon head on top.

"'Tis a lakly day," she cried.

I thrilled to hear the English tongue, e'en though she lied; the sleet stung like needles.

"Them brutes mighta helped ye."

She pointed at fifteen pairs of giant oarsmen who seemed too busy placing their own seats at their rowing stations to bother with me. I liked their appearance: pale hair and beards, savage silver eyes, bearskins around their middles and huge bare feet; not handsome, exactly, but reassuring. My new friend pushed my head low or I would have been struck when a long oar swung close.

"They're s'posed to warn ye!" she cried.

When the oar was safely past, I stood to search for Bonel on the shore. There he was; I waved, but he didn't see me.

Now the Vikings swung their long oars dangerously close to other passengers' heads. Two sailors at the stern lifted decorative shields from the seaside of the ship, shields that had concealed oarlocks. Seawater immediately sloshed onto the

deck through the oarlock holes. At the helm, the captain—
called Sven, according to my new friend—studied a needle
floating on a plate. The male passengers sat in the hold on
boxes of merchandise they'd dragged aboard.

Now Bonel waved. When I stood to wave back, something nipped my calf.

"What the . . . !" I clutched my leg.

"Sorry, dear, dinna worry, it be anely my duck, not dangerous, ye understand, but he resents yer blocking his view."

The duck, in a slatted crate, was big as a small sheep.
White with yellow beak and feet, he frowned with beady
black eyes. He struck again—I moved forward.

"Tch! Henry!" She looked up at me proudly. "A Saxony
duck, he'll bring a guid price tomorry, you'll see."

"You're going to sell him?"

"Aye, at the Smithfield Market just outside London
Town."

My skin crawled; Smithfield! I was on my way home!

"I hope they doona eat him. He be a great breeder."

She then introduced his mate in a matching crate as
Clémence and herself as Madame Eglantine. "Married to a
Flamand called Soren, a turrible mistake. Still, my da had no
coin fer a dowry and when Soren got me in a family way . . ."

The anchor was raised, the ship heaved.

"Ahoy!" cried the woman. "The tide be ebbin', richt fer
sailin'!"

Bonel stepped into the water. Was he going to swim?

Madame Eglantine chattered nonstop about our sailing,
which I only half-followed, for my mind was distracted.
Bonel and Theo and Queen Eleanor and King John and Enoch

tumbled widdershins as the oarsmen bellowed a fiendish chantey
to the smack of oars on water. The *Drage* hissed over the heavy
swells; Bonel grew smaller and smaller. Four brawny sailors
braced the mast with mast partners as four others untied the
sail. Madame Eglantine proudly pointed to the cross designs of
leather sewn on the white muslin sail to increase its strength.

"Oh, they be canny seamen!" she cried.

Henry bit me again.

Though long and narrow, our Viking ship wasn't painted
blue, but was a polished oak with a golden glow. Gold—not
red sleet—not fire. I felt safe.

Madame Eglantine and I leaned comfortably against our
dragon pole.

"Ye war wise, Sister, to wed Jesus; a hard terse doesna
compensate fer the beatin's that go with it." She paused.
"Still, my da put my youngest sister in a convent and she
starved in a year. Mayhap she war too hungry goin' in, but . . .
werse than any madhouse, it war."

"Did anyone else die?"

"Aye. Mast nunneries simply gi'e free funerals ond graves,
ye know. Did ye ha'e enow to eat?"

"Too much; the Sisters were fat." I described Queen
Eleanor's kitchen at Fontevrault, the only nunnery I knew,
which I called St. Michael's at Nantes.

She crossed herself. "I niver sailed wi' a haly Sister befar,
sae excuse me yif I seem to blasphene, I doona mean naught."
She smacked my knee. "Ye bring God's blessing on our journey, no doubt aboot it."

Though I nodded, I hadn't attended Mass in more than
two years.

"I wouldna travel on the Lord's Day, Sister," Mistress Eglantine apologized, "except that, after six weeks of Lent, ye ken, the market will be that eager fer meat."

She made sucking sounds with her lips; the doomed ducks quacked in response.

Easter, it was Easter Sunday; I hadn't seen Theo since last Wednesday. Had Lady Matilda taken him to Mass today? He was luckier than the ducks in any case, for at least Theo wouldn't be served up on someone's platter tomorrow.

Mistress Eglantine had seven children; therefore, she was fat and toothless, but her eyes were a bright happy blue, her pink cheeks firm, and she could sing like a bird, which she did frequently. Though I admired her shrill voice, her matter was disturbing:

> A seal-suave mermaid swims in sparkling waves
> A glint! A glare!
> Now dives down in darkest depths
> Oh where? Oh where?
> Up she swims in serpent green—
> Red eyes aglow, gums afoam
> From fangs of fearsome sheen!
> Roars with glee and drags us doon!

"*Avant le hel!*" shouted a blond giant, and we turned to the left.

Almost at once, he sang out again, "*Sus le hel!*" and we turned right.

We were at sea.

Mistress Eglantine informed me that though Ostend was the most excellent port in the north, it could have benefited from a Roman seawall such as she'd once noted at Dover—had I seen it?—because the Channel could be rough indeed, especially at takeoff. Boats from Ostend also had to contend with blasts from the North Sea and icebergs aplenty, as well as the monsters she'd sung about. Once, a storm had delayed her for three days before she could even board her ship. She always felt more secure once she could see England's shore approaching.

I surveyed the retreating hills of Europe. Suddenly, I again saw Bonel high on a bluff, his hand raised against a whipping line of trees.

"Be that a friend?" Mistress Eglantine asked.

"A brother who . . ." I couldn't speak for a lump.

"Yer brother? He mun be hard to leave!"

"Yes, he is."

When I looked again, Bonel was gone.

So was Europe.

Our fellow passengers were dressed in short tunics and colorful braies and boots. Most of them were merchants, according to my friend; they sat in the hold on heavy wooden boxes containing their goods and held others on their laps, wrapped with their arms and legs. That one in the yellow and blue was Master Edgar, who sold finished woolen goods to London; next to him and just to the left was Master Randolph, who might be a knight, though Mistress Eglantine wasn't certain. In any case, he carried arms to sell. Other crates contained salt, meat, bread, and wine. The knight (if he was a knight) and Master Edgar were regular passengers.

The steady slap and roll would have put me to sleep if the sleet hadn't pricked my face.

"We be beyond the troughs!"

Mistress Eglantine explained that the floor of the Channel in the north had deep gouges on the European side, but a shallow shelf next to England. Add to that, the English side had warm seas. She always felt safer once they were past the depths and were in the shallows.

"The days be lang," she repeated, "which be a good omen as weil. Nicht can bring winds."

We rose and fell on the billows, the wind blew, Mistress Eglantine fell quiet, and I slept. Once I woke—it was still light—and I removed Mistress Eglantine's sharp chin from my shoulder. My habit was wet from her drool. Her ducks, free from their cages, waddled among the other sleeping passengers, cleaning their crumbs off the deck. What did it matter? The ducks should be permitted a bit of freedom on their last day on earth.

I planned to think of Theo, but I fell asleep again. Perhaps I dreamed of him, for I woke myself briefly by laughing.

It was twilight. We were passing an island.

"Be that a landmark?" I nudged Mistress Eglantine.

She roused herself for a moment. "An iceberg."

"Impossible!"

Then she sat upright. "Boot we shuld be headed south!" Then she discovered her empty cages; her ducks, now sleeping with their heads under their wings, perched next to the captain. "Oh, weil." She snuggled into my shoulder again.

I watched the iceberg as long as I could see it. One of the blond, barefoot sailors was also watching it; his face looked worried. Mistress Eglantine had been right; as darkness fell, the wind rose. Even with two tunics, and Mistress Eglantine as windbreak, my teeth chattered. The *Drage* shivered, too, as it took the billows directly on with a steady thump. The sail had been lowered; the sailors again used their oars.

Though dark at sea level, the sky high above us still glowed. It was a strange sensation, sailing in a black world under a luminous sky. The rocking motion, the rhythm of the snores, the slap of waves lulled me into forgetting the iceberg. Again, I slept.

I was wakened by shouting! The Vikings—where were they in the dark? What were they saying? Were they speaking Viking? Or Danish? Crates crashed! Where were their owners?

Because it's night, I thought groggily. *Deo gratias* that we're on a Viking ship.

This time icy foam woke me thoroughly! I tried to stand in the lurching ship. Lightning flared over an oil-black sea. The mast broke with a giant splinter right in front of me—had it hit the other passengers? Where was Mistress Eglantine? I groped in empty air. Only water! Wind! The dragon pole lay flat across the prow—could it be raised again? Oh God, where were the Vikings? I screamed—a wave broke over me like a jaw! Mistress Eglantine! The jaw clamped— I swallowed salt water.

I grabbed the pole at the dragon-head end. Together we

slid into the sea. The ship sucked behind me and I kicked with all my strength! Theo! Enoch!

My head hit my saddlebag. Gagging and swallowing, I looped its handle to my belt. Kicked forever—*O Deus juva me,* did I move? *Keep your mouth shut—don't swallow water!* Theo, oh Theo, don't give up, God help me, I'll pick you up.

Where was Dover?

My foot touched solid ground.

A sandspit or the shallows of England?

I stood—I pushed my dragon pole back to sea. An orange sun crept over the horizon before me. Crept over the *mountain!* Land! But where? Something heavy bumped my knees—Bonel's saddlebag. I couldn't undo the wet knot at my waist.

With waves licking my ankles, I stared at a rounded blue horizon—England, it could only be England!

Now sobbing, I staggered onto sand dunes. Only when I was on a dry beach did I look back to sea; the ship was gone.

Crates of cargo and supine merchants littered the beach. I stumbled among the bodies looking for a sign of life—all were dead, some hideously injured. Even Lord Randolph the knight, if he was a knight. They sprawled on bleached bones, showing that we hadn't been the first to wreck on this beach. Bones and bodies, except for Mistress Eglantine. I looked three times before I gave up. Vultures circled low.

I felt guilty for surviving. Mistress Eglantine had thought

I would bring good fortune to our ship because I was a nun. But I wasn't a nun. Was this God's way of punishing me for my disguise? Was He offended?

I knelt to ask God's blessing for the dead and to thank Him for His mercy toward me. *I won't forget,* I promised.

Where was I? To my left and to my right stretched a wide expanse of sand. The beach was enclosed by two long arms reaching into the sea, forming a bay. Was there a bay above Dover? I was too tired to seek my whereabouts just yet.

I sank upon a high dune away from the human graveyard. To my right rolled a series of dunes stretching to infinity; to my left was a rocky promontory, with stunted trees atop and perhaps a hill behind it. The rocks, I thought. I should go toward the rocks. After I'd rested.

But I couldn't rest—I was agitated. Theo, I had to reach Theo.

I curled on the warm, dry dune.

A flat spoon nudged under my nose. I pushed it away.

"Quack! Quack!"

I dozed, it came again: "Quack! Quack!"

I lay in a stupor. A duck—was it possible that Mistress Eglantine had survived? I sat up.

"Quack!" the duck sounded urgently. Henry or Clémence? I couldn't tell.

"Lead me to her."

My heavy saddlebag still struck my leg every time I

stepped. What had happened to Theo's document? I reached inside. It was dry, everything safe. Smart Bonel, to anticipate water damage. After I'd cared for Mistress Eglantine, I would examine all my treasure. The duck waddled confidently, turning his head from time to time to be certain I was following. He headed to a pile of kelp.

"Quack! Quack!"

Tangled in the weed was a dead bird. I leaned closer; the other duck.

"He's dead," I told my guide gently.

He nudged the supine duck with his bill, and I changed my mind.

"Almost dead," I amended. "There's naught I can do."

He quacked vociferously, alternately nudging the duck and pulling at my skirt with his bill. Impressed by his determination, I decided there was only one way to prove my point: I picked up the sopping fowl, whose cold, webbed foot curled around my finger; I carried him to a higher dune, and wrapped myself around him.

With a purring whimper, the first duck forced his way under my arm as well. We all fell into a deep sleep. I was wakened by a soft conversation. With quacks and a variety of other noises like purring, laughing, even words, the ducks conversed under my arm. When I sat up, I could no longer tell the sick from the well: they were identical.

The sun had descended—the air chilled. The dead bodies still lay on the beach; two had been licked by the incoming tide. I should search them, I thought dully, remembering Bok, but I couldn't. Several had lost their eyes to seabirds. With a shiver, I turned away.

"I lead, mates!" I said. "You follow."

Still chattering and splattering in the sand, the ducks waddled after me.

We walked around the rocks without having to climb over them. We did have to climb over a fallen oak tree in our path, however, which took all our strength. On the far side of the tree stood a tall daub-and-beamed house, built on stilts below and with an ancient thatch on top. The bottom part was a cow byre, and there were several white beasts who mooed when they saw me.

"Is anyone home?" I shouted.

"Quack!"

"Not you—be quiet."

A shutter on the top floor opened. "Who's there?" called a woman's voice. "Do you have a duck to sell?"

No face appeared.

"I'm a nun from St. Margaret's Abbey in Nantes and yes, I have two good ducks to sell, but only for laying, not for the table!"

"Stay right there—I'll be doon."

In time, two ancient dames walked around the corner of the house.

"What's your name, Sister? Did you walk from Nantes?" It was the voice from the window.

The women were so alike that they must be sisters: tiny creatures who didn't reach my shoulder, with wrinkled faces and bright blue eyes under brown woolen scarves tied low across their foreheads, full brown tunics protected by black aprons to their ankles. Their bare feet were splayed.

"Nantes is in France, and I was shipwrecked; Sister Angela at your service. I was on my way to London to join King John's Crusade to the Holy Land, when my ship was wrecked at sea and . . ."

"France?"

"Close to Paris."

"And you drifted so far north?" the first old lady said. "Usually our shipwrecked guests come from Scandinavia. Isn't that right, sister?"

Sister nodded.

"We're Abigail and Alysoun of Sky-field," the first said. "May we offer you hospitality?"

"Can my ducks have shelter as well? They're the only other survivors and . . ."

"Of course." Abigail clucked sympathetically. "They would survive, wouldn't they? Ducks can swim."

I'd thought of that, of course. Yet my survival—the dragon, the shelf under the sea—seemed a miracle greater than the ducks'.

I followed the sisters and the ducks followed me around the house to where a double door gave entry.

"Our cows live on the ground floor," Alysoun explained, as we stepped into a pitch space redolent of milk and cow pats, sweet breath and hay. Memory surfaced: Theo, when we'd hidden in France, the friendly sound of swishing tails, and Theo getting his fill of milk at last. Oh, how could I get to London from here? Was Lady Matilda giving him fresh cow's milk?

As if she caught my thought, one sister said, "They give us milk; we give them a home. A fair exchange, isn't it, sister?"

"We should pay them rent," her sister argued gently. "They warm our quarters in winter and give us curds, cheese, butter . . ."

One sister nimbly climbed a ladder against the wall.

"Quack!"

"Leave the ducks with the cows," Alysoun called down. "I'll bring them grain and water."

The instant I reached the first level, she climbed back down with a small sack of oats and a crock of water. The cow smell was less distinct here, the warmth greater.

"Quack!" came the grateful sound from below.

"Are you hungry as well?" Abigail asked. "I can give you bread and beer. We have a bit of sausage if that's to your taste."

Oh, it was. More than anything at Bonel's, I'd missed my pork. Rachel had said that Jews didn't eat pork because it caused leprosy. She was probably right, so I would get leprosy!

Alysoun climbed back. "Those ducks are almost human, aren't they?"

"Aye."

The sisters brought forth an apple pudding and a bit of cheese.

When I'd finished eating, Abigail said gently, "Tell us all about your shipwreck, dear."

I tried, unsuccessfully because of my emotions, so said simply, "A miracle."

They gazed in awe. "You're the first person since we were children who's survived such a disaster."

"And he was a holy man as well, you remember, sister."

Alysoun nodded.

Abigail took my hand. "You're a saint, Sister Angela. God preserved you for some great purpose."

Since I'd been feeling guilt for my survival, I thrilled at her words. "Do you think so?"

They both nodded.

"A miracle," Alysoun assured me, "and to be accomplished right here in Dunsmere."

"Dunsmere?" I sank to the floor, unable to stand. "Did you say Dunsmere?" Practically the same as saying Wanthwaite!

Dunsmere was their closest village, though they'd been there only once, when they were children. Their father, a worldly man from Denmark, had taken them to the fair.

"How far?" I asked.

Less than a day's ride, across the ridge and onto Dere Street. Their voices continued; I heard them as through a fog.

Dunsmere, I was close to Dunsmere, God was rewarding me!

At my insistence, they returned to to their memories of Dunsmere with its green and its church. My eyes filled.

I'd heard a tale, once, of a shipwreck on a strange strand and how one woman alone had been saved to make a miracle. I was that woman! Wanthwaite was my miracle! Aye, I would have to travel to Dere Street anyway to go to London and it would be only a week at the most and Theo was safe for a month! This was the proper order, Wanthwaite first, I was about to see Wanthwaite.

And Enoch.

Though I protested that the nag the sisters gave me in exchange for my ducks was too much, the horse was a bad bargain. She trembled and stumbled on the path up the ridge until I apologized profusely for my existence; I would get off and lead and felt I should offer her my back! The sisters called her Shark—they named all their animals for fish; the ducks were now Minnow and Trout—and maybe Shark could swim better than she could climb. Nonetheless, we reached the top of the ridge. Looking down at the smiling sisters and their new ducks, I waved and called, "Thank you!" again.

There was a dramatic drop to my left, and a vertical hill covered with spring growth to my right, an ancient path along the top of the ridge. The vista below thrilled my very bones, a bright green mixed with forests, a handsome castle looming in the distance, the beating heart of England. I felt the miracle of my survival all over again: England, Wanthwaite, Enoch. *Enoch and England, Enoch and England!*

At Haute Tierce, I stopped for my repast beside a cloud of purple frangia. The sky at eye level was a deep blue with two vertical clouds. The contrast between the blue and the white made me gasp with wonder. No place in the world has such skies as England; French skies are beautiful in their way but always muted with a metallic overtone, such as copper blue or silver blue or bronze blue. This was purity itself, where the very idea of heaven must have been born.

Heaven, survival, Sister Angela, the miracle of Enoch. I laughed aloud.

At midday, I heard the gurgle of a spring below. I slid down to a small grassy dell before a pool, where I opened my saddlebag. The money bag contained well over a hundred livres, a fortune. Though Bonel had Sea Mew, I must repay him—not even a king could give away so much money. Then the jewels, a mix of uncut gemstones and finished jewels in their settings: the familiar lion and eagle pendants, a moonstone set in silver—how did he know my favorite?—various pendants of semiprecious stones, then gemstones of emerald, beryl, topaz, amethyst, two small pale rubies, an Egyptian turquoise, and I know not how many more. "Too much, too much," I moaned. These I would certainly give back, since I had no intention of seeking employment in London.

A small stream bubbled among cowslips to form a pool. I removed both my habit and the new tunic beneath it—there was no one to see except a comical toad on the rock opposite —and I doubted if even he could see me, since his eyes stared in opposite directions. After I'd drunk and washed my person, I dipped both tunics to remove seawater and stretched them upon a bush while I slept.

The sun was still high in its run when I woke. The toad had leaped to a closer rock, and perhaps he could see me now—I put both tunics on again, the habit on top. They were still a bit damp, but no matter. My unbraided hair was also damp as it fell free to my waist.

"Goodbye, Mr. Toad. Thank you for your company." I reached past his puffed cheeks to stroke his beating throat, and froze. This was the toad my mother had called the golden leopard-prince; though mainly covered with yellow spots outlined in black, he had faint scarlet lines between his eyes, meaning he was poisonous. Fortunately—like some spiders and snakes—he was not aggressive, but if one should be bitten or eat him in a stew, that would be farewell forever. I backed very cautiously to my hillock and out of sight.

Riding through white and yellow and pink flowers on all sides, I reached my descent just when the sun had lowered to eye level. Slowly, I guided Shark down the steep path to Dere Street, which seemed haunted. I imagined Dame Margery waving goodbye from her bush after Roland de Roncechaux had murdered my parents, pictured Enoch rounding the bend for the first time, blowing his pipe. Oh, I couldn't breathe, couldn't think. After how many years? Was I still beautiful? Aye, Bonel had said that I was. Surely Enoch . . .

Every stone, every tree sighed *welcome home.* My blood churned, my eyes pooled. If only Theo were with me! I had only my flatulent Shark to savor the moment with me.

There was the path to Dunsmere. Now Maisry beckoned eerily; a flock of crows gave warning.

Here were the fields where Maisry and I had flung black mud at one another; long curved furrows gleamed in the retreating sun. Enoch had plowed early.

Here was a break in the low stone wall Dame Margery and I had followed.

"Hoyt!" Shark turned.

I stopped before the ford where the Wanthwaite River gurgled over the stones. I dismounted, removed my habit. Oh, to have a reflecting pool! I ran my fingers through my waves. Was it unseemly to show my hair? Yet Enoch was my husband—hadn't he said a hundred times how he loved my pale locks? I dipped water to my heated face, then mounted again. Shark walked cautiously across the ford.

On the far side, I dismounted again. I pulled the neck of

my new tunic downward to display my throat, pinned the moonstone set in silver on the ruff. Up the spinney, *Enoch and England.*

Chickens clucked with contentment on one side; I missed my ducks. A new lamb bleated somewhere in the hills—an orphan lamb deserted by his mother. *You're not deserted, Theo—tomorrow your father and I will come!* The soft lowing of cows, a horse whinnying in alarm. The dovecote. I smelled the pigs, though they made no sound.

I walked across the moat bridge, somewhat surprised that the iron gate was open. Below this bridge, my injured father had bled to death. Dame Margery had sat close, mourning Maisry's death.

I passed the donjon, the cheesehouse where my wolf, Lance, had been caged. Yet there were happy memories as well. I'd walked this very path to become Enoch's bride. There had been pine torches then as there were now. Were they expecting me? But how?

I tied Shark in the stable. When I returned to the path, the thump of the kettle and the shriek of the pipe filled the courtyard—aye, they must be expecting me.

Eagerly, I ran past the schoolroom, the chapel, the privet hedge, the geroldinga apple tree now in blossom, straight to the Great Hall! I stopped at the entry.

What a party they'd prepared! Drunkalew as mice, Highlanders flung their skirts and leaped to the beat. "Cum, my buxom burdie, fling a foot!"

"Ho-la! Gae aft, lass! Gi'e a hap, stap, a lowp, then a cuchie!"

I couldn't stand still—I jiggled to the piper's beat!

"Grab her hurdies!"

My eyes searched—Gruoth had seen me, and there were Edwina and Thorketil. All dressed in their best brechan feiles! Round and round—I grew dizzy. Where was Enoch?

"Lip the lassie!" shouted a high tenor voice.

"Gi'e her the skean dhu!"

"Swape!"

Enoch thrust a broom into the hands of a short dark-haired lassie jigging before him, aye, Enoch! Taller and leaner than I remembered and dressed in his best kirtle and skirts, I knew that red-gold hair as if it waved to *my* shoulders, had felt that beard against my face!

Then I froze. Goddes halp, this was a wedding, aye, Enoch's wedding! I tried to find a shadow—I kicked a torch! But there was another—where could I go? Where could I hide?

Enoch grabbed his bride most ardently—he kissed her full on the lips!

"Alix!" Gruoth screeched.

Death had attended the wedding—I was death. I was not the welcomed survivor, but the bad folet Lucinda. The guests froze. The pipes whined to silence.

Enoch stared wildly at me and fell to the rushes. Blood spurted from his head. The black-haired lassie knelt beside him.

5

I SPENT THE NIGHT ON THE RUSHES WRAPPED IN GRUOTH'S ARMS close to his pool of blood. He, of course, slept in his *wife's* arms up the stairs in the room my parents had shared. Gruoth assured me that Enoch had believed I was dead; otherwise he would never have married, would he? Or at least he would have gotten an annulment first.

I managed with great effort to learn the bride's name: Lady Fiona of Loch-Baver, close to Inverness.

And yes, she was rich; she'd inherited vast estates from her father and later her first husband.

And yes, Enoch had courted her for some time; two years, in fact.

I announced myself delighted for his good fortune. Of course, he would be returning to Scotland now. Could Gruoth and her husband, Donald, accompany me to London the following day?

I didn't really change so abruptly, but what could I do? I'd always been a good actress; some would say liar.

When I entered the stable at dawn, I almost fell over Enoch. He was squatted in a corner with a huge white bandage around his head.

We stared at one another in the gloom.

"Are you badly hurt?" I asked courteously. My voice sounded like a horse's whinny.

"Nay."

He stood. Enoch. Not an apparition or a dream, but Enoch. Had I glorified him in memory? I didn't think so—just the opposite. He was a Scot, of course, which he couldn't help and which explained his red-gold hair and his outlandish skirts. His eyes were the blue of the English sky, I'd gotten that right. How could I have forgotten his red, red lips and his hairy arms, his strong hands with their sensitive fingers? His beard was trimmed short (for his bride?), and he had two new thin lines between his eyebrows.

"Waesucks!"

I supposed that was a compliment, but maybe not.

"Be ye a folet?" he asked.

"A witch?" Did I look that bad?

"Ye doona luik real." He continued to stare. "Lak ond unlak Alix."

"People grow up, milord."

"Aye," he agreed. Then, after a pause, "Ye're a lady."

As opposed to the child he'd left at Wanthwaite, aye. I waited in vain for a real compliment. So much for my new tunic and silver pin.

I couldn't get around him. "Would you mind?"

He knelt in front of a nest of straw. "Ich be afeared he's dying."

I started. "Who?"

"My wolf, Dingwall." He hesitated. "It war meant fer ye— Ich brought her back fram Scotland quhan ye war . . ."

Stolen away. In spite of myself, I was touched. I knelt beside him. The wolf, lying on a sheepskin, was definitely dying. Her suffering was palpable, her expression almost human. Looking at her silver mask and yellow eyes, I began to tremble. Was it the wolf, or was it Enoch? We both rose together.

"She doesn't look good, Enoch. What's her trouble?"

He stroked her muzzle, then turned to me.

"Waesucks!" he said again.

He startled himself as well as me. It was a moment of intimacy that neither of us expected or wanted. He licked his upper lip. "Ich be nocht sartain, boot Ich think she war bit, mayhap by a rat, mayhap a snak."

Now I had the woodly thought that he was referring to King John as a snake. I touched the wolf. Mayhap a toad? No, toads don't bite, and I doubt if a wolf would eat a toad. Nor spiders—a snake. There were few adders this far north, but there were a few.

I forced myself to peer through the gloom at the horses. Shark looked only slightly better than the wolf, but there was a line of fine healthy steeds against the wall. I signaled to the stable boy to saddle a black mare.

"That be Fiona's," Enoch said, his voice now hostile.

"Your wife's? Thank you for warning me, milord." I signaled for a bay mare.

"She canna be my wif if ye're alive; Ich thocht ye war daid," he said defensively.

I couldn't stop myself. "After you go north, I hope to resume my life here. Not as your wife, of course."

"Ich thoucht ye daid becas King Richard died twa years ago."

Soothly. I didn't want or have to explain. Theo, oh, Theo—I'm coming! All the pent-up emotion I'd felt for Enoch and England now centered on my darling boy. Yet I must explain to some extent.

"The present king looked on me as a rival to the Crown and tried to kill me."

"Rival? Boot ye be female!"

I stumbled on quickly. "As you can see, he failed, but I was delayed. To be honest, I planned to resume my life here as I'd left it. Well, that's impossible." I took a deep breath. "You're wed to another—I must accept that fact—but *Deo gratias,* I still have Wanthwaite."

And England.

"Nay, Alix, Wanthwaite be mine ond that horse ye just saddled be mine!"

"You have your estates in Scotland, Gruoth told me." I was now seated on the bay. "This horse and all the animals at Wanthwaite as well as all the furnishings, grain, ale, and foodstuffs were left me by my parents, and they're still mine." I couldn't resist a jab. "Your Lady Fiona's vast estates, I am told, make Wanthwaite look paltry. I congratulate you on finding such a rich lady!"

I'd touched a nerve.

"Quhat Fiona ha'e be nocht yer affair!" he roared. "Ond Ich nocht be wed to her yit! Boot quhen I git my annulment, this property be mine!"

I feared he might be right, but I would fight for Wanthwaite! If the canon law supported him, well, I would find another law! Come to think of it, I could kill Enoch after I'd killed King John.

"Wanthwaite be mine! Bought fer a goodly sum, ye recall. Fiona ha'e deeded all her land to me, boot we'll live in Wanthwaite! I'm makin' her an English baroness!"

No time to argue now. I raised my quoit and kicked my steed.

He grabbed my bridle. "Yif ye claim Wanthwaite, quhy do ye lave it nu? Quhar gang ye? Ond quhy?"

I'd been afraid he would ask, yet I know not where the lie came from that I uttered. "To tell the truth, I must go to London to pick up the Crown Jewels Richard left to me. I'll return at once." I felt pleased with myself. Plausible. Impersonal. Safe. And I knew about jewels. A perfect lie; I hadn't lost my skill.

He still held my bridle. "Quhar be they in London?"

My jaw dropped for a beat—what could I say? A good lie stays close to the truth.

"I'm meeting someone—er—at Baynard Castle. Aye, a lady at Baynard Castle." I raised my quoit. "Let me go, if you please!"

"Quhy a lady? Quhy didna ye carry them yerself?"

Oh, he was shrewd. "I mentioned King John, didn't I? He feels—with a certain justification—that the Crown Jewels should stay with the Crown. Therefore, I was forced to send them with my friend. I'll be in the city only one day before I return."

"This lady mun be a fool to tak swich a risk. King John be muckle dangerous."

Oh, *Deus juva me,* he was! I forgot Enoch, forgot everything but Theo! Was it possible that the king had stopped Lady Matilda de Braose? Had Queen Eleanor deceived me?

Should I have taken even a day to come to Wanthwaite?
Enoch was waiting.

"Yes, he is dangerous. I must hurry!"

He didn't release my bridle.

I tried to assuage him. "I'm truly sorry, Enoch, that our
marriage turned out as it did, and I thank you for the wolf."

He led my steed into the courtyard. Gruoth and Donald
awaited on the moat bridge. If Enoch saw them, he said
nothing. He pulled off his bandage; his wound was no longer
bleeding, though his hair was matted.

"We're still wed, Alix, because I didna sake an annulment
yet, quhich manes that yer property be mine. Them Crown
Jules be mine."

Eyes blue as the English sky and as hard. "I'll give you
one jewel." One of Bonel's jewels.

"Ye'll gi'e me nothing! I'll tak quhat's mine! I'll ride to
London wi' ye!"

"No! You can't! You mustn't!"

He wrenched my bridle away and gave it to the stable boy.
"Wait richt here!"

The instant he disappeared into the Great Hall, I pulled
free and rode to Gruoth and Donald.

"Hurry!" I shouted.

We slipped sideways on the melting rime in the park. To
think that just last night I'd climbed here with such hope.
Theo! Theo! That was my hope now! My spirits soared. Theo,
my sweet companion for years to come. Then his wife and
grandchildren! Bliss, bliss, my golden babe!

We'd no sooner reached the lane leading to Dunsmere than I heard male voices and the fast clop of horses behind us—Enoch and his Scots galloped after us as fast as ever they could. I glanced again and almost fell from my saddle! Lady Fiona rode on her handsome ebony filly by Enoch's side—he was bringing her to London! She would witness when I picked up Theo? Never! Never!

I pressed my horse faster and faster—Gruoth and Donald struggled to keep up. I sobbed openly—there was only one road to London, and Enoch knew it! *Deus juva me*, why had I dangled jewels before his greedy eyes?

When we reached Dere Street, Enoch's party crowded in front of us and stopped so we couldn't pass. He and Lady Fiona dismounted and whispered. Then, to my horror, Lady Fiona walked briskly toward me. She clutched my rein—we stared at one another. Well, I admit that she was beautiful in the Scottish manner: violet eyes—same shade as the violet, plaid cope clasped with silver at her shoulder—perfect pale skin, large white teeth, a chin that was a little too long and too sharp for absolute beauty (like a Lochinvar ax). Most surprising, she was older than I was and even older than Enoch, though she was still youthful, a rich widow from the Highlands, where Enoch had known her husband.

"Lady Alix," she said in a voice so soft I could hardly hear, "I be Lady Fiona of Loch-Baver, clase to Dingwall, which be clase to Inverness."

Dingwall—wasn't that what Enoch had called the dying wolf? I felt sick.

"Enoch tald as me ye war daid, or I would niver ha'e wed him in Haly Church."

I made no comment. Gruoth had told me of the many months Lady Fiona had spent at Wanthwaite—I was surprised she bothered getting wed at all.

"Ye're still his wife legally, boot he will get an annulment fram Haly Church quhan he returns fram London Town."

"Doesn't an annulment take a great deal of money?" I asked sweetly. "Are you paying?"

"'Twill be asey fer him quhan he has the Crown Jewels," she replied. "Quan he's free, I'll be back."

"In the meantime, I'm his legal wife."

Her violet eyes widened; her voice became steely. "Nocht fer long, because ye're a well-known houri. Everybody in England knaws aboot you and King Richard."

I felt sick. Was that true?

The Church controlled marriage laws, but didn't the assize court control property? Very well, I would let Enoch go—and good riddance—but not Wanthwaite.

Lady Fiona had gone back to Enoch, where they spoke in low tones. Both were dismounted; both glanced at me from time to time. I tried in vain to push my steed past Enoch's Scots. Then, suddenly, they gave way because Enoch was back at their head. Lady Fiona was leading another small group of knights toward the north, toward Scotland.

Enoch and England, a sour mantra now. Of course, England was still the same. It was a beautiful morning.

Thorketil, Duncan, Donald, and Wallace were the only men I recognized in Enoch's party, former friends all. Now none of them smiled or spoke to me. Did they feel guilty for not

fighting the English when Bonel had snatched me years ago?
Did they, like Fiona, consider me a houri? Besides these four,
there were six strangers, one of them an older man, all Scots.
Aye, I would have cultivated them if I hadn't been distracted
by Enoch. I knew not whether it was the sense of intimacy or
revulsion that so obsessed me: his appearance, his smell, the
way he moved, his voice and laughter. Above all, there was
memory of things not seen or smelled. Not just how he'd
protected me on the road as my "brother," or even more on
the Crusade. But later: his feel in the dark, his body on top of
mine, the bliss—almost anguish—that we shared.

Did he remember as well? He must—how could he forget? And why was he angry? I had the reason to be angry! I
hadn't chosen to go with King Richard, had I? But Enoch had
chosen that Scottish hag Fiona! How could I forgive him?
Easy. I couldn't!

Yet Wanthwaite was an unexpected problem.

Should I approach Bonel's friends in London now? No,
no, Theo must see Wanthwaite no matter what; I must bring
my baby home. And yet—another problem—were either
Theo or I safe in Wanthwaite? King John was still very much
abroad. I frowned. King John might not know my whereabouts in France, but he could find me easily at Wanthwaite in
England. How tenacious was he? He had the Crown, after all,
and I'd heard somewhere that he'd wed. Did his bride satisfy
Raoul? Would he still seek me? Theo? My heart thumped;
Queen Eleanor had moved for some reason, and there was the
peasant girl waving in Rouen!

I hadn't noticed when we began our climb in the foothills
of the Pennine Mountains. Now I was plagued by another

memory, of when Enoch and I had first ridden this road together, how I'd suspected him and how kind he'd proven to be. I'd been so raw after the slaughter of my family. Oh, I wished there were another road to London!

"We be gang high," Gruoth's uneasy voice jarred me back to the present.

"We have to cross the Pennine Mountains," I explained. "We'll soon descend."

She pointed to the vast valley we'd just left. "Be we lakely to fall over the edge?"

"Of course not."

"Than quhy do they call these mountains 'fells'?"

Donald squeezed her fat knee. "Doona be concerned, Lady Alix. Gruoth be a-skeered of hights; she's fram the lowlands."

Enoch and England. I still had England, I thought again: the sky was certainly blue and the earth a dazzling green. And Enoch? As I watched his easy roll in his saddle and his pipes flopping on the horse's rump, I recalled his sweat in the dark, smelling slightly of boiled lamb, the way he ran thistles between his teeth, how his toes overlapped slightly on his long feet, the way he emanated heat (for he was never cold), the way he jumped into icy water every day he could find it. Aye, once I'd known him better than I knew myself. Now he was a curious mix: a stranger who evoked intimate memories.

As I watched him now, he struggled out of his wedding finery and into a bearskin vest, his half-cape held by the silver cat of his clan; he pulled on deerskin socks laced over knarry calves, and placed his fur hat with horns where his bandage had been; and, finally, his Lochinvar ax, his gavelock, and his

bow with a quiver of arrows. If you like savages, he was magnificent! At the same time, I prayed that Lady Matilda de
Braose never saw him.

Oh, Theo, brave sweet Theo; my eyes stung. Why did I
think of Enoch when I had a love of my own, love without
duplicity, the love of a small son for his mother and a mother
for her son. Yet when I opened my eyes, there was Enoch.

So I closed my eyes, and there was King John. Someone
in the commune had revealed my presence, which meant that
John was still seeking me. Queen Eleanor's revelations—
true? Why would she be false? John must think I was in Normandy—why else would he close the ports. How many
young women in red, I wondered, had paid the ultimate
price? How many boy children? (My heart thumped—Theo,
oh, Theo!) I'd promised the peasant girl in red—and John
was looking for me as I looked for him. Where was he? My
stomach became a ball of ice. *Aye, hide, baby brother, for one of us
will pay with our life and it will not be me!*

Would I—or John—have my present dilemma if Bonel
had not existed? Did I forgive him for his original role? Moot
questions; I would never see him again. Despite his brave words,
I knew it was true. As for the king's attitude toward the Jew, I
could only hope he never discovered how Bonel had saved me.

I concentrated on the dangerous mountain path. We would
not tumble into the valley, as Gruoth feared, but the narrow
way tilted precipitously and there were many roots. We
stopped at Haute Tierce at Meg's circle of stones on a flat
mountain plateau.

My mother had worshipped stones. My mother—my mother. I fought morbidity. Her decapitated head, her poor raped body. Because of her, I'd learned the law about rape, about murder, and I'd turned to the moot court—did it still exist? Now I must learn the law about annulment. Perhaps about murder. What law governed a king's death? The king *was* the law, he was the assize.

Enoch tore off a piece of Gruoth's ham, left over from his wedding feast. Likewise the oatcakes he stuffed into his mouth.

"Didn't you bring your own sustenance?" I asked coldly.

"Aye." He grinned with his mouth full. "Gruoth brang me my ham quhat I cured last fall." He held up a cake. "Ond these be made fram my estate below the oat line."

I walked away.

Though the sky was still bright, the path became difficult to see, as if I were again sailing on the North Sea. By the time we stopped to make camp, I was so exhausted that I failed to recognize the site: the very same narrow cave between rocks above a foaming tarn where Enoch and I had stayed our first night together. Was this deliberate? Aye, Enoch glanced in my direction as he pulled his knights inside. Then he hung the selfsame skin before the opening. Gruoth and Donald and I fought the wind in vain with our skimpy pelts on a line.

We ended wrapped in furs on the rocky ground.

"We don't need to be so close to Enoch," I said.

"'Tis safer," Donald pointed out.

Enoch, reeking of heat and haggis, emerged from his cave.

"'Tis a starry nicht," he said pleasantly.

"Aye," Gruoth answered.

"A guid breeze offen the moors."

If you call a gale a good breeze; I pretended to sleep.

Now I must scheme. Could I persuade Gruoth and Donald to stay with me after I'd picked up Theo? I needed their help badly. Would they fight against Enoch if it came to that? I must hire at least thirty people to run the estate, ten of them knights. Could I enlist help from men in Dunsmere? Would *anyone* fight the king on my behalf?

And how would Enoch react when he learned the truth about the jewels, about Theo? I would pick up Theo, and Enoch could make of it whatever he wished.

Enoch took my arm to guide me across the shallow Thames at Oxenford, the first time he'd touched me.

"Tal me, Alix, did ye e'er see Richard's jules?"

"Aye." I pushed his hand away.

"Con ye recall quhat they were?" He took my arm again.

"A pearl of great worth . . ." and I stopped. The pearl was Theo.

"Ond rubies ond diamonds?" He had bathed in the Thames—his hair was still wet. "King John ha'e demanded a thousand marks in scutage. 'Twould be amusin' to pay him fram his ane inheritance." He stopped. "Except I doona knaw how to dispose o' fine jewels."

He needn't worry.

When we joined Icknield Street, I approached him. "Lord Enoch, forthwith you will address me as Lady Angela, if it please you."

His blue eyes studied me. "Quhy?"

"Lady Angela. Do you promise?"

"Aye, yif ye call me Saint Peter."

"The lady I'm meeting is expecting a Lady Angela."

His eyes narrowed. "Ha'e she ne'er seen ye before?"

"No, she's a friend of a friend." I hesitated. "And of King John's, which is why the friend thought she could be trusted." I hesitated again. "The jewels are in a packet—she doesn't know the content. She merely has the name I told you."

"Ye entrusted swich a prize to a straunger?" His brows shot up. "Ye've changed less that I thocht."

For once, I agreed with him.

He placed a heavy hand on my shoulder. "Yet ye ha'e changed."

Eating worms and hiding in bushes while someone tries to kill you will change anybody.

"Ye're still shifty, anely moreso."

I replied mildly, "This lady is expecting a Lady Angela."

"Angela maybe, boot nocht an angel," he agreed. "Quhat did Richard think quhan ye became a houri growed? He liked his boys young!"

My eyes filled. "Why did you refuse to release me when he asked? He offered you money, Wanthwaite."

"Ye shuld thank me!" He turned away.

"Why are you so greedy now?"

"I be nocht greedy—I'll gi'e ye that horse."

Gruoth tugged on my sleeve, wanting me to explain the

wonders around us. From Icknield Street, we could now see London spreading below us on the far side of the city wall. I pointed to the Thames, winding through the city, as a reference point.

Enoch interrupted my description. "Con ye pay fer yerself ond yer people at the inn, Lady Angela?"

"Yes."

"Ond I tak it ye doona wish to gae through Newgate."

My heart thumped. If the king had searched the commune in Rouen and knew I'd fled . . .

"No, if it please you . . ."

So we bypassed Newgate, though it lay directly on our path. I grew totty: I was now breathing the same air as Theo; I could feel his presence. I kept my eyes on Enoch or I would have fallen from my steed as we hugged the wall leading toward Smithfield, the route we'd taken before when led by Enoch's doxy. Now, as then, the roaring mill at Old Bourne below us stopped conversation.

We reached Smithfield in good time. The horse fair was not in progress, meaning it was not Monday. Venders sold a few horses, however, though the nags were used mostly to display equipment such as fancy saddles and bridles. Some were studded with semiprecious jewels—rough work, in my opinion, but work that might be easy to secure. Sidesaddles designed for great ladies (*sambue*), especially, were heavily studded. Aye, in an emergency I might support Theo for a few months while I sought legal help.

Enoch led us to the horse pool, where we dismounted to let our steeds drink. Gruoth again questioned me about the sights, but I waved her off, now heartsick when I saw a young boy selling ducks—poor Mistress Eglantine. How were Henry and Clémence faring with the sisters? Better than they would have fared at Wanthwaite, where we had so many mouths to feed. Poor Mistress Eglantine, I thought again. The shallows of England had done her no good, nor had my religious garb. Had she suffered? I hoped the mast had struck her, that her demise had been swift. I turned my back to cross myself and say a prayer for her soul.

At dusk, Enoch led us to Aldgate, where we all stopped as he surveyed the situation. When the guards *aleoir* stopped an unruly group of tipplers who had a courtesan in their midst, he signaled that we should slip through.

Once on the other side of the high wall, we had to dismount in order to make progress through the disorderly mob thronging the street. We linked arms in order to stay together, and wide-eyed Gruoth pulled on me to explain the puzzles and verses smeared in human excrement on the eighteen-foot wall; I could read only one for her: *Sal be a houri.* When she asked the meaning of *houri*, I pulled her forward as swiftly as the crowds would permit, saying that curfew would soon ring. Now she gaped at the spires of St. Paul's looming on the horizon. I explained the importance of the great cathedral that dominated London, only to find that she had been distracted by a large yellow-stone house with ornamental portals—was it also a church?

"No, private; the yellow stone is imported from Caen," I informed her.

She was struck silent at the sheer wealth of the city. She was so diverted, in fact, that she accidentally stepped into the stream washing down the middle of the road. Donald and I cleaned her foot at once lest she become infected. The stream was awash with dead dogs and cats and fowls, human garbage, offal and animal shit and waste, even the stinking body of an old man whom hogs were eating apace. We Christians would be lucky if leprosy was the only disease pigs carried.

"Quhar cum all them swine?" Gruoth cried.

"Nobody knows exactly; they breed faster than flies and die faster, too—today's street cleaners will be tonight's pork pies." I suddenly yearned for a pie from the famous pantry along the Thames. "Tomorrow there will be new pigs."

We turned off Newgate Street onto the even more crowded Thames Street beside the river; I suspected (correctly) that Enoch was leading us to Jasper Peterfee's Inn of the Red Fox, where we'd stayed before. Now Gruoth was intrigued by the private ports carved into the banks of the Thames. She'd never seen such a grand river—even in Scotland—or such tall boats. I was struck by one craft myself, a merchant ship with a tall mast anchored in Queenshithe, Queen Eleanor's port. I'd seen this very ship before, aye, in La Rochelle!

Great ladies and gentlemen dressed in fine brocaded tunics, some decorated with sparkling gemstones cut in facets and cabochons, strolled on the Strand for the evening vapors. I counted six lion pendants.

"Be he the king?" Gruoth asked as we passed a tall wight decorated in gilt.

"No, probably a duke."

Aside from the fact that the king would never stroll unguarded, King John was a short man. Yet he was here; his red banner flew over his palace of Bermondsey on the other side of the river. Had he followed me here? Or Theo?

I shook as if with palsy.

Now we passed one castle after another, each with tall, forbidding walls against invading armies. Only one castle had a dock on the Thames—Baynard Castle, it had to be! So huge, so ancient, my heart squeezed, I lost breath. Shading my eyes against the low sun, I found tiny slits that might serve as windows. Did I see a small hand waving?

The sun set; Baynard Castle loomed as a menacing black behemoth above the swift-flowing Thames, now white as milk. White as death. I moaned aloud.

"Quhy be ye stopped?" Enoch stood beside me. "This be Baynard Castle."

"Do you know it?"

"I knaw Lord Robert fitzWalter quhat owns it."

I was astounded. "How do you know him?"

"He be one of our Brotherhood."

"A clan brother? A Scot?"

"Nay, milady. Remember that I'm an English baron nu fram Wanthwaite in the north. Sae is Lord Robert; he ha'e the honor o' this castle, boot his real hame be in Dunmow, close to Wanthwaite. There be aboot forty o' us barons in the northern Brotherhood."

"It sounds like a clan."

"'Tis mar a financial organization." He considered. "Aye, we ha'e a clase financial relationship, lak the Jews. We gi'e pledges o' money whan a brother be unable to pay his scutage or quhan crops fail or quhan one be under attack." He gazed at me significantly. "Notice, milady, e'en yif the wives inherited the estates, the men mun run them."

"Is bigamy also a requirement?" I asked sweetly.

As he turned away abruptly, I caught his sleeve. "Are we going to the Inn of the Red Fox?"

"Aye, I hope ye have coin to pay fer Gruoth and Donald."

"I told you I do."

We entered the inn in a long slow twilight. Inside, everything appeared exactly the same as I remembered. Though Master Peterfee now wore white hair atop, he still swung on his ropes, spry as any spider, though instead of eight good legs, he had no legs at all. I looked automatically for my wolf, Lance, whom I'd left with the innkeeper, though I knew he must have died by now. In his place, however, a large gray wolf curled on a pile of straw in the corner; he growled from his chest, then whined. He trotted directly to me, rubbed my hip, then put his paws on my shoulders and mouthed my face.

"Wolves lak ye," Enoch observed.

"Isn't he sweet?"

"Not at all!" Master Peterfee was astonished. "I keep him tied because he be fierce." He tried unsuccessfully to pull the wolf off me. "That be Wolfbane, son o' a wolf I once had called Lance." Master Peterfee, who didn't recognize me, of course, was still amazed. "He's never that friendly. I never see him act so."

The wolf retreated to his corner, where he watched me, whining softly.

Since it was too late to send to the river pantries for pies, Master Peterfee offered us a bit of dried fish to share. After we'd all eaten, he showed us to our rooms: I'd hired a double for Gruoth and Donald and a single for myself, a most luxurious choice since most travelers—for example, Enoch and the Scots—lay on the floor in one room together. I would soon share mine as well with Theo.

I sat in the dark and listened to bedbugs rustling in my mat. Curfew rang; I couldn't see my own walls. I could no longer wait—what to do about Enoch? If he hurt Theo . . . Theo'd never heard a cross word from anyone. Yet Enoch would never . . . not the Enoch I knew. Did he like children? He'd liked me when I was a child.

I paced till and fro. A strong breeze came off the Thames, along with bawdy songs and shouts as ruffians took to the streets. Tomorrow, tomorrow—all would be over.

I stopped. Why wait until tomorrow? I must do my deed tonight! Aye, that was my solution!

I fumbled in my saddlebag for my nun's habit. I added a dark veil over my face I'd not worn with Bonel. Then I cautiously opened the door; all was silent in the dark hall except for drunken songs coming from Enoch's quarters, *Deo gratias.* I glided silently to the top of the stairs, carefully avoiding the web of ropes Jasper Peterfee had hung from the ceiling. The lobby was empty; Wolfbane growled from his corner. I snapped my fingers, tore a rope from its peg, and leashed the brute.

Together, we stepped outside.

6

THE LANE IN FRONT OF THE INN SLOPED TO THE THAMES IN TOTAL
darkness. Wolfbane snarled, then lunged behind me. I sensed
a presence; someone was following me. A Scot? Enoch? Probably. I stopped and started—my follower did likewise. It
took all my strength to pull the wolf forward.

It might not be Enoch himself—his manner was more
open—but one of his knights, and at his order. Well, no help
for it. In fact, I was grateful for his presence when we reached
the Strand. Though still dark, torches blazed along the path,
casting long wavering reflections in the black Thames and
bodies sprawled drunkalew on the crowded way. My follower
was my human wolf.

In fact, the Strand was a virtual hell, complete with fiends
and staggering rowdies and criminals lurking on the river-
side. The women were as dangerous as the men. Wolfbane
snarled constantly, and twice he leaped at someone's throat.
Though I kept him on a tight lead so he wouldn't actually
kill, he frightened even the most inebriated from my person.
There were no horses or carts, only vomiting humans mixing
with pigs and wild dogs in the center gutter. Then Wolfbane
was attacked by a pack of canines, and I became the protec-
tor; I kicked hard at snapping muzzles and would have
sustained several bites except that Bok's boots stopped all

teeth. After the curs had retreated, I knelt briefly to feel Wolf-bane's muzzle—he licked my hand—before I braved the street again.

I walked on the river side of the street, where there were fewer people. The city side contained taverns and stews and mysterious boarded houses, all of them spewing human scum onto the street. In the distance, Baynard Castle loomed as more of a change in elements than an actual edifice, a solid darkness against a more pellucid darkness. I glanced over my shoulder: The Scot was still following me.

I walked as briskly as I could, making signs of the cross before staggering sailors and their aging wenches. Then, slowly, the taverns and hostels grew more infrequent; I had to leave the river to go around large castles between me and Bay-nard, and official torches reflected in the fast-moving Thames, so at least I could see my way. Then, gradually, it became more difficult to advance because every castle was heavily guarded. Castellans asked for proof that I was a nun in my French abbey; I wheedled my way through by saying I was from Fontevrault in Aquitaine, a place they knew not at all, though they understood the name of Queen Eleanor. I could no longer see my Scot—perhaps he hadn't been so persuasive as I had. When I stopped by a torch to get my bearings, Bay-nard Castle still loomed in the distance.

In fact, the castle seemed to retreat. I rested, trembling, against a wall in the shadow. I was near my goal at last and now practical problems rose in my fantastick cell. What was I going to say when I reached the castle? Would Lady Matilda—would anyone—admit me at this hour? And if I did gain entry, would Lady Matilda release Theo in the night? And to a nun instead of Lady Angela? On the one hand, I hoped she had the discretion to be cautious; yet I had undeniable proof of who I was, for Theo would recognize me.

So, if—when—I got him, then what? I must take him back to the inn to get my horse! *Benedicite,* I should have tied my horse somewhere more accessible, aye, and I must return Wolfbane. Should I leave the horse and purchase one on the road—I had the money! Very well, I had my horse and I had Theo—then what? No gate was open at night! My chest tightened. Think! Think! Aye, I must leave at once, this very moment. King John and Enoch were in London, both after me for different reasons—I must escape! Oh, I doubted not that Enoch would follow, but King John had taught me how to be evasive.

I left my wall. The street widened; horses had passed this way recently. Now I saw my shadow knight again; he'd just waited for me to show myself. He was canny, ducking in and out of wall niches, and persistent. Wolfbane saw him, too. The wolf growled; I tugged him forward.

As I got closer to Baynard Castle, a line of pine torches lighted my way. Their acrid smoke choked my breathing and my eyes began to run. How strange, when I'd endured the foul fumes of the street just a short time ago. Wolfbane made choking sounds. As breathing became more difficult, I stopped. Sparks drifted onto my sleeves.

Baynard Castle was on fire!

Men rushed past me, shouting and carrying buckets! Pushed against a wall, this time to make way, I stared in disbelief at circling sparks overhead. Ten black horses from the direction of the castle trotted smartly down the middle of the street. I flattened myself against the wall—had they rescued anyone? Did one of them carry Theo? A red glow played over their black bodies—the king's knights.

I hurled myself into their path!

"Stop! For God's' sake, stop! Baynard Castle is on fire! There are people inside—children!"

One cracked his whip across my face.

I staggered back and almost fell. My eye would surely have been gone if my veil hadn't protected me.

I ran as fast as I could toward Baynard Castle! A line of men were sloshing water from the Thames in a pitiful effort to stay the roar.

"Tak keer, Sister!" A rough arm pulled me against a wall. "Canna ye smell the smoke?"

Aye, I could smell! And see! My heart stopped—the peasant girl in red! She grinned and shook her fist! Was she saying that King John had done this? Was she admonishing me again to kill the king? But oh! If Theo were burned! I burst into loud wails!

I staggered back to a wall, too weak to move. Where had this crowd come from? Not routiers or whores, but commoners all, out to see the fire. There is no more seductive sight than flames—everyone loves disaster. Sobbing uncontrollably, I pushed hard through the rabble and ducked under chains. Some guards gave way—albeit reluctantly—to my habit.

The heat was overwhelming. The arrow slits—what I'd hoped might be windows—belched red flames and smoke. No small hand waved. People pushed me perilously close to the river to make room for the bucket brigade.

Maybe on the other side—I pushed three people onto the ground in a desperate effort to see. A spark burned through my sleeve—I pounded out the flame. I jerked off my veil, which was also flammable.

Sparks and flaming wood fell like rain. My peasant girl went mad—I waved to her frantically! Theo, oh, *Deus juva me*, I must find Theo. I stooped under a rope barrier. My shadow followed.

"Sister, stop!"

I ran toward the warning voice—a guard!

"Is anyone dead?"

He pushed me back. "I don't know! Leave or I'll arrest you!"

"Please! Please! In Jesus' name—there were children!"

"No children that I saw."

"And a great lady—Lady Matilda de Braose!"

The guard relaxed somewhat. "Why didn't you say so? She and her family left this afternoon."

So stunned I could hardly speak, I whispered, "Left for where?"

He was gone.

My heart dropped to my boots. I should be glad—aye, I *was* glad—that Theo hadn't been burned. But why had Lady Matilda left so abruptly? She knew I was coming—we'd said a month. Why hadn't she waited? Had she had warning? If so, by whom? And about what? Was her exit connected to Theo? Did she know who he was? Had King John discovered his whereabouts? What was her real position toward the Angevin family? Would she hold it against Theo that Richard was his father? She and her family were close to King John, and if he . . .

The wolf, hacking from smoke, collapsed at my feet.

I had to carry the heavy wolf back to the inn, where he struggled to be put down. When I pulled him to his water bowl, he drank voraciously. When I tried to leave him on his pile of straw, he howled so loudly that I pulled him up to my room. Wolfbane rushed inside, snarling for the kill!

"Waesucks, git him offen me!"

I jerked the rope hard. "Wolfbane, no!"

The wolf licked my hand.

"Quhy do ye bring swich a vicious animal whar he con hurt people?"

"Not people—invaders who hide in my room!"

"Would ye radder we gae to my room?"

"Say what you have to say—and be quick!"

"Alix, ye be a liar ond a cheat!"

My heart stopped.

"Ye sneaked out at nicht to git my jules fer yourself."

I could have wept with relief—he still didn't know. "It wouldn't matter, Enoch. The lady's gone. She left this afternoon."

"Left? Quhy?"

"I don't know!" Now I couldn't stop tears.

"Quhare?"

"I asked the guard—he didn't know either!"

"She stole my jules?"

I didn't answer.

"Ich tald ye ye shuld nocht ha'e gi'e them in a packet lak that, ond to a straunger! She mun ha'e opened it ond . . ."

"I hope your friend Lord Robert fitzWalter wasn't injured."

"Nay, I hope nocht." Enoch was quiet a long time. "Waesucks, Alix, this be serious. We need halp. I'll ask the Brotherhood."

He groped his way to the door.

"Enoch, I'm keeping Wolfbane with me tonight."

"A guid thocht. I'll wrap three times in the marnin sae ye know ye're safe."

My dark room smelled of smoke.

My window was a dull gray when he knocked.

"Ich ha'e a pork pie fer ye!"

Wolfbane growled.

Holding the wolf, I opened the door.

"Waesucks!" he said.

"Benedicite!" I cried.

His hand where the wolf had bitten him was wrapped in a bloody rag, mayhap the same one he'd worn on his head after his fall at Wanthwaite. I had no cover for my eye, though it throbbed and hurt.

"Con ye see?" he asked.

"Aye."

"Ye shuld cover yit! Eat this—I'll be back!"

I fed the pie to the wolf.

Enoch returned with a clean rag, which he tied around my head, covering my eye. "I'll put a little egg yolk on it quhan we finish our interview."

"Interview? Where are we going?"

"Master Peterfee told me as hu one of my Brotherhood be here in the inn, Baron Eustace de Vesci of Alnwick Castle in the north. Ye remember."

Where my father had once defeated the Scots. He waited; I made no comment.

"Didna ye tal me oncit that yer father fought at Alnwick? That be Lord Eustace's estate."

"Is he a Scot?"

"He war born in Normandy, boot his wif be a Scottish princess."

"How can he help, Enoch?" Time was passing.

"He knaws yer Lady Matilda." He considered. "Least-ways he knaws her husband, Lord William de Braose."

I had a sudden suspicion. "Is this Lord Eustace a friend of King John's?"

"Aye, lak all barons. John be our king nu. He be better than King Richard war—leastways he be in England."

Benedicite, I'd trusted Theo to a friend of the king's—yet what choice did I have? I could only hope that this Eustace was an honorable man.

Enoch and I climbed to another story above ours; Lord Eustace's apartment covered the entire top floor of the inn, a luxurious area I hadn't known to exist.

An obsequious hunchbacked manservant, Master Stane by name, admitted us; perhaps his deformity made it seem he might kiss Enoch's feet, certainly not mine, for he managed to sneer at me through his smiling, tipped head. Lord Eustace de Vesci stood outlined against a bright window. My defective vision must have distorted my view or my opinion, for Lord Eustace seemed as deformed as his crippled manservant.

Oh, he wasn't hunchbacked, nor did he carry the set smile of Master Stane. He was excessively tall, aye, yet fleshy as well. Not fat, but pudgy, soft, blurred. Standing against a window in a cloud of dancing dust motes, his hair appeared the color of wet sand, likewise his eyes; his lips were full, his hands were long and nervous, and he wore a tartan over his tunic.

"Lord Enoch," he said in a husky supercilious tone, "I thought you asked for an audience for yourself and your wife. Where's Lady Fiona?"

"In Scotland," Enoch answered. "This be my ferst wif, Lady Alix of Wanthwaite. I havena got my annulment yit."

"The famous houri?" lisped our host. "May I look?"

Was he asking Enoch or me?

Without waiting for a reply from either of us, he walked around me, pinched my arm, and would have fondled my backside, I trowe, if I hadn't turned.

"Yes, a luscious beauty, like a dewy rose. Innocent appearing despite . . . I can see why the king wanted her, though it's less easy to understand why she would want a weasel. Or perhaps she didn't—did you?"

He was fortunate that I didn't strike his wet-sand eyes.

But he now jabbed at my bandaged eye, then at Enoch's hand, then at my eye again. "Been fighting, you two? Begun your punishment, Enoch? You should kill her, my lord, cheaper and faster than the Church. Then you could be with Fiona at once."

Though Enoch flushed deeply, he stayed with our purpose. "King Richard gifted Alix wi' the Crown Jewels of England."

Lord Eustace hardly knew whether to continue his scorn or become deferential. The Crown Jewels would make me one of the richest ladies in England.

"Ond the present king wants 'em."

"And you want me to take them to him?" Lord Eustace stammered, overcome with the honor. "I pride myself that King John is my friend and we trust each other absolutely—and yet, how would I explain my possession of Richard's jewels?"

He'd crossed the Scot at last. Enoch now roared, "They be nocht Alix's jules! They be mine! Them be *my* jules, Lord Eustace. 'Tis small enow payment fer quhat that wallydrag did to me."

Lord Eustace stood as if struck. "Aye, I see what you mean." Then he paced around me again. "Such a deceptive wife, hard to believe she was ever a baroness. Of course, not all of us can be married to a princess of Scotland." He stopped as if in wonder at his own good fortune. "Margaret is, Margaret . . ." He was too overcome to list Margaret's virtues beyond her accident of birth. "Aye, Lord Enoch, aye, you've earned the jewels. The riches. What can I do to help you? Anything for a brother!"

Enoch finally explained about our problem with Lady Matilda de Braose, her abrupt departure from Baynard Castle, the fire—which astonished the lord—and our need to learn her whereabouts.

Lord Eustace rushed to his window and pulled away the oiled linen. The room instantly filled with the acrid stench of smoke. Hacking through his lace sleeve, he then asked myriad questions: How had the fire started? Was the entire castle destroyed? Had anyone been hurt? What had happened to their other Brother, Lord Robert fitzWalter? Aye, so far as he knew, Lord Robert had been in residence. Yet he knew nothing of Lady Matilda. He'd had an invitation to sup with Lord Robert on Thursday next.

When we could get him off the subject of Baynard Castle and Lord Robert fitzWalter, he finally returned to our request. To give him credit, he really tried.

"I don't like Lady Matilda personally." He screwed his brow as if he didn't even remember her. I held my breath— what was wrong with her? Was she harsh on bairns? "My real friend in that family is her husband, Lord William, one of the bravest and most loyal lords in the kingdom. Yes, he and Matilda both are close to King John, I believe."

My heart sank—was she close enough to betray Theo?

"The last I heard of Lord William, he was at his honor in Limerick, Ireland. She may have followed him there."

My heart sank further.

"And yet, that seems strange, doesn't it? I mean, I don't like her personally, but I would never accuse her of thievery. No, no, she's honorable." He paused again. "She might not give the jewels to you, Enoch, if she thought their rightful owner was King John." His brow screwed. "And yet—you know how rumors fly, especially in the Brotherhood."

"Lord William be nocht a Brother," Enoch interrupted.

"I know, but . . . Well, we help one another with money, so when I hear that a lord needs money, I pay attention."

"Ond Lord William . . . ?"

"There's some gossip. Lord William claims that the king gave him Limerick in gratitude for Lord William's capture of

Arthur of Brittany. The king claims that he gave him a loan, only, and now he demands his money back."

"What has that to do with Lady Matilda?" I asked.

Though he heard me, he answered Enoch. "If he learned somehow that Matilda carried jewels, or perhaps if he simply learned she was in London . . . well, we all know the king."

No one knew him better than I did. Oh, Theo!

"Sae yif she left becas she larned aboot the king's greed, qhuar would she gae?"

"King John is not greedy. Don't misunderstand me. And he's morally upright, unlike his brother." Lord Eustace was again before the window, peering out. "She might follow Lord William to Ireland, but I don't think so. She inherited vast estates in Wales, which is her native home. Yes, if I were you, I would try to find her in Wales."

"Wales be vast. Quhar in Wales?"

"I don't know. Lord William's brother, Bishop Giles, head of the cathedral at Hereford, would know, and Hereford is close to Wales. Ask him."

Within an hour, we were on the road again, now traveling as one unit. Another difference was that Wolfbane now traveled with us.

7

Wolfbane's charred ruff grew back; Enoch removed his bandage from his hand; and Gruoth said I had only a tiny pink scar above my eyebrow—I'd been fortunate. Most of the time, Wolfbane trotted behind my horse; when he tired, I let him ride pillion. We followed a ridge across England, together except that Enoch's knights still ignored me, and I didn't learn their names. Thorketil, however, became friendly again and told me the news of his wife, Edwina. From Thorketil I learned that the Scot had accepted the wolf because Jasper Peterfee had been willing to reduce our tariff at the inn if we would take him. He didn't reduce my tariff, but no matter; I loved the wolf. He kept my mind somewhat off Theo.

Enoch, quite naturally, avoided Wolfbane. He watched me, however, over the heads of the other Scots when we stopped to eat. I suspected that he suspected, though exactly what I wasn't certain.

Hereford was on the far side of England and I was too totty to record the days it took to get there. We stopped only for food; Enoch once sent Gruoth down the steeps to a village on market day. A cross was raised in the square to prevent thieves, but Enoch said that the cross didn't work against the merchants. He pronounced the dried fish Gruoth bought back as being at least five years old.

As we approached Wales, I became wild with anxiety. How dare Lady Matilda spirit Theo away when we'd had an agreement? Her friendship with King John loomed more and more ominous. On the other hand, suppose she was a reasonable woman who'd fled for her life and Theo's? What could have frightened her so?

King John. I could think of no other justification.

On our fifth night out, Wolfbane growled.

"Control yer wolf—I need to talk wi' ye."

Enoch squatted beside me; the wolf licked his hand as if in apology. "We're near unto Hereford, Alix. We mun git our stories straight fer Bishop Giles."

"I won't argue about who should get the jewels, if that's what you mean."

"Ich doona think ye shuld mention the jules at all," he said quietly. "Didna ye say that the jules be wrapped in a packet? That she doesna knaw quhat she has?"

"Aye."

"Than Ich doona think the lady be runnin' becas of the jules."

Oh, he was shrewd. "Then why?"

"Ich doona knaw. May niver knaw. Mayhap somethin' to do wi' the fire."

I could hardly speak. "What are you going to say to Bishop Giles then? How justify our pursuit?"

He was quiet a very long time. "Ich doona knaw."

I offered my hand. "Whatever happens . . ." He stooped to hear me. "I'll give you your share of my jewels when we find . . ."

Bonel's jewels. Not royal perhaps, but real and valuable.

His face was in shadow. "Mast generous, Alix. I war aboot to offer ye a jewel to halp ye git started."

The small city of Hereford was located on a flat plain, under the shadow of hills on our left. Behind Hereford Castle, the gate was open to rural traffic: farmers and herdsmen with flocks passed through without difficulty. Enoch surmised it must be market day. Though our small contingent moved closer, we still camped outside the wall while Enoch went to seek an appointment with Bishop Giles.

He would see us this same afternoon.

We entered the gate immediately after Haute Tierce. As in our previous village, the town sported a cross to keep evildoers away. We stretched out on the grass in its shadow until time to enter the cathedral.

We could hardly climb the steps, so crowded were they with beggars and lepers. We entered under a pointed arch into an anteroom, then the vestuary, then a large high-ceilinged room with shafts of sun shooting through swirling dust.

The bishop was alone.

He turned when he heard us.

Though not young, he was a muscular well-built giant, with the figure of a knight. His drawn gray face belied his physique, however; this was a desperate man. His anguished expression fought for resignation. My heart squeezed, my breath became shallow.

"What do you know?" he blurted.

And I knew we were doomed—he wanted information from us!

He struggled for control. He'd received our message asking about Lady Matilda—did we have news of her whereabouts? Was she safe?

At that question, Enoch understood the hopelessness of our quest as well as anyone, but he asked bravely where Lady Matilda might be found. We'd followed her from London. Had Bishop Giles heard of the fire?

The bishop was appalled. He knew Lord Robert very well, had even heard of Enoch and the Brotherhood, and he feared it might be an attack on their organization. He didn't think, however, that the fire was directed against Lady Matilda.

"Is she trying to escape you?" the bishop asked bluntly. "Maybe she doesn't want to see you!"

Enoch repeated that we'd missed our rendezvous with the lady at Baynard Castle and why.

"Do you represent King John?"

We all stood dumbfounded, though I doubt if Enoch had the same thoughts that I did.

"The king has nothing to do with it!" I cried. "She carried jewels for me from Rouen!"

Enoch groaned.

"If you suspect that she stole them, you're wrong!" Bishop Giles said stiffly, "I can assure you that she's an honorable lady."

He then broke into harsh sobs. Gruoth put her arms around him; the rest of us stared, beyond speech.

Did we know Lord William? he asked when he could speak.

No.

After a further silence while the bishop regained control, he said to Enoch, "I doubt if the fire had anything to with my sister-in-law. More probably, it was directed at Lord Robert fitzWalter himself, who . . ."

Enoch interrupted, "Quhy?"

"Nothing to do with your Brotherhood . . ." He fought for control again. "King John . . . the king . . . he's angry, you see, that Lord Robert keeps London as a commune." He blew his nose; I saw by his sleeve that he'd wept many tears.

Finally, he came to the point: She'd passed through Hereford about a week ago in a terrible hurry, he told us. "She didn't confide in me—to protect me, I now think—and I don't know her destination."

King John, King John, oh God, let her enemy not be King John.

"We be fram Scotland," Enoch said. "Our king be William."

The bishop was again weeping.

Enoch put an arm over his shoulder and spoke in French. "We know that your brother fought most bravely for King John in Normandy."

Bishop Giles looked up sharply. "Yes, he captured Arthur of Brittany for the king."

I cried aloud!

"She's probably in Wales, where she's hiding from John. No doubt the king has heard of her treasure."

I forgot the ephemeral jewels, for Enoch was finally getting directions to Wales. Theo, surely I would soon see Theo, perhaps this very day! If I did, I promised God, I would ask Lady Matilda de Braose not a single question about why she'd fled London.

We left the worried bishop with many vows to tell him what we discovered.

We rode through a wood to the border, marked by the fast-moving Wye River. We stopped at its edge.

"Wales luiks yust lak Scotland, doesn't it, Donald?" Gruoth asked her husband.

"Aye, the sam bleak fells."

"The ford be this way," Enoch said, turning upstream.

In a short time we saw a clear path across the river where rocks were exposed and rivulets churned among pebbles. Now we had difficulty with Enoch's knights, who wanted to take their spring baths in warm southern waters. We finally managed to cross in good time.

Enoch followed Bishop Giles's instructions upward and to our right. A few squatting Welshmen watched us from behind rocks; they were pale as Druids and had hair like weeds, but seemed friendly withal. Streams tumbled down the mountainside to join the Wye, and when we passed under a falls, we all received our spring baths.

We climbed to a wide high plateau. Old oaks created a pleasant forest in the deep shadowed grass. Enoch looked up at the sun, down into the grass, and pointed. In single file, we walked our horses to a second river, really a moat.

"Bagnor Manor," Enoch said.

Welsh knights guarded a narrow swaying bridge. After an interminable time during which each party tried to understand the other, they let us pass. Now herds of tame deer bounded away when they saw Wolfbane; two old bucks watched us pass along a twisting lane. What had Theo thought when he'd seen such wonders?

A long low manor stretched before us, easily three times the size of Wanthwaite. Built entirely of oak, it was cunningly beamed to form a pleasing pattern. Though there was no wall, nor even a fence, there were two guards wearing the Welsh green at the entry. We dismounted so they could take our horses while I held Wolfbane on his lead.

A manservant, also in green, greeted us at the door, then indicated we should wait for the butler, Geraldus by name, who shortly appeared. Speaking in heavily accented French, he demanded our identities, though the presence of females reassured him. Enoch, answering in equally accented French, said that we were Lady Angela's party, that Lady Matilda expected us.

Were we from King John?

My heart stopped.

No, said Enoch; Lady Angela was from the north of England and had never met the king.

In that case, Geraldus was sorry to disappoint Lady Angela; Lady Matilda had been here for two days only, then left.

"With her family?" I whispered.

Geraldus addressed Enoch: yes, with the family she'd brought from Normandy.

"Ask him where they went!" I begged Enoch.

Geraldus didn't know himself, nor did he know why she'd come here at all when she wasn't expected for nearly a month, and yes, she'd seemed worried. He suggested that Lady Matilda's personal monk might know more. She'd established a small Cistercian abbey on the premises, and he knew that she'd visited it during her brief stay. The place was called Margam Abbey; the monk was Father Davyyd.

Before dawn, Enoch and I were again riding silently among the oaks, now swathed in mist. I was filled with foreboding. Enoch, too, was facing disappointment, though hardly of the same depth.

We passed Margam Abbey three times before I saw a tiny passage carved into a rock with the sign of the cross above it. We crawled to a low oaken door with a magic twist of iron hanging in its middle. Enoch knocked and bellowed, "Father Davyyd," again and again before a small bent man answered his summons. Obviously Welsh with his pale skin and weedy hair, he wore the black robe tied with a rope of his order, and walked on the bare feet of a hermit. He seemed so antique that I was startled when he spoke with a young, strong voice. Enoch introduced himself as Lord Enoch of Wanthwaite and me as Lady Angela from Durham, who'd had a rendezvous with Lady Matilda in London, which that lady had missed. He hoped that Father Davyyd could inform us of the lady's whereabouts, for the case was urgent; a fortune was involved.

Were we from King John?

The question chilled.

When Enoch answered no, I realized that he, too, understood our danger. Or Lady Matilda's.

Father Davyyd lapsed into a Welsh argot that Enoch understood, for he answered in a similar tongue. The monk pulled forth wooden benches for our comfort and then brought lathed oaken mugs filled with local elderberry wine. We sat and talked of many things—or the men talked, I was quiet—as Father Davyyd tested our honesty. Suddenly, the monk put down his mug.

"Follow me; I have something to show you," he said in French.

He squeezed on his hands and knees through a hacked tunnel and into a larger cave with a hole open to the sun. Even with air, the floor was moist with mildew. Father Davyyd turned a desperate face.

His voice trembled. "Lady Matilda fled Bagnor at my advice. She wasn't safe in Wales! She's had warning, you see, that King John wanted her male children to be given over as hostages against her husband's debts. She knew well what that meant, because . . . Read this."

He pointed to a rock in the wall with new chisled letters. I read aloud, putting the French into English: *After King John captured Arthur and kept him in prison for some time in the castle of Rouen, and after dinner, on the Wednesday before Easter, when he was drunk and possessed of the devil, King John slew his nephew with his own hand, and tying a heavy stone to his body, cast it into the Seine. It was discovered by fishermen in their net and being dragged to the bank and recognized, was taken for sacred burial in fear of the tyrant to the Priory of Bec, called Notre Dame de Prés.*

"I knew it couldn't be a fisherman!" I screamed.

Father Davvyd sobbed. "Now you understand, Lady Angela. Lord William de Braose, who captured Arthur for King
John, was appalled at the prince's fate, as was Lady Matilda.
In London, King John demanded the children she had with
her be given over to his routiers as hostages to 'show that she
did love him'; she replied, *Why should I give my children as hostages
when the king murdered his own nephew, whom he should have protected?'*"

Enoch caught me when I fell.

"She ha'e the falling sickness," he explained. "Hit's werse
when she's shocked. Ye con see the marks on her face whar she
fell in London."

But Father Davyyd wasn't interested in my condition. "I
advised Lady Matilda to seek the protection of the king of
Scotland. Perhaps you may find her there. Isn't the king in
Edinburgh?"

Scotland, at least four hundred miles to the north.

Enoch thanked Father Davyyd profusely for his help, *Deo
gratias,* for I couldn't speak. He even made a contribution to
his tiny cell. Then we were among the oaks again.

"The king of Scotland will protect her, ye'll see."

I didn't respond.

"Mayhap ye shuld gae back to Wanthwaite and wait for me."

"I must go to Scotland."

Enoch stopped and dismounted. He looked up at me.
"Do ye want to tell me the truth, Alix?"

After a period of silence, he remounted.

One of Enoch's knights took Wolfbane to Wanthwaite.

Several knights, including Thorketil and Dugan, wanted to return to Wanthwaite when we reached the turnoff. Their horses were exhausted.

I spurred my mare—Enoch galloped after me. Thorketil and Dugan followed. Gruoth had never wavered.

We met a shepherd traveling south; aye, King William was in the capital; aye, the weather had been bonny in Scotland four days ago.

We passed through Durham with its stone bridge. Something was important about the city—ah yes, it had an ecclesiastic court. We rode close to the coast with its melancholy associations when we entered Scotland, then on to Edinburgh. The countryside was indeed like Wales: high cliffs, deep purple chasms, and a fast-moving sky. Tarns and falls and inlets from the sea were everwhere. We passed through Edinburgh to camp close to its port, called Leith.

Enoch and Thorketil rode back to the city to seek an audience with the king. They returned that same eve.

Enoch took me aside. "Be ye sartain that this Lady Matilda be nocht a criminal?" he asked.

"Why? Oh God, tell me!"

"King William turned the lady over to King John ond the Scottish king wouldna do swich a thing unless . . . She ond her brood be in prison at Windsor Castle!"

"Windsor?" I lost all caution. "I must go, Enoch! Must save him!"

Well, I'd just let it slip that something human was at risk—I didn't care!

"Ye shuld wait in Wanthwaite while Thorketil and I . . ."

"No! No! I must go! Your king is . . . Your king . . ." I couldn't finish.

"I'll tak ye, Alix. Doona wape, I'll tak ye."

We camped in a field near to Windsor called Runnymede— well named, for it was a waterland with many leets draining into the Thames River, just below Staines. Our camp was on a shallow pond with a dead tree in the middle. Gruoth—who wouldn't leave me—hung our blankets on limbs close to the pond. The dampness cooled my hot body. Dugan caught fish in the Thames, which Enoch turned on a spit. Though we couldn't see Windsor Castle, we could feel it close by.

In early morning, Enoch and Thorketil rode at once for Windsor. Thorketil knew one of the guards at the prison; they would beg for an audience with Lady Matilda. At the very least, they could get information.

I heard their plan, heard them leave. I twisted damp leaves; Theo was in prison. I'd never seen a prison—was he in chains? Why would anyone—even King John—want to put a baby in prison? John had been a baby once. A tiny lisping boy. And John himself had at least one son I'd heard of— named Henry. If he ever saw Theo . . . Who could resist Theo? Did he know who his father was? Perhaps John had given orders about Lady Matilda and didn't know she had a babe in her custody. Aye, that was probably the case. Would Enoch approach King John if I asked?

Thus my fantastick cell worked throughout the day, now morbid, now hopeful. Dusk had fallen before the Scots appeared in the gloom. I tried to read their slow-moving figures: they seemed puzzled.

"Did you gain entry?"

Enoch dismounted. "Into the prison? Nay."

"You didn't talk to a guard?"

He squatted beside me. "Aye, to a mon Thorketil knawed. Alix, the lady had no jules on her person. Or mayhap John tuik them. Air ye sartain . . . ?"

"On her person? Is she dead?"

He sighed heavily. "Gi'e me yer hond, Alix; 'tis a gory tale."

"Tell me." I knew by his tone: Theo was dead. Something died inside of me. The very worst, the very worst, my own life was finished.

His voice was gentle, the tone you use to speak to an idiot. "Wal, it could be werse, remember."

What could be worse than death?

"King John be famous fer putting his prisoners in lead copes and sinking them slowly into brine. That be a turrible death!"

All death is terrible.

"He sank forty prisoners at the castle in Forte after he starved them."

"Lady Matilda," I whispered. "Was she at Forte?"

He put his hand on my cheek.

"I mun say that the lady war courageous. Quhan they tried to starve her . . ."

"She had children! Even John couldn't . . . "

"She had three childer wi' her, two older—one luiked to be a cnicht—ond one a babe. The babe died ferst, o' course."

I heard him in a distance.

"The lady ond her older bairns et him."

"Before or after . . . ?"

"The guard be sartain he war dead ferst . . . I doona knaw hu lang the older ones lasted."

"The baby was eaten." My words tolled in my ears.

"Aye. Whan the guards buried them, the babe had no face at all."

He caught me when I fell.

Magna Carta

Book Two

8

I WANTED TO DIE, I TRIED TO DIE, I DIDN'T DIE. JOHN HAD WON.
I cared nothing for my own life, only Theo's, and Theo was
dead.

Mayhap I survived because I was in Wanthwaite again
with the Scots, who took most excellent care of me. The
malaise I'd experienced on the journey to Hereford and beyond now deepened to a catatonic state. People talked as
through a haze, and, though I was aware of conversation, I no
longer responded. Gradually, the Scots stopped addressing
me. I replayed in my head every single night and day that
Theo and I had lived in the Jewish commune together. When
I got to the night he'd left, I started on the very first day
again, when he'd been brought to me in his swaddling clothes,
and the more I thought, the more I remembered. I carefully
refrained from imagining his time with Lady Matilda.

The Scots gave me the fattest cuts of pork, fresh salmon,
and honey cakes, while they ate beans with pork fat or
turnips with the same. They informed me that the crops were
good this summer, that we had plenty of pigs and sheep to
carry us through the winter months, just as if I were their
mistress. Gruoth tended my needs; most important, she informed me that my two leopard bags—the one with coins,
the other with jewels—were hidden under my bed, though

she hadn't opened them. I asked her about Theo's document, but she didn't know—she couldn't read.

When it chilled at nights, someone put a furry beast—Wolfbane—into my bed to keep me warm. Indeed, he did keep me warm, as most any beast is warmer than a human, but I also think he kept me alive. That dumb animal loved me—you would think I kept *him* alive. Perhaps I did, for he was a skeleton when he came and soon developed thicker fur and fat. He snuggled on top of me, licked my face, groaned in the dark, rested under the cover and back on top of me all through the night. Aye, he knew nought of God or Jesus, but he was my spiritual support e'en so. He loved me when I needed love.

Then I began to gain a little from the rich food, especially from suet cakes that were prepared for the Nativity. When I rose one winter day, I found my tunic snug. I covered myself with an old fur cope belonging to my mother.

I was a little unsteady on the stairs, but stood upright as I walked through the Great Hall. The Scots gaped at me in astonishment; Gruoth rushed to my side, but I pushed her off. Outside, I stopped a moment to adjust to the wind's bite. My eyes watered, my chest hurt when I breathed, and my feet soon lost all feeling. Nevertheless, I bent against snow flurries and pushed forward, across the moat, through the spinney, and down the park.

I fell heavily. The snow deepened around me as I struggled to stand; I finally was upright again. However, when I passed under a flailing ash, I broke a stick for support. Down and down I slid, toward the ice-covered river where my father and mother lay at rest. I knelt beside their graves to pray. When I'd finished, I edged sideways to a level spot where I would dig a grave for Theo. Over and over I punctured the frozen ground. My stick broke.

"Try this." Enoch lay his thwittle on my shoulder.

I struck the turf with his dagger—the blade splintered. I covered my face with my mittens; hot tears mixed with tiny ice shards. What a failure I was: I hadn't been able to save Theo's life, and now I couldn't even dig his grave.

Enoch knelt beside me. "Cum back to the Hall quhar it's warm, Alix. Ye shouldna be out here on yer ferst day outa bed."

Theo's soul rose in a snow swirl; he smiled, shook his pale ringlets.

Find my mother and father in heaven! I ordered him silently. *They were murdered as well—they'll help you!*

"Lat me halp ye oop. It cums a blaw."

I'd forgotten about Enoch—what was he doing here?

I liked the cracking ice on whipping black branches, the upward draft of snow.

His hands pulled me to my feet.

"I must—Theo!"

"War that his nam?"

"Aye."

His voice was sympathetic. "Ye be totty, Alix, creepin' oot of yer bed in swich a storm. Theo will wait."

Faceless Theo would wait. His mortal coil was in a prisoners' grave. Had he been alive when they ate him? Can you live without a face?

I faced Enoch with his frosted beard. "I had a baby by Richard, Enoch."

"I knaw."

"He's dead."

"Cum."

"I killed him. I knew that the king was after him and I should have killed the king first, you see."

"Aye, I see. Cum, befar ye freeze."

Enoch's hands held me upright as we fought our way up the park, slipping, falling, grunting with my weight. Drifts held the Great Hall's door closed. At Enoch's shouts, Scots pushed it open from the inside. Gruoth ran to me. When had she become pregnant? I'd had a baby, Theo, one baby to last me forever. She thrust a methier of hot mead into my hands.

"'Tis her ferst time oot o' her bed," Enoch announced to the company, who already knew it. The Scots had been tactful all these months when I was catatonic on my pallet, especially Gruoth. Even Enoch, insofar as he'd left me alone.

He may have given me Wolfbane, though; aye, I thought he had.

The mead went to my head. When I tried to walk, I stumbled.

"Lat me halp ye, Alix." Enoch placed a firm arm around me and led me up the steps.

I was not so drunkalew that I didn't wonder at his kindness, especially after I'd told him the truth. Aye, on the road as well—he must have surmised that something was amiss about the jewels long before we went to Runnymede, for I thought the last time he'd mentioned them had been in Wales. Something—Enoch was not stupid.

I welcomed the familiar cold and dark of my room. I fell across my bed.

"Waesucks!" Enoch, on his hands and knees, scooped

handfuls of snow from under my window. When he'd finished, he placed a fur pelt across the opening, which billowed and flapped. Now the room was darker than before.

"Where's my wolf?"

"Aye, I'll bring him to ye."

By the time he returned with Wolfbane, I was already alseep. He put Wolfbane in my bed nonetheless.

It was late March before I realized that I was pregnant—aye, very pregnant! How could this be? An immaculate conception? Was that what John had said? Or no, Mistress Eglantine and the sisters who'd thought I was a saint whispered *maybe*. Was Theo returning to me? Tears ran down my cheeks.

Deorling! Someone had called me Deorling.

Deus juva me!

I stared at Wolfbane, lying under my covers. His tilted golden eyes stared back. The wolf knew the truth! I played for three heartbeats with the notion that the wolf had turned into a man in the dark, that he was a wolf-man, then pulled back the fur cover.

"Let me see!"

I lifted one of my own pale hairs from my mat, brushed short wolf hairs into a pile, then found one red curl. I moaned aloud.

Enoch, it must be Enoch.

And I'd thought he was my wolf—why hadn't my real wolf protected me? Had Enoch enchanted him somehow? I'd heard oft of a wolf in sheep's clothing, but never a Scot in wolf's clothing!

Wait until I told Lady Fiona.

And yet—that was the least of it—I was going to have a baby. Enoch's baby. How could I have been so stupid? Grief was a luxury I couldn't afford. Now, *think!* What else? I pressed my brow—Lady Fiona, Lady Fiona—she'd been here—she already knew—aye, I recalled her face bending over me. Was it a scheme? What scheme? Was she barren? Were she and Enoch plotting to use my body for their own purposes?

My head pounded. *Benedicite,* what had ailed *me?* I'd been in a melancholy disposition . . . I moaned aloud. Of all the terrible things that had befallen me, my kidnapping, King Richard's lies, Theo, this was the worst! I would murther that heinous Scot, aye, without so much as a Hail Mary for forgiveness! The varlet deserved to die!

Yet, again, what was his purpose? His kindness these last few months now took on a sinister cast—but what? He wanted Wanthwaite and he wanted Lady Fiona—how did this help him? I couldn't fathom his purpose. At least I had no illusions about his welcoming me with open arms—however belatedly—nor did I think he was a necrophiliac on top of being a bigamist! But why?

He would tell me before this day ended! Before *he* ended. I reached under the bed for my dagger.

Sitting alone in the Great Hall, Enoch watched me tread very carefully down the steps.

I pulled a bench opposite him.

"Hu de ye feel?"

What a question! "Why do you ask?"

Gruoth entered at that moment with a mug of hot spiced wine; Enoch waited until she'd retired to the kitchen.

"Wal, ye been oot in the cald several times nu—do ye ha'e quinsy?" His lips were very red, his eyes very blue.

"No, milord. Your baby's safe."

His face turned scarlet. He pretended confusion. "Babby? My babby? I doona knaw . . ."

"That you raped me? That houghmagandy makes babies? Except in one instance, of course: perhaps the Holy Spirit entered my body as He did the Holy Virgin's!"

"Ye're no virgin, haly or otherwise! Boot raped!" His astonishment quickly turned to anger. "Ich raped ye? Ich coudna rape ye yif I wanted to—ye be my wif!"

"Yet you did, milord, I know not how many times! I was in melancholy disposition and didn't . . ."

"Ye war in a swoon!"

"But not completely totty, so much the worse for you! I recall that Lady Fiona came into my room. Aye, well you may blush!"

His fingers rapped on the table. "Very weil, I made ye wi' child. Ond ye're richt, Fiona knawed all aboot it ond quhy."

"Ah, a reason! Not pleasure, but some scheme—what scheme?"

"I'll tall ye aft ye calm doon!"

"Does Lady Fiona realize how this complicates our annulment? Do you?"

Enoch had always been difficult for me to read: when pushed, he played the Scottish buffoon or pretended outrage; the ardent lover was a new role at this time, though I remembered . . . Now he became the hard lord of the manor.

"Quhat's between me ond the lady be our business, not yours. Boot she knaws aboot our houghmagandy and quhy."

"Since I was the victim, I demand to know why as well!"

"Later." He rose.

"Enoch, I'll not play games. This is serious. You deliberately made carnal love to a sick woman not your wife. My fantastick cell founders—what could be your reason?"

"Hu fer along be ye?"

"I'm not certain. Perhaps five months. Why? Do you want to eat your bairn's face?"

He paled. I thought he would strike me! Then he suddenly became the outraged victim!

"Yer wolf bit me oncit!"

"But not on your terse! Pity!"

"I ha'e to ride south today," he informed me coldly, "boot I'll be back wi'in ten days. We'll talk then."

"I take it that I'll have to learn to sleep alone while you're gone. Or will one of your knights service me—I'm insatiable, as you often point out."

"Ye ha'e Wolfbane." He walked to my bench. "Alix, bath Fiona ond I be happy that ye're wi' child."

I slapped him before he finished. What a travesty!

While Enoch was away, I rode into Dunsmere to consult with Father William, a young priest I didn't know. I told him my situation as well as I knew it myself and found him as baffled as I was. Enoch was right about the canon law permitting him to refuse to take me back, and he could even kill me within the law. On the other hand, since he'd made carnal love to me, the situation had altered. Holy Church was most particular in protecting children, especially the present pope, Innocent III; Father William doubted if any annulment would be granted that would make the child a bastard. On the other hand—he began to sweat—the situation was strange in the first place since King Richard had stolen me on false pretenses from my husband. That was surely a sin and might be illegal as well; yet kings might be above the law, or perhaps they *were* the law, he wasn't sure even about the canon law. My best option was to consult the ecclesiastical court at Durham; if I couldn't ride north in such weather and in my condition, the court would visit Dunsmere this spring.

He could tell me nothing about the moot court, of course, except that he doubted if it existed.

There was no possibility of my riding north, for we were truly in a late blizzard. At the very height of the storm, Enoch returned. Thorketil managed to save his feet from frostbite by soaking them in hot water, but an ugly sword wound on his shoulder began to fester.

"I thought summer was the fighting season," I greeted him. "Or did you get this in Scotland?"

"Ich got it in the south, fightin' yer king."

We stared at one another, both of us thinking of Theo.

As his wife—though the term was shaky—I bathed his wound. With my hot poultices filled with agrimon and aloe, with a neat cut to drain corruption, the wound healed. The day Enoch climbed slowly to his room in the tower—the room I'd occupied as a child—he signaled that we would have our talk.

I went to my own room to prepare. By now, everyone knew I was gravid. Edwina, who was about my size and had had three children, had lent me her laying-in tunics with their cunning side panels. I thought for a wretched moment of my tight red tunic and nun's habit.

"Ach, 'tis the happiest news there be fer a woman!" Edwina assured me.

There was little I could do to prepare for the interview. I dabbed lily water on my wrists and temples, straightened my braids, then rapped. When there was no answer, I opened the door cautiously.

Enoch sat upright on his bed, leaning against the wall; his eyes were closed. Across his lap lay Theo's document!

His grave, I thought, overjoyed, *I'll put it in his grave.*

When I reached for it, Enoch's eyes opened.

"Sae ye see it."

"It's mine, Enoch. My only tangible proof that Theo ever lived."

"Be that the anely reason ye kept it? It says here that Theo—Richard's son—war to be king. Did ye plan as he shuld be king?"

"At first, yes." My old hurt and hardness came back. "King John and his mother thought otherwise." Yet I was confused. "I gave up such dreams long ago, Enoch, but it's proof that Theo lived, that King Richard was his father!"

"Ond that Theo war his heir!"

"Yes." Enoch sounded like King John.

"Do ye plan to claim the thrane fer him?"

The wound must have affected his fantastick cell. "Of course not; I just told you . . ."

"Ye tald me in the snaw that ye planned to kill King John."

"Aye, as retribution." I lost voice. "I should have done it before . . .'

"Ich doona belave ye, Alix. Ye brought the document ond the babe hame fer me to mak the claim!"

I gazed out his window, expecting to see the peasant girl in red. "Never! I was betrayed by King John and his mother—I accepted the rebuff. Perhaps Richard wouldn't have, I don't know, but I did!" I paused. I didn't see her, but I spoke anyway. "It didn't make any difference, as you saw. John killed him anyway."

"Quhat will happen after ye kill the king?"

I knew he was humoring me, but no matter. "I suppose I'll be thrown into a dungeon. I don't really care, Enoch. John must die." My voice trembled. "I should have done it sooner."

"Ich meant, quhat will happen to England?"

"I don't know. I hadn't thought. The whole world will be better off without John."

"Quhen did ye forgit your law studies in Paris?"

I laughed bitterly. "At once, I think. Are you bringing up our annulment again? It may be difficult, since you raped me."

"I didna rape ye!" He clutched his shoulder. "Ond I war referrin' to English law. John murdered Theo, quhich be a crime; he shuld pay, boot he willna pay."

"I agree. The law won't punish him—I will."

"Thar be another way, Alix." He slipped off the bed. "Schal I tal ye true? The babe ye carry nu will rule England!"

His wild blue eyes were completely serious.

"Enoch, I am not a queen, and this babe will not be royal."

"It be Richard's babe, no? No one knawed the identity o' the babe at Windsor."

Was he serious? "*Benedicite,* Enoch, everyone knows that Richard died two years ago! This could hardly be his baby!" I had a sudden insight. "This is why Fiona came, isn't it? This is her scheme as well as yours!" I felt sick.

"Aye."

He then meandered on about England being governed by law instead of physical force, about fairness and I know not what. I interrupted him.

"Enoch, your child is . . . your child, not Richard's . . . will never rule England, and if you try, remember Theo's fate."

"Ich be thinkin's o' my Brothers' fate."

"Brothers?"

"I tald ye, the Brotherhood."

I was dumbfounded. "You would do this to me—to your own child—for Eustace de Vesci?"

"Not just Eustace. This be serious, Alix. We be meetin' here in September."

To my knowledge, none of their wives had been abducted for the king's pleasure. And from what I'd seen, none of them sympathized with me much.

I spoke slowly, as if Enoch were an idiot. "Aye, King John is also serious. And what can any infant do about financial matters, which you say is your Brotherhood's business? I'll not have a babe of mine murdered again! Do you understand?"

"This babe be mine by law! My son qhuich ye ond Fiona knaw, boot the English Court doesna knaw. King John doesna knaw. Ye wull say it's Richard's."

I was too amazed to speak.

"Sit on the bed. We mun talk."

My heart thumped. "Only if you promise not to . . ."

"Doonna be daft."

Feeling slightly foolish at the same time that I was defiant, I sat.

"Ye askit hu I becam wounded." His eyes closed again.

He'd been called by the Brotherhood to save the castle of Lord Robert de Ros in nearby Yorkshire.

"You said the south."

"Ich didna want anyone to knaw."

"Enoch, please don't try to change the subject! This baby complicates our annulment and . . ."

"Quiet!" he roared.

Though the battle had been fierce in York, he had been the only baron who'd been seriously wounded.

I shuddered so hard I shook the bed.

"Did the king mistake York for Wanthwaite?"

"O' course nocht! Quhy do ye ask?"

Because John must know where I lived and the document . . . I sighed with relief.

"It war aboot forest rights. The king shoulda ta'en his complaints to the assize court."

"Perhaps he prefers to fight. He's a killer."

"Aye, twa assaults this same month. Both fer forest rights."

"Forest rights?" What had this to do with my pregnancy? Or Theo's document?

"He's attacking the barons becas he wants their lands forsooth. The barons air talkin' of civil war. Nu, do ye understand?" His face suddenly twisted. "Lond be nocht the anely reason. Thar be things mar important."

What was more important than land in Enoch's eyes?

"Sae they're meetin' here—the Brotherhood—ond I want ye shuld speak aboot yer babe!"

I reached for my document.

Enoch held it aloft.

"I ha'e promised to gi'e the barons a different way to rid themselves o' this monster. They'll lose a civil war. They be comin' here in September, as soon as the crops be in."

"To hear me speak about my baby with the gestation of an elephant?"

He flushed deeply. "Ye'll do it, Alix."

I stared blankly, not knowing what to say. Had he gone woodly with his wound?

"Ye'll hald up this document ond tal them ye're expecting Richard's bairn!"

Expecting—Theo? I laughed at the absurdity, not at the actual suggestion, which was almost tragic. "And what reason will I give for my late delivery? Richard's been dead for two years, Enoch!"

"Aye, that be yer problem."

Englishmen were not naive. I said so.

"The word be nocht *naive,* it be *desperate.*"

We stared at each other.

"I could resolve their desperation by killing the king."

"Ond I could kill ye." He wasn't japing. "After my babe be born—Fiona would mother it."

I trembled violently. "Never!" I opened the door.

"Ye'll do it, Alix!" he shouted at my back. "Ye con invent yer ane reason fer takin' sae lang!"

Back in my own quarters, I chilled. Without his saying so specifically, I understod that Enoch was still enraged about Richard.

Enoch and England.

I sank to the mat where he'd lain beside me. I looked at my long tapering fingers—not swollen, *Deo gratias*—and rolled to my side.

I couldn't sleep. Enoch was a Scot, a murderous and ambitious Scot. Could he become king of England? Was I to be forever the means for men's ambitions? I must be careful.

Of course, I might die in childbirth—many women did—or the baby might die. Yet I wanted this baby, wanted it to survive, which meant also that I should kill John.

9

As soon as Enoch was able to mount his destrier again, he armed himself heavily and left Wanthwaite, whether to fight about forest rights he didn't say. It was the fighting season, in any case. He looked formidable on his huge warhorse, not a comical Scot at all, but a savage cutthroat.

He put Thorketil and Edwina in charge of our fields and forests and women's work. Much as I resented being put in an inferior position on my own estate, I knew little of the actual business of Wanthwaite, and this was really my first summer at home. Though I'd been the ostensible head when still a child and Enoch had been in Scotland, I shortly realized how much had changed since that time.

The principal change, of course, was that I was expecting a child myself. I should have been happy, even though it was Enoch's seed, and indeed my condition took my mind somewhat off Theo. And I wanted this bairn, aye, really wanted it, and there was the rub. The more I considered Enoch's goal for the throne, the more I felt that this bairn was doomed. Most of all, I was absolutely blank when it came to explaining my two-year pregnancy. Even the Scots here in our household knew how babes were made and how long it took.

Therefore, I was distracted when Edwina explained a new plow to me. Activities in the bed were sometimes referred to as "plowing"; when Edwina waxed enthusiastic over the steel blade from Germany that cut the soil more efficiently than wood, my mind drifted back to last winter, when I'd confused Wolfbane with Enoch in my bed, as if I wouldn't know my own husband! The German blade was important, for it permitted horses to pull our plows instead of oxen, which meant that horses lived in the stables and oxen were released into our woods. The blade also meant that we could finally grow oats for our own table as well as for animals. The oats created destriers in place of small horses, and the oatcakes made us fat.

"When do you expect your bairn?" I asked Edwina.

"Late autumn or early winter, same as you. This is the best time of life for a woman."

Best for her, perhaps; I feared King John's knife.

She went on: Oats fertilized our soil in some way, so that we had fallen into the newfangled way of rotating our crops. All because of a German blade!

We also began rotating beans with other vegetables (Gruoth had discovered that beans replenished the soil, and it had naught to do with a German blade), and I dreamed of how my little boy would learn such new techniques.

Then reality hit. Instead of pondering German blades, I should be preparing a new grave for my fetus next to Theo's. I should also dig my own grave. If the barons didn't slay me on the spot, Enoch would.

In short, I could think of nothing to explain my delayed condition.

Despite these dour thoughts, my appetite grew with everyone else's. Our winter diet of beans and turnips plus whatever we could kill in the forest was also our diet in July, a fallow month while we waited for autumn harvests. I remembered vividly that the Jews wouldn't eat beans because they caused blurred vision, and while my vision seemed normal forsooth, I suffered flatulence.

Summer was the fecund season, and we women compared our bulging bellies, for we seemed to have conceived all at the same time. I wondered briefly if Enoch had prowled from one mat to another, but, of course, these women flushed and boasted of their husbands' prowess, especially Margaret with Havelock. Edwina suggested we oil ourselves to prevent stretch marks. I rubbed myself, even though no one could find marks—Edwina warned that sometimes they came late. While others chatted about names and possible sex, however, I stayed awake at nights trying to scheme some way to save this babe. I imagined all sorts of methods that John might use his routiers against us. I was now convinced that the king had murdered Theo quite intentionally.

Thorketil made coarse, loving jokes about Edwina's cabbage shape; Donald complained that he could no longer find Gruoth's slit in all that flesh; even Havelock stroked Margaret's lump lovingly. Enoch was seldom on the estate during this fighting season, but, when he was, he asked me only if I'd devised a credible argument about how I could still be carrying Richard's babe.

I dug a proper grave for Theo next to my parents and planted it with wild rose hips from the forest. When I spoke to him every evening, I told him he would soon have a little brother in the grave next to his to keep him company.

The barons of Enoch's Brotherhood agreed to meet at Wanthwaite. My spirits plummeted. I vascillated between defiance and sullen fear. Enoch told me again that his friends were desperate, but I couldn't imagine anyone desperate enough to accept such a woodly tale. I concluded that Enoch must want me dead—and so did Lady Fiona—but wasn't there some more direct way to do it? Then I thought belatedly that Fiona was indeed barren, and they wanted this babe for their own purposes.

Aye, they might want the babe, but not me. I resigned myself to death.

The autumn rains began early and threatened our grain. Everyone went to the fields to fight the mold at the same time that we must arrange for accommodations inside. Our horses joined the oxen in the fields as we transformed the stable into a hostel. We removed as much manure as we could, covered with clean straw what we couldn't. My former schoolroom and the chapel were already prepared.

The first two lords arrived together: Richard, Earl of Clare and William de Fors, Earl of Aumâle, each with five knights. They were followed quickly by the Earl of Norfolk with ten knights. Twenty-three more giants arrived, fourteen with bandages, all on huge fighting destriers, which they immediately put in the stable. The lords were courteous and condescending, making it clear that Wanthwaite was a paltry estate compared to their great palatinates. And Enoch was right, they were desperate men. The pall of melancholy soon hung heavy in our Great Hall.

These were Enoch's "Brothers"; they would have been my associates if I controlled Wanthwaite. And they were England. I might rant about blue skies and flowers, but a country is its people. Well, England should be proud. Most were fair (showing their Viking ancestors), most were tall, most had deep voices, all were courteous. Though garbed in fighting gear, many wore rich chains with crucifixes, and silver or gold rings. The Scots stood out in such company. Equally brawny and fierce, they wore capes over their shoulders, short plaid kilts, bristly socks with straw in the woof to their knees. One lone piper droned in the corner, and for the first time I realized how sad the bagpipe was. Sad their pipes might be, but the Scots were prancing with glee compared to the English.

At noon, Lord Robert fitzWalter of Baynard Castle and Dunmow arrived, thus giving the signal that the meeting could begin. Lord Robert, an impressive man of medium height whose bright black eyes took in every nuance of behavior, not only controlled London (though he wasn't mayor), he owned vast estates all over England and Normandy; only King John had more wealth. To me, he was simply one of the last people to see Theo alive—I watched him hungrily, but dared not approach him directly, though his black eyes sought me out, then held. He wore a blue tunic pinned with a gold dragon on a heavy chain and trimmed with miniver, despite the hot humid air.

I watched for Lord Eustace de Vesci from Alnwick, the only baron I knew, though a most unpleasant wight in my opinion; in everyone else's view, he was one of our important guests because of his connection to the Scottish throne. I prayed he wouldn't come, for he knew quite well I hadn't been gravid when he'd met me in London. And I recalled as well that Lord Eustace was a friend of the de Braose family because he was a friend of King John's.

I need not have worried—if he came, I didn't see him. Mayhap Enoch had had the same thoughts that I had.

To my astonishment, however, Bishop Giles of Hereford was among the lords. Certainly, he couldn't be a member of the Brotherhood, nor did he have the vigor of our lords. Yet he'd changed, for he'd once appeared brawny as a knight. What had happened? Was it because of Lady Matilda? He'd lost a third of his previous weight; his bishop's robes fell in thick folds around his frail body. His eyes were no longer tearful, however, nor did he share the melancholy of our other guests; this was an angry man.

"That be the plaid o' the king," Gruoth whispered.

"Where? King John?"

"King William o' Scotland. Lord Eustace be wed to the Scottish princess. He be wearin' her plaid."

That was Lord Eustace? I gasped—I couldn't believe the man she indicated was Lord Eustace! But aye, the same narrow nose, the same thin lips, eyes the color of wet sand, even the same smiling manservant. I'd heard of people turning white overnight from grief but never seen it before—and he was even thinner than Bishop Giles.

Lord Eustace approached me. My heart squeezed—was there no place I could go? I fully expected some crude comment about my condition, but, to my amazement, his supercilious voice was respectful. "Lady Alix, thank you for your hospitality." He knelt before me. "And thank you for so bravely giving us hope in this desperate time."

Desperate time. For whom? Not for him, for me.

Or maybe Lord Eustace's crops had failed or a child had sickened; if the man had to suffer some disaster to make him human, then I was grateful for his tragedy.

I exchanged no other words with anyone that day. Men kept arriving; Gruoth kept whispering their names. All seemed weary, and all seemed low in spirits.

Early on the second day, Enoch announced that the official meeting would begin. Though he thanked his Brothers for traveling great distances at this busy time of year, his voice, too, was grave. He knew well their sacrifice, but he also knew their universal shame; he promised the journey would be worth their trouble. For their convenience, he hoped to complete our business in a single day.

Universal shame? What shame? That a few had been wounded in battle?

Father William arrived from Dunsmere dripping water on our floor—for the rain had increased—to open our meeting with a prayer. I hadn't invited him—had Enoch? He smiled approvingly at my inflated middle.

Enoch replaced the priest at the podium; he wanted to state the limits of the law of feudalism so we all shared exactly the same understanding. I sighed; Enoch *would* introduce his beloved law into our meeting. Was rape against feudal law? He intoned: The king owned all of England, and the distribution of estates had an ancient history and was never disputed; we all thereforet paid a *feu*, which might be considered a rental fee for our lands, though such rents were limited to the land itself. He looked up significantly: The *feu* did not give the king rights over our wives or children.

My heart raced. Had this meeting been called simply to expose me as King Richard's concubine? Was Enoch still that angry? Was I to become an exhibit with my distended belly?

Through my lashes, I studied the barons. They were paying attention, aye, to a fault. Yet hadn't Enoch himself told me that their biggest complaint concerned the forest laws? Wasn't that part of feudal law?

Yet I grew more and more uneasy. Every exit, I noted, was guarded by a Scot.

"Hear! Hear!" murmured the barons.

"We didna sign away our wives and dochters!" Enoch thundered. "They be nocht diseissed to the king! Niver!"

Enoch then called Bishop Giles of Hereford to begin. Now I was completely confused: Bishop Giles had no wife or children that I knew of, nor was he connected in any way to the tragedy of my abduction. Of course, there was the de Braose case, but that had naught to do with these barons.

"My brother, Lord William, died last week in Normandy," the bishop began. "He was murdered, not by the sword, but by a broken heart."

My tears gushed. As with Theo's death, I wanted to die—after I gave birth.

Then the bishop's theme turned to Lady Matilda and her children, a tragedy well known throughout England by now. A tragedy and a scandal—even here in Wanthwaite we'd heard rumors of the king's villainy.

"William died of a broken heart," Bishop Giles continued through tears. "The king had made gifts of lands and money that he later claimed were only loans; he demanded exorbitant repayment—or death."

"Stay to the pint!" a Scot shouted. "Women and children!"

"Isn't the death of my sister-in-law and her sons point enough?"

"Aye!" cried the barons.

Bishop Giles sat down. A heavy silence fell over the company.

Enoch now introduced Lord William Marshal of Pembroke Junior, son of the famous Earl William Marshal, who rivaled Lord William de Braose and Lord Robert fitzWalter as the richest man in England. Though the son walked boldly, towering over most of the other knights, he was the youngest man in the Hall by far, hardly more than a boy.

He stood in front with his eyes lowered, as if not certain why he was here. His cheeks were fuzzy. Then he raised his lids to reveal fiery orbs.

"King John," he said in a boy's broken voice, "demanded two of my brothers as hostages, one of two years, one of four. In deference to my father, he placed the younger one—two years old—in his own court under the care of Queen Isabella. The older, however, Roger by name and only four, was sent to Corfe, where he perished in a leaden cuff. My father, though deeply hurt, remained steadfast in his vows to the king. But I am my own man. I mean no disrespect to my father, but I loved my brother, and I don't think any man born of woman, be he king or no, has the right to murder another man's child. I have wept my last tears, however, and now I am angry. I cannot serve such a tyrant."

This case, less known than the de Braose tragedy, shocked the company. His situation also seemed parallel to mine. What did his mother feel? I had company.

An even taller man came forward, a blond giant like the men in Ostend, and as richly attired as Lord Robert.

"Saer de Quenci," announced Enoch.

Edwina whispered, "He and Lord Robert lost Vaudreuil to the French; King John claims they betrayed him!"

Not mentioning Vaudreuil, Lord Saer spoke instead of King John's prurient and destructive curiosity about the private lives of his subjects. He claimed that the king rode the countryside in disguise and picked up gossip from taverns, which he then used as blackmail.

"For example, Lord William de Bellevoir was estranged from his wife. The king put his human hounds on the scent of this scandal. They learned that Lord William had another lady—also married—and the king threatened to expose him if he didn't give a huge sum of money, what we call blackmail. Lord William sold land and paid the king, whereupon the king trumpeted his indiscretion anyway. Now Lord William, his wife, and his friend are dead. I call that murder."

Edwina whispered again, "'Tis true."

Now I had no doubt that Enoch would expose me as a victim of King Richard, thus claiming that the evil is in the Plantagenet blood. How I hated King Richard at this moment! Though not so much as I hated King John.

Lord William de Lanvalle took the podium. When one of the older de Braose boys, Gilbert by name, had been murdered at Windsor, he had left Lord de Lanvalle's daughter distraught, for she and Gilbert had been betrothed. Though he could do nothing to stem her grief, Lord William did try to recover the large dowry for the wedding, which the king had seized. When Lord William had requested that the dowry be returned, the king had not only refused, he'd threatened the life of his daughter.

A murmur of shock followed this presentation, which Lord William immediately stopped with a peremptory gesture.

"I'm not yet finished!" he shouted. "My chief forester wants to speak!"

The company was appalled to have a commoner at the podium, but the forest laws was what I'd expected.

The forester, a brawny young man with no hair, dressed in the green of his trade, was in place before anyone could complain, however. Master Enderby, as he introduced himself, was an inarticulate man with a chubby face and a wandering eye.

"I thankee all fer lettin' me speak wi' the gentry," he said humbly in a raspy voice. "I know my cas may be unimportant to the laks of ye, but I thocht ye micht lak to knaw that the king abuses us lowly folk as weil as the gentry.

"The king's men ha'e told me oft enow that his greatest income be from fines collected for forest infractions. Therefore, I turn over every poacher as I find, never mind if he be starvin'. I draw the line, howsomever, at my wif. My wif—" He couldn't go on.

Lord William hastened to his side. "His wife recently offered the king two dozen eggs if she might be allowed one night with her husband."

We were all shocked to silence.

Then, to my even greater astonishment, Enoch called

Lord Eustace de Vesci to the podium. Eustace's sandy hair was now streaked with white, and he'd lost weight to rival Bishop Giles. His voice, no longer supercilious, had diminished to the point that he was difficult to hear. I would prefer his former condescension to this pitiful creature.

"My Brother lords, I'll be brief." His voice stopped—he seemed not to know where he was. Enoch rushed to his side. "Unhand me!" Lord Eustace would have struck Enoch except that the Scot twisted away. Lord Eustace didn't speak, however; he panted as if he would swoon. Then he seemed to melt; he sat on the floor sobbing like a babe. When he swooned altogether, Lord Robert and Enoch carried him outside into the rain.

Where he had stood, a pillar of fire now shot to the smoke hole. Inside its flames, the peasant girl in red raised her fist. I heard the crackle, felt the heat—did it come from within? I nodded grimly. I knew at last what I must say.

When Enoch and Lord Robert returned, Edwina announced loudly that we would break for Haute Tierce. The entire company breathed a sigh of relief and were soon eating pork and cheese pies and sipping ale, after which they slept.

When we reassembled, Enoch again took the podium. Lord Eustace felt too weak to talk, so he'd asked Lord Robert fitzWalter to do the honors in his place.

Lord Robert walked gracefully to the podium, swinging his golden chain, which was encrusted, I saw, with tiny diamond facets. The company fell silent. This man, more than any other, represented the power of the Brotherhood.

"My friends," he said in Parisian French, his voice low and musical, "Lord Eustace apologizes profoundly for his sudden weakness. He has endured much, as some of you already know, and I can only hope that I can convey the depth of his agony in his place. King John spends much of his time on the road with a huge contingent of servants and knights and family members in the manner of all royalty. Unlike others, however, this king keeps his itinerary secret and therefore appears at our estates unannounced. Hospitality under such conditions and especially at certain seasons poses a hardship on the host, however flattered he may be."

He paused for wine.

"In January—I believe it was January, yes, that's right— King John arrived at Alnwick unannounced, expecting hospitality. Lord Eustace and Princess Margaret moved with all haste to accept their guests. They supped, they prepared rooms, they did everything they could at such short notice.

"After their evening supper, King John indicated that he was ready to retire. Lord Eustace offered to accompany him to the lord's own suite of rooms, which servants had prepared for the king. The king stopped him; he never slept alone. Could Lord Eustace spare his own wife for the king's pleasure?"

The entire company moaned.

"Lord Eustace stammered, too shocked to be articulate. Then his wife, Princess Margaret, stepped forth swiftly: of course she would be most honored to share the king's bed. She would join him as soon as she could change her chemise."

Again he sipped.

"She left; Lord Eustace paced in a small closet throughout

the night. In the morning, she assured him that she had sent a handmaid in her place. Yet the king said nothing, and Lord Eustace has become the broken man you saw."

He seemed finished. Yet he still stood at the podium. When he began again, it was in a different voice, more like the broken tones of Lord Eustace.

The flames flared again.

With the smoke coiling around him, Lord Robert spoke of Lady Matilda's visit to Baynard Castle just before the castle was burned, and shortly before she and her children were starved by the king at Windsor. He didn't mention Theo by name or even his presence with the lady. Instead, he described her in detail: her lusty humor, her courage, her energy.

"Hear! Hear!" A few barons obviously had known Matilda.

"How Lady Matilda earned the emnity of this mad king is still a mystery, though his emnity seems easy to attain. I personally suspect it was her knowledge about the death of Arthur of Brittany. I wonder how many people in Rouen suffered her fate?"

Did he know about Theo? Aye, I thought he did. The flames crackled louder—I looked at my sleeve, expecting to see a spark—but it was all in my fantastick cell. Again he had to stop for the barons to quiet, this time to an ominous silence, whether from the mention of Arthur's death or the suggestion that the king's vengeance had spread, I didn't know. They looked to him as a sage, however.

"Lady Matilda's presence had nothing to do with the loss of Baynard Castle, however. I was warned—I knew it was coming. And I warned her when I heard that the event was near. It has been rumored that the king's men threw their torches because he would not permit London to be a commune. London is still a commune, milords! It will stay a commune so long as I live!"

There was a stamping of boots on rushes.

He held up a hand; the Hall fell silent. Then, like Lord Eustace, he lost control of his voice. "That was the reason the king gave, I say, and there's an element of truth, but only an element." He paused so long that I thought he was finished. "I had a daughter—her name was also Matilda." His voice became difficult to hear. "For those of you who met her, you know that she was the most beautiful maiden ever to tread the earth." He continued in a whisper. "And she was my favorite child. Oh, I have sons and daughters married to great heirs all over England, but Matilda was . . . special, the fruit of old loins. King John saw her, lusted, asked for her in his bed. I refused. He set Baynard Castle aflame."

The flames around Lord Robert crackled.

"The flames didn't touch Matilda—with my cousin Guy de Mandeville's help, I spirited her out of the city and up to my estate at Dunmow. But I underestimated the monster's persistence. King John followed us. I didn't know. He found Matilda alone. I hope he didn't have her—I hope he didn't murder her. According to my apothecary, she drank poison of her own free will." His shoulders heaved. "She died."

Barons and knights sobbed openly. I was too angry to weep.

I understood at last: *desperation.* I walked to the front. Enoch introduced me as his wife and the former concubine of King Richard of the Lion Heart.

Now I stood in the midst of crackling flames.

Softly at first, I began to speak. I spoke not of a great passion; rather, I concentrated on Richard's determination to leave an heir, of his forcing me to sign a contract agreeing to give him a son for his own purposes, his wound and the certificate naming my son as the future king, then the betrayal of both the dead Richard and my embryo son by King John and Queen Eleanor.

Enoch watched me intently.

"After King Richard died of gangrene, I had only a scroll and a sacred order to make my child king. I still have the scroll."

I took a deep breath.

"Yet while the dead king was still lying on display, I had to flee for my very life."

I described in gory detail King John's pursuit, his drunken proposition, my biting of Raoul, the deer trap, Bok's decapitation.

"You will think me dense—I think of myself as dense—for not connecting King John's threats with these tragic events. I'd been seduced by the Plantagenet view that he was a silly boy, mischievous but harmless. Then, at La Rochelle, I had an epiphany."

I described my yearning for sardines, my loathing of wormy bacon, then the dead peasant girl and the grapes.

"In my sandy grave, I faced the truth. King John was willing to kill every young woman in the kingdom to assure that Richard's child would die. Silly and young he might be; he was also cunning, powerful, ruthless, perhaps mad. At that moment, I swore two things: to escape and to kill him before he could kill me or the son I was carrying."

I described my pact with the flaming peasant girl, my nun's habit, my efforts to hide along the road. One knight rushed from the chamber when I described the difficulties of eating worms. I could hardly hear my own voice in the flames' crackle.

"At that point—I think it was then—my babe stopped growing. I didn't give birth, didn't know what to do, so I simply continued on my way north to Rouen with a dead fetus inside me. After a time, I sailed back to England."

I glanced at Enoch. "I had long accepted that I carried a dead person inside my womb. And yet . . . recently . . . my unborn babe has quickened. I can't explain it—maybe it's because I'm home, safe. All I know is that I'm growing apace and will soon give birth to King Richard's son, the rightful prince of England."

Did the barons believe me? Aye, for the same reason they believed that Lord Eustace's wife had sent her handmaid: because they wanted to believe. Enoch's face was pale; his hands trembled. Like Joseph, he accepted Mary's son as coming from God. I went to the kitchen court.

He followed me. "Air ye sartain?"

I turned.

"Aboot the quickening?"

"Oh yes, that."

"May I feel?"

"You amaze me, Enoch. Not only do you half-believe that this is Richard's child, you behave as if you want it to live."

His face reddened. "O'course Ich do! Ha'e ye gone tinty?"

"Have you forgotten Theo? I haven't won, Enoch, even if I escape John, even if I get him before he gets me."

"Ye'll have another son." His eyes were moist.

"Then you didn't understand: King John will kill this babe as surely as he did Theo. And me as well."

"Nay, Alix, he may try, but he willna succeed."

Lord Robert pushed his way past cheese pies. The great baron looked deeply into my eyes with tears in his own. "Theo was a beautiful boy, my dear, a fit son for such a beautiful mother and great father. And he was happy, I want you to know that."

"Thank you, my lord." My voice fell to a whisper. "I'm sorry about your—"

"I know." He pressed my hands, then went on: The barons had voted to accept Richard's son as their new king.

"As for the boy you call Theo, that's the name I will give my son."

This time there were flames instead of tears in his eyes. "Good girl."

I congratulated Enoch. His mad plan was going forward. John would be displaced and replaced.

Yet my spirits drooped. I wanted my bairn to live.

I wanted to live.

Which meant . . . ?

Shortly before the Nativity, I rode into Dunsmere with Donald and Gruoth beside me. Gruoth led us directly to a small hut on the lane where Dame Margery had lived. Inside a dark room, we huddled close to a fire pit under an open smoke hole. A short gravid woman surrounded by children introduced herself as Dame Queenhild.

"Rip!" She pulled a small boy away from the fire.

"That's a most unusual name, Rip," I commented.

"Rip for Ripple," Dame Queenhild explained. "All my childer be named for water whence we all cum. The boys be Rip, Current, and Tarn—water what moves—and the girls be Spring, Mere, and yif this one be a female, 'twill be Well, the deep water ye see."

Like the sisters on the coast naming their cows for fish, everything from water. Or, I recalled my water breaking in Rouen. Aye, babes swam in water; water was their element.

"'Tis a bonny thought, Dame Queenhild."

She then agreed to serve as my wet nurse, probably in November. When we started back to Wanthwaite a light snow began to fall.

Enoch followed us.

10

In like manner, I found Dame Berdeth in Dunsmere to serve as my midwife. My "prince" was now extremely active; I could no longer sleep lying down. Nor was I any longer of sanguine disposition. I would have him and instantly lose him.

"Alix, oncit ye told me hu ye escaped from Wanthwaite when that Sir Roland de Roncechaux attacked." Enoch stood in the door of my room.

I forced myself awake. "Yes. Why?"

"Ye sayed as there war a labyrinth summers on the estate."

"On most estates, I believe."

His pale face frightened me.

"Do we need to hide?"

"Shaw me."

He supported me on our way to the stable. Once inside the dim interior, I felt the eastern wall with my hands.

"Here, aye, here. Push to your right."

Half a wall slid open to reveal a rough earthen hole. I hadn't been in the labyrinth since that awful day my parents had died—I felt sick.

"It's a tunnel down to the Wanthwaite River," I said in a hushed voice—the place seemed like death to me—"big enough for a horse. Maisry and I used to play in the cave at the bottom."

Aye, with stick horses. My hands shook.

"Be the cave wisible below?"

"You've never noticed it, have you?" He waited. "I think not; honeysuckle vines mask it during the summer. During winter, snow drifts conceal it." I tried to recall playing there during winter months. "Ice forms well inside."

"Be there also a door?"

"At the bottom? Not unless you put one there."

He stepped inside. "'Tis muckle hot!"

"And filled with rats and spiders." He returned quickly to the stable. "Why are you asking these questions, Enoch?"

"The king." He put his hands on my shoulders. "Yif we're attacked, Alix, I want ye shuld bring all the womenfolk here ond stay till I say it's safe."

His serious tone chilled me.

"I'll soon be in labor."

"Ond ye mun protect our prince."

"Something's happened, Enoch. Tell me!"

Before he could answer, I clutched his arm. "Quick, Enoch! Send for the midwife!"

"Air ye . . . ?"

"Aye!"

We reached my closet just as the babe descended. Unlike the Jews, my English help used the birthing stool. Clinging to a rope, I pushed—my babe dropped! It was so sudden—so easy—that I couldn't believe my eyes when Dame Berdeth held up a mewing waxy triangle. She swung the babe to Gruoth's waiting hands.

"Careful!" I cried.

Enoch's wet face came close.

"What are you doing here? Leave!"

"Hu do ye feel?"

"Better than you do, methinks."

"What will ye call it?" Dame Berdeth shouted.

"Richard. He's Richard II!"

Enoch licked his lips. "'Tis a wench," he apologized. "We mun try agin."

I laughed helplessly. A daughter, I had a daughter. Oh, *Deo gratias,* a daughter! A worthless female! Not the next prince of England after all! Who wanted a queen on the throne? What father wanted to raise a dowry for his daughter? She would be all mine.

Of course, there was still the problem of King John. Never mind, for the moment let me revel—I had a daughter!

Once she'd had her wax removed and Gruoth had bitten her cord, Enoch cradled her against his neck. Then he held her at arms' length to gaze in wonder. "We'll nam her for my mudder. This be little Garnette."

"Her name is Leith."

"Leith! Quhat sart o' a nam be Leith?"

"Leith, the port of Edinburgh."

Deep water for a girl, and the last place I'd been when Theo had still lived.

"'Tis a beautiful nam fer a beautiful gal!"

Leith now lay by my side. After his first enchantment with her, Enoch had disappeared, to tell the barons the sorry news, no doubt.

"That's men, my dear," I told Leith, "a fickle breed, every one."

She opened one lapis eye. Poor thing looked like Enoch. His snub nose, his red-gold hair, his stubborn chin. Yet she was my daughter, too, for she had dimples in her fat cheeks. She gave forth a bleat; Dame Queenhild rose from the dark corner.

"Little Leak wants the nipple."

"Leith, her name is Leith." Which she knew quite well— she was jealous that she hadn't thought of it.

Leith burped on cue and was back.

And so was Enoch, who entered unannounced. He'd sent Donald with the bad news.

"May I lie beside her?" he asked humbly.

"No!"

Too late, he placed her on his chest.

That was just the beginning. The very next morn I had to run after him to the stable, where he placed the infant on his huge fighting destrier. He would hold her, he said; he wouldn't let her fall! If Dame Queenhild hadn't supported me, poor Leith would have tumbled to her death or been frozen in the storm now brewing. Enoch couldn't bear to have her out of his sight. If she couldn't join his world, he would join hers. At first it was surprising, then touching, then irritating. He knew naught of the care of bairns, which didn't stop him from challenging all of Queenhild's decisions.

We didn't mention the sore topic of her sex, though I knew he must be disappointed. Poor barons, poor England, poor Alix, who was discovered to be a fraud.

Lucky Leith.

In the weeks that followed, I was absorbed with my new babe. Enchantment, however, quickly gave way to reality. Leith was healthy, quick in her development, and quite pretty in the Scottish manner. Enoch's "babby" had red-gold curls, very red fat cheeks with dimples that came and went, and startling blue eyes with long dark lashes. Everyone commented on her beauty. Her temperament was a different matter. She had definite likes and dislikes and expressed herself with loud screams. Though she had no teeth, she bit down hard with her gums. She scowled as often as she laughed. Everyone in the household was wary of her except Enoch. He doted on his faultless daughter.

Though I assumed that the barons had been told of her disastrous gender, I had no response except from Lord Eustace. The great lord of Alnwick sent a blunt message to the effect that since mothers determined gender, it was my fault. On the other hand, I had not deliberately had a girl child nor had I wanted a child by Enoch at all. Therefore, I returned to my former opinion of Lord Eustace.

As if to compensate, Lord Robert fitzWalter sent a knight with a basket of pasties and a missive saying daughters were a great solace to fathers as they grew older. He might better have said to mothers, but I was pleased nonetheless. Meantime, Leith's wet nurse became resigned to Enoch's interference.

"'Tis because she's his ferst bairn," Dame Queenhild observed. "Wait till 'tis the ninth."

There would be no second, let alone a ninth. The mother of Enoch's next child would be Lady Fiona. Let her have the son to be England's prince, I thought grimly. At least she wouldn't take this babe from me and become the queen mother.

Leith's birth raised a problem concerning my annulment, for I could foresee a battle with Enoch about who would take her. In ordinary cases, which mine certainly was not, the father owned all children, but Leith had been trumpeted as King Richard's child. I put off thinking about it just yet.

As time passed, I defended her prickly nature (which seemed to improve as she gained fat) and took pride in her obvious quickness of mind. Thorketil built a cradleboard on which we hung her in the Great Hall when we assembled. All the Scots made much of her from a distance, though they stroked the other babies hanging on the wall, for our summer planting had come to fruition. Leith scowled when awake, though she didn't scream.

Then to my astonishment, Lord Robert fitzWalter rode into our couryard to see her, all the way from Oxford.

"You came just to see Leith?" I blurted.

"Of course!" He dandled her on his shoulder, where she promptly vomited, whereupon he gave her back to me.

"A delicious girl," he opined, as Gruoth rubbed a small white trickle from his shoulder. He slapped Enoch's back. "Enjoy her, Enoch. They grow so fast."

Enoch was flattered at the attention from such a great man—though he hardly needed the advice.

As I watched Gruoth rub, now with water, I slowly realized that Lord Robert had not come to see Leith at all. Indeed, he'd been a game sport to dandle her at her age (and especially with her disposition, though he couldn't know that). But if not Leith, why? His shadowed eyes had purpose. When he changed the subject from babies to politics, I paid close heed. He spoke redundantly about the de Braose case, which had roused public outrage against the king, especially since the king refused to acknowledge any wrongdoing.

This was not his subject. I waited.

"Where is the king now?" I asked. "Still in Rouen?" It was not the fighting season, so there seemed no real reason for him to be in England.

I thought Lord Robert wouldn't answer.

"No, he lost Normandy to France."

Enoch and I were too shocked to speak. Lord Robert told us about battles and castles in Normandy.

"Be the king in London Town nu?" Enoch asked.

"How does the French King Philip treat his Jews?" I asked at the same time.

It was Lord Robert's turn to be surprised. "I have no idea." He turned to Enoch. "No, Dover. I'm told he's amassing a fleet to invade Normandy in the spring, or perhaps the summer."

We were silent. I was thinking of Bonel and the commune. Once, when I'd visited a witches' coven in Paris, I'd heard that King Philip was generous to the Jews. Was this still true?

"So you're no longer disturbed at the king's licentiousness? Or domestic issues?" I asked.

Lord Robert bared his teeth. "Always, milady, always. For it's been rumored that the reason the king lost Normandy was that he played in bed with his new wife until the late afternoon while his knights waited in the courtyard. Thus he lost Normandy a castle at a time." He paused. "It is also said that she was a child of eight years when they wed."

I smiled at Enoch. "No doubt he raped her."

Enoch turned deep red.

Lord Robert took me seriously. "Oh no, I think not. Queen Isabella is said to be a perfect bedmate for the king." He paused. "The important news is that he wants to take back Normandy."

"That takes ships," Enoch observed.

"And money. And men," Lord Robert agreed. "Mark me! Retaking Normandy will become his entire purpose as king. And he will want us—his barons—to take it for him."

"Boot . . ."

"But . . ."

"Indeed, you understand my point. We signed fealty at his coronation, which meant a willingness to fight for England, to defend England. Not to fight abroad, however, not to invade. No Englishman wants to die on foreign soil."

"Is Normandy foreign?" I asked. "Isn't it part of England?"

Lord Robert sighed. "You touch a vexing legal point. Most of the gentry come from Normandy or have estates there, many would say their roots."

This news was the real purpose of his visit, though Enoch had the same questions that I did. Were English barons sailors? Surely this would be a sea battle.

Enoch turned to me. "Ich war tryin' to tell ye, Alix, qhuan Leith cum, that day in the labyrinth, that King John be determined to tak Normandy back. He wants English barons to do the job ond they've refused."

"So you've already been approached."

Our eyes locked.

Lord Robert cleared his throat. "Enoch is not the only one to refuse, Lady Alix. No English baron will fight in Normandy!"

"Are you saying that they're English, not Norman?"

"Good girl, you spare me explanation." He glanced at Enoch. "You're a fortunate man, Enoch."

"Aye," Enoch agreed without enthusiasm. Lord Robert then repeated himself several times in different manners as if we were deaf or dense. He finally ended. "Many barons, even some of our Brothers, are originally from Normandy, and at the moment their problem is whether to pay King John or King Philip the scutage; France demands payment, of course. Others claim that Normandy isn't our native land, England is."

"Did they change their minds because of the French victory?"

His voice became intimate. "The late King Henry II spent hardly any time here, Richard even less. Think, my dear, you were there. After Jerusalem, King Richard stayed to fight the French, who have always claimed Normandy. As a result, many Englishmen stopped thinking of him as an English king." He paused. "I'm told Richard couldn't even speak English." It was a question.

He was right, but I said naught.

Enoch rescued me. "The king wull release us fram service yif we pay scutage. He con use that money to hire mercenaries."

"He needs English manpower, even with foreign help. Before he takes Normandy, you see, he plans to attack the Low Countries."

"Flanders?" I cried. "He wants to fight the Vikings?"

"It seems madness, I grant you. Why should we pay good money to indulge him?"

Abruptly, I rose to leave, then sat again. This man was angry, and not about domestic issues.

"I refuse to pay a tyrant," he said softly. "Remember, he murdered my daughter."

So it was still domestic issues. Our scheme had failed—what did he have in mind?

"He tried to kill Alix's babe quhan she war in Fontevrault," Enoch added grimly. "My little Leith."

For a moment, I didn't know what he meant. Then I realized he referred to my time in Fontevrault Wood when I'd carried Theo.

Lord Robert rose abruptly, as if he, too, was offended by the lie.

"Well, I've accomplished my purpose." But he still stood at his bench. "Except, my Lord Enoch, a few more words in private?"

His "casual" request sounded ominous.

I lifted Leith off the wall at once and walked up the steps to my closet. Yet my head was spinning. What did Lord Robert want? What was the real purpose of his visit? Certainly not Leith! Then I heard rustlings and men's voices below.

I peered into the darkness. How strange, at least a dozen men beat their arms against the snow in our courtyard. Even stranger, my peasant girl from La Rochelle burned in their midst. Lord Robert's patrician French rose—then another voice I knew well, Lord Eustace de Vesci's! Now I was truly frightened—why had he stayed outside in the cold? Why was the peasant girl burning?

And there were other lords—aye, lords, not knights. This was a meeting of the Brotherhood. After a long argument in which voices occasionally rose, the knights and lords remounted their steeds and rode silently across the moat bridge.

I slipped down the stairs to catch Enoch when he returned.

He pulled me into the snowfall outside.

"They want I shuld murther the king," he whispered.

Kill King John? Enoch?

I forgot John's character utterly and thought only of Enoch. Forget our muddled history—he was a good man, and he was going to die!

"Come to my closet!" I whispered.

We huddled on the edge of my mat beside a snoring Leith. Wolfbane growled, then went back to sleep. Warmth from the fire below rose even as our conversation chilled. The actual assassins of planning and purpose were Lord Robert and Lord Eustace; Enoch was their means, though they would take responsibility. Their *infant perdu*, I thought, remembering the Crusade. They'd made their plan: they had it on good faith that King Llywelyn of Wales planned to attack England here in the north, which would deflect King John from his Normandy or Low Countries ambitions; John would be riding north on Dere Street sometime during the early summer to meet the Welsh, and Enoch would shoot an arrow into his heart as he passed Dunsmere Lane.

I was appalled and said so. "This is a plan to get you killed, Enoch! John is guarded—and he'll have his entire army with him! They'll slay you at once!"

"They'll ne'er see me! I'll be hid!" Enoch spoke as if not believing his own words. "Lord Robert ond Lord Eustace ha'e a plan."

"What plan?"

"They'll tal me soon." He sighed. "It do same odd aboot Wales, since the Welsh king be wed to the English king's bastard dochter. Boot they swear it be true. Quhan King John rides north to meet him, I'll slay him daid."

"Whereupon the king's guards will slay you dead and Wales will attack with no opposition! And why do the barons call themselves the assassins when you will do the actual killing?"

"They made the plan. They'll tak the blame."

Their plan was woodly. Lord Robert and Lord Eustace would station themselves on Dere Street about a mile south of Enoch; after the deed, they would wait for him to join them, whereupon all three men would ride to the very same ridge I'd used after my shipwreck and dash to a boat waiting to transport them to Normandy. This flight was how they would "tak the blame."

"The king's men canna follow us to Normandy—ye heard Lord Robert explain why."

"Enoch, are you so bedazzled by your Brothers that you can't see the flaws? To begin, how can you be certain that John will march north? Everyone remarks how he changes his movements without warning—Lord Robert himself admitted that the king shifts purpose for no reason. And look at how he descended on Lord Eustace!"

"Aye, boot Lord Robert ond Lord Eustace ha'e spies wi' the king, o' course. That's hu they knaw that the king o' Wales be gang to attack King John here in the north; King Llywelyn hisself ha'e sayed so."

I knew naught of the Welsh king's steadiness of purpose, but I certainly knew that John was easily distracted.

"Has John asked his barons to fight Wales?"

He became uneasy. "He ha'e hired mercenaries fer the job."

Mercenaries who would kill Enoch with no conscience whatsoever. During my time with King Richard, I'd learned the rudiments of warfare with hired killers.

"By fleeing to Normandy, Laird Robert and Eustace be admittin' guilt."

"Are you going to Normandy as well?"

"Aye."

How passing strange; I'd fought to leave Normandy for Enoch and England, and now he would be *in* Normandy.

"So you'll be admitting guilt as well."

"Nocht as much as they do."

"Why not, Enoch? You have reason to kill the king, which he'll remember if he lives. Do you think John has forgotten Fontevrault Wood?" He didn't answer. "Have you considered Leith? In the unlikely event that you do get away and that John still lives, she and I will receive the full thrust of royal wrath. Do you want her destroyed?"

"Ye spoke o' some peasant girl and burning, by quich Ich tought ye meant to kill the king."

"You're right. But not sloppily, not this way. You're going to die for no reason! If you insist, let me do it, Enoch. I can shoot an arrow, and I don't matter."

"I wull cum back fram Normandy—quhan it blaws over."

"I should be the one!"

"Except ye canna place the arrow lak me."

"Then teach me."

He rose. "Good nicht, Alix."

For the first time since Leith had been born, I clung to his arm. "Don't do it, Enoch."

"Eustace ond Robert wull be wi' me," he said stubbornly.

The following morning, he sat before the fire with his bow on his lap and made new arrows. Thorketil checked his points for him. By the end of the week, the snow had melted sufficiently so he could go outside. He placed turnips atop snow mounds and aimed again and again. When snow started to fall, he came inside; the snow melted, and he practiced once more. The Scots watched. They seemed to know his purpose, though I'm certain he confided in no one.

"Don't do it!" I implored. "Teach me—John will blame me anyway."

"He willna blame anyone quhan he be dead."

But his guards would.

In late snowstorms, Enoch shot blossoms off our geroldinga apple tree. When the grass turned bright green and budding leaves were everywhere, Lord Robert arrived with two of his knights.

Despite Enoch's stern orders to stay home, Leith and I followed the men to Dere Street, where they arranged a blind. I knelt behind a bush to watch. Lord Robert knew we were with Enoch, but he barely glanced in my direction; he was serious.

Enoch, still on horseback, aimed an arrow from behind a prickly barberry bush. Lord Robert, pretending to be King John, rode into plain view in front of Enoch. Lord Robert's knights watched from the shrubbery.

"Hu do ye knaw that the king willna be surrounded by guards?" To that extent, Enoch heeded my warning.

"Oh, he will!" Lord Robert replied. "You should have one fast aim, nonetheless. But only one."

They then rehearsed in earnest: four knights flanked a horse carrying a straw bale (King John), which made Enoch's aim more difficult. On the sixth try, he shot through the bale's "heart."

"Good shot."

Lord Robert broke a branch of the barberry where Enoch had stood.

"What happens after he shoots?" I asked innocently.

"He's to join Lord Eustace and me." Lord Robert was dismissive, almost surly.

"You wave your arm southward," I insisted. "Won't the king's army be stretched for many miles to the south?"

"Don't be concerned, my dear, this is man's work."

Betraying Enoch was man's work?

I smiled with "feminine" deference. "I suppose I'm still under the influence of King Richard when it comes to military matters; I have opinions."

His glance sharpened. "Such as?"

"King Richard would have conceded that you might escape—and you might not—but that Enoch is doomed. That you planned it that way."

Our eyes held. "Enoch will go with us to Normandy."

I stopped being "feminine." "You are sacrificing Enoch! No matter whether he hits or misses the king, he's dead!"

Lord Robert rode close and spoke through his teeth. "I didn't know you loved him so much."

My face heated. "He's Leith's father."

"Is he?" His smile broadened. "You have myriad fathers for your children, sometimes for the selfsame child!"

"Methinks you speak from a 'masculine' view, which means that men father many children."

His voice became buttery again. "In any case, I'm not going to let this sweet babe become fatherless. I have Enoch's sailing all arranged, my dear, I promise you."

I would have felt more secure if Eustace de Vesci were not part of the plan.

And I knew from my peasant girl that I should be the assassin. Yet why? What did it matter who killed King John? Many of us had good reasons; potentially, many more would join our sorry number. The important thing was that he should be removed.

Two weeks later, Lord Robert's knights, Sir Jérome and Sir Gilbert, came without Lord Robert to escort Enoch to his site once more. To everyone's discomfiture, I followed them. Spring growth now completely obscured the opening on the verge, even the barberry bush. Enoch was pleased, but the knights slashed at limbs to carve out a clear place for him to kneel. I went onto Dere Street to look up; he should wear green. When he fell to one knee and raised his bow, I decided that it, too, should be green. Lord Gilbert thrust me roughly aside as he rode by in the person of King John. Though he had his same dark blond hair and blue eyes as the king, he was taller, which skewed the purpose.

The knights then pointed out where they'd hacked a narrow path running parallel to Dere Stret to the spot where Lord Robert and Lord Eustace would be waiting for Enoch. The three men would cross Dere Street in the presence of John's entire army, who presumably would not yet understand the significance of their stopping because they were in the rear.

"How lang will we be exiles in Normandy?" Enoch asked. "Since John be dead, con we return soon? Will we still be in exile?"

A good question: Who would be king? Would he forgive the assassins? Would the pope?

"Lord Robert and Lord Eustace both have grand estates in Normandy." Sir Jérome avoided a direct answer. "I would give much to hunt in those forests again."

Which meant yes, he would be an exile.

"What happens if Enoch misses?" I asked. "Won't the king's men search the bushes?"

"He won't miss."

"Then he hits. Won't they still hunt?"

"He'll be gone!" Sir Jérome reminded me haughtily.

"May we see the exact spot where Lord Robert and Lord Eustace will wait?" I asked.

Both knights consented to lead us to the rendezvous.

We rode silently for several miles along Dere Street until we came within sight of the path leading up to the ridge.

The knights stopped.

Sir Jérome explained again that soldiers in John's army would be too far from the event to be suspicious when Enoch appeared.

"How many heartbeats did you count from the blind?" I asked Enoch when the knights rode on.

"Twenty-three thousand five hundred twenty-seven."

About sixty more than I'd counted. We stared at each other: Why would Lord Eustace and Lord Robert wait that amount of time for Enoch?

Yes, Enoch was their *enfant perdu.*

He increased his marksmanship practice.

The Scots watched him silently. Occasionally, Edward or Thorketil would advise him in low tones.

Then Sir Gilbert rode in to report that the king might be going to the Low Countries before fighting King Llywelyn of Wales after all.

He dashed away before we could even question him. Enoch rose from his kneeling position and spoke to Thorketil, whereupon his friend instantly rode south. He returned two weeks later: King Llywelyn of Wales still planned to attack, probably close to Durham. King John still planned to march north; the assassination plan was in place.

Yet we remained confused. What had Sir Gilbert meant by his visit? I prayed he wasn't a spy.

King John wasn't idle during this period. Geoffrey de Mandeville, Earl of Essex and cousin to Lord Robert, was murdered by one of King John's routiers; the castle of Henry Bohun, Lord of Hereford, was burned in the last week of July; Robert de Vere, Earl of Oxford, and Geoffrey de Say, Earl of Clare, sent runners all over England to warn of impending civil war. Would John's death prevent such a disaster?

One late eve when Enoch and I huddled in a corner over our ale, I spoke out. "Does the baron's choice to make you the assassin have something to do with me, Enoch?"

He pretended astonishment. "You? Quhy?"

"Simple. The king knows that I live close to Dere Street. Perhaps your Brotherhood wants to get rid of me for your sake."

He put down his ale. "I doona knaw."

But he didn't deny the Brotherhood's opinion of me. We both fell into melancholy disposition.

I spoke first. "Or mayhap the barons are angry about Leith's sex. This may be vengeance."

He shook his head. "As ye sayed, most be fathers. They knew that half o' babes be females." He stood. "I war chosen in part becas I'm guid and in part becas I live at Wanthwaite, quhich be conwenient."

Yet I lived here, too. I shuddered, remembering France. If Enoch missed, I had no doubt of my own fate. I couldn't hold back tears. "I'm sorry if I've gotten you into this horror."

For the first time since he'd raped me, he put a hand to my shoulder. "Ye're wrang, Alix. 'Tis nocht you or Wanthwaite, 'tis all o' England. Ond I be chose becas I'm the best mon with the bow. Ond John be riding clase." He paused again. "Those be guid reasons, but in truth, the anely way to cure England be to change the law."

Yes, he was good at bowmanship. I was also good, for I'd been practicing for hours every day. If Enoch missed—if John rode up our berm . . . well, I would be waiting.

Enoch leaned over his baby.

On August 17, King John and his army left London for Durham, north of Wanthwaite. Sir Jérome and Sir Gilbert kept us informed of his progress.

By coincidence, the ecclesiastical court from Durham was visiting Dunsmere soon after John passed—if he did.

"The king wants to visit the new Scottish king Alexander before he fights Wales," Sir Gilbert informed us.

Enoch was outraged. "Be ye sayin' that Scotland be with King John?"

No answer.

Sir Gilbert was back in four days: King John had assembled another army at Dover to try to take Normandy. Perhaps he would give up Wales altogether. Then Lord Eustace sent "good" news: King Llywelyn was finally poised to attack England, and King John was finally marching north on Dere Street.

Our day to assassinate him arrived.

"Leith and I will go with you," I announced.

"To the labyrinth!"

"I want her to be with you to the last heartbeat!"

His eyes filled, his voice broke. "Tak keer of her yif . . . !"

I mounted my saddled horse. "You can't stop me, Enoch!"

We glared at each other. Blue woad dripped down his face. "Yif she screams?"

And I knew I'd won.

"Ich doona want ye shuld see me killed eider, Alix."

"We're speaking of Leith! She may see you kill King John! Imagine the glory!"

"Ye wull hald yer hand o'er her mouth so she doesna cry out," he conceded, "boot nocht her eyes! I want her to see!"

My heart broke. I saw myself as a small girl gazing into the moat where my father's life blood drained into the water. I knew firsthand what it is to lose a father! And my mother— if Enoch failed, I hoped Leith and I went with him. I wiped my eyes.

"I willna die." He patted me awkwardly. "Ye forgit I'm a Scot."

That was one thing I never forgot!

I'd persuaded him to wear the hunter's green, and now he ordered that I again wear my nun's habit because it was black; Leith likewise was to be wrapped in a black shawl. He smeared our faces and hands with blue woad to make us "inwisible," and instructed that I keep my eyes slitted so the whites wouldn't show. In short, we became a typical Scottish family going to war: I should be grateful he didn't insist we ride naked.

Tears ran over his woad. "I want her to remember me at my best!" He hesitated. "Ond ye, too, Alix."

Silently, I put Leith on my saddle in front of me. Once Enoch was intent on his mission, I slipped a honey teat into her mouth, on which I had placed a small dose of mandrake disguised with ciciley. Her bright blue eyes soon closed.

"Hu be my babby?" Enoch whispered over his shoulder.

"The rhythm of the horse has put her to sleep!"

The quiver moved up and down on his great square shoulders.

By the time we arrived at the rendezvous, Leith slept soundly. Lord Robert and Lord Eustace were nevertheless frantic at her presence, and equally outraged at mine. I calmly hid in a second blind I had fashioned some days ago for Leith and me, a labyrinth of greenery where we could stay, concealed, then escape through a back opening. I pulled her deep inside. The arrows I carried punctured my habit.

The barons, also with black-smeared faces, dismounted without glancing in my direction—did they see me? They knelt in Enoch's blind overlooking Dere Street, whispered in French, mounted their steeds, and rode south on the tiny path.

A robin's shrill song warned us of the approaching men.

Enoch took an arrow.

Hooves clopped softly on Dere Street. Human voices rumbled. Someone laughed.

"Quhy be he cumin' fram the north?" Enoch whispered over his shoulder.

I nodded as if I understood, which I certainly did not.

Aye, from the north: the familiar skirl of a bagpipe, the shrill of a fife, and the drummer's beat, the Scottish royal tap. Enoch lowered his bow. I put my hand over Leith's nose to quiet her snores. Around the bend came the flash of royal plaid, sun on silver, an army of ten Scots flying the Scottish flag, a harmless royal dress band. Harmless except—we remained as quiet as cats. Now they were opposite us, big burly men with hairy knees.

They stopped directly in front of us. They must know we were here. My heart thumped.

The leader signaled silence. Within moments we heard what they heard, an army approaching from the south—John's army. What a disaster! We couldn't let the Scots witness Enoch's act. In fact, I doubted very much if he would shoot in their presence. Leith didn't cry; I did.

King John's army became noisier. Glints of gold, then the king himself, exuberant though sober, straight in his saddle, his profile handsome and lethal; he looked finally like the dangerous killer he was. Sun blinded off his golden helmet and his jeweled raiment. His lips were tight under his short curly beard, and his jaw had chilling purpose. No longer "baby John," he was a thick-torsoed, menacing man. And vain. His middle was obviously girdled under his tunic to make him appear more slender. Only his eyes were the same, black-fringed and jewel-blue.

He was as surprised to see the Scots as we were.

When a Scottish officer dismounted to talk to the king, royal guards thrust themselves close around the monarch. Then, before they could parley, another musical army marched from the north singing a madrigal. Both the Scots and the English looked dumbfounded; then the Scots hid in the foliage on the other side of Dere Street.

John and his routiers climbed up the berm directly to Enoch's blind.

For a moment, John's eyes looked straight at Enoch, who seemed to melt into the foliage. No, he was inside my blind. John's gaze followed him—did he see him? Aye, he did, and me—he saw me. I slitted my eyes and covered Leith completely—but he saw her as well. Then he turned his back. Why hadn't he spoken? Killed us?

Enoch squeezed my hand and drew us back farther. John's guards were examining his blind, and by their agitated movements showed they knew exactly what it was. Would the Scots be blamed for stopping him?

They waited—the madrigal was fast approaching—all of us watched Dere Street.

Light male voices rose like a cloud of birds in close harmony. The Welsh—it had to be! And yet, would King Llywelyn be so careless as to sing his approach?

I watched John's back.

The music grew louder, the voices more jubilant.

Enoch pushed his steed silently as any serpent to my horse and pulled us deeper into the brush. King John gazed only at the approaching Welsh.

By the time the singing army rounded the curve, we could make out a haughty child-woman dressed all in white sitting sidesaddle, her filmy train trailing over her creamy mount's rump. For a giddy moment, I thought she was the young Eleanor of Aquitaine, for the profile was the same. Yet this woman wore the white and green of Wales and a shining band on her head.

"Joanna!"

She slipped off her steed as John leaped onto Dere Street

and embraced her. Another of his whores? No, whispered
Enoch: This was Queen Joanna, John's bastard daughter and
wife to King Llywelyn of Wales. As she spoke in low earnest
tones to her father, the small Scottish contingent revealed
themselves as well. The Scottish chieftain and Queen Joanna
spoke to John with high excitement—Joanna even shook her
father. King John remounted his stallion and pounded south
on Dere Street. Joanna and the Scots turned back toward the
north.

"Quick! We ha'e been betrayed!"

Enoch pulled my horse behind his in a fast canter.

No one followed us. After we'd passed Dunsmere, Enoch
slowed. Blue woad ran down his neck.

"They be after the barons!"

"Who? Scotland? Wales? Are they allies?"

"The sam traitor mun ha'e tald both!" He seemed distracted. "Quhy wuld the Scots warn John?"

How could he ask? Hadn't they betrayed Theo?

"Nay, it war the Welsh dochter," he concluded. "She tald
the Scots, and they wouldna... There be a new Scottish
king; mayhap ..." He didn't finish.

Had Lord Robert and Lord Eustace escaped to Normandy?

"John knows about Wanthwaite! Hurry, Enoch! The
labyrinth!"

When we reached the park, we slowed. Wanthwaite, Wanthwaite, sanctuary, home, the heart of the world.

The baby flailed fretfully, but I gave her no more mandrake.

By the time we entered our courtyard, Leith, sucking her thumb, lay her head on Enoch's chest. He sang a Scottish lullaby.

> *Upon the midsumer evin, murriest of nichtis,*
> *Imuvit furth allane neir neir as midnicht was past . . .*

I joined him:

> *Besyd ane gudie grein garith, full of gay flouris*
> *Hegeit of ane huge hicht with hawthorne trees.*

A horse's head appeared through a bush.

"Someone's here." I reined my horse.

Enoch instantly turned to the labyrinth.

Very quietly, he shifted the sleeping baby to my horse and reached to his quiver for an arrow. Something rustled from the direction of our schoolroom. Enoch slid to the grass.

Lady Fiona ran to his arms. "Enoch, oh, Enoch! Ich cum as soon as I received your message! Be ye all richt?"

11

ENOCH HAD SURVIVED THE ABORTED ASSASSINATION—WOULD I survive this?

"Greeting, Lady Alix," Lady Fiona said in her soft burr. "I trust I'm not intruding."

"Not at all. Any wife of Enoch's is always welcome." I pointed to Leith. "Part wolf, but of course you know all about that."

At that moment, Wolfbane leaped joyfully to lick my face.

Followed by the beast, I pushed past the loving couple to the kitchen, where I washed the blue woad off Leith and me.

Enoch followed me up the stairs to my closet. "Ich didna knaw she ware cumin', Alix, I swear."

"But you did alert her about your assignment?"

"Aye."

"Then she probably told the Scots. Did that occur to you?"

"Niver!" But I saw I'd hit a sore spot.

"At least your runner wasn't intercepted by John's men, which must be considered a victory of sorts. And the lady obviously cares about Wanthwaite—or is it you?"

"Ye're a cynic, Alix."

I turned slowly. "No, milord, a realist. I have to be, don't I?"

"Ich didna inwite her here. Ich war just as surprised as ye."

"I doubt that, milord."

After he left, I instructed Gruoth that henceforth Leith and I would take our repast in my chamber.

I hid my arrows under my bed with my jewels and money.

Yet I was too agitated to remain without news. What had happened to Lord Robert and Lord Eustace? Had they gotten away? I sank to a corner with long shivering sobs: Had John seen me? Leith?

Aye, he had.

At my insistence, Gruoth rode into Dunsmere. There she learned that the barons had escaped, though no one knew their whereabouts; nor did they know where the king had gone. No, there was no war with Wales that Gruoth knew of, at least not here in the north.

She did have one piece of news, however: Father William said that the ecclesiastical court from Durham would be in Dunsmere within two days; he'd made an appointment for me to meet with the head, Bishop Peter, first thing in the morning. Could I come?

I sent back word that I would be there.

With Leith in front of me, we left Wanthwaite while it was still dark. A heavy rainfall gave us further protection from view. Though we had to wait an hour in Dunsmere, it was still dark when I was ushered into the small office to meet with the bishop. Bishop Peter spoke only in the vulgar Latin that I remembered from my Crusading days, and for a while we chatted about the Holy Land and the need for another Crusade; he hoped the present king would lead it as he'd promised.

Finally, however, we came to my situation, and his responses became perfunctory. Only when I mentioned King Richard did he began to listen. He dandled Leith, asked many questions, offered us ale and cheese, asked more questions. Despite the interesting diversions on King Richard, my case was clear: Enoch owned both Leith and Wanthwaite; I had behaved like a houri and must leave my family. I argued desperately to no avail. By the end of the day, the problem remaining was that only a husband could get an annulment. Therefore, our interview was a waste of time.

But not quite: Enoch would never pay the exorbitant fee for the dissolution. I gave the bishop two of Bonel's gold pieces and told him that Enoch would be in touch.

I then returned to Wanthwaite in rain and fog, where I carried Leith to my room.

Three weeks later, Enoch rapped on my door: Could he see Leith?

No.

Please? He missed her.

Leith, recognizing his voice, screamed.

And received the mandrake.

He finally left.

Then he sent his emissary. Again I heard the soft burr followed by timid knocks. She meant me no harm—couldn't we be friends? She knew my history—did I know that she was a widow? I shrugged silently; I daresay most Scottish women are widows from the clan wars.

Yet I opened the door.

She gazed in astonishment, unprepared to see me.

"Come inside."

I peered down at the Great Hall, but there was no Enoch.

Lady Fiona was not as tall as I was, yet I realized again that she was many years older. She was exquisitely groomed, however. Her black brows were plucked to a thin line, her skin a pasty white from a popular boar-grease concoction, and she smelled of Scottish heather. Though I tried, I couldn't catch Enoch's odor on her.

"Quhat a pretty babe," she said softly. "May I?"

She picked up Leith before I could answer, and blood spurted as Leith sank new teeth into Fiona's flesh. When I'd finished my apologies and dabbing, I invited the lady to sit at the far end of my mat, away from Leith.

"She looks like Enoch," I answered her comment. "Do you have any children?"

God had chosen to make her barren, though she loved bairns. I studied her expression, her voice, her eyes. I didn't like her—how could I?—but I could grant her a certain sweetness of manner. Leith would be safe with her.

She'd come to see if we couldn't be friends.

Why should we be friends? Did she want a ménage à trois as well as bigamy? These were thoughts, not words, for I must be careful.

Then she roused my attention: "Ich would lak to say farewell."

"Farewell?" I took her hand. "Before you leave, I have a proposition, Lady Fiona." I turned to the wall to say it.

"Aye!" she replied. "Aye, I'll keer fer her, ond gladly."

Later, from my window, I watched the couple talk

earnestly. When they glanced upward, I withdrew. I heard rather than saw Lady Fiona call for her horse.

In a short time, the expected knock came to my door.

"Lat me in, Alix; Ich want to see Leith."

When I opened the door, he dashed to the baby.

"She ha'e mar hair!" he accused me.

"And more teeth," I agreed.

He walked her till and fro, cooing and talking in Gaelic; she didn't scream, which was her highest compliment. Finally, he sat on the edge of my bed, still dandling Leith on his knee.

"Ich mun talk wi' ye."

I nodded. "I hope you'll listen first."

"Lady Fiona be gan."

"I know." I then told him my proposition: There were two weighty problems in our household, the problem of our marriage and its future, and the problem of England and its king.

"King John be nocht yer problem," Enoch protested.

"I assure you that he is, milord. He saw me in my blind— saw Leith and me both. The fact that he didn't kill us simply means that it wasn't his chosen moment. It will come."

I had his attention. "Leith!" Then he said, "The barons will settle King John."

"Do they plan another assassination?"

He shook his head.

I began to pace. "Enoch, I've been thinking about England. The one meeting of the Brotherhood I attended concentrated on John's invasion of their domestic scene. He isn't just a seducer, however; he's a killer. The death of Lord Robert's daughter was the real cause of this assassination attempt."

He frowned. "Quhat's yer pint?"

"Obviously Lord Robert wanted revenge. With or without John's life, however, his daughter's still dead. There may be a second attempt."

He grasped my wrist. "Lat me speak! Lord Robert ond e'en Lord Eustace mun learn that killin' John willna solve all their problems. John, ond aye, his famous brother ond their father befar them, ha'e all disdained the very heart of our laws! Aye, John mun behave different, but we mun ha'e laws in place to control him!"

"The heart of the law, as you call it, doesn't even mention the treatment of women." I sighed. "Have you forgotten that I studied law on the Petit Pont with you? English laws hardly exist—in most trials, there's only canon law."

His face dropped. "No! No! Ye're wrang! I grant that mast judges doona knaw the old laws which may be hearsay, ond therefore there mun be new! John can be controlled anely by law!"

If he wanted to be controlled—I'd just faced canon law in Dunsmere.

"Very well, you must change the law. Or articulate what may already be writ somewhere. And when you do, we must resolve our personal difficulties"—my voice dropped to a whisper—"Wanthwaite, Leith."

He didn't argue.

"John hates me personally, Enoch, face it. You must protect Leith—do you think I should leave?" I held my breath. "Return to Europe? I could go at once—it may take months, e'en years, for you to change the law."

He looked up with red eyes. "No. Yif he touches ye or Leith, I'll kill him."

"He's not easy to kill." I waited. "I am. Leith is."

He didn't argue. How could he? After several sighs, he finally spoke. "The anely way to settle our condition be through the law."

This time I fought hysteria. He was following my design, to confound the law of the land with our personal situation.

He went on about the advantages of a legal solution, simply because of the odds against us if we fought with arms. Enoch might not be another King Richard, but he knew his military matters. And clan warfare was closer to the civil war we faced if we attacked John than anything Richard had experienced. The fact was that the king held twice the number of castles as the barons, and he had the power of the throne, meaning he could reward men with land. From anyone else, I would have seen the "law" as an evasion of these facts, but, with Enoch, I knew I was listening to a true believer.

"You said there was no more unclaimed land for the king to dispense."

"Nocht here, boot in Ireland."

The Irish might not agree.

"Don't the same odds apply if you try the law? John controls the courts. And he's notorious for breaking laws."

"Nocht the canon courts."

Probably not, though I recalled vaguely something about his father and Archishop Becket. Then I held my breath— was this a subtle reference to my visit to the bishop? "Do you think the pope will help England?"

He took a long time to answer. "Ich doona knaw."

"Enoch, I started by saying we had two problems. Never

mind that I'm a woman—I'm English, and I care about a decent government. However . . ."

"Gae on," he said after a time.

And I gushed, started, and stopped, utterly confused about how to put it, but I felt—thought—we should settle one problem at a time!

"Sum udder country?"

"Our personal problems. Our marriage. Leith."

I thought he wouldn't answer. "Quhich one ferst?"

England, oh, yes, England! What choice did we have? I mean, we couldn't live behind palisades forever in fear of attack from our own monarch. Oh, yes, England must come first. I held my breath.

Enoch rose slowly. "Air ye sayin' that we shuld stay wed until . . ."

"Aye, only in form, of course. The way we've been . . ." I laughed breathlessly. "Brother and sister, aye, brother and sister."

"No houghmagandy."

"No."

We stared at one another. The moment throbbed.

"Boot ye'll stay at Wanthwaite?"

I turned to hide tears. "Aye."

He sighed. "I'll ride to Edinburgh fer books on the law. This be a serious problem."

I nodded.

Leith, I would have Leith and Wanthwaite a little time longer.

❖─◦◦◦◦◦─❖

So I went to the Great Hall that evening as always. Though the Scots stared, they said nothing; in fact, Gruoth gave me the biggest portion of pie with my ale. They were still talking about the assassination attempt, which they'd been discussing for weeks and about which everyone agreed: Enoch had been betrayed. Thorketil suspected Eustace de Vesci, while Gruoth believed it was a hermit who'd sung a song about King John's assassination before the event. How had he known? A folet? God hisself? No matter, said Gruoth; John believed the threat because it had come from diverse sources.

"Boot hu did the hermit hear?" Enoch asked, dismissing the supernatural. "Summun clase to the plot betrayed us."

This must be true. The Hall grew darker.

"Has anyone heard from Lord Robert or Lord Eustace?" I asked.

Enoch rose. "A knight be comin' tomorrow to tal us summit." He left the Hall.

The following day, Enoch waylayed me in in the cheese house. "Be it possible that the king suspects ye in the plot?"

"Aye, I told you he saw me, Enoch." Then I realized the import. "Why do you say so?"

He didn't answer directly. "We mun ha'e mar security." His eyes moistened. "Fer Leith. Quhan yer Theo . . . We mun secure Wanthwaite . . ." He reddened. "Ond we mun be mar nice to each udder. Ich want Leith to remember . . ."

We both wept; I wanted her to remember her mother.

"You think you'll be able to find a legal solution?"

"Ich want to avoid war, boot . . ."

"You'll do it, Enoch. And I'll help you, I promise."

But what law could stop a king? Yet there must be some price for wrongdoing, even if—especially if—that law was broken by a king.

What had happened to Lord Robert and Lord Eustace? Did they have to be included in our legal attempts? After what they'd done to Enoch? I despised both of them. A bigamist Enoch might be, but that gave them no excuse to throw him to John's dogs.

Or me either.

That same day, when I walked briskly into the Great Hall with Leith in my arms, the Scots were discussing the law.

"Precedent. Law is custom based on precedent. King Henry I wrote a charter o' the barons' richts." Enoch's brow furrowed.

"The barons, oh yes. Their pathetic rights!"

I thought of the legal solution to our marriage. An ancient law. I must accept the dissolution because it was legal— and the pope had ways of enforcing the law. Who would enforce England's new law? Would we even have a new law? Didn't John have to accept it?

"The king terrifies me." I whispered. "He's not stupid— he knows he breaks the law and custom at every turn, and he doesn't care."

No law could protect me if he chose to murder me. Theo was lying in a mass grave at Windsor. Would I join him?

Enoch watched me. "Do ye think that he micht kill Leith?"

I started—Enoch had read my mind. "He saw her, Enoch! When he saw me, he saw her! She doesn't claim the throne . . . unless . . . he may have heard something of my speech to the barons."

He gripped my hand. "I'll never lat Leith . . ."

Die, as Theo had died.

The next morning, a runner came from the Channel; Enoch and I were to follow him to the ridge—the very ridge I had taken from the sisters' house and that Enoch had been supposed to use to escape—where we would meet a knight who would bring news of Lord Robert and Lord Eustace.

The runner, an anxious young boy dressed in dun, was exceedingly relieved when we agreed to go.

"Git Leith ready," Enoch ordered.

Since I saw no reason why she shouldn't accompany us, I did so. The ridge was as safe as Wanthwaite. By midmorning, we gazed down at the shimmering valley below, sweet as I remembered it.

I hugged Leith. "A few more feet and you'll be able to see a castle."

"I see it a'ready!" Enoch spurred his steed to an outcropping.

I gasped! Flames shot around the castle! Tiny black figures darted in and out. Other men in red and gold fought against them desperately.

My peasant girl in red waved from the flames. I drew back.

"Royal mercenaries," said Enoch.

The black figures outnumbered the castle knights. Faint screams rose eerily after people had been pushed into the moat. Even from this distance, we could see blood flowing from a decapitated body.

Leith was fascinated—I put my hand across her eyes.

A knight with a black noseguard pushed against my steed. We'd been seen! Enoch raised his ax—then apologized.

The knight was Sir Alexander of Lord Robert's household, the man we'd ridden to meet. Without speaking, he pulled beside Enoch to view the conflict below. The black villains dragged two screaming women onto the moat bridge, where they raped and killed them, then threw them into the water below. More blood. The villains were fast and efficient. Then two little girls received the same treatment. Then two boys.

"Quhat be the villain quat leads?" Enoch whispered.

"Falkes de Bréauté." One of John's most notorious brutes, found in a Norman prison.

"Whose castle is it?" I asked.

Sir Alexander wasn't certain.

He then informed us that Lord Robert and Lord Eustace were safe in Normandy; the king knew their acts and had formally exiled them.

"Hu did the king larn they war his assassins?"

"From a hermit." Lord Alexander turned on his frisky steed. "Lord Robert now suggests we exploit the king's struggle with Pope Innocent III. It's his only hope."

Both Enoch and I looked blank.

"The pope has put the interdict on England and excommunicated the king—that was his punishment."

While we digested this incredible news, the knight turned back to the battle below. It was Lord Fallaise's home, he believed upon reflection; strange, for that lord had ever been loyal to the king.

When the sun was high, he rode back toward the Channel.

Enoch and I watched the mayhem below a while longer until, as if stung by the same thought, we turned back to Wanthwaite. *King John was sacking castles in this area.*

"What do you think this Lord Fallaise did to deserve such treatment?" I asked. "Is he part of your Brotherhood?"

Enoch pondered. "Mayhap he couldna send the ten knights the king demands fram his vassals." He sighed. "Mayhap the varmint wants the castle. Do he need a reason?"

I was thinking of those children who'd been raped and killed. Nature took enough babes without people doing it. Leith had survived her first year, unlike several other infants at Wanthwaite. I wondered about my own mother. Had she had other children? Had I not been an only child after all, but the only child who'd survived? I pulled the sleeping Leith closer.

Enoch stroked Leith's hair. "He be comin' close, Alix."

"Can we defend ourselves?"

Nottingham had resisted the king and York had not. Both had paid an equally terrible price.

We'd reached our descent to Dere Street.

"Where does he get the coins to pay mercenaries?" I asked.

"He pays wi' jewels. He ha'e the largest collection of jewels in the kingdom." He glanced at me. "Though nocht the Crown Jewels."

I shivered in the sun. Jewels. It couldn't be a coincidence, it was fate. Could John be bribed? If so, what was his guarantee? I reviewed Bonel's jewels in my mind; only my rubies might appeal to John; though small and pale, they threw light like hot coals.

Enoch and Thorketil built a wall on the far side of the Wanthwaite River. Then they pounded tall, pointed palisades slanted to impale horses. I sent the women to clean out the labyrinth. By the end of the month, it, too, was lined with rough palisades, and the sliding door was oiled with a strong lock inside. Meantime, the women had beaten most of the rats to death; what they missed, they turned over to two large feral cats.

Thus we prepared.

"Be it possible to rule a country wi'out fightin'?" Thorketil asked two days later. "Otherwise, why have a king at all?"

"Law replaces fighting," I said. "The king or someone could enforce the law."

"Does law replace a king?" he pressed, as if he hadn't heard.

The concept of a king was strong; every clan had its chief, every tribe its leader.

"We mun fight to enforce the law!" Enoch cried, showing his Scottish bias. "Our men con defeat any king!"

"We go to court to enforce the law," I said. "We don't need a king."

Everyone stared, but Enoch instantly capitulated. "History be on yer side, Alix. Whan Richard war in Normandy, his justiciar Hubert Walter ruled England wi'out an army and wi'out a crown, and he used the courts richt enow." He laughed bitterly. "Boot nu we be ruled by a king here in England. Quhan auld Hubert finally died, King John sayed, *Nu fer the ferst time, I be truly king of England.* By that, he meant he would fight!"

The killing had begun.

"Perhaps if he retook Normandy, he might leave England alone," I said.

"Aye, except he'll ne'er take it becase he doesna fight weil." He sighed. "'Tis perplexing." He fretted his brow. "His fantastick cell be better than mast, they say, boot warriors doona need to be canny, just to be brave."

"And lucky," Thorketil added.

"Aye." Enoch drank again. "Ond they mustna gae to sleep on the job. The king gaes fishin' or fades . . ."

"Fades? How?"

"Gits distracted, loses purpose, taks a nap; I doona knaw." He stared without speaking.

A few weeks later, Sir Guy d'Avent rode into our park to enlighten us about John's quarrel with Rome; Pope Innocent III favored the French king in the constant wars between France and England. His point in repeating this old news was to find some way to exploit it.

"The French king ga'e the pope money fer his favor," Enoch said flatly.

The knight admitted that this was true.

How did this effect Bonel, who now lived under French rule? Did he give King Philip money?

On the other hand, said the knight, King Philip refused to give up his concubine and return to his queen; he sought an annulment to his marriage from Rome in vain.

"This pope doesn't permit annulments," the knight said.

Enoch and I exchanged glances.

The pope was therefore wavering in his backing of Philip against John. I personally thought that John must be more villainous than Philip—how could the pope waver?

Because of money. This pope was gifted in the collection of gold.

Furthermore, John refused to accept Cardinal Stephen Langton, the pope's choice to be archbishop of Canterbury, which put the pope in a dilemma. Not only had Stephen Langton been born in Lincolnshire, which would give us an English archbishop, but Langton had taught law at Paris University for twenty-five years. The quarrel echoed the more famous case of Becket.

Enoch raised his brows to me: Did I remember this Langton from our years on the Petit Pont?

I remained silent, though I thought maybe I did.

"Thankee fer this information, Sir Guy," Enoch said courteously. "Ich wish the pope weil, fer I like that this Langton taught law."

Sir Guy lowered his voice. "I have a message from Lord Robert in Normandy. Lord Robert wants to find a noncombative solution to our problems, if possible—he knows your ideas. He thinks Stephen Langton might help us."

Enoch stiffened. "'Tis nocht a religious problem."

"Nevertheless, Lord Robert thinks Pope Innocent may be our only hope."

"At quhat price? The barons canna pay! They nocht be King Philip!"

"They might if Cardinal Langton can find a legal way to restrain King John."

Enoch studied the knight thoughtfully. "Be this Lord Eustace's idea as weil?"

"So I was told."

To depend on Eustace!

Sir Guy grew stern. "The cardinal will be traveling through northern England in a few weeks."

"Close to Wanthwaite?" I asked, understanding for the first time the knight's mission.

"Yes. He wants to meet your Brotherhood here."

Enoch nodded curtly, though he had obvious reservations. "I'll ride back when I have the exact date."

After the knight had left, Enoch sighed. "Ich doona lak dealin' wi' the Church. Even yif the pope and this Langton con help, quhat be their price?"

When I visited Dunsmere two days later, the church bells rang as always when villagers straggled to Mass. Was Father William ignorant about the interdict? Edwina said that burials, marriages, and christenings were also taking place as always. I suggested to Enoch that we have Leith baptized before word reached the priest.

Sir Guy returned on a sunny April day to tell us that Stephen Langton was now close by with a company of priests. He would be here soon; we should have our arguments ready. Yet May and June passed into July and still there was no sign of our visitor.

Then one lazy afternoon in early July I took Leith to the green to make clover chains. By now she could toddle, and she laughed more than she screamed. Bees buzzed around her clover, but she was not afraid, nor did they sting her.

Like Theo, she was a good baby insofar as she ate well, slept well, and didn't sicken. Both seemed extensions of me, for our bodies curled around each other most naturally. Yet they'd had different fathers, and that showed as well. Theo had been a straight, imperious little boy—even when in the womb—and gave orders to all around him. Leith achieved her goals slantwise, by weeping or dimpling or cooing or turning her head upside down to seduce her victim. Both were intelligent; both had sanguine dispositions. To give Leith credit, however, she seemed faster to talk.

The greatest difference, of course, was that Theo was dead, Leith very alive.

"Redbird!" she now cried.

I followed her finger: yes, a redbird, a cardinal to be exact! I counted the men in the train behind him, for I would have to offer them hospitality: twelve priests, like the apostles, except that half of them wore small tight hats. And the one in front wore a patch over one eye.

Bonel! It was Bonel!

12

"Tak Leith to the labyrinth!" Enoch's pike pricked my neck.

I pushed it away. "You've drawn blood!"

"Do ich ha'e to ask twice?" The pike dug deeper.

"It's Cardinal Langton! Don't you remember what Sir Guy told us?"

"Ich remember that yer parents war killed by routiers posing as priests!" He paused. "Ond sum o' those men doona even luik lak priests."

Though not in full armor, Enoch carried his pike and his quiver of arrows; he mounted his bay stallion. Behind him, his knights were lined at the privet hedge.

"I know it's Cardinal Langton, Enoch! I recognize one of his followers!" Bonel was with Cardinal Langton, though probably not a follower. I suspected, by their long beards and twisted hair, that the other Jews were rabbis.

"Quhich one?"

"The one with an eye patch. Bonel, the Jew, you remember . . ."

"The Jew quhat stole ye, aye." He lowered his pike. "To the labyrinth!"

The stable was already crowded with silent women and children. Leith cooed in excitement, whether at the labyrinth or my pounding heart I didn't know. I'd never expected to see

Bonel again. Memories flooded back: his body sheltering mine on the flats of Flanders, his black figure waving goodbye, Mistress Eglantine . . . No doubt Cardinal Langton's men would soon convince Enoch of their credentials, but what were Bonel's credentials? What was he doing here? Had he been responsible for setting the meeting at Wanthwaite? The labyrinth door groaned open.

"It's all right! You can come out now!" Thorketil called.

Pushing Leith into Gruoth's arms, I walked hastily to the courtyard, where the prelates stood by their horses, talking in Latin to one another, though I could see no Jews. Nor could I find Bonel.

In the center of the Great Hall, the cardinal, resplendent in his scarlet robes despite a hump on his shoulders, slaked his thirst, metheir after methier. I gave him only a cursory glance: medium height, saturnine, the smell of sanctity. Searching for Bonel among the priests (the rabbis were still gone), I sidled into the kitchen. Where was he? Did we have to greet in front of Enoch? Yet why not? What had either of us done to be ashamed of? Hadn't he risked his very life to save Theo and me? Had he ever made demands? Yet why would he travel so far north to a small insignificant castle if not to see me? Why, for that matter, would he come to England at all? Though he'd said that his favorite port was Boulogne, he'd often forsworn our entire country because of York. Yet there was that kiss—not goodbye, he had said. Yet why shouldn't he kiss me goodbye? Because he was a Jew? Jews and Christians are the same species, not dogs and cats. Yet most mysterious, what was his connection to the great Christian, Cardinal Langton?

I went back to the Great Hall to greet that cardinal, finally, myself. He paid absolutely no heed to my presence at all, as if I were a bothersome fly—yet even a fly deserves a slap. His deep voice rumbled with authority as he spoke of the meaning of faith over acts. According to Sir Guy, he was here because of Lord Robert and Lord Eustace, men I had good reason to distrust. Sir Guy claimed that this renowned legal expert, Langton, would help us find a noncombatant solution to our problems with King John. The knights sounded like Enoch, and a pox on the whole lot. Even with all the evidence and experience, they still didn't understand John's character. Might as well pass a law forbidding snakes to suck eggs. No wonder I doubted their judgment. Hadn't they assured Enoch that the assassination would work? That he would escape with them to Normandy? That catastrophe had exposed Leith and me—what else?

Not for the first time, I pictured Leith being raped and tossed into our moat. I suppose I should be happy to have Stephen Langton's help—if he could help.

Yet why the Jews? Why Bonel?

I pushed my way into the crowd of men in the Great Hall, where I took care that everyone was served. Bonel simply was not in the Great Hall, so I returned to the courtyard. Still no Bonel.

Edwina caught my sleeve. "Help me lay these mats in the chapel and schoolroom, would ye?"

The two of us worked quickly to transform the rooms into hospitality areas. Bonel found me there.

"Alix!" He stood in the doorway of my former schoolroom.

"Greeting, Bonel!"

He studied my person while I studied his. Handsome, exotic.

"I'd forgotten how beautiful you are." He smiled. "Or perhaps I've never seen you completely happy before?"

"I was happy in Rouen," I protested, "happier than I am here."

His cheeks flushed.

Edwina looked at both of us and left.

"You're tired," I said hastily. "No, more than tired, you're worried."

"True on both counts."

"What brings you here, Bonel?"

"Ever the gracious hostess!" He laughed. "As you remember, I'm presbyter for the English Jews; the Jews of Bristol summoned me for help."

"This isn't Bristol. Why Wanthwaite?"

"Cardinal Langton is going with me to Bristol, and he was visiting the archbishop of York."

I waved a dismissive hand.

He continued in a low voice. "To see you. Satisfied?"

The moment throbbed.

"I'm glad."

Both of us spoke at once. He insisted that I continue.

"Tell me about Bristol. I haven't seen you so upset since you told me about your escape from York."

"A number of Jews in Bristol . . ."

Enoch burst into the schoolroom. He studied Bonel's yarmulke, then his eye patch. "Be this the Jew quhat tuik ye to be concubine fer the king?"

"Yes," Bonel admitted quickly.

"A Jewish *pimpereau.*"

"A what?"

"I doona knaw the Hebrew word; *pimpereau* be French fer summun quhat gaddirs women to service rich men fer a price. Quhat did King Richard pay ye?"

Bonel, though tall and muscular, was not armed, or one of them would surely have been dead. He glared at Enoch. "You're a bastard, milord, utterly unworthy of the prize you have."

"Ye want to buy her? I'll sell her chape! I nade money."

Bonel left abruptly for the Great Hall.

Enoch turned to me. "Ye ha'e a woodly effect on men, I'll gi'e ye that."

"And you have a woodly effect on women," I said. "All of us get away from you as soon as we can—except your beloved Fiona!"

I ran after Bonel.

"Do ye intend to git away?" Enoch called after me.

Bonel took my arm just inside the Great Hall. "Where's Theo? Is he as happy here as you are?"

"I pray that he is; he's buried at Windsor."

"Buried!" Bonel's good eye filled. "Oh, Alix, I'm so sorry!" He pulled me to a corner. "Where and when can we talk alone? I have to know . . ."

"Tonight, just after the moon rises. I'll meet you in the cheese house."

"Which is where?"

"You passed it just after you crossed the moat. A small structure shaped like a tower."

I walked rapidly into the kitchen. When I was composed, I carried more methiers of foaming ale to refresh the riders not yet served. Bonel was now conferring with a prelate in the corner; with difficulty, I turned my attention to the cardinal. I studied Stephen Langton, dazzling in his regalia, but it wasn't his position that attracted me. I'd seen him before on the Petit Pont—belatedly, I remembered one afternoon at the back of his class—and knew him to be a dull pedant, albeit well informed. He certainly couldn't compare to Master Malcolm, our special instructor from Scotland, a humane and original thinker. Be as it may, this man was our hope, not Master Malcolm. He carried his prestige as cardinal with supreme condescension, diminishing his followers to sycophants. His scarlet robes ballooned in a large aureal around his person; his gold headpiece above his long narrow face made him a holy icon, not his pronouncements, which were as trite as I remembered. Past middle age, he had weary eyes under heavy brows, which emanated authority; he was a close friend to the pope. Speaking in Latin, he patiently answered questions of the eager sycophants around him.

He must have heard about me and King Richard, for he carefully avoided looking at me. Then Edwina offered him ale and I changed my mind, for he ignored her as well. The cardinal despised all women!

It was too late in the day to even consider an official meeting with him, which was just as well, for (the cardinal informed us) a few barons in the area would join us tomorrow. Meantime, Enoch talked to him about the university in Paris in his Scottish brogue, which the cardinal courteously seemed not to understand.

I waited for the night.

The moon rose early. I edged sideways along the narrow shadow where Scots snored on the floor of the Great Hall. My skirt brushed Edward's nose, bringing on a fit of sneezing, but he didn't wake. Enoch was up in his room, *Deo gratias*. Once outside, I still crept close to the walls. Finally, I opened the door to the cheese house.

Into Bonel's arms. We stood absolutely still, our hearts racing. I didn't think, only felt; then I did think about what I felt, which was that I was no longer alone.

"Tell me about Theo," he whispered.

I began with the shipwreck that had detoured my trip to Wanthwaite, instead of going to London . . .

"It's my fault!" Bonel cried. "My fault entirely! If you knew how I prayed that you had picked up Theo before Lady Matilda was caught!"

"So you know!"

"Everyone knows."

I reminded him of how stalwart Vikings were supposed to be, how my own shipmates had confirmed that the *Drage* was the best coastal ship afloat.

"But there was a storm, sleet—remember? Even for Vikings, it was a dangerous sea!"

"How do you know about Lady Matilda?" I changed the subject.

"She and her husband were important nobles in Normandy. The whole duchy talks of nothing else. And Theo, oh God, Theo."

We fell quiet, remembering.

Then I resumed my sad recital.

"Enoch is married to someone else?" he interrupted.

"Yes. He followed me to London because I made the woodly excuse of Richard's leaving me the Crown Jewels . . ."

"They went to Otto!"

"I know. I even quoted Maimonides."

"Richard should have left you something."

I told him of the London fire, Enoch's insistence that he be included in my riches, Hereford, Bagnor Manor, the Cistercian abbey, the revelation about Arthur of Brittany.

I interrupted myself. "He was our snag on the Seine, wasn't he?"

"Yes."

"A warning."

"Oh God, surely that had nothing to do with Theo!" he cried. "And I couldn't tell you . . . the fishermen were terrified."

"So they knew?" And it had everything to do with Theo, because he was with Lady Matilda.

"It was pretty obvious. He still wore his Brittany tunic with royal markings and . . . he was black and blue around the face. Then Rouen filled with rumors—the king beat him to death in a drunken rage. Pretty hard to keep an event like that secret."

"What about Queen Eleanor? Did she know?"

"I can't be certain; she died soon after we saw her, you know."

I didn't know—I suspected.

"Obviously, Lady Matilda had learned about Arthur from her husband," I said. "And despite her flight and caution, it brought her own demise. We're in the grip of a madman, Bonel."

"I can't argue. Oh God, Theo! He never hurt anyone!"

We still stood with our arms around each other, and—despite our melancholy subject—our hearts continued to race. It was getting dangerous.

Bonel recognized it, too. "Is there someplace we can sit? This may be a long conversation."

We found two cheese barrels.

We continued to discuss the de Braose tragedy, for both of us were thinking about Theo.

"At Runnymede, Enoch must have guessed, or perhaps even earlier. I became comatose and . . ." I fell silent. "It seems impossible that the queen would permit her own son to murder either Arthur or Theo."

"I feel at fault."

"You? Nonsense! Without you, I . . ."

"No! No! You don't know my culpability. Someone informed on you, remember? I should have guessed!"

His anguished tone stopped my protest.

"Esther betrayed you, Alix." His voice shook.

"Esther?" For one moment my mind was blank—who was Esther? Then I remembered: Bonel's fiancée. "Betrayed me? When?" I started to add *why* and stopped myself.

"I'm not certain. I learned it from the priest who baptized Theo."

"That long ago? Did the priest tell the king?"

"I'm afraid not. As a matter of fact, when the priest proved discreet, she went higher herself."

"Did she go to King John?" My heart thumped.

"She may have; I have no direct proof except . . ."

"Except what?"

"The queen thought he'd been informed. That's why she moved so quickly."

I wondered if Queen Eleanor and Lady Matilda had exchanged information. Well, both were dead; I would never know.

"Why did Esther hate Theo?" I couldn't hold back tears. "She hardly even saw him, to my knowledge. Did I do something?"

"For a perceptive woman, you're obtuse at times, aren't you? She was jealous, just plain jealous."

"She was very beautiful."

"Jealous because of my attentions to you. I should have guessed, though I doubt if it would have made any difference. I didn't break with her, but I kept postponing our nuptials. She knew why." He made a sound. "Everyone knew except you."

"Oh Bonel, I knew." I spoke haltingly. "I'm ashamed . . . I suppose I thought it wouldn't hurt since I'm not Jewish."

"You're female, that was enough."

"Enough for her to tell King John? To murder me? And Theo . . ." I shuddered. "I'm glad you didn't marry her. Or— are you going to?"

"I'd kill her if I could find her."

The irony hit me violently: ironic that I'd struggled to reach Bonel for safety, only to be betrayed by his closest friend; ironic that the queen had put Theo into the care of Lady Matilda de Braose, the only woman in all England the king was determined to destroy.

Fortune's wheel. You can't escape your fate.

I buried my face in Bonel's shoulder. "Help me, please; I want to die before the king finds me. I can't escape any more than Theo could, oh please . . ."

"He won't find you, Alix, I promise you on my own life." His voice was chilly.

I pulled away. "I bring disaster to others. Theo was with me before he was with Matilda de Braose; there was Richard before him, and before them my mother and father. I may be Death stalking the world and not know it."

"Stop it, Alix! You gave life to every one of those people! And to me!"

I shivered. "I don't give life to King John—he's marked me for death. Me and everyone around me." Through the smoke hole open to the sky, a faint star flickered beside a cloud.

"John is still jealous of his romantic brother, and jealousy is a strong emotion, Alix—I should know."

"You've never killed anyone!"

"No? In my heart I have, many times. And sometimes I get my way. Maybe I'm Death, not you."

"Whom did you ever kill?"

He pulled my head into his neck. "I wished Richard dead, and he died. Now I wish Enoch . . ."

"Enoch doesn't have to die. And you have no reason to be jealous. He . . ."

"He what? Finish your sentence."

"We're no longer man and wife—he married someone else."

"Then I don't understand. Where is his wife? Why are you still acting as his lady?"

I explained that our quarrel now was over Wanthwaite, which we agreed would be resolved after a new civil law was established. We both recognized that the threat of King John must be resolved.

"Then we'll fight. I don't want to give up Wanthwaite, and he claims that he bought it."

Bonel laughed. "An old-fashioned motte castle in the wilds of northern England, a place, nothing more. I doubt if it will stand another generation."

"Yes, it will."

"And you would run it alone?"

I didn't answer.

"I took care of you once. Remember?"

"You take care of everyone, Bonel."

"I help Jews, if that's what you mean. That's my calling."

"You gave me money, jewels, training—all those things Maimonides talks about, and I'm not a Jew. You saved my life when I came to Rouen, you . . ."

"Stop! Next you'll say that Jesus was a Jew, and I'm the Second Coming!"

I laughed.

"Are you sure it's just Wanthwaite that holds you?" He slipped his arm around my waist. "Weren't you holding a new baby when we arrived?"

My heart squeezed. "Aye, my daughter, Leith."

"Is she Enoch's?"

"Yes, but . . . It's not what you think!"

He withdrew his arm.

I was ashamed to admit that I'd been raped, but I finally did. Worse was when I tried to describe my fantasy about the wolf, then Enoch's woodly scheme, and my participation.

"Do you still love him?"

"Love him?"

"Have you forgotten how you raved about Enoch and England?"

Still ashamed, I pretended I had.

"I stay only because of Wanthwaite, even though it's old-fashioned, as you say," I repeated. "And, to be honest, because I'm afraid to be on my own. The king——"

"Must know you're here, yet Enoch agrees to let you stay?"

I described our arrangement to behave as brother and sister.

Bonel seemed dubious. "With a child? What does Leith think? What does your household? What do you?"

Desperately, I described the aborted assassination and Enoch's hopes for a legal solution for England. It was complicated and the marriage was complicated; we simply couldn't handle both problems simultaneously.

"Though many others do." Bonel's voice became formal. "Your scheme—even your voice when you describe it—sounds as if you're trying to hold him. Are you sure you've recovered from your early feelings?"

"My very earliest feelings were about Wanthwaite; that's what I still love, that's all. And Leith, of course."

"Does Enoch still regret losing you?"

"His pride was hurt—he's a Scot. Hurt about Wanthwaite, I mean. He'll get Leith—I want Wanthwaite." My voice dropped. "Regret losing me? No, men are different."

"Where affairs of the heart are concerned? I doubt it."

"He loves Lady Fiona."

"So why don't you leave? Why doesn't he?"

He obviously didn't accept Wanthwaite as my reason. "And go where?"

"London is one possibility. Should I make another list of jewelry centers?"

"I still have your first list." I dropped my voice. "It's hard to lose Leith."

"Take her with you!"

"How could I? I finally know the law, Bonel. Canon law." When he didn't answer, I continued. "Before I leave, though, I've agreed to help settle this matter between the king and the barons. You witnessed York, Bonel, know how violence . . . it could effect the survival of England."

His voice tightened. "Not much of a loss if it goes."

"Oh Bonel, have you looked around you? England isn't the kings, this one or any other, it's the air, the animals, the trees and rivers, and the people, all the people . . ."

"The Jews?"

"The Jews, yes!" My voice shook. "The children."

"Stop! You've not seen much of the world, have you? Children are everywhere . . ."

"I saw the Holy Land, remember; nothing but sand, heat, and cobras."

"And crocodiles!" He laughed. "I was speaking of central Europe. Alix, I . . ." He stopped himself. "Jews are undergoing another Diaspora, except that this time a few countries actually want us. I'm considering several places myself—there's an estate high in the Carpathian Mountains overlooking a lush valley—I've seen it—it could be paradise if . . ."

"If?"

"You could bring Leith—I would be her father, and then we . . ."

I felt faint. "Leith?"

"Do you still have the money I gave you?"

"Yes."

"Then use it! I'll send instructions—I'll meet you in the south—maybe Italy—oh, Alix!"

Again he clasped me close. His whole chest shook with his heart.

"Do you expect me to convert?"

He laughed. "Do you expect me to?" He stroked my hair. "Is that *yes?*"

I drew back. "Are you sure?"

"I take that as *yes.*"

"I must get an annulment, then steal Leith."

"Can you do it?"

"And I must fulfill my agreement about England."

He pulled away. "Be more specific."

"I've told you: the law, the king . . ." He still seemed cold. I changed the subject, sort of. "Why are you riding with Cardinal Langton?"

"We met on Dere Street and rode the last few miles together."

"That's not why. Is Cardinal Langton going to help you in Bristol?"

"Not at once, but I'm betting he'll be the next archbishop of Canterbury, and, as archbishop, he could be of enormous help."

"Explain."

"He will be the ecclesiastic ruler of England; John dare not cross him."

"Suppose he agrees with John."

"A risk, I grant you. His reputation is that of a shadow of Pope Innocent III; he takes his orders from Rome, and the pope is neither liberal nor compassionate, though I don't know specifically about Jews."

"Does the pope back King John?"

"You said you knew the law? The pope will challenge John's power here in England—some kings succumb for a personal reason, such as Philip of France; some don't. Popes don't have armies, of course, but kings have, and their armies do his bidding."

"You haven't answered—does he back King John?"

"As we speak, no; he backs King Philip of France against John."

"Why?"

He laughed. "Do you know about bribery? Philip paid the pope more than John. And John, at heart, is not religious. For him, it's a pure power play. Philip may feel the same, but he's smarter. It's all about power, Alix. You'll learn. Especially if you become involved with the barons' rebellion, you'll become well acquainted."

"You know we're already under the interdict."

"The pope's power at work, Alix. So long as the pope punishes England, John loses power. Ergo, John will give in. The first and easiest capitulation is to accept Stephen Langton."

"Can Langton be trusted?"

He hesitated. "About what? Jews? Barons? I've never heard that Stephen Langton had an independent thought or did an independent act. He conforms."

"He's compared to Abelard."

"No! Abelard was much the more original, I assure you. And rebellious."

"And he ended in disgrace."

"Forget his escapade with Héloïse. His *Sic et Non* challenged absolutism, which is what you're about. The law is flexible; kings are not. Nor are popes. And Langton is the champion of accepted dogma. He can quote St. Augustine word for word, and he accepts it; the same for canon law, papal history, and the present pope's mind. He's a pedant, not a scholar."

"You sound as if our cause is hopeless, Bonel."

"Oh yes, if you depend on Langton, it's hopeless." He laughed softly. "Or maybe I'm just trying to nudge you out of green, green England." He became serious. "We Jews have tried for generations to shake the system of Church dominance so we can exist, with little effect. I don't know the details of the barons' plea, but I see no reason to think they'll be more successful. Aside from the pope, people are loath to change. John knows that, and he exploits it with military might and superstition."

Was it possible that our situation would worsen? Could Bonel be right?

"It's growing light, Alix."

"It's a white night; it means nothing. I have much more to say about my—our—estate."

A cock crew.

"Can we meet here tomorrow?"

"Yes."

"Then you go first." He rose.

The instant I was on my feet, he clasped me close. We didn't speak.

I went as I'd come, hugging shadowed walls. The Scots snored deeply from their sprawled positions on the rushes. When I reached my room, I stumbled over Enoch, who leaned against my door.

"Sae yer *pimpereau* lat ye cum back."

"Stop calling him that! He took Theo and me into his commune! He helped me escape from Rouen—I owe him everything."

"Wery touching. He halps ye escape the situation he made. Ich suppose he luvs ye as weil."

"Would you move, please?"

Once I was inside my room, I locked my door.

Cardinal Langton stood in the center of the Hall. Three knights entered: Sir Guy and Sir Alexander, and a stranger.

Enoch edged in their direction. "How did Lord Robert arrange this lofty visitation from his estate in Normandy?" he asked in French.

Sir Alexander replied. "He wrote to the pope that his assassination attempt was made only because King John had been excommunicated, and he refused to be ruled by a heathen. His reason appealed to both the pope and to Langton."

I groaned to myself: power or hypocrisy?

"Very clever," Enoch commented mildly.

At that moment, Bonel entered the Hall flanked by two rabbis. He didn't look in my direction; he didn't have to. He walked to Cardinal Langton and conversed in low tones.

"Who's the Jew?" Sir Alexander asked. "What's he doing here?"

Enoch gave Bonel's name and ignored the second half of the question. Soon Sir Alexander stood with the cardinal and two prelates behind a small table; the unruly crowd began to take on the look of an orderly meeting.

Though I hadn't alerted him, Father William suddenly entered. When he stepped to the front as if expected, Cardinal Langton greeted him most courteously. The priest called a blessing on present company. All talking ceased. The priest then departed, and Cardinal Langton gazed at us from heavy, ringed eyes. He began to whisper in Latin.

Bowing courteously, Enoch approached the table and interrupted in French. "With all due respect, Your Eminence, most of present company cannot follow Latin. Could you address us in French or English?"

The cardinal replied haltingly in French. "Naturally, we speak Latin in Rome; I fear that I have quite lost my facility in French or my native tongue. Is there no one present who can translate?"

"If you will accept a woman, Your Eminence, my wife, Lady Alix, is gifted in Latin. In fact, she apprenticed in Latin."

An old jape between us—I could have killed him.

Langton nodded. I think he knew that his voice didn't carry, no matter what his tongue. I took my place beside him.

"As you can see," he addressed the throng through my voice, "I am Cardinal Langton of Rome, though I will soon be your archbishop of Canterbury, your ecclesiastic leader in England."

Was that a hope or a fact?

"King John prefers another man, but, of course, Pope Innocent will prevail," he added hastily. "I mean no irreverence to King John, who is my lord by divine right as he is yours, but such an intelligent monarch will concede that the pope has precedence."

Enoch again stood forward. "Lord Robert fitzWalter asked you to speak to the barons' cause. Do you understand our grievances?"

Langton hesitated. "Not exactly. You took an oath of fealty to the king before God."

The barons remained ominously silent.

Enoch spoke in French, which I translated into Latin for Langton. "We want to codify England's laws to conform with custom. We plan nothing revolutionary, just clarification."

Langton seemed bored. "You already have the canon law to guide you. Every priest in England knows it, or has access to it. What more do you need?"

Enoch's blue eyes flashed dangerously; the cardinal either didn't see or didn't care.

"Canon law covers family matters such as birth, marriage, and death, and . . ."

"God rules the world, my friend; the pope is God's emissary to the world. If Pope Innocent tells King John what to do, then the king must obey."

"So tell the pope that King John must stop killing his own subjects! Or taking our children as hostages, then killing them! Or demanding our service in foreign wars! Or . . ."

"Pace!" the cardinal interrupted sternly. "Your king is inviolable, annointed by God Himself. You can make no demands whatsoever."

Enoch was now shaking with rage. "We were speaking of the pope making demands! However, since you shift the authority to us, we can and we will demand the right to live under law! You say that we already live under canon law! How does canon law protect us from tyranny?"

Enoch's vehemence startled Cardinal Langton.

"Tyranny? How is obedience subjection? Can you explain?"

And Enoch cited atrocities against people and in places I'd never heard of. The cardinal, obviously shaken, thought a long time before he responded.

"If what you report is true—and I will check, you understand—the pope should be advised."

"The pope is in Rome—we can't wait."

"You should make a charter of your complaints. If the pope agrees, then the king should be forced to sign it."

"Ond yif the pope doesna agree? We ha'e to live! We ha'e customs!"

Enoch was too furious for French, and I chose not to translate his question.

But Langton had understood. "Local customs can hardly be construed as universal law."

"When a man is accused of wrongdoing, is a trial by a jury of his peers a local custom? I say it should be law!"

The cardinal flushed. "Such a man should be tried by canon law, and by priests. We strive for repentance, not punishment."

"Yif a man kills a man's wife and children, 'tis nocht enough fer him to say he's sorry!"

"It's enough for God," Langton replied gently. "We strive to improve a man's soul, not to punish his body."

Enoch turned dangerously red. "King John has na soul. Mayha we havena as weil, boot we ha'e bodies. We doona want to drown or burn! Quhat will ye do fer our rights?"

Langton didn't reply.

Enoch reverted to French. "And if the king covets a man's land and the man refuses to give it, should that man say mea culpa?"

The cardinal flushed. "You skew your example."

"No, I do not! Under the king's law, which is the law of covetousness, that man who wishes to hold his land would be killed."

"Our Savior didn't concern Himself with land ownership. Or money."

"Soothly!" Enoch was no theologian, but he knew about money. "Our Lord beat the moneylenders with a whip, didn't He?"

It was Langton's turn to redden.

"Our local customs, as you call them, keep order in our community. We won't tolerate the king or anyone else destroying our system!"

The two men mixed eyes.

"Are you suggesting anarchy against King John? Against the pope?" Langton showed his shock.

And he had reason. Enoch stood nose to nose with him. "We want to avoid anarchy! We don't want war! And we seek your help! But don't insult us with talk about souls or God or repentance! We're serious!"

"So am I! So is God! The king *is* the law."

"Kings die and the law still goes on."

Cardinal Langton rubbed his eyes wearily. "Are you worried that King John will die?"

Not worried, but certain. John would die.

Enoch mumbled, "Aye, but we can't wait."

"At that time, you can draw your charter. Law is malleable as situations change."

"Yet in God's eyes, the situation never changes."

"I didn't say that." The cardinal smiled through steel. "As we speak, Hungary, Germany, and Denmark are writing new laws! They are challenging the very concept of royalty, so you seem part of a new wind blowing through Europe." He leaned forward. "Yet they don't live under King John. What could their reason be?"

"Will you help us or not, Cardinal Langton?"

There wasn't a sound in the room.

"Help you what?"

"Write a charter addressing those laws that apply across the land. We want to live in peace as our forefathers did, nothing more. But, with this king, we find ourselves in perpetual warfare, either against strangers or against the king."

Langton flushed. "I admit that I have my own problems with this king; I don't want to comment today. Can you wait?"

"No, now."

Sir Guy suddenly rose. "May I add, Your Grace, the requests of Lord Robert fitzWalter and Lord Eustace de Vesci?"

Langton stared coldly at the knight. "They are in contact with the pope."

There was astonished muttering in the Hall. Enoch lifted his arms for silence.

Enoch pushed closer. "We speak to you alone, Cardinal Langton, and not to Pope Innocent III. This is outside the Vatican's concern."

"Canon law is universal. Unchanging, ever wise," he muttered. He looked up through bloodshot eyes. "Very well, if you insist."

The barons and knights and priests didn't breathe. Even Enoch seemed overwhelmed with his success. Fortunately, Edwina called the company to repast—it was Haute Tierce.

Speaking in Vulgar Latin, Cardinal Langton blessed our meeting, which had been called to do God's work after we'd rested, to keep the peace, for we were the children of the prince of peace. His thin, husky voice expressed his intense personal commitment. Like the Angevins, this man wears rich red robes; like them, he creates a music with his voice, I thought. And, like the Angevins, he seemed slightly false. False because he'd promised to help us with law and still spoke of canon law.

Four more barons arrived.

The cardinal suddenly asked, "Where is our host?"

Enoch stepped forward.

"Lord Enoch, I found this letter from Pope Innocent III in my sack during our repast, and I want especially for you to hear it. Where is the woman who translates?"

I came forward.

The cardinal turned to his audience. "This is a letter from the pope himself."

I read slowly: *"If you pay to King John the loyalty that is due to him, you can be sure that this is pleasing, both to God and to us. But because you should order your loyalties to your earthly king so as to never offend the Heavenly King, you ought to be on guard to save the king by faithful advice . . ."*

Loud stamping and jeering stopped my reading.

"He wants we shuld advise him?" Enoch shouted. "Aye, we will!"

I pulled Enoch back before he could have a stroke!

Langton sank in the front row with his hand to his eyes; the Jews moved forward.

Bonel was speaking with an archbishop—a stranger—in a far corner. Then he took the podium. Langton raised his head. Bonel, speaking in French, first introduced the archbishop in the corner as Archbishop Geoffrey of Norwich, King John's justiciar of Jews. The bishop drew hostile gazes because he came from the king. Was he a spy?

"Thank you for permitting me to speak," Bonel addressed us. "Though I quite honestly know little of your plaints, it seems we have common cause. We Jews, too, live under the laws of the land as applied by the king, whoever that may be; we are called the king's men. And, like you, we experience differences in our treatment when the crown goes to a new king, though every king presumably follows the same law. Is that the canon law? I don't know. We, too, follow a religious law, the Torah. Therefore, it seems to me that canon law couldn't possibly apply to Hebrews. We are certainly not the pope's men. Nevertheless, I see analogies in our situations; if you see them, too, perhaps you can profit.

"You all know deadly attacks have been made against the Jews here in England in the king's name and in your Savior's name and sometimes the pope's accusing us of trafficking with a devil whose existence we do not accept, poisoning wells because we place our own wells away from latrines and are spared bouts of fevers, drinking the blood of children who actually die of natural causes; perhaps you agree with these attacks or others and have even participated in them. I could answer such allegations in more detail, but this is not the place. What I share with you is my despair of your law, for the king is supposed to protect us under that same law. When Christians attacked Jews, King Richard at least pretended to be shocked; this king is the attacker.

"Yet both kings share a single purpose: to steal our money. Did I understand correctly that the king is claiming your lands? Your castles? We have no land or castles, alas; we do have money. The Church itself makes Jews rich by permitting—nay, ordering—them to lend at interest—almost the only work we are permitted, but I won't go into our history here—and the kings depend on our money to fight their wars."

He had everyone's attention.

"We were first brought to England from Normandy during the Conquest, specifically so we could supply the new king with money to fight; in return, he and his ancestors would protect us from the mobs. Yet, in fact, they treat us brutally—I'll give you an example in Bristol in a moment—and now the king is treating you brutally as well. The thrust of this king's reign is to regain Normandy, nothing more. To wage an attack across water is very expensive, as you know. We pay money; you pay with your lives.

"Yet we pay with our lives as well. In Bristol today lie three Jewish corpses, men who bled to death when the king extracted silver from their teeth. Furthermore, their homes go to the king rather than their families; their widows and children are destitute. The assize law protects these families, but who enforces the law?

"Cardinal Langton is right when he says that precedent should make you eager to fight for the king, not against him, but something has happened, and I don't speak of any political wind or even our pitiful situation. King Richard stayed in Europe and you lived without a king; through years of royal neglect, you have become independent Englishmen.

"In our case, we are homeless in England or anywhere else. If we refuse the king our money, he takes our lives, or permits you to do so. We are not a military group, nor do we have the pope to defend us.

"Can we win justice? Can you? I don't think so, not with this king. We Jews had a thousand years of relative peace. Now that peace is ended, and I speak of another wind blowing through Europe: anti-Semitism. Can we prevail against it? Can you win? Frankly, I think you have right on your side, but I fear the answer must be the same for you as for us: not with this king. I mean no disparagement when I say that we are all Jews together."

He sat to absolute silence. Then Enoch moved forward to speak to him in urgent whispers. At first Bonel rejected whatever Enoch was saying, then abruptly rose. Enoch took his arm. The two men left the Hall for Enoch's closet.

Bonel was not in the cheese room when I arrived that night. At first I thought nothing of it—it had begun to rain, so he couldn't time himself by the rising moon. I pulled the barrels away from the smoke hole so they wouldn't be wet, then wiped them with my hands, thus getting a splinter in my right thumb. Finally, I sat. Though it wasn't cold, the constant patter of rainfall plus a whistling wind oppressed my spirits. Where was Bonel?

I'd just opened the door to leave when he entered. He apologized profusely for his delay—he'd had business with Bishop Geoffrey—had I been waiting long? I assured him that I'd just arrived myself; I noted that he didn't embrace me. After I'd helped him wring water from his tunic, we sat stiffly on our barrels in silence. By then, I knew something had happened.

"What was your business with Bishop Geoffrey?" I asked courteously. "About your difficulties with King John in Bristol?"

"I would call having teeth extracted to the point of death a difficulty, yes."

Yet he'd known this a long time. He was lying.

He meandered on about the widows, the children, all the

things he'd told us this afternoon. He said nothing about the
Carpathian Mountains.

"Do you think Stephen Langton will help the barons?"

He spoke at length; I heard nothing.

"Any more than Enoch has helped you," he ended.

"Yes," I said brightly. "I suppose there's an analogy. What
was the status of the Jews in England?"

"Haven't you heard anything I've said?" he replied gruffly.

"Of course I have." I'd also heard what he hadn't said.

"Normandy is now part of France."

"I know."

"Odd, Normandy has historically been a Jewish haven, I
don't know why, probably something to do with some
Roman emperor."

"Julius Caesar?" The only emperor I knew.

"I've leased a large farmhouse in the Low Countries for
my commune. We're crowded, for more arrive each day, but so
far we're surviving."

Had he told them he was leaving for the Carpathian
Mountains? Where were they exactly? I dare not ask. My vital
spirits fell.

He went on: The reason that King Philip had expelled the
Jews was because he wanted the backing of Pope Innocent,
for the king with the pope behind him was usually the win-
ner. This pope hated Jews.

"And he's won," he finished. "France over England."

"Do you think King John will turn to the pope?"

"Without question."

I felt guilty, though not because of the pope. Perhaps
Bonel didn't want this mountain estate after all—and he

didn't actually own it, did he? Was I supposed to say something?

"Bonel, you say you live on a farm in Flanders—why not
here? Why not come to Wanthwaite? I'd love to give you sanctuary—repay you if I can for your generosity when . . . and
all the trouble I caused."

"Thank you, dear Alix." He squeezed my hand. "And no
thank you."

"Why not?"

"Oh, my dear, are you truly so naive? You fear and hate
King John with good reason. England may be beautiful—
even Wanthwaite—but all dungeons look alike. Do you want
me to become a prisoner?"

"Of course not!" I sat for a few heartbeats, then jumped
up. "What happened? Tell me, for God's sake!" I burst into
tears.

Bonel instantly put his arms around me, but it wasn't the
same, wasn't the same!

I shook like a leaf. "Why don't you like me anymore?
What have I done?"

"Oh, I do like you, more than like, I do, but Alix . . ."

I drew away. "I'm sorry, I didn't mean to force you."

"You're not." He drew back as well. "I meant what I said
last night, Alix, about Leith, about the Carpathian Mountains . . . then my speech today reminded me—I would prefer you not to suffer a Jewish fate."

What could be worse than the fate I was facing? "That's
not it," I said dully. "Something happened." We were silent a
few heartbeats as my fantastick cell raced. "What did Enoch
say to you?"

"Enoch?" He sounded guilty.

"Did he talk about our Crusade? About King Richard?"

"Only in passing." He hesitated. "He's more interested in the law."

"Our annulment? Did he try to borrow money?"

He shook me slightly. "Stop! Let me ask a question: Will you come with me now? First to Bristol, then back to Europe?"

"I would, except that I gave my word: after the barons get satisfaction and I'm released from my vows . . ."

"In a word, no."

"I didn't say that! Bonel!"

"It's stopped raining—we should leave."

"But . . ."

"Oh, Alix!" He groaned. Then he kissed me—passionately—again and again.

Why did it feel like goodbye?

And I knew the reason. "Did you like him?"

"I did, in spite of . . . he reminded me of a Jew."

I was astounded. "How so?"

"Cleanliness, for one thing. He's the cleanest English Christian I've ever met."

"He's not English!" And might not be Christian, but I had no proof.

"No, he's Scottish. He made that clear as well."

"What did you talk about?"

The barons' attempt to bring King John in line with the law, Stephan Langton, the influence of the Church.

I tried to keep him talking. "Enoch's no more the pope's man than you are!"

"No," he agreed.

Enoch worshipped nature. He read signs in everything.

"At least he doesn't impose it on anyone else."

"No," I conceded. "Neither do you."

"No, Jews don't proselytize. Maybe we should, for our own safety."

He then astonished me further by revealing that Enoch had invited him to Scotland, where Jews were welcome, especially in the Highlands. Enoch thought that Jews and Scots were similar: devotion to tribes and clans, intelligence in law and history and science, love of the land where they were born.

"Do you agree?" I asked.

"I've never been to Scotland. Have you?"

"Aye, when Theo . . ." I forced myself to describe the country as it had seemed. "It's wild, deeply shadowed, poor soil. Not a rich country, but it has a charm."

"Windswept beauty," Bonel mused, "but poor land for growing. People who are born on a desert are forced to develop other skills."

He wasn't even considering a move to Scotland. First, and most important, he didn't agree with Enoch's appraisal of the religious/political situation there.

"He doesn't want to admit that Scottish kings were seduced—or terrorized—by the Angevins. The Scottish king—Alexander?—is not to be trusted."

Thinking of Theo again, I agreed.

The second reason was the remote situation of the country. Besides moneylending, the Jews depended on trade with the Middle East. Most of their jewels came from there, and all the spices they sold in Europe. Plus artifacts of silver and brass, cottons from Egypt, silks from the Far East, all kinds of luxuries. Like moneylending, this monopoly wouldn't last forever, but at least, for now, it was all they had.

All very informative, but off my subject.

"Did Enoch talk about me?" I finally asked.

"Yes." He was silent so long that I thought that was all he was going to say. "Like King Richard, he thinks you are mentally brilliant, considering that you're a woman and weren't born in Scotland."

He laughed; I didn't.

"He echoed your statement that the two of you had agreed to postpone your personal arguments until you resolved the political situation."

"I wanted the time, Bonel. I've been to court! I'll lose Wanthwaite, lose Leith."

I waited; he didn't comment.

"It's starting to rain again—we should hurry."

"Alix . . ." He held my sleeve, then released me.

I stepped into the rain first; I hardly noticed the drops in my despair. Oh, I could understand his preoccupation about his community, but that had been with him for months. No, something had happened since last night; it could only be Enoch.

"I'll write, send you money, send you a map," he called softly. I waved my hand in the dark and kept walking.

Our entire household gathered in the courtyard to say farewell to Cardinal Langton and our other guests. I stood in Enoch's shadow, for the sun was warm after the rainfall. Cardinal Langton spoke to Bonel, then with Bishop Geoffrey, and finally he thanked Lord Enoch for his most gracious hospitality and hoped to see him in Canterbury one day.

"I hope so," Enoch replied in French. "Or mayhap we'll see each other in another meeting about our charter."

Bonel then thanked Enoch as well. "And thank you, Lady Alix." I nodded without speaking.

"We're old friends." He stopped. "I hope this is farewell, not goodbye."

Again, I nodded.

"I'll write you, if I may."

"Please do, milord," I whispered.

The men formed a line, horsetails flicked at flies, one stallion dropped fecal matter close to the hedge, and they were gone.

Carrying Leith, I followed them briskly down to the new palisades, where I stopped as they disappeared down the lane.

Bonel didn't look back.

The second day, I waited for a missive. I couldn't believe that Bonel had changed so drastically, not after all this time. I told Dugan that a runner might come for me and, if so, he was to take the missive and deliver it to me privately. Of course, there was nothing.

Enoch, however, received a missive from King John's court demanding service or scutage or he would be disseised of his lands. Enoch tossed the notice into the Wanthwaite River, then turned to me.

"Be ye expecting summit?"

"No."

"Jist hopin', eh?"

"Won't you be imprisoned for ignoring that summons?"

He studied me speculatively. "Ich doona think sae. No baron in the north be acceptin' the notice." He grinned. "Rumor says that the king ha'e abandoned his invasions of Normandy fer noo."

We continued to stare at one another, and I had another suspicion: What had Bonel told Enoch? I ran up the hill.

Time passed and nothing came for me.

13

FATHER WILLIAM RODE TO WANTHWAITE UNANNOUNCED. WHEN
I welcomed him while he sat on his donkey, I gave thanks that
Enoch was in the forest, for I suspected the priest's mission. I
was right. Though he began with the great Cardinal Langton's visit and the important meeting we had convened, a real
honor for Dunsmere, he quickly came to his point: Was
Enoch going to seek the annulment that was his? A runner
had come from the ecclesiastic court in Durham about the
gold pieces I had given for the annulment; the bishop didn't
feel right, keeping them, if Enoch didn't want to go forward.

"Keep them," I whispered, afraid that some other Scot
would hear. "Only say nothing yet. Enoch wants his freedom
from me, but I'm not quite ready to leave my home. Or
Leith."

Father William looked confused. "Does that mean that
your husband wants to keep his bastard?"

I almost struck him! How was my daughter a bastard?
Enoch hadn't sought an annulment before she was conceived!
I hated Father William!

Sensing that I was upset, the priest patted my head, then
left me much depressed.

Lady Fiona had promised that she would accept Leith—as
a bastard? If I had difficulty forgiving Enoch for his act, what

about her? Could she ever forget? And would Leith become
the hated symbol of Enoch's attack? Bastard! Look at King
John and his bastard daughter Joanna—he was kind, wasn't
he? If a king cobra could be generous, why not Lady Fiona?

Bonel had accepted Leith as he had accepted Theo. My
tears flowed. The Carpathian Mountains, a paradise high in
the sky. He'd meant it, I knew he had. But why hadn't he written? Was it because of Leith? Because she was Enoch's? Tear-
less now, I paced in the cheese room where we had met.

When I left, hours later, I'd concluded that Bonel would
write soon. And he would include Leith in his invitation.
Would Enoch let her go? Probably not, if he knew. Aye,
Bonel had many chores to do for the Jews. I wouldn't hear before next spring at the earliest. Yet I agonized. I'd had so many
losses in my life, I couldn't bear another

The nutting season distracted me: we spread pelts under
the trees to catch the nuts. Then the lightest among us—I
was one—climbed and shook the branches till nuts rained
onto the pelts.

> Alas, let nuttes fallen free!
> Ond in that freedom cum to me!
> Far to stay stucken on the tree
>> Certes war folly!
>> Cum!
>> Maken our mouthen jolly!

We culled the nuts for worms, then trampled them with
our wooden clogs to remove the skins.

As for the men, Enoch and his knights often left Wanthwaite fully armed. To survey the countryside, Enoch said,

then added that many northern barons had been reduced to penury because they'd paid the scutage. One day he pulled me into our forest to show me a dank earthen cave under a circle of nut trees.

"Yif ye're attacked ond I'm nocht here, bring Leith to this hole."

"What about the labyrinth?"

He looked at me coldly. "Here. Pull this brush in front. Swar to me."

I swore. Nuts lay drying on the cave floor.

After the Nativity, the wassail threw a bank of snow into my bedroom so deep I couldn't get the door open—Gruoth had to rescue me. The blizzard departed in a week, leaving wet, dreary months of winter still ahead. Many of our company rode to Scotland to see their families, for it wasn't the fighting season. Leith was a hot gleed in my bed. Did it snow in the Carpathian Mountains?

Then, slowly, the Scots returned. Hours of bright blue sky broke the monotonous gray, followed by birdsong. I began to watch for Bonel's missive again.

Enoch saw the runner before I did. From the moat bridge, I watched him waylay the yellow-garbed man on the far side of the river and take a packet from him. He glanced briefly at its contents, gave the runner something for his pains, and rode in my direction.

I hid behind the cheese house until he'd passed, then surreptitiously followed him into the Great Hall in time to see him fling the missive carelessly into the fireplace.

I pulled the smoldering packet from the flames.

Enoch turned on his bench. "Doona burn yerself—Ich

con tell ye quhat it says. The king demands that I cum to Portsmouth beach to sail to Poitou. He plans to fight the French thar."

At a glance, I saw that the packet was indeed addressed to Enoch.

The next day, I took my position on the moat bridge again.

A second runner appeared at the selfsame hour with another missive for Enoch.

I accepted it this time, however, and handed it to him.

"Be ye expectin' summit?" he asked.

"Of course not! Why?"

"This be the second day ye ha'e hovered by the river."

"I was planting lilies on Theo's grave!"

"'Tis fram Lord Robert fitzWalter, yif ye're interested."

"All the way from Normandy?" I was interested and amazed.

"Fram Dover. He's back in England. The king ha'e forgiven him, him ond Eustace, fer trying to assassinate him." His blue eyes clouded. "Mast strange." After a time, he continued. "Lord Robert wants I shuld cum to his estate in Dunmow, ond he's mast particular that ye cum, too, to translate Latin. He's inwited all our Brotherhood to meet wi' him thar."

"About the charter? Is Cardinal Langton coming?"

"He doeesna say."

Every instinct screamed that we should stay home! Lord Robert had betrayed Enoch—I knew it! I couldn't forgive him.

Enoch read my thought. "Ich be surprised that the king would forgive him after he tried to kill him!"

"Because Lords Robert and Eustace blame you! And so does the king!"

He rose and patted my head. "Thankee, Alix, fer defendin' me. Lord Robert ond Lord Eustace didna shoot the arrow, 'tis true, boot no one knaws that I war inwolwed."

"How can you be so certain?"

"It cum to Gruoth in a dream." His grin widened. "A dream poot there by a hermit. How do the hermit knaw? Waesucks, you tell me!"

When we left two weeks later, Leith rode on my horse in front of me.

Dunmow Castle was not a great distance from Wanthwaite if we'd followed a straight path, which we didn't. On Dere Street we turned north, as if going to Scotland, then immediately to our right, where we ascended another ridge. Again, we beheld a vast valley below; Enoch led us down a path to the opposite side of the ridge. Even here, we didn't follow the path, but fought our way through melting ice, broken limbs, steep mounds.

Six knights galloped in our direction, whirled, asked our names, then waved us forward with one knight leading us. We went through three such points before we began following the curtain wall guarded by a high gate with more knights, then a moat, another gate, another wall, and we were inside a park.

We reached the actual castle of Dunmow in a low winter mist rising from hoary grass. The park reminded me eerily of the park at the de Braose estate in Wales with its ancient oaks bending like Druids, and its herds of tame deer.

Enoch's conversation with the armed men at the final gate was muted in the fog. The swirling mists briefly opened to reveal a tall stone castle. I nudged Leith awake so she could see the splendor before us.

We entered a great Hall four times the size of Wanthwaite's. Leith's eyes were wide with wonder: the Hall was ablaze with wax tapers wreathed in smoke. Two huge fireplaces blasted intolerable heat, and the cacaphony of shouting male voices was also intolerable. The mix of hot blasts in front of us and cold from the rear, the choke of smoke, and the smell of spilled ale and wine everywhere made me totty. Against the wall, jongleurs banged tambours and scraped viols in vain. Lord Robert signaled wildly from the back wall; he looked hale and happy. Exile agreed with him.

A servant removed my furs and disappeared; someone thrust a goblet into my hands. I felt naked in my new shimmering multihued tunic with the moonstone at my throat. Except for Leith—now in Enoch's arms—I was the only woman in the hall. A billowing tapestry from Toulouse whipped from a wind behind it; where had Lord Robert found it? I must purchase one for Wanthwaite.

Then Lord Robert was beside me with his free arm over my shoulder. "Welcome to Dunmow!" he cried. "Thank you for coming!"

"I feel honored, milord, that you included me."

He laughed. "Did you expect me to defy the great Cardinal Langton? He described your linguistic talents. No, to tell the truth, I couldn't deprive these men of your delicate beauty! You must be aware of their stares. Of course, they dare not appoach you, not with your doting husband shooting murderous looks in all directions."

Which he was—to protect Leith.

"How were you able to return from Normandy so quickly?" I asked directly.

"Our sojourn *was* short, wasn't it?" he hedged, laughing. "You'll see Lord Eustace here in good time."

"How did you manage to be forgiven for such a heinous crime?" I insisted.

He smiled. "The pope persuaded the king."

"Did he persuade him to forgive Enoch as well?"

But he'd gone to greet three new barons who'd just entered the Hall, men I'd not seen before.

Enoch stood on the far side of the Hall, holding Leith aloft. The newly arrived barons gave their furs to serving men, then disappeared into the crowd. Sipping my fine Madeira and smiling vacuously, I tried to appear poised. Then two new barons entered, whom I did know: Lord Eustace de Vesci and Lord Robert de Ros. They were related through their wives, both Scottish princesses. Lord Robert de Ros directed them to a corner where Lord Robert fitzWalter waited; all three men spoke behind palms.

Then Lord Robert fitzWalter was back by my side. "Come, my dear, my wife is most eager to meet you."

He pushed through the throng to a board groaning with fresh game. Behind it stood a fashionable lady.

"Gunmora, this is the baroness of Wanthwaite I told you about. Lady Alix, my wife, Lady Gunmora."

My first thought was that Lady Gunmora was much too young to have been the mother of Lord Robert's daughter, Matilda, who'd had such a tragic end. Though far from beautiful, the lady was fashionable: She was richly attired in a black tunic open at the sides, trimmed with the white weasel of the far north. Her brows were plucked almost away, and she wore a cone-shaped hat with veils trailing to the floor.

"Lady Alix, though we've not met, I've seen you from afar. In Normandy, at my uncle's estate. Your beauty is legendary."

She must have seen me with King Richard.

"Quho be yer uncle?" Enoch asked from behind me.

"The Lord of Baloyne—do you know him?"

"Nay, except that everyich one knaws aboot him." He whispered into my ear, *"Richer than auld Midas!"*

Lord Robert, the richest baron in England, had just become richer by marriage.

She took my arm. "So beautiful and so intelligent at the same time. Quite a miracle."

She meant well—why did her words sound insulting?

She then made much of Leith, who was also intelligent though hardly beautiful, except in Enoch's eyes. "When Robert told me you might bring your baby, I made special preparations; I hope you'll all be comfortable in the quarters I've arranged. Upstairs. A private chamber. Our other guests will roll their mats in the Great Hall."

She pulled me toward a winding stair. Glancing over my shoulder, I signaled that the Scots should follow. Still chattering in a high affected voice, Lady Gunmora led us to a corridor, open on one side to the Great Hall below and on the other to a series of doors.

"This is for you and your lord," she told me, opening a door to a small closet. "Your household may place their mats here in the hall, close to you."

Enoch was already placing Leith on the far edge of a high bed.

"You are most thoughtful, Lady Gunmora," I thanked her.

"Leave someone for your child while you partake of our poor repast." She turned to the Scots. "All of you!"

Gruoth indicated that she would stay with Leith, and I promised to send up meat.

Again we followed our hostess to the Great Hall, now louder and more crowded than before. Lady Gunnmora's voice rose: Had I heard of Lord Robert's latest loss to the tyrant?

"Castle Baynard?"

"Oh no, his castle at Bennington." The instant he'd landed, the castle had been torched. He swore revenge.

I thought the fighting season was finished.

She claimed the season meant naught to the king.

"Why did Lord Robert come back from Normandy? Doesn't he have fine estates there?"

But Lady Gunmora had slipped away.

I spied Lord Robert in a corner talking seriously with Lord Eustace. Something in Eustace's furtive expression alerted me: Had their present freedom been won in exchange for naming Enoch as the killer? Had King John been told of his presence here? Silently, I slipped behind a billowing brocade embroidered with bluebirds and flies, the better to hear.

The barons immediately moved away, however, so I stepped into the company again. They had disappeared. In the distance, Enoch talked earnestly to an unknown knight-errant who stood in a splay of saffron. I pushed toward him, greeting on my way Lord Robert de Ros, Lord Henry Bohun, and Lord Robert de Vere. Enoch had also disappeared. I passed my hand across my damp forehead.

Someone tapped my shoulder. Cardinal Stephen Langton smiled at me, only he was dressed entirely in a monk's black robes instead of his usual bright red habit. Was he in disguise?

"Lady Alix, I thank you for coming."

"You're most welcome." I studied him closely; he knew the truth about Lord Robert and Lord Eustace—did he know about Enoch?

He displayed a few gray snags. "I hope you don't mind translating for these oafs. I've been without a clerk at Canterbury for several weeks, or I would have brought someone else. You're better than my ecclesiastical clerks in any case because of your acquaintance with legal terms."

I realized he was flattering me. For what purpose? "It's been many years since I wrote Latin—I may have lost the facility."

"Discretion is all you need know. King John would punish all of us if . . ." He glanced around the room.

"I'll not betray you, but . . ." I breathed deeply. "Are you certain of our host?"

His smile faded. "Lord Robert? Why? Do you have information?"

I shrugged prettily. "None at all. I just thought you might know why the king had forgiven him so readily."

"I plan to make an announcement about his release on the morrow." He belched lightly. "Then you'll do it?"

"Aye, if you wish . . ."

He was gone. Could I leave as well? Where was Enoch? I'd just reached the stairs when Lord Robert banged a gong for attention.

"Hear ye! Hear ye!" he cried. "My Lady Gunmora and I welcome you most warmly to Dunmow."

Most warmly indeed; I brushed my wet brow.

"We invite you to partake of a feast!"

I continued on the stairs, stepped over Scots sprawled in the Hall, and pushed the door to my closet unsuccessfully. On the third try, it suddenly gave way.

"I war asleep on the floor," Enoch's hulk informed me.

After I'd rolled Leith to the edge of the bed close to Enoch, I climbed over her to lie next to the icy wall.

Enoch collapsed onto the floor again; then his hand reached over the edge of the bed to Leith.

Tired as I was, I stared into the darkness, unable to sleep.

The following morning, Gruoth took Leith outside to see the deer; I descended for a little food. Lady Gunmora was nowhere in sight; I ate heartily of an exceptionally tasty pig's stomach shaped like a hedgehog and stuffed with ground pork, ginger, nuts, and apples. Stephen Langton appeared at my side. I moved away.

Fresh logs did not yet smoke and the aroma of fine Portuguese wines seemed fresher than the Madeira of last night, or perhaps I was simply more rested. Lord Eustace brushed close without speaking; still much aged, he appeared healthy and as surly as he had in London, which again made me suspicious. Had he and Lord Robert betrayed Enoch?

Servants staggered into the Great Hall carrying a heavy table, which they placed close to the door. Cardinal Langton gestured that I should sit on the stool behind it and next to where he stood. He pointed to a sheet of vellum and a stylus.

"I want you to make notes of what's proposed rather than recording every word. Can you do that?"

"If you indicate what you think is important, yes."

"Of course."

When he finished praying, he raised his hands. "I bring you great tidings!" he paraphrased Scripture, "for you see before you the next archbishop of Canterbury!"

Joyful shouts filled the Hall; everyone seemed genuinely pleased.

I was pleased that Bonel's wager was confirmed.

Langton continued. "My good fortune is matched by my host's. He is back in his own country with a full pardon, as is Lord Eustace de Vesci!"

And my own joy faded. Was Langton's appointment connected to their release?

Enoch shouted, "Has King John died?"

I froze. John might have a spy in our midst!

Archbishop Langton's smile held. "The interdict has been lifted from England!"

I frowned; we were getting to the crux.

"The pope demanded from the king that he forgive the barons! That he permit them to return in peace!"

"War the interdict his only concession?" Enoch echoed my thought.

Archbishop Langton smiled.

Enoch called out again, "When the king agreed to take you as archbishop, did the pope lift the interdict?"

Langton continued to smile. "Oh, much better than that, Lord Enoch! The pope was pleased, of course, to have me at Canterbury, but my appointment wasn't enough to lift the interdict."

Now the barons fell silent. Enoch was blunt. "What did the king give up to get the pope to forgive the assassins?"

Langton turned his smiling face. "Are you not canny?" he asked in English. Then he went back to Latin. "When John lost to King Philip in Bouvines, which I'm certain you know, he realized at last that he must have God on his side."

I didn't follow for a moment—John had lost in Bouvines? Many in our audience already knew this, though not Enoch or me. Again I thought of Richard—Bouvines was close to Poitiers.

Langton continued. "Pope Innocent has always favored France, but John struck at a good time."

Langton was evading the real reason: Lords Robert and Lord Eustace had betrayed Enoch. What else could it be?

Lord Eustace pushed his way to the front. "This has to do with the king's lubricity. When John stole Queen Isabella from the count of Lusignan, Hugh shifted his loyalty to King Philip. King John was defeated at Bouvines because of his weakness for women!"

He left abruptly. Poor man, still obsessed about John's sexuality.

Archbishop Langton seemed genuinely astonished at the claim. "I know naught of the king's courtship."

Many of the barons present had attended our first meeting at Wanthwaite. Therefore, Lord Eustace easily roused their suspicions.

"When the pope refused to lift the interdict upon my appointment, the king offered money, and it still was not enough."

Enoch looked directly at me. Leith's faint shouts from the deer park cut the silence.

Archbishop Langton beamed at his audience. His voice fell to a whisper. "The pope agreed to free your brothers only when the king finally agreed to give up all of England! Your country is now a papal fief!" He laughed aloud. "All of England is now ruled by the pope!"

Two barons ran from the Hall. Others fell to an ominous silence.

Enoch called out the crucial question. "Do we write our charter fer the pope then?"

Before Langton could answer, Lord Robert pushed his way forward. "Tell these men the truth! That this is the very first I've heard of such an outrage!"

Langton flushed deeply. "If you consider it an outrage, shame! It had to do with your release only indirectly!"

"Quhat did then?" Enoch insisted.

"Lord Robert sent a missive to the pope, saying he'd tried to assassinate the king because he could not bear to serve under someone who was excommunicated! Needless to say, Pope Innocent is not excommunicated!"

Lord Robert bowed his head. "That's true!"

Enoch wasn't satisfied. "Boot quhy did the king sell England?"

Langton winced. "You put it so crudely. England has always belonged to the Church, as every country does."

"Hu much?"

Langton didn't answer.

Enoch raised his voice. "How much did the king pay the pope for lifting the interdict and his excommunication?"

"To lift the intedict, forty thousand marks," Langton replied quietly. "And twelve thousand a year ever after. Plus one hundred thousand marks to cover the Church's losses for the years of the interdict."

An ominous silence fell over the barons.

Enoch slipped into French. "You and your pope have your way; we are supposed to pay the king's debt. And England is now under canon law?"

Langton flushed angrily. "It always was."

"And the debt? Tell us who will pay the king's debt to the pope?"

"England is a rich country."

"Indeed, until the Normans gave away all our land."

"The Church owns England."

"King John does not agree. He will demand scutage from his barons to pay Pope Innocent, then continue to engage in foreign wars, continue to murder his subjects. Your pope is a fool—but we are not."

I'd never seen him so angry.

Langton, too, was in a rage, only he closed his eyes. When he opened them again, he'd gained control. "We've been called today to speak of a charter of your complaints to the king."

But the barons were muttering to each other: They'd traded one tyrant for another, though the pope wouldn't burn their castles—just take them. One voice rose: The pope might hire some other country to grab his land, maybe France. What difference did it make to the barons if they fought John's foreign routiers from Brabant or the pope's French soldiers?

Langton again spoke of our charter. I dipped my pen.

"The pope drew up a charter for his agreement with the king in the matter of England becoming his fief, which gives us a precedent."

"He can't bend King Philip to his will!" Enoch interrupted. "Maybe we should invite Philip to be our king!"

Langton finally showed rage. "The pope has brought your king to heel—you should be grateful!"

Well, the barons weren't grateful. They argued all through the morning, but the day was won by Archbishop Langton. "You have no choice but to accept the pope's truce!"

Which was true. Pope Innocent ruled the world.

"Will ye mak us a charter, yea or nay?"

"John must accept the restrictions of a Christian nation!"

We adjourned to rest.

We returned, still a smoldering company, for the barons had been talking among themselves.

After Stephen Langton's prayer, he asked that the barons please list specific grievances that might become chapters in our charter.

Still surly, the barons listed what we all knew. I recorded as fast as I could, but I had trouble with "judgment" since there is no *j* in Latin; I thought *indicium* was correct, and, for "court," I substituted *forum basilica.*

It took most of the afternoon to list grivances, and even then we hadn't come to the crux of the problem, which was John himself. Or was that the pope's duty?

At dusk, Archbishop Langton closed our session with another prayer. Lord Robert then called for fine Jerez from Spain, but the party was off-key. Lady Gunmora slithered among us in her long train in the style of Tars, the jongleurs sang of love, the pipes and tambours rang, but no one ate, drank, or listened. *England was a papal state.* Ominous.

I caught Langton as he retired to swallow some medicinal seeds.

"Archbishop Langton, may I speak with you?"

"Of course, my dear." He burped gently into his palm; he had a sour stomach.

"Do you know the Carpathian Mountains?"

My question surprised him. "Mountains, you say? Carpathian? Are they a branch of the Alps?"

"I know not. They're in Europe, mayhap close to Italy. I thought that since you've lived in Rome . . ."

"And traveled extensively. Carpathian—do they have some other name? The Apennine Mountains run through the Italian boot."

I changed my gambit. "Do you recall when you rode to Wanthwaite with the Jew, Bonel?"

"Of course, not a year ago." His eyes narrowed. "If you're asking whether he is in the Carpathian Mountains, I would venture to say no. Most Jews of Normandy went to southern France, I believe. Bonel made a very moving plea for the Jews, as I remember."

"Yes!"

"Yet he included many inaccuracies."

"You don't believe that the Jews are persecuted? That King John . . . ?"

"Oh yes, I'm sure the king is dangerous to the Jewish community. We expect their expulsion from England at any time. Bonel was telling the truth about the problems in England." He took more seeds.

Yes, Bonel had been accurate about England, I thought, but not about Langton, whom he'd believed would help.

"Then what inaccuracies?"

He smiled with condescension. "Well, let's begin with King Philip of France. It's true that he's expelled the Jews from time to time, but it's also true that he's always readmitted them."

"Because he wants money!"

"*Benedicite,* be patient. You sound like your husband. The king of France is not the main enemy the Jews have in that part of the world, it's the barons. What about your own barons?"

I was unable to reply. The problem seemed dense—I wondered how much Bonel knew. Enoch had said that the Scots accepted Jews, which was the only word I'd ever heard on the subject.

"King John may be the simple monster you've painted—though by my own personal experience, he's more complex—but you have to understand that this struggle is about power.

The barons everywhere want power, and that includes power over the Jews. In France, they have it."

"Power over the Jews?" Not in my experience.

"Over the Jews' money, my dear, not their worship. Bonel understands: Expulsion is not his main problem; impoverishment is. The French barons are brutal. The Jews can exist only because they have money and the kings want to grab their riches before the barons can get it, and vice versa. Northern Italians are becoming moneylenders themselves, another way to attack the Hebrews."

Suddenly I felt sick. "So you don't know where the Carpathian Mountains might be?"

"If they exist at all."

I studied the dark bags under his eyes. "How do you feel about the Jews, Archbishop? Should they live among Christians?"

"I'm a man of the Church." He saw my expression. "Don't worry for Bonel's life, only his riches. The present danger for the Jews is penury."

I had jewels and money, both from Bonel—how could I return them?

"Can't the pope help? You know him—can't he . . . ?"

Langton sighed. "Pope Innocent believes in the universal Church. He doesn't care about the Jews' riches, but he is nevertheless intransigent about the sanctity of Christ." He wiped his face. "So am I, of course, but I would never . . ."

"Never what?"

"In his recent Lateran Council, Pope Innocent forbade any marriage between Christian and Jew."

He waved to someone and walked away quickly.

14

Enoch already lay on the floor beside a sleeping Leith. "Quhat war ye talkin' aboot wi' Langton?"

"Bonel the Jew. The archbishop thinks Bonel may be in danger."

Enoch grunted. "I sayed as hu he culd stay at Wanthwaite."

"Did you!"

He didn't reply.

"Have you ever heard of the Carpathian Mountains, Enoch?"

"Be that whar carpets cum fram?" He laughed at his jape.

After a long silence, he spoke again. "Do Leith's breath sound richt to ye?"

I leaned over the baby. Soothly, her breath rattled. And there was a scratching sound in her chest. "I hate to wake her."

"Wull slape do mar guid than medicines?"

"Go downstairs for hot water, Enoch. And bring a taper if you can—I have herbs with me." I also had eagle stones, the head of a goat-milker bird, and powdered snake. As Enoch held the taper, I worked over our little girl.

"Quhat war that stuff?"

"Only lemon balm meddled with swine grease. It should relieve her breathing."

Soothly, she was better by morning, though still wheezing. With Gruoth's help, I treated her with bugloss, a stronger herb. When she passed blood, I added the cuckold pint. Now I worried about the herd of deer in the park, for many ailments come from animals. Upon questioning Gruoth, I learned that she'd found a pinecone for Leith to offer to a deer, and when the animal had refused it, Leith had eaten it herself.

"Tell her to leave," I said to Enoch, "and you go as well. This is going to be unpleasant."

Gruoth left; Enoch stayed. Together, using fingers dipped in the oil of the salmon we'd had at Haute Tierce, we dug the wood from Leith's anus. When she had fallen to an easy sleep, we spent the rest of the morning hours cleaning the mess.

"Thank you, Enoch."

He looked up through red rims. "Thank ye, Alix. Ye ha'e saved my babe."

"Our babe."

We stared at each other.

Thus I was late to our second day of discussion. The barons were now indisputably hostile to Langton himself. The archbishop flushed at their refusal to speak, but remained secure in his superior authority. By the end of a week, I handed Archbishop Langton a short list:

1. FOREST LAWS
2. TRIAL BY A JURY OF ONE'S PEERS
3. INHERITANCE
4. WEIRS

5. SCUTAGE

6. MARRIAGE PRIZES

7. WIDOWS

8. DISSEISE

"They didn't include the freedom of the Church," he said.

More important, no one had mentioned the dire situation with the Jews. As for the Church, I was aware that the argument had begun with Becket, but so far as I knew it didn't affect the barons.

"I'll begin putting these in chapters, appropriate to a charter. I'll send a runner to Wanthwaite with a copy when I'm finished. Perhaps your husband can comment."

At least Leith recovered.

Our small party left Dunmow as we'd come, through a series of spiked gates and harsh questions. A weak sun now melted the snow in our path, and the acrid smell of smoke from a burning castle had diminished. Putting aside the bitter arguments behind us, I pondered on Bonel, and why he'd told me that wild tale about the Carpathian Mountains. Or was it a dream? If so, his or mine? Mine, I decided, for he'd made it clear on the second night that something had changed his mind.

Less than half a day from Dunmow, Enoch suddenly pushed us off our path.

"Hide! Sommun be following us!"

We scambled behind a cluster of rocks.

Within ten heartbeats, Lord Robert and Lord Eustace

pounded into sight. The lords rode directly to the rocks where we hid.

"Come out and talk!" Lord Robert called.

I remained on my horse with Leith while the men dismounted to parley. Lord Robert, his shadowed furrows clearly visible in the sun, looked most distraught. "What think you, Wanthwaite, of this archbishop?"

Enoch hesitated.

"Langton and John are in the hands of the pope!" I called. "Will Innocent back our claims?"

Lord Robert squinted at me.

"John would go against the pope if women or money were involved." Eustace sighed heavily. "England is a papal fief—is John even relevant?"

Lord Robert's face twisted. "Would any charter have saved my daughter?"

Or Theo?

Enoch answered. "Law be the wave of the future."

Lord Robert's furrows deepened. "Except we don't live in the future, Wanthwaite; we live now. Law is an abstract and acts are real."

"Is religion an abstract?" I called. "You used canon law to escape Normandy. Could you have used civil law?"

Lord Robert finally told the truth. "Canon law plus money, don't forget."

"Ond ye made England be a papal state lak Lombardy. We shuld address our charter to the pope?"

"No, to King John." Lord Robert paused. "John dealt with Rome because he was desperate, but mark my words, he won't be true. Yet Innocent trumped John in his choice for archbishop; John has a real adversary. Question is, will the charter bring them together?"

I pushed my horse forward. "Think! John's interdict, his excommunication, the exchange of money, France. The pope cites God as his authority and John claims to be a Christian prince, while both buy the military, give women and children no power . . ."

"Don't make a speech concerning women!" Lord Eustace interrupted.

"Alix be totty!" Enoch put his hand on my arm.

I threw it off. "I would suggest, milords, that the king and the pope have common cause; one augments the other, and neither cares a straw for your complaints. Will Pope Innocent approve our charter? Will the king sign it or respect it? The answer is no. Will you proceed anyway? Yes. Only see that you include women and children and old men; I should have added Jews."

Enoch pushed me aside roughly. "Listen to her! Alix learned aboot government in Aquitaine."

It was the first kind word he'd ever said about my sojourn with King Richard.

Lord Robert conferred with Lord Eustace. "We know it's a game of quid pro quo between the pope and the king. We think we should deal with the pope; he may be misanthropic about women or Jews, but he isn't mad. And, despite his obvious intelligence, we believe that John is insane. Can the pope control him? I say we have no choice."

Lord Eustace nodded. "And we're fortunate to have Stephen Langton to represent us to both the pope and the king."

I kicked my mare to move on; I was disgusted. I'd told the truth about Fontevrault Wood—hadn't they listened?

Enoch had the last word. "Ye gave the pope England! That's his language, nocht religion or law! He wrapped his forgiveness o' ye in cold cash." His steed bumped mine. "Ond we'll pay."

A thin plume of smoke rose on the horizon.

I stopped. "*Deus juva me!* Help them!"

"They died at least a week ago," Lord Robert shouted. "Doona throw away yer arrows yit."

"Lord Enoch will not act as your assassin again!" I cried.

Lord Eustace galloped to my side, then pulled at my reins. "Lady Alix, may I speak to you privately?"

"I'll tak Leith," Enoch offered.

Lord Eustace led me to the shadow of a rock. "Lord Robert and I excuse your folly because you love Enoch to distraction. As my own wife loves me and Lady Gunmora loves him. But you make it hard. I have never and would never do anything to harm Enoch."

Before I could reply, he returned to Lord Robert.

"Quhat did want wi' ye?" Enoch asked finally.

"He says that they won't try assassination again."

"Ich tald ye!"

Another meeting of the barons was called in late autumn at the castle of Robert de Ros, Lord of Yorkshire. Archbishop Langton would not be in attendance, and therefore there was no reason for me to translate Latin; Enoch insisted that I go to care for Leith.

Lord Robert de Ros's castle was even grander than Dunmow, though not so well appointed inside, and his lady, another princess of Scotland, had the unfortunate name of Lady Fiona. Our little party had its own closet with a mat for sleeping, and the food was most excellent. Whatever Archbishop Langton's deficiencies might be, we immediately saw his value in this noisy slipshod meeting. Lord Robert de Ros steered us almost exclusively to the unfairness of the forest laws, his particular peeve. His best hounds had been shot dead by the king's men; otherwise, there was a paucity of new complaints.

The archbishop wrote me that he'd had the great good fortune to stumble on King Henry I's charter as he was sorting the records at Canterbury. The charter, written in Latin, was in terrible shape: torn at the edges, with water damage on the script itself—some of the words were illegible (the original black ink had faded to red, and it was scripted in tiny cramped letters, illegible to old eyes), but he hoped I could make out the meaning. Indeed, he would appeciate my reading it and reporting back to him. Perhaps I could even copy it in larger script?

I took the enclosed document, wrapped in fine linen as if it were a newborn babe, and continued to read the rest of Langton's missive. The archbishop had news he knew I would want to hear: Bishop Geoffrey of Lincoln—did I remember him? the king's justiciar for the Jews?—had received a letter from Bonel. He was somewhere in the Middle East and must be thriving, for the good news was that he'd married! The wife's name was Miriam of Tars or Tarsus, he wasn't sure, but apparently an excellent match. He hoped I would be relieved . . . I stopped reading.

Enoch came home late with a large elk, enough to feed us for a month. I told him of my missive about King Henry's charter; he seemed relieved. I also told him about Bonel. Enoch was happy and claimed he liked the Jew in spite of his noxious behavior in stealing me; he wished him well.

As for my honest feelings? *Enoch and England.* I'd thought I'd found an escape from shattered dreams in Bonel. Now that the escape had ended, the dream of Bonel was just that, a dream. I tried to be happy for him—aye, I was happy. Wasn't I?

Yet how could I be merry when I thought of my own future? Once this charter was settled, I would lose Wanthwaite, Leith, and—aye—Enoch, in a single day. Bonel had prepared me for such a future; I should have been satisfied.

Alone in my dark closet, I fumbled under my mat for the letters Bonel had given me of his contacts in London. Tomorrow I would study my jewels again.

I prepared to leave. I cultivated Thorketil, who was obviously of Danish descent though he'd been born in Scotland, a thin, blond giant with a long saturnine face, an intelligent man, though he spoke rarely. Next to Enoch himself, Thorketil had the most knowledge and had the most authority concerning Wanthwaite. His wife, Edwina, was my surrogate when I had to be away. Tall and slender, she made tunics for herself, which she pretended didn't fit, then passed them on to me. She and Thorketil had three boys; the youngest, who played with Leith, was only two.

Though I felt most compatible with Edwina, Gruoth was my best friend. Tubby and sweaty and toothless, she still had the wonder and enthusiasm of a young girl. She served me, adored me, sacrificed herself at every opportunity, so it was Gruoth I began to prepare for my exit. I asked her to guard Leith every day; I taught her my best recipes and my herbal medicines.

"Ich doona want to knaw more," she said one day. "I doona want to tak your place."

"What an idea! Have you told anyone?"

"Aye, Ich tald Enoch."

Enoch watched me as if I were about to steal our buried treasure; he was worried that I would steal Leith, that was the truth.

One of Edwina's nieces, Nicola, came to live with us. An exceedingly pretty and lively girl, she soon reformed the male habits, so they washed and refrained from spitting on the floor just to be in her presence. She was wonderful with Leith, which gave me a second nurse for my little girl.

I examined the jewels and concluded they might be less valuable than I'd first thought, especially my rubies. Though blinding in full sun, they looked pink instead of red, and they were small. My diamonds, though even smaller, sparkled prodigiously because of their excellent cut. Mayhap the same hand had cut my rubies. My pearls were faintly pink and exceedingly large and smooth, better than the gray pearls Bonel had bought in Brugge. Mine were probably from the Mediterranean.

Enoch read Henry I's charter with great interest, then with disdain. Filled with generalities, it addressed none of our concerns.

I didn't take it to our next baronial meeting at Carlisle, close to Scotland. The small Carlisle castle was claimed by both King Alexander and King John in a bitter quarrel. Archbishop Langton would not be in attendance. The barons who did attend, including Lord Robert and Lord Eustace, were deadly serious. Still, without the archbishop, we accomplished little.

Archbishop Langton summoned me to Durham to deliver my translation of the old charter, to Enoch's delight.

"'Tis a beautiful city to shaw Leith!"

"Neither of you is coming!"

"Ich war gang there anyway! Thorketil lined op a team of oxen we mane to buy!"

"Send Thorketil then!"

Two days later, Enoch, Leith, Gruoth, and I set out. We arrived at Durham in good time and, once he saw me established in a monk's dorter, Enoch took Leith and Gruoth to a church inn.

The archbishop was leading a prayer service for the monks when I found him; tapers shed little light into the low, arched sanctuary. Since women were strictly forbidden, I remained quietly in the shadows until he was finished. When the other monks had departed, the archbishop removed his miter.

"Lady Alix, are you there? I thought I saw you."

He led me to a small office at the back of the sanctuary, where I saw my familiar vellum and ink. He had great difficulty even recognizing the original of King Henry's charter when I laid it before him.

"Could you see it?" he asked anxiously.

"Aye, though it's in terrible condition, Your Eminence."

At least the charter was short, a brief coronation speech filled with vacuous generalities and not much else. Yet Henry I was said to be a good king, though he had no real charter.

"Sometimes I can make out three letters, and I need a good Latinist to suggest the fourth. The first chapter, published August 5, 1100, reads: *In Christi nomine promitto haec tria populo Christiani mihi subdito. In primis me praecepturum en opem pro vribus impersurum ut ecclesia Dei et omnis Christianus veram pacem nostro arbitrio in omni tempori servet—*' "

Langton interupted. "I recognize the exact words—it goes back to Ethelred. That's only the introduction—read me from the charter itself."

"Yes, I will," I said, humiliated. " '*Sciatis me Dei misericordia . . .*' "

When I finished this, the archbishop was smiling. "Do you understand what you just read?"

"The English Church is free."

He laughed gently. "Meaning that Rome controls all appointments and legal matters concerning Church governance and property. Didn't I tell you?"

"Wanthwaite is not Church property."

"Are you certain?"

I was.

That was my only meeting with the archbishop. Within a week, I was finished. Archbishop Langton assured me he would write me where and when the next meeting might be.

Enoch and Leith and Gruoth were waiting outside the walls with a team of oxen; we began our jouney southward that same afternoon.

Enoch was happy with his purchase; I was thoughtful.

15

SIXTEEN CASTLES BURNED THAT SUMMER. THOUGH MOST WERE IN the south, we were terrified. Enoch built a tower atop our highest fell as a lookout; we couldn't see approaching armies, but we could see smoke.

Nicola had a friend in Oxenford who sent word that the tower of Oxenford had burned. Lord Guy de Mandeville was killed, and the money he'd paid the king for the Duchess of Gloucester was not returned to his family.

"We're in civil war!" Lord Robert cried as he galloped into our courtyard—we didn't need to be told.

Yet wasn't a civil war waged by rebels against the authority? What did you call a war of a king against subjects? Enoch claimed that the barons were fighting back, albeit unsuccessfully. But they never attacked the king's castles or his men first. Had I forgotten that we believed in the law? Our charter was our rebellion, not the sword.

Yet someone was fighting; wounded knights arrived at Wanthwaite all the way from Wessex or Essex. Knights usually cared for each other in the field, but these wounds were deep, some near fatal, and I'd developed a reputation afar for my healing arts. Edwina and I transformed the schoolroom and chapel into medical hospices. I sent women and children into the woods to gather aloe and lemon balm.

Our meetings about our charter accelerated as often as we could muster nobles who were not fighting. Archbishop Langton could rarely attend, but we all referred to him as our leader. Yet—hadn't he been instrumental in making England a papal state? On the other hand, that very fact gave him access to the king, which we would soon need.

Our new oxen fell to their knees, rolled over, and died. This could not be King John's fault, but Enoch blamed him nonetheless. Thorketil and Dugan and Enoch and I all worked throughout the night, bleeding the sick beasts, even forcing Pliny's famous concoction of *Comeleon* mixed with pepper boiled in wormwood and drunk with hot honey, which had saved the lives of two knights. Though we may have slowed the oxen's deaths somewhat, they still died. Enoch was beside himself. He sent Scots in all directions searching for other oxen; while he was waiting, he borrowed a pair from Eustace de Vesci. Thorketil returned with ten young healthy beasts who'd escaped into the king's forest when a castle had burned, close to the castle of Lord Robert de Ros, which had been attacked.

The new beasts were put to work at once to plow fields too long fallow, while we women dug into the wet black soil of our vegetable garden with sticks. When Enoch and I were summoned to Nottingham for a few days by the archbishop, I left the other women to plant for me.

Archbishop Langton had begun to outline our charter to conform to others, for our emphasis on precedent and custom must be proved by other documents. That was not the law, but it was the accepted tradition.

"The king luiks on our charter as a peace treaty," Enoch said. "Mayhap that's quhy he's tryin' to get the upper hand in the field."

Both the pope and the king wanted peace, or so they said.

Langton referred to England as the "patrimony of St. Peter," which must obey the holy law; yet he took our complaints about John's brutal methods seriously. And so would Pope Innocent, he assured us. Langton promised to send his first draft of our charter to Rome—a journey of six weeks there, then another six weeks back—a long time, he granted, but perhaps God had a secret purpose.

Which meant twelve weeks before my marriage must finally be resolved. Twelve weeks with Leith, at Wanthwaite

And, finally, with Enoch.

When I showed my jewels in London, must I include my pink pearls in my application? Was I not permitted one memento of Bonel? Or of King Richard? In any case, the jewels must be preserved in case of attack. I hollowed a round of cheese as my hiding place, then placed the cheese inside a barrel.

I didn't know I'd dreamed of the Carpathian Mountains, until I stopped dreaming.

In January, Archbishop Langton summoned the Brotherhood to the castle of Lord Robert de Ros in Yorkshire, where we'd met before, though now the castle was half in ruins. Langton was visiting Archbishop Geoffrey of York, however, so it seemed the best place to rendezvous. Enoch and I agreed for once to leave Leith with Gruoth, for the wind was blowing a blizzard. We wrapped our faces in woolen scarves, but our eyelashes froze.

I cried aloud when I saw the castle from a distance, only a high smoking chimney still intact, the tower gone, the walls, the moat bridge. We labored toward the bleak treeless ruin with the wind at our backs. When we crossed planks to a wooden wall that had been erected on one side of the Great Hall, I looked back on moors and shallow valleys. Opalescent, shadowed, mysterious, and dangerous, the other lure of England.

Lady Fiona met us with royal dignity, despite her rough long Scottish kilts. Inside the Great Hall, barons shouted and toasted in high glee. Never mind that the makeshift thatch above leaked small snowdrifts in the corners, never mind that huge snarling hounds occupied the only warm places by the fire, spirits were high—made more so by hot mead. Lord Robert de Ros came forward to meet us accompanied by three young daughters, all wrapped in fur: Mary Alice, Mary Angela, and Mary Margaret, Scottish princesses all.

Lord Robert fitzWalter thrust methiers into our hands. "Where's that little pink pearl?"

I started. My pearls were not little!

"Leith be at home," Enoch answered, "becas o' the weddir."

Lord Robert punched my stomach. "Another one on the way? You make beautiful heiresses, Lady Alix!"

"Nocht wi'out me!" Enoch cried.

Lord Robert laughed. "You want me to punch you as well?"

The de Ros daughters now lay on top of the hounds. Two were quite young, but the one called Mary Margaret was fast turning into a beauty.

Another round of hot mead was passed; my feet began to thaw. At least the weather guaranteed a good turnout, since knights weren't fighting and lords weren't overseeing their planting. Therefore the meeting was attended by twice the number of barons as we'd had at Dunmow, which now seemed long ago.

Archbishop Langton staggered into the Hall through the kitchen court, carrying a stack of leather folders, which he placed on a small table.

These were documents of laws and precedents he thought we should know.

I read the charter of Henry I first. When I stopped, the barons waited, as if not believing that this was the entire document. Langton beckoned Lord Robert fitzWalter to read another charter of Henry I, concerning London. The charter declared London a free city for all time, with its own rule and its own trade and franchises.

"Hear! Hear!" cried William de Mowbray, who was London's mayor.

"You see what long life a charter can have," Langton said, "and yet how little effect on everyday lives at the time it's written." King Henry I had been a brutal despot, especially in London, efficient and clever, but nonetheless a tyrant.

"Boot he left a legacy," Enoch pointed out. "London be

free, fer example. Ond we can use his words and fergit qhuat he did."

Yet Henry—or even the present king—shrank in villainy when compared to the despotism of King Stephen. And King Stephen had nevertheless listed the rights of his subjects in a charter. Enoch opined sotto voce that Stephen had become king only because the English so hated the Angevins. Other charters were read. Robert de Ros took exception to a common theme: that the forests of England were a personal and peculiar possession of the king's.

"The point is," Langton suggested, "that charters may be signed and proclaimed, only to be followed by anarchy. Are you certain of your approach?"

When no one spoke, he continued. Tacitus of Rome had written a learned treatise on the law (though, Enoch whispered, the great law of the Roman system had been its strong central government). He also mentioned German law, and the laws of Wessex, of Alfred the Great, of Athelstan, of Edgar. And London wasn't the only city with a record of independence: Newcastle upon Tyne also had an ancient charter granted by the parliament of Scotland, much to Enoch's satisfaction.

"You have just heard the precedents you sought," said Langton. "Are you ready to proceed?"

There followed a melee of shouted accusations against John, King Philip, even the Holy Roman Emperor. The air was cloudy with sour breaths. Yet our cause remained opaque.

We stopped for Haute Tierce.

In the afternoon session, Lord Richard de Percy urged greater focus on our purpose. "Haven't we already written a list of categories on which we agree? Shouldn't those be our basis?"

"Indeed, we have," Langton replied. "Lady Alix, would you read them in English, then French?"

I read our short list.

After a long silence, Lord Robert rose. "Where we differ from King John is only in application. We should make that clear."

Langton sighed in relief. "You're right. We should look forward to modern application. Though the eternal verities don't change, the circumstances wherein they're applied do change. As St. Augustine teaches us: '*The human mind needs Divine Illumination to know the truth.*' The sun illuminates the earth."

Enoch had gradually become a deeper and deeper red. "This shell of a castle be illumination enow!"

"All governance depends on holy inspiration."

"So you think we shuould forget the charter and pray?" Enoch stammered in French.

"All law stems from God, who gave us a tablet of commandments. Divine wisdom provides the design whereby we shall create the artifact, which is our uniquely human gift. We make tangible that which the Holy Spirit suggests. Surely you want to know that your artifact contains truth."

I doubt if a single baron could follow his reasoning except Enoch, who could hardly speak. "A pox on your St. Augustine! Didn't he write about two cities, one of light, one of darkness, where the devil lives? King John is the devil, and yet the pope will deal with him! We'll contain his evil with a charter if we can, but we won't stop at prayer! Do you understand my French?"

He slumped to the floor and leaned against my knees, but he wasn't finished.

"We willna fight the king's foreign wars. Poot it in!"

Lord Robert nodded; Langton just stared.

"Yif we want to fight abroad, we'd better follow Caesar."

Most of the barons had never heard of Caesar. They would have known King Richard as a military hero, but Enoch wouldn't evoke his name.

It took most of the day to get beyond the foreign-war issue. Lady Fiona asked, Did widows have to remarry just because the king wanted money? Her husband hastily interrupted: What about the bailiffs' behavior when a man died with debts? Sir Hubert asked, Could a knight's service be inherited?

Gradually, our first draft of a charter was formed. Added to my original eight points, we had twenty-five more. Now very sober despite the mead, the barons each signed their names.

As we rode through heavy drifts again, I said to Enoch, "How dare you lean against my knees! I will not tolerate such intimacies!"

He pretended not to hear.

"You behaved as if I were your wife!"

"Which ye air until the Church says ye're nocht!" He turned a very red face with very blue eyes. "Besides, ye're my sister."

"Aye, sister." I was near tears.

"I lean agin my real sister so."

"Did you also rape her?"

I galloped ahead through the snow.

In April, King John sent his reply to our charter: He refused to even read it.

In May, Langton suggested that Enoch and I, plus twenty-five other barons, retire to Staines on the Thames, close to Windsor, and stay there until the king had to give in. I must again act as scribe to make necessary additions and deletions. Langton would reside at Windsor with the king; he would ride back and forth to Staines as need be.

Since Staines was across the river from Runnymede, I couldn't bear to attend this final phase of our charter; I would stay at Wanthwaite and guard Leith. Then Enoch convinced me that we would both be safer in Staines than in Wanthwaite, which was due for a sacking.

The bridge across the Thames at Staines was heavily manned. Royal guards in red protected the gate on the Windsor side; then one must pass a series of small towers along the riverfront, each with four knights, some in red, the same as the guards, some in black, meaning they were foreigners, according to Enoch. We stared at them from the market town, but only Langton dared ride past them, and even he was stopped twice.

Enoch put us in a church inn with other barons, and, as Bonel had done in Flanders, he placed me against the wall with Leith between him and me. Lice and spring fleas and rats gnawed at our mats; Enoch brought us a stray cat. Nothing could protect us from freshly oiled piles of armor, which fell on us twice.

During the day, I led Leith to a small grassy knoll above

the river where she might play while I worked with a flat rock as my table. On the second day, Archbishop Langton found me there. "You were right, Lady Alix."

I didn't like his tone. "About what, Your Eminence?"

"The king insists upon changes."

I smiled as I took his list. This was an improvement over the former dismissal of the charter.

He walked away before I could ask if he'd heard from the pope—something we all wanted to know. If he had and the pope was negative, dare he go against Innocent III?

On reflection, I suspected that Langton was using the pope's delay to mask John's own decision against us. John didn't want to grant any of our wishes, yet he wanted to appease the pope. If the pope backed us, John would have to comply; if not, it would give the king an easy excuse to condemn us. So long as he heard nothing, the king could dally.

I confessed my suspicions to Enoch when we took our usual stroll along the river. We glimpsed Windsor Castle in the distance.

"Why would the pope side with a madman? Why would Langton?"

"It doesna matter quhether the king be mad or sane," said Enoch. "He be king."

Which was true.

Yet I stared at the curve in the river; beyond that point lay Runnymede. And at that castle in the distance lay Theo. It seemed distant in time as well, and yet only yesterday.

When Langton took the final version of our charter to the king, he was gone four days. He came back, a drawn, trembling man: He had never seen the king truly angry before.

Other barons arrived; other chapters were added in a frenzy not to omit anything. We expanded to sixty demands. Langton sent to Canterbury for a larger leaf of vellum.

"This has far outgrown former charters. We'll call it our Great Charter (Magna Carta)."

We didn't get our next submission back at once; the king objected to chapter 16 (*Nullus faciendum majus sercicium de deodo militus, nec de alio libero tenemento, quam inde velli*); the king changed *velli* to *debatur*. A difference too subtle by far; was he simply stalling? Would he ever sign?

The king insisted we add a chapter at the beginning announcing the freedom of the English Church, and we saw the heavy hand of Langton, for John didn't care a bean about the Church, except as it might help his cause. And had this truly been the king's idea? I still didn't know what "freedom" of the Church meant. That John and his progeny controlled the English Church instead of Rome? Or that Rome controlled it? Which was freedom?

We stopped at sixty-two chapters, all neatly numbered and as short as we could make them with clarity.

The king again turned them down.

We changed only one chapter, the one referring to fish weirs.

Then suddenly Enoch insisted on another chapter. "S'pose the king doesna do quhat he says? We mun ha'e sum way to enforce our charter."

He was right; once John had signed our charter into law (if he did), the king had to conform to our demands! And Enoch had caught the weakness: The king might sign and yet refuse to obey; this was John.

A chapter was added giving the twenty-five barons who signed the right to enforce the law. I was amazed when the king didn't object.

But he did amend chapter I, about the freedom of the Church; we accepted his correction. The barons were elated that whatever his changes, he was accepting the principle of a charter!

Langton took another "final" document to Windsor with its corrections: The king now wanted to amend chapter 9, the one about widows being forced to remarry. We studied his objections and conceded his points where we thought they wouldn't hurt.

He next attacked number 16 and I saw a pattern. He deliberately substituted vague terms where we had been exact: *evil customs* for *illegal acts;* the constant addition of *ought* instead of *must;* the vague use of *freemen.* Again I heard Richard's voice: never underestimate his intelligence.

Yet intelligence is not the same thing as sanity; administrative skills are not the same as governance; editing is not the same as invention.

Nevertheless, the day came when King John accepted our Great Charter. He insisted that we relinquish our only copy, however, so that his scribes could copy it to conform to the king's other royal papers. I stayed up all night making a second copy for us, in case the king lost his.

We waited while the scribes laboriously made their five

THE PRINCE OF POISON

copies. Now Langton perused King John's official copy to be certain that nothing had been changed. Nothing had. We were ready.

No, one last request: All the barons who were to sign, as well as the king, were to read the final document carefully. And did they comprehend—for it was not explicitly stated—that this charter ended all hostilities between the king and his rebellious lords? For that was his sole reason for signing: to promote peace in his beloved realm. In short, he regarded it as a peace treaty.

We understood.

The date was set for June 15.

The day before June 15, six knights plunged into the Thames to take their yearly baths. Others splashed their faces, their armpits, their parts, and trimmed each others' beards; all polished their armor. Few barons did likewise, for they were discussing the charter to the last moment. Finally, we formed a line to cross the bridge; Leith and I rode in the middle beside Enoch, who had argued persuasively that I deserved to witness the great occasion since I'd labored so faithfully. And since he truly believed that this was a momentous event in history, the most important in Leith's lifetime, he insisted that she go, too. He promised to keep both of us out of sight.

I was very aware that I was riding with a small army, the very first time since I'd gone on the Crusade. Lord Robert fitzWalter led us, followed by the twenty-four other barons who'd agreed to sign in the presence of the king. We'd had as many as forty barons at first; many had dropped out from fear. Or they'd been bribed. I'd given Leith a honey teat with just a trace of the mandrake; she might see the ceremony, but I didn't want her to draw the king's attention our way.

Many natives rowed small skiffs on the Thames beside us; the sky was clear, the air balmy but not hot. New green leaves and grass dazzled the eye in every direction. Even burly, fully armed knights seemed small boys playing at war. Yet when we were forced to ride single file on the far side of the bridge—the king's side—my heart thumped like a kettle. We had finally entered the devil's domain; knights stationed at the small towers, foreigners all, stood with drawn swords. Peace might have been declared, but no one had told these swine.

Runnymede was poignantly familiar in early morning sunlight. Beams shot low through giant oaks; white-barked poplars trembled in an elusive breeze. Tables and benches were placed on a level grassy area on the Windsor side of the pond. Theo, Theo, I thought, as if his death had just occurred; I felt his presence here. Enoch led Leith and me up a small rise, where he placed us behind a clump of gooseberry bushes, allowing both cover and the ability to see. Leith was now asleep. Enoch rode back to the barons. Enoch had refused to sign the charter with the barons because he might be Scottish by law, but he stood in the center of their group.

This is the end for me, I thought. The only person whose life will change completely. I continued to muse: No, King John's will. Then I looked at my sleeping little girl. And Leith's. How ironic that I would lose both my children at Runnymede.

The faint bleat of wooden horns sounded in the distance. Six huge black stallions rode into view, accompanied by a host of knights guarding the prelates who rode with them; fourteen scribes followed, carrying five copies of our charter wrapped in scarlet silk, held high above their heads. When they were dismounted, a second fanfare announced Archbishop Langton in full Canterbury regalia; he was followed by a host of papal dignitaries, including two cardinals in the familiar red tunics. Once he was dismounted, Langton instantly conferred with the first group.

Finally, the horns blasted an unmistakable royal fanfare. My heart stopped. An army of white stallions mounted by knights in red paced slowly over the hill and down to the benches. And finally, at last, there was the king himself. Like the cardinals, he wore a full-length scarlet tunic. I crouched lower, my heart now a hammer. How odd, a lady rode pillion behind him, her arms clutched about his waist. Was it his daughter, Joanna? His queen? She turned a ghastly smile— the peasant girl in red! Odder still, both the girl and the king were covered with white worms! I moaned softly. The girl disappeared and the worms—real small creatures close by— devoured the gooseberries. The king's scarlet cape trailed on the ground behind him. The cape was heavily embroidered with hounds tearing apart their prey. John's head was burdened with a heavy helmet that might be real gold. He projected cold rage.

I'd never seen him truly angry before, not even in Fontevrault, where he'd played the vicious clown. Today he bristled with vitriol. The barons caught it, too—their fright was palpable. For the first time, I thought that Langton might be right about preferring the pope: This was the prince of darkness. He looked neither right nor left, spoke to no one.

Two knights helped him dismount; he took his place be-hind the table. His hands, heavily ringed, lay flat before him as a priest read our charter in sonorous tones.

The reading devoured most of the morning, during which the king moved not at all. Two legates then unrolled the five copies and two other legates affixed the Royal Seal to each one. A golden container of ink was placed before the king; he signed his name five times, after which twenty-five barons did the same. When the king rose, the barons came forward for the kiss of peace. John, still silent, stared at each one from his jewel-blue eyes; I thought he wouldn't kiss Robert fitzWalter, but he did. Then, in a blaze of noon sun, all the royal parties turned to Windsor whence they'd come, this time the king first. I watched, fascinated in spite of myself; at least the girl in red had truly disappeared.

The king paused. For one terrible heartbeat, he gazed directly at my gooseberry bush. Our eyes met; he didn't smile. In an instant, he rode on.

The barons began to talk to one another in a general melee of glee. Yet Lord Robert and Enoch remained somber. How could they be mirthful? After so many murderous years under this king? Who believed King John? How many felt, as I did, that he'd been memorizing their faces and names?

And he'd seen me.

16

THE SIGNING OF MAGNA CARTA SIGNIFIED THAT AT LAST ENOCH
and I could resolve our marital difficulties. Therefore, I was
surprised when he suggested that we show Leith London
while we were so close.

"What a bonny idea, except . . ." Leith put her finger in
my mouth.

"Ye doona want to?"

"Of course I do!" So we would discuss our annulment
later. And I had my own reasons for visiting London.

"Quhat be ye up to, Alix?"

"Are you afraid I'll still find the Crown Jewels?" I meant it
as a jape, but I had to turn away. Theo, oh, Theo.

"Ye have ulterior motive."

He was perceptive; I must be careful. Yet why shouldn't
he know?

Still, soothly Leith might never have such an opportunity
again, certainly not with both of her parents.

"Luik ye, Leith, that be the biggest city in all the world!"
Enoch pointed proudly over London's city wall.

"No, Paris is," I said.

"In France, maybe, boot I speak of England."

"You said the world. Paris has at least a hundred thousand people, London only about thirty-five thousand."

"Mun ye always be contrary?"

Leith pointed at the Thames. "River!"

"She knaws the Thames!" Enoch cried. "Be she nocht list?"

While his eyes glowed in pride and she flashed dimples, my heart broke. To lose my parents, Maisry, my friend Roderick, King Richard, my own Theo, even Bonel, though he still lived, now Enoch and Leith—would the list never end?

We went through Aldgate—the first time I hadn't been frightened to enter London. Yet something terrible was amiss—at this late date, was I experiencing my mother's second sight? I felt I was walking into a trap, John's trap. He'd seen me at Runnymede, I knew he had. And on Dere Street during the assassination attempt. My fear grew. I was becoming tinty with fear, for if he'd seen me at the assassination attempt, wouldn't he have acted? Yet I trembled; the uncanny trumps logic every time.

Enoch booked the same room we'd shared long ago when we'd first met, the room he'd shared with the Scots when we'd sought jewels; I, again, claimed the annex as my own. He seemed puzzled—the crawlspace to the annex was more suitable for Leith than for me.

"Leith would be frightened without you." At that moment she gripped his lower lip and he forgot me.

The following morning, he called through the tunnel: Would I please hurry, he wanted to take Leith to see St. Paul's Cathedral while the morning was cool. I called back that I had the flux; he should take her alone.

"Aye, sae do I!" he called back. "Too muckle celebration o' our charter! Cum, we'll splatter togeddir!"

"You go! My stomach is cold!"

"Ich doona belave ye, Alix!"

He started through the tunnel.

"You'll be sorry if you come here!"

He backed out.

In a few heartbeats, I heard Leith's voice outside.

I donned a plain brown smock, tied my head with the same material, and examined my saddlebag to be sure I had Bonel's letter. No one saw me depart.

Turning away from the Thames, I followed a winding lane toward the rising sun, East London. The day waxed hot—sweat poured into my eyes, yet even at this hour my narrow path thronged with people. Many sidled sideways, all pushed, and I did the same. Then the arches above that joined houses cast black shadows, which helped at first, then became dark alleys; I concentrated on puddles of slime and avoided the ubiquitous hogs, for to slip was to become instant pig mash, but even upright I had to avoid packs of bone-thin snarling yellow dogs. Once I climbed up a pedestal with its statue long gone while hungry hounds attacked a baby pig. Continuing, I stepped over two dead humans, too noisome even for the dogs. Yet their faces were eaten away—like Theo's. One old sow was finishing off an entire corpse.

The bell at St. Paul's clinked—were Enoch and Leith in the vestuary?

I took out Bonel's letter: "Jewelry Lane." None of the black corridors branching left and right was marked. When my path ceased at a grimy wall, I turned around. Now moving slowly, I found smudges at eye level; one read "Jewry Lane."

Did "Jewry" mean jewelry or Jews? A toothless hag shoved me with her basket; when I asked her, she said, "Both."

Sidling sideways, I studied one locked wooden door after another; many had smeared names, one marked "Y. Berengarius."

Y for Yossi? I knocked.

A peephole opened at once.

"*Que voulez-vous?*"

"Bonel!"

The peephole closed.

It opened again. "*Vous êtes une amie de M. Bonel?*"

"*Oui!*"

The door opened; I stepped inside.

"*Vous n'êtes pas Juive!*"

M. Berengarius definitely was Jewish with his telltale yarmulke. The room, though cramped, was spotless. Somewhere above, a chicken was boiling. I thrust Bonel's letter into Yossi's hand, then told him rapidly in French that Bonel had collected me as a hostage when King Richard was captured in Austria.

"So you're English?" asked M. Berengarius.

I was. Then, skipping my amorous history, I said that Bonel had protected me for more than a year in the Rouen Commune, where I'd learned the art of gemstone cutting, and told him how he'd finally sent me back to England.

"Hostage? You must be noble."

"A baroness," I conceded.

"Aren't you rich?"

"Things changed while I was away," I said vaguely. "I need employment."

"According to this letter, Bonel wants me to hire you."

"Aye, Bonel said that you have a shop for cutting and design."

He touched my cheek. "What is such a beautiful lady doing in trade?"

"I don't plan to sell—Bonel said you did that."

"Cutting gems is dirty work, sometimes dangerous."

"I'm not afraid, M. Berengarius. Bonel knew that—he quoted Maimonides."

"Wait here."

He retired through a door behind him. Outside, someone fell heavily. The small Jew returned with an even smaller woman garbed in the familiar blue. She was Rebecca, his wife. Would I repeat to her how I knew Bonel?

When I described his experiences in York, her hand reached for mine.

The Jewish couple again retired through the back door, and this time they were gone so long that I despaired.

M. Berengarius returned alone. I'd said that I'd learned the craft of cutting gems in Rouen. How could I prove it?

I handed him one of my sapphires. I hadn't cut it, I admitted, but I could describe exactly what had been done, including a close evocation of the original gemstone. He asked sharp questions about the use of saws versus the use of hammers.

Then he took the sapphire to show his wife.

This time he returned with a jug of fine ale. Did I know where Bonel was now?

I thought he was in the Middle East, married to a woman named Miriam, but I could be wrong on both counts. I'd not seen him or heard from him for many months.

M. Berengarius's expression softened. Yes, Bonel lived on the outskirts of Cairo; yes, he'd wed an Egyptian Jew; I might be interested to know that Bonel himself was now in the jewelry business. In fact, M. Berengarius and Rebecca bought many of their gemstones from him. Of course, Bonel continued his work with Jewish refugees, especially those from France or England, but he was more of a businessman. And a family man, he added slyly.

I said I was very happy to hear such good news of my friend. And, indeed, I was.

"Next time I write, I'll tell him that we've taken you into our business," Berengarius said.

"Then you'll . . . ?"

"Of course, if we can agree on terms. And we owe him—he finds us many fine stones."

"I know, Egyptian turquoise."

He smiled.

"If you mention me, could you tell him, please, how happy I am for him? How I had worried?"

Aye, he would do that. Could I wait one more heartbeat?

When he returned this time, it was with an offer. On Bonel's high praise of my skill, and because M. Berengarius and his wife couldn't handle their supply of gemstones, which therefore cut into their profits, he was willing to try me for a month without pay, after which I could have a percentage of whatever I created.

I accepted on the spot. Could he recommend a nearby house where I might rent a room?

He seemed surprised. I would live here, of course, in a room above the store. He and Rebecca would share their vittles, poor though they might be. In short, I could expect no cash, but I was being offered room and board. He then invited me to share the boiled chicken, which should now be ready.

Tears came to my eyes: I was in a commune again.

He even agreed to a few weeks' delay during which time I would return to my home for supplies, including a small cache of jewels.

When Enoch greeted me suspiciously at the inn, I told him that chicken broth had cured my flux.

Now London had new charms: we took a boat up and down the Thames to gaze on its many parks and castles from the river; we visited the horse fair on a Monday, gazed at the White Tower, even at Bermondsey Castle, where the king was not in residence. I memorized every event for future reference, as I'd unconsciously memorized every day of Theo's life. Leith, too, was memorizing; she gazed at Enoch's happy face with love, laughed at his japes, clapped her hands with joy. I forgot Lady Fiona; she would have her father. Then he suggested we go to Cornwall.

"Enoch, have you forgotten . . . ?"

"Doona ye think Leith shuld see wonders wi' both her parents?"

The same argument—I turned away.

Cornwall was soothly another country, more strange than Wales. Enoch held Leith firmly while she peered down cliffs at the churning sea, pointed out caves and quaint dwellings. We gazed at strange gashes in the hills—tin mines, Enoch thought. One stormy night, we watched a ship crash into the dangerous rocks along the shore. At last, however, even Enoch admitted it was time to return to Wanthwaite.

Now I demurred. "We made an agreement, milord."

"Doona spake of swich things in front o' Leith."

I didn't argue. Let him handle the inevitable conversation with his daughter; let him introduce her to the idea of Lady Fiona as well. I hoped she would remember me, aye, I did, but I also recognized that from this point on I must stay out of her life.

When Enoch told me that our return to Wanthwaite might take all summer because it was a rare opportunity to show Leith the wondrous castles between here and Wanthwaite, however, I was beyond astonishment. A whole summer—would M. Berengarius hold my position for me until autumn? Then Leith clapped her hands at the prospect of seeing great castles, and I succumbed. Yet I asked Enoch with my eyes what was in his mind? His bland eyes gave no reply.

At the first opportunity, I sent a runner with a missive for M. Berengarius, telling him I would be delayed.

England was a summer garden. *Enoch and England,* I recalled as if in a dream. I'd fought to return; now I must leave the countryside. Leave Enoch and Leith.

Enoch gazed over Leith's curls. "Castles be magic fer a little gel!"

It was true—I recalled how Maisry and I had pretended that an old catapult was a dragon. For Leith, mayhap dungeons and torture chambers in the bowels of castles would seem the homes of invisible giants; mayhap the towers and walkways would guard secret lovers. Or, instead of military fortresses, she might see crouching dragons.

Our first castle was in Northampton, a castle I'd never seen. As we approached, we choked on the stench of burning flesh.

"Do they ha'e a pig on a spit?" Leith asked.

Enoch pulled us off the path. In a moment, he became a warrior—I hadn't realized that he carried his pike!

"Dinna move! Ond be quiet!"

While I pulled my steed behind a bush, Enoch rode up a steep mound where he could see.

He returned.

"The castle be on fire!" Sweat poured down his face.

"The king again?"

"He ga'e the kiss of peace to the barons." His frown deepened. "Boot mayhap thar be some personal quarrel between the king and Northampton we doona knaw."

Never underestimate his perfidy.

We made a wide swath off the road through brambles and thorns. Then, suddenly, tiny folk blocked our way. As featureless as mushroom, they stared with frightened eyes. One man spoke in a difficult mumble: They were serfs, and when the king's army had attacked, the master had told them to hide in the wood. Was it safe to return now?

"King John—war he here?" Enoch asked.

Aye, the king himself. The man shuddered: a terrifying

sight it had been. The man, called Rupert, believed all the gentlefolk were dead. He stopped. And the house servants. And the peasants. What we saw before us was all that had survived. A woman joined him with an even more difficult dialect: They had sick and dead among them.

I gathered Leith close. Rupert—the small man who spoke—had I seen him before? Surely not, and yet . . .

Enoch abruptly rode into the gloom and disappeared. I was astonished—why hadn't he taken Leith? Suddenly, an arrow whizzed close to my ear and lodged in the heart of the man called Rupert. Several serfs screamed—he collapsed before I could shield Leith! The woman who'd told us about the dead ran into the crowd. When Enoch finally returned, he slid off his steed without speaking and wrenched the arrow from the dead man's chest, wiped blood on the grass, and salvaged his weapon. Horrified, I realized that he was in his war garb: horned hat, thwittle, a sword, even blue woad. The woad—or something—made his blue eyes wild. I jerked Leith's head in the opposite direction. She struggled back— she smiled.

I turned furiously at Enoch! Was this Scottish blood? Was my little girl contaminated?

"What ails you?" I cried. "How could you murder a harmless serf in front of your own daughter?"

"Nocht harmless." Enoch pushed the dead body with his foot, then thrust his hands up the man's sleeves and removed two sharp daggers. "He cum close sae he could use these!"

I gasped! Not at the daggers—I recognized the man myself! Lying in profile—that nose—like a parrot's beak—one of John's knights in Fontevrault Wood!

How had he gotten here? Who else among the serfs knew? How had Enoch known? More important—Leith. She was gazing calmly at the dead man. She wore no brechan feile or blue woad, but she was a Scot.

Enoch deliberately led us on a parallel path some distance from Dere Street. Yet when we reached Frothingham far to the east, we found smoldering ruins and the same desperate mushrooms in the forest. This time I helped Enoch test every one of them by demanding that they give their names and occupations; their accents proved they were English. Like the other serfs, I noted, they appeared to be young—no old people and few children. I deduced that such people at the extremes of life died soonest, though perhaps the middle group killed their ancients and their babes for greater mobility. In any case, from that point, our mushrooms proliferated exactly in proportion to the burning castles we passed. We had to stop in Nottingham to forage for food.

Enoch had no illusions about the danger: John had been here, might still be here, but our case was desperate. He hid our serfs in the famous nearby Sherwood Forest and told me to bring Leith and follow him. He assured me that he would hide us in some safe place while he entered the town with three hand-chosen male serfs; he would be more comfortable knowing we were near than leaving us with the mob. The serfs he selected understood Enoch's instructions, and they had the same fierce eyes. Enoch knew Nottingham well, since we'd had one meeting there with Stephen Langton, and he hugged the city wall to an opening into an ancient churchyard.

He signaled silently that Leith and I should hide among the tombstones, but not enter the sanctuary.

The wet grass was long, the graves overgrown around smooth gray stones; it was easy to conceal ourselves among a bed of rhubarb plants. Enoch and his three "knights" left.

Though hardly peaceful, the graveyard was silent; far in the distance, I heard male voices cry out. Then a low moan nearby.

A huge milch cow grazed among the tombstones.

"Moo-moo," said Leith.

I put my hand over her mouth.

The moan repeated.

"Be sommun thar?" Hardly more than a whisper.

I pushed Leith deeper into our rhubarb. Very quietly, I crawled on all fours toward the voice. A very old man lay prone in his own blood beside a lopsided stone cross, a cow herdsman to judge by his rags. His eyes were dim with pain: His right hand was cut off.

"*Benedicite!*" I quickly threw the amputated part into the bush. "Who did this terrible act?"

King John—oh, not the king himself, but one of his foreign routiers; he'd said that old Tom had had a hand in the new charter—this was his reward!

"I knaw naught o' no charter."

But I did.

He couldn't read or write—how could he make a charter? Mayhap the routier had been confused, mayhap the king objected to Tom's bringing his cow into holy ground to graze. Yet hadn't the priest said he could? Hadn't his da and his da before him brought their cows here? Kept the weeds down, especially on old graves where no one came to tend them. Would I tell the king so?

Enoch tapped my shoulder. He took in the scene at a glance and signaled I should follow. I started to speak—he put a hand over my lips. Old Tom was now twitching in his death throes. Only one serf followed Enoch.

We had beef and milk and sour cherries that night. We all took small portions and packed the remainder for tomorrow. Enoch, now a Scottish chieftain again, circumvented castles as we marched north, though he sought survivers in the forests.

We happened on Rockingham by mistake. Though it looked to be an old burn, we found one of the original family still alive, an ancient female, the grandam of the castle, who had hidden in a dry well. She died on the first day we rescued her.

We passed close enough to know that Dunmow was burning, then York.

"But he already sacked it once!" I cried about York.

"Stay here; I'll see yif I can halp."

He returned hours later. Lord Robert de Ros still lived; he would say no more.

We both now had a single thought: Wanthwaite.

Once off Dere Street, we passed the lane to Dunsmere without comment; we smelled smoke.

On the near side of the Wanthwaite River, a few palings still burned—Enoch signaled our followers to stay back. He carried Leith as we walked silently on foot up the park, into the spinney. An eerie sensation of déjà vu gripped me—I expected to find my dead parents at the top.

Wanthwaite was no more. Flat. Not a wall remaining. Smoke still rose from where the kitchen court and the Great Hall had stood. Our new tower overlooking the fells didn't even smolder—nothing remained but cold ashes.

Enoch heaved with sobs. I pulled him to my shoulder. Neither of us spoke.

Leith, also sobbing, squirmed between us.

When he'd recovered sufficiently, we approached the ruins cautiously. Where were the people?

Enoch pointed to our wood. No one came.

We both whirled at a rustling behind us. A man, utterly black with soot, came toward us with outstretched arms. I recognized a woman behind him.

"Nicola! Oh, Nicola!" I clutched her close.

"I came to warn you," said the man with Lord Robert's voice, "and found this! I thought—Nicola thought—oh God, who are they?"

"'Wina!" Leith screamed.

Deus juva me, she was right! On the spit—one of Edwina's flaxen braids was still intact on a shriveled piece of meat! She and Thorketil—it had to be—were splayed on a large iron spit we'd used for boars.

Nicola flung herself into the ashes. Lord Robert pulled her away.

All of us wept, but I was most aware of Enoch. Those sobs weren't about a title or money—he loved Wanthwaite.

"They must have pretended . . ." I gasped.

"Aye!"

But why?

We turned to the labyrinth. There we found Gruoth and Donald and Dugan and most of our household, all wretchedly hungry, all besmattered with waste! Then our serfs and peasants came from our woods. Everyone was dazed; everyone glad to be alive.

Edwina and Thorketil, we learned, had deliberately pretended to be Enoch and me to gain time.

The following day, Donald accompanied me to the sisters' house by the sea. We returned with six pigs, my two original ducks, plus ten others, one cow, and two nags. I'd taken Bonel's money, which had survived inside its leopard sack, but the sisters refused to accept coins. While we were away, Enoch had constructed an open-sided hut in the forest for our new dependents. Gruoth had overseen the cleaning of the labyrinth, where the rest of us slept. We now used our new metal blade from Germany to make our plows easier for men to pull. Our oxen had been slaughtered, of course, as well as our horses.

The serfs ate raw birds that they caught with their hands. Everyone else used arrows; we didn't eat our catch raw, though it was difficult to start a fire. We gathered sufficient berries and roots to serve with our game. The men built a crude shelter where the Great Hall had been. Then Agins, a carpenter from Dunsmere who knew how to do wattle and daub, quickly constructed one cottage for us, then three more.

The cheese house had burned, but not the cheeses. On

the pretext of searching for food, I found my cache of jewels intact. I thrust them in a sack.

The assault on Wanthwaite—indeed, on all northern barons—changed our assumption that our charter had made any difference. If anything, England was more dangerous than ever. I knew it; Enoch knew it. And Lord Robert knew it as well.

After my first gratitude that he'd come to warn us had passed, I marveled that he would stay in such wretched conditions.

"Dunmow be burned," Enoch reminded me.

"But he has so many castles. Surely one must be intact."

"Aye."

One evening as we shared mead in our cottage, Lord Robert looked out on our patchy late oats. "Our charter is worthless. You know why, don't you?"

"Tell me."

"The king added a clause that it would be in effect only fifteen days, and he kept his word."

I jumped up. "Did Stephen Langton know?"

"That would be my guess. The pope wrote that if John signed the charter, he would no longer be king. I daresay this was Langton's version of a compromise." He pressed his lips. "He's the pope's man."

"Whar be the wallydrag?"

"Somewhere in Europe, beyond all our reach." Lord Robert continued: King John had harried all the way up to Scotland, and sooner or later he would come back.

Despite our bravura, we all fell silent. There wasn't much more to destroy in Wanthwaite, but there were still people.

"Harrying be the werst kind o' attack there be." Enoch looked at me.

"Stephen Langton," Lord Robert mused. "Yes, it explains . . ."

"He had two masters," I said bitterly. "Pope Innocent and King John."

"But not us."

"No."

Nicola spoke shyly. "What will you do? Write another charter?"

Enoch ignored the question. "Sae the king ha'e heavenly permission!"

"You don't believe that!" I scolded.

"Nay, this king doesna need permission, nocht fram heaven nor fram auld Clootie."

"You're right, Enoch; he would have done it anyway." I couldn't contain tears. "But to burn Wanthwaite!"

After a silence, Enoch changed the subject. "Hu fares Eustace?"

"I'm riding out tomorrow to check." Lord Robert walked into the darkness.

He returned within a week.

"As I suspected, the king went into Scotland."

"Did King Alexander defeat him thar?" Enoch asked eagerly.

"Rumor says that the Scottish king surrendered at Berwick; all southern Scotland is now under John's rule." Lord

Robert put a sympathetic arm around Enoch's shoulder. "At least the Highlands are free."

Enoch groaned.

Lord Robert continued. "Not all castles were razed, you know. If the lord was in residence, John offered a way out."

"York's wasna burned," Enoch agreed, "nocht completely."

"Do you know why?"

Neither Enoch nor I could answer.

"King John's men raped and killed one of York's daughters, the one called Mary Margaret, I believe, and threatened the other two. Lord Robert de Ros begged for clemency, whereupon the king said he would spare the family and castle for ten thousand pounds, *to show that you do love us.* I believe Lord Eustace de Vesci gave a like sum. I hate a man who either seduces or kills a lord's family!"

Nicola abruptly left.

"Ich doona belave that Eustace . . . !" Enoch jumped to his feet. "Eustace would fight!"

"Would you, Lord Enoch?" Lord Robert's face crumbled. "Lady Gunmora is dead."

Enoch was too stunned to speak. So was I. We gazed silently at the bucolic scene before us. Two larks dove into our grain.

"She was a fine woman," Lord Robert continued in a choked voice. "Furthermore, if you came up Dere Street, you saw only half the destruction. From Scotland, John harried down the other side of England with equal ferocity; he razed close to fifty castles to my knowledge."

The larks rose again. Then sang.

Lord Robert's eyes were bloodshot. "What do you suggest we do, Lord Enoch? Call a meeting of the twenty-five barons who signed our charter? Assuming that they're still alive, do you think they'll accuse the king of breaking faith? Evoke the Magna Carta? Technically, he was within his rights: He waited the fifteen days."

Enoch replied heavily, "Can Magna Carta help at all in this case?"

"You know it can't."

Enoch stood. "Ye be suggestin' somewhat."

"Any treaty is only as good as the people who sign. We made a pact with the devil."

"Yif ye're suggestin' assassination, find anudder mon."

The moon rose over our plowed field before Lord Robert spoke again. "I don't want you to kill the king, Enoch."

"Then who?" I asked.

He took his time. "No one; the king will die a natural death sometime."

I laughed. "You have a long wait for that event. His mother, Queen Eleanor, died at eighty-two."

"But his father, some say, died young of natural causes," Lord Robert repeated. "Others say John murdered him. In either case, John's death must be natural when it comes."

I heard his tone, not his words. "You mean, *seem* natural."

"Seem, be, the same thing."

"Seem, murder, the same thing."

"Sum Scottish kings war murdered."

Again we were silent.

"I still prefer the word 'natural.' "

"To *seem* natural is still murder."

Lord Robert put his hand on my arm. "Do you have the skill?"

"Oh yes. Now ask if I have the will."

"I willna have Alix be the assassin!" Enoch shouted.

"Hush! Of course not, I agree. But neither do I want her to be a victim, as Gunmora . . ."

Or Theo.

"The king moves constantly," I said slowly. "I don't mean his invasions or his harrying, but just his ordinary life is on the road. No one knows where he is."

"Or where he'll suddenly appear," Lord Robert agreed. "Remember Eustace's story of how the king arrived at Alnwick with his entire entourage?"

Enoch muttered, "Leith . . ."

"Do you want her to suffer the fate of Theo?" I rose. "Where is the king going after he finishes harrying? Do you know?"

"Dover Castle, I think. He's gotten wind of the French invasion."

"Quhat French invasion?"

"Most of the barons want to invite another king to rule us; Prince Louis of France, for example. They see the problem as we do: John is hopeless."

"Quhy nocht King Philip?"

"Prince Louis has a more legitimate claim. He's married to Lady Blanche, Queen Eleanor's granddaughter. But this Prince Louis . . ."

"Is another foreigner," I finished for him, "and you feel we've had enough invasions from the Continent. England is for the English!"

"You read my thought!"

"Aye," said Enoch, forgetting that he was Scottish.

Again we sat in silence.

"It won't be easy," Lord Robert warned. "He's clever."

Never underestimate his intelligence.

"No one ever knows where he'll be," I repeated.

"No king should be abuv the law."

"He's much too clever for a frontal attack." Lord Robert stood. "Clever, but still vulnerable. He must have some weak point."

"He eats and drinks to excess."

Lord Robert shook his head. "Poison leaves traces. Unless you know one . . . A natural death . . ."

"Ye want Alix to be yer assassin," Enoch declared.

"Oh no, I happily volunteer—I'll do anthing she tells me to. As I said, *seems.* The actual person may be difficult . . ."

Enoch spoke so softly I could hardly hear him. "Ich doona want her to tak the blame."

"If we're clever, there shouldn't be any blame," I said.

"Exactly so," Lord Robert approved.

"Do you have any notion of where the king will be when he finishes his harrying?" I asked again.

"Dover."

I rose. "Then I'll prepare to go at once."

"Nocht wi'outen me." Enoch rose as well.

"And Leith?"

"She'll stay here."

By which I knew he was serious.

I was serious as well.

And terrified.

And elated.

Who Killed King John?

Book Three

17

Through the gray-green frets of a thornbush, I studied the guards at the curtain wall of Dover Castle. Six people applied for entry while I watched; three were turned away. Finally, when two guards had departed the gate, leaving only one on duty, I heaved my bosom and waddled forward. The guard turned dead eyes in my direction and asked perfunctory questions in a thick foreign argot: What was my business with the king? I pretended not to understand and repeated Queen Isabella's name again and again. How long did I intend to stay? It depended, I had come to serve the queen, I replied in langue d'oc. My name was Lady Marie-Françoise; I was from Aquitaine. He stared at my papers uncomprehendingly, then at my burgeoning belly and my many moles with obvious distaste. Still, he was uneasy; he clawed my papers with his dirty paws. When I cried suddenly, "Queen Eleanor!" he waved me through.

Panting, I paused for a moment inside the gate to permit my heart to beat normally again. I was Daniel entering the lion's den, for wasn't King John in residence? Aye, the red flags fluttering above said he was, which I already knew. At the same time, I was triumphant, for hadn't Enoch begged me to reconsider? Hadn't he argued against my plan for days?

Yet soothly I was still far from inside Dover Castle. I stood now in a narrow alleyway between the new curtain wall and the older castle wall, also gated, also guarded. I crouched behind a shrub to prepare for my second assault. My hip pads had slipped, and one of the moles on my face had dropped off somewhere. I found the purple pimple in the sand, and lost my bust—*Benedicite,* I must add a second strip of linen to hold it in place. My abdomen had also slipped a notch, not enough for anyone to notice, but enough to affect my walking. I minced as if holding my water.

The second set of guards—ten in number—were more literate and more diligent. Dressed in the familiar black and red of the king's official guard, each one examined the pass I'd received from Queen Isabella; then they checked my person with hard piercing eyes (though not with their hands, *Deo gratias*); one seemed to know me—was he from Beynac?—but surely not. They engaged me in conversation in langue d'oc; chirping and huffing, I must nonetheless have sounded like a native. I lowered my eyes, however, pretending that something had entered one, for Enoch had warned that my silver eyes might give me away. The guards passed me through.

The castle proper was still a mile away. The lane was almost invisible in the patchy grass. Though I'd studied this park many times from above, it had appeared less rough and not of such great size from a distance. I glanced over my shoulder, then hiked my left breast.

The whole area sloped subtly uphill from the Channel; the ancient Roman lighthouse, though still to my left, was more squat and more decrepit when seen close; the half-dead linden trees cast faint shade, the soil was rocky and sandy.

Dover Castle itself was neither a country house nor a castle so much as a tall, forbidding military fortress. Pocked with arrow slits, the square behemoth loomed ever taller as I neared, a hundred feet high. More, for the base sat in a declivity between two small hillocks. A perfect abode for the king of darkness. My entire body trembled; I looked over the wall behind me to find the inn of St. Martin's, where Enoch and I had taken residence. The faint outline of its thatch reassured me.

A red flag with three snarling lions waved above the entrance: aye, John was in residence.

Again, I faced a group of guards, Brabantian routiers, no doubt whatsoever, yet tall and blond as Vikings. They probed my credentials again, repeating the same questions in Norman French while I replied in langue d'oc; we didn't pretend not to understand one another.

Then one disappeared inside the tower; when he reappeared, it was in the company of four knights. I struggled not to gasp—I knew these men! Alberic de Marines, Evrard de la Beauvrière, William de Gamache, Baldwin de Béthunes—all knights from king Richard's court. *Deus juva me*, to face men I knew well and who knew me, especially Baldwin—oh, certes they would see through my silly disguise. Why hadn't I anticipated that John would take over Richard's household?

But they hardly even glanced at me. I was almost hurt, then bemused: I was getting a taste of what lay ahead in my later years.

They gestured me through the castle door, chatting and japing in langue d'oc about some tournament, as if I weren't there. Now their indifference gave me opportunity to examine the castle, for my life might depend on familiarity with its design.

Dover Castle was a hollow square with a private garden in its center, thus forming still another wall around the family's private space. Memorizing my entrance as if it were an exit, I noted that the small rooms nearest the door had windows overlooking the park; the rooms themselves, obviously for storage, were piled high with rusting armor, the outer windows accessible only if one climbed over the armor; there were actually four such rooms before we entered what must be the Great Hall. A long, narrow dark room constructed entirely of Caen stone except for red-tiled floors and with no windows whatsoever, it nonetheless boasted Toulousian tapestries depicting tournaments on the walls, and we passed a long table in the center, nothing more. At the far end of the Great Hall, my guides signaled I should wait. In a few heartbeats, Richard's top butler, an older man named John Williams, stared at me with milky eyes.

I held my breath; if anyone recognized me, he would. Whether it was his fading vision or the darkness or my disguise or the fact that neither of us spoke that saved me, I didn't know. At a signal, I followed his rapid pace through a series of fourteen more dark storage rooms, some piled with more armor, some with rugs and hangings, at least two—maybe three—with crates of foodstuffs. John Williams turned to be sure I didn't stumble when we stepped briefly into the garden, then back into the tower.

He spoke over his shoulder, "The queen's quarters."

I nodded, with my eyes lowered. The tiled flooring was

now polished, the storage rooms dedicated to feminine wardrobe. Herbs and flower juices masked any noisome human odor. More Toulousian tapestries disguised the walls, these with beautiful damsels kneeling amid flowers, and sleepy unicorns. In the distance, a countertenor sang his sad plaint of love to the pluck of a lute.

Master William turned again. "This is the queen's Great Hall."

A large chamber opened before us and I could no longer lower my eyes, for I must see. *Benedicite*, never had I beheld such riches, such beauty. Flowered tapestries billowed across deep, flowered carpets underfoot. If the black tower was hell, this was heaven! Small tables loaded with cakes surrounded an indolent queen stretched on a long couch. She held out her hand and smiled. Such beauty! Such sweetness! I clapped my hand over my mouth to keep from crying aloud! Blue green tilted eyes, hair thick and black as any Gitano's, teeth white as ivory, lips like cherries . . .

"Lady Marie-Françoise, at last!" She sang rather than spoke.

She swung off her chaise, whereupon her rich tunic fell open to display high pointed breasts and a black furry animal between her legs. The queen was naked!

She laughed—I tried to hold my gaze on her face. Beautiful, aye, very white whites of the eyes, long curling fingernails and toenails.

"Look all you please!" She laughed again. "Do I remind you of Queen Eleanor?"

And I understood—or thought I did. Though Eleanor

had been ancient in the years I was with Richard, I'd heard rumors of her licentious dress when young. Only what was this
beauty doing with a murderous king?

"Well, now you know why I accepted your application—
as everyone knows—I'm quite besotted with my departed
mother-in-law. But why did you seek me?"

So soon! I swallowed nervously. "I was curious to see one
of such beauty, but I admit to an ulterior motive. I pray you
can gain me audience with the king."

"Same as everyone." She dismissed me on the spot.

Though surrounded by a dozen laughing young beauties,
each in rich attire, each sipping Bordeaux from a silver goblet,
I felt utterly rebuffed until one young lady stepped forward
and introduced herself as Lady Damiana; could she please
show me to my quarters?

Thank you, yes, I said, and hoped I hadn't alienated the
queen forever. I followed Damiana again through the same
small rooms until we reached the ladies' quarters, a dark
space covered with mats for sleeping with the curtained
queen's bed at one end. Where did the ladies go, I wondered,
when the king visited his lady? I thanked Damiana profusely
and declined her invitation to return to the queen's Hall.

"There will be more music," the lady argued, "and fine
fruit to go with the cakes. Are you certain?"

Yes, I was weary from a long journey.

In short order, I lay alone in a closet. In the distance,
music wafted softly, followed by women's laughter. I crept out
through the series of small rooms, out through a high window
above the arms, and into the garden. The queen's quarter was
the only room with light. Doubled over, I crept forward to the

sound of music. Once there, I removed one of Bonel's small diamonds from my false breasts, held it to the queen's torchlight, which it reflected brilliantly, and turned it thrice toward the top of the hill. I waited for twenty heartbeats before a torch arched three times in reply.

Enoch knew I'd entered the castle safely.

The queen was haughty and remote the following day, as if I'd never viewed her naked body. More disturbing, she made no mention of my request.

I glimpsed the king myself, however, on that very same day. I quickly ducked behind a bush to view him through the wands, and I didn't believe he'd seen me. He talked earnestly with two prelates, then led them into the chapel at the far end of the castle. Though his back was turned, I saw at once that he'd lost weight since Runnymede; no longer a slender boy to be sure, he was nonetheless well proportioned, almost a normal man. Harrying is good exercise, I thought. My heart thumped like a kettle. To see him, fat or slender, was to recall Thorketil and Edwina, Lady Gunnora, the peasant girl. Theo.

On the third day, Queen Isabella summoned me to her side to ask questions about Queen Eleanor. Now most demurely gowned in a white tunic sparkling with brilliants at her throat, her manner was condescending. Did John remind me of his mother in appearance? They had the same coloring, did they not? And the same intelligence?

I granted the coloring, both with honey-blond hair and similar smiles, but pleaded ignorance about intelligence.

Though I knew Queen Eleanor to be exceedingly intelligent—intelligent enough to conceal her sharp intuitions—
I'd never met the king except for having seen him from a
distance. If she could get me the interview I sought, I would
make a special effort to appraise his mind.

Her green eyes were flecked with brown dots. "I trowe,
Lady Marie-Françoise, that you may be more crafty than either the king or his mother." Didn't I know that her word was
good? Please be patient.

I was crafty enough not to remind her that she hadn't
given her word. Was she giving it now? No, I would not be
patient with an evasive queen. Intelligent or no, I was determined.

The days passed. Though I learned her habits, the queen
evaded me. Except for my purpose, I would have avoided her
as well, for she irritated me with her false hospitality. Nor did
I see the king again. The entire atmosphere at Dover was
poisonous—everyone seemed false. Lady Damiana and Lady
Festalle became friends of a sort, but both were discreet
about the queen, by which I gathered that something was seriously amiss. Did John abuse her? I knew better than to ask
them about the king. Sometimes at night, I crept into the garden. Once Enoch signaled again; it was a question asking if I
was still all right. I signaled back that I was, though I was far
from certain.

One morning I met the queen in the garden by accident.
Since we couldn't escape one another, she took my arm and
resumed her queries about Queen Eleanor. Of course, their
coloring was different, but did I not think their features similar? Even the king said so, which was one reason he'd fallen in

love with her at first sight. Did I know their story? And he'd told her that first day that she reminded him of his mother. I was stunned. By now I was certain that it would be hard to find two women more far apart than Isabella and Eleanor: one dark, one fair, one seriously seductive, one playful and evasive with men. Yet I did sense that Isabella shared Eleanor's political ambitions. And, while I had no proof in either case, I suspected that both hated their husbands. For, despite her descriptions of their courtship and certain intimate details about their honeymoon in Normandy, Isabella despised John. She didn't have to say so; I knew. Yet, instinctively, I couldn't sympathize with her.

On another occasion, Queen Isabella had her four children by John with her. Now I was truly shocked at her disdain. Surely no one was responsible for one's parents—I thought of Theo and King Richard. The oldest, a blond boy called Henry after his grandfather, struck me as a sullen lethargic child, whereas the youngest, a girl, named Joanna (after her father or her bastard half sister?), was as beautiful as her mother. All the children were subdued in manner; all feared Isabella.

Once, while alone on a bench, Isabella told me the tale of Hugh de Lusignan, her fiancé before John had seen her. If she'd married Hugh, she asserted, they would have ruled Lusignan, Poitou, Angoulême, even Aquitaine, and by her tone, she considered these counties to be infinitely better than England. Though I bristled at the insult to my beloved country, I could agree that that part of Europe certainly excelled in charm and sophistication. Despite her own proclivities, Queen Isabella had married John because her mother had seen him as a better match than Hugh; as for Isabella herself, she admitted that she'd been intrigued by the prospect of being Queen Eleanor's daughter-in-law. Also, she'd believed then that John shared her enchantment with Aquitaine, that they would live there as Richard had done. He was an Aquitanian in his bones, she claimed. She didn't mention the vaunted physical attraction between them.

I would have avoided the queen after that except for my project. I next viewed her from the shadow of a bush where I was once again repairing my face. Padding the body under layers of clothing is a simple matter compared to maintaining more exposed parts. I kept wads of tree gum in my mouth to extend my cheeks; I'd pasted the usual dead snails on my gums and bits of bark on my skin to serve as raised moles, and even added two dried grapes for special repulsiveness. Yet I had no mirror, nor did I entirely trust Enoch's approval. Therefore, I sought the shade.

Queen Isabella, walking alone, passed quite close to where I was hiding. Her breasts were decorously bound in some white stuff again, her kerchief was high on her neck, and she wore a sleeveless tunic embroidered with parrots and turtle doves. Even her wild black hair was braided and looped. As she passed, I realized how young she was, still hardly more than a child.

"Lady Marie-Françoise, why are you hiding? Are you spying on me?"

Startled, I stepped into the path. "Why no, Your Highness, of course not. I dare not expose my skin to the sun, that's all. I break out in sores of the most hideous nature."

She stared at my face, which was no doubt blotchy. "I apologize; I'm accustomed to spies, you see." She peered closer. "Your skin, indeed, looks flushed. What a burden for someone born under southern skies!"

"Thank you, Your Majesty."

She sank to the grass. "May we talk?"

"I should like nothing better." Now that I had her sympathy, however, I retired back into the shadow.

"You called me *Your Majesty*—do you think of me as a queen?"

This was the last thing I'd expected. "Of course; you're married to the king, and you're . . ."

"When I married my Lord John, Queen Eleanor still received the queen's gold as the queen of England; after she died, King Richard's widow, Berengaria, was called queen of England and received all incomes from Gascony plus an allowance she forced from the king; John's first wife, Isabella of Gloucester, still resided in the royal palace at Winchester after our marriage and received incomes from her estate as well as gifts from the king. I receive nothing, have nothing from England, am soothly impoverished, so how am I a queen?"

I was aghast. I certainly wouldn't compare my lot with Queen Isabella's, for they were at different social levels and had different causes, and yet there were similarities; Enoch had stolen my lands and title and, except for Bonel's generosity, I would have nothing.

"Do you not have incomes of your own?"

She laughed. "Oh yes, in Angoulême, where I'm the sole heiress. I let moneys accrue there so the king can't seize them." She fell silent for a long period. "It's strange: John's father and his male line were kings and his mother was a famous duchess, yet I am better connected than any of these other queens: My mother was cousin to King Philip of France and to the king of Hungary in the Carpathian Mountains."

"Carpathian?" I breathed.

She didn't reply. "By her second marriage, she became connected to the king of Jerusalem. Wouldn't you say that that's better than the Plantagenets?"

"Indeed."

"I'm a poor little queen. Without a pence."

Abruptly, she rose and wandered out of sight. Though much depressed to learn that the Carpathian Mountains actually existed, I continued to wad my wax until she returned.

She bent to my bush. "My mother, Alice, was a famous beauty."

"Was? Is she dead?"

"Just recently, yes. She wed three times, the last time to my father, the Count of Angoulême."

"Usually men outlive women."

She laughed. "And you're from the south? Most men die in battle before their wives."

I didn't argue, though childbirth took women, not men.

"Yet my first fiancé, Hugh of Lusignan, is still alive." She then recounted how she and Hugh had been betrothed while she was still a child; her father had wanted them to wed, but Hugh had refused until she reached puberty. Unfortunately for Hugh, John had had no such scruples; he'd married her within a week of first seeing her.

Queen Isabella was so luscious, so developed, that it was difficult to think of her as a child.

"What year were you born?" I asked.

"In 1191, the year my mother married my father."

She'd been eight when she'd married John. Even political advantages couldn't excuse such debauchery.

"He taught me everything I know." She laughed again. "About the body, about power. Or are they the same thing?"

She wandered off before I could reply.

I decided to be more aggressive. The next time I accosted her was inside the tower. "Your Majesty, you spoke to me quite openly about your lack of riches."

"Or control as queen," she added. "Yes?"

"Then you'll surely understand my desperate need to see the king, for I, too, am impoverished, and I support my grandchildren in Aquitaine. For that reason, I came here to sell some of my jewels to the king. Won't you help me?"

"You want me to set up an appointment with him."

"Would you?" My voice became breathless, as if this were the first time I'd asked.

She touched my cheek. "How are your sunspots?"

"Not too bad since it's been raining. And thank you for asking, Your Majesty."

She withdrew her hand. "I'll see what I can do, though I make no promises. The king is occupied—he expects an invasion from France momentarily."

Which I already knew. Prince Louis of France had accepted the invitation to take over England; the barons had promised their cooperation when he landed.

The queen turned to leave, then paused. "What sort of jewels do you have? Brooches? Pendants?"

"I have a single ruby with me as an example, though I have more. No, it's not set." Why mention my small diamond?

She lost interest. "I'll try."

Days became weeks, but while I saw the queen daily, we had no more private conversations. Though the month was now August, our proximity to the Channel kept the weather cool and moist. I became accustomed to maintaining my disguise. I now spent every afternoon in the garden—still under my shrub, so I could avoid contacts—and often enjoyed watching small children at play. These were John's hostages under the queen's care, though she was never present. Then one day the queen's children joined the six little hostages—babies really, for two could hardly walk.

I thought of Leith.

I thought of Theo.

As the summer waned, so did my disguise. Though I never lost vigilence, twice I picked up black spots that had fallen from my face onto the floor. No one remarked on the accidents, which doesn't mean that no one noticed. I continued to wait on the queen in the early evening when she invited her ladies for a merry conversation, but I rarely saw her to speak to privately. Isabella was undoubtedly a seductive woman (though she never displayed her breasts again), beautiful in her face and figure, most excellently gowned, clean to a fault. It did strike me as odd, however, that I never saw her with the king. Were they estranged? Was he involved with some other lady?

Had I chosen the wrong messenger? When could I see him? Who else could get me an audience? I became alarmed that weeks passed and still Isabella made no mention of my desired audience with the king. Had she simply forgotten? If I hadn't had that brief glimpse of John, I would suspect that the king was not in residence because I never saw him with Isabella. In the dining *salle*, I ate with the other ladies two tiers below the royal platform and was careful never to look back, fearing that turning my head might release another wart, but I could hear. The king was not present.

Then one afternoon I ran into the queen and a stranger in the garden. Her friend was a man a few years older than she was, obviously a man of the south, possibly from Angoulême or Aquitaine, for, like her, he had thick black hair, startlingly white teeth, and clear green eyes with flecks of brown. Like her that day, he was dressed most elaborately in a scarlet tunic topped with a gold cape, and he wore gold boots on his feet. They could have been twins.

"Oh, Lady Marie-Françoise, I'm delighted that we happened on you!" the queen cried with obvious dismay. "This is my brother—Lord Peter de Joiny—who comes from your part of the world! Gascony, was it not? He knew Lady Mamile!"

He kissed my hand lightly. "Have we ever met, Lady Marie-Françoise? You look familiar."

My heart stopped. "I think not, my lord, though I could be mistaken. Did you ever visit Mercadier in Beynac?" We then tested each other's veracity by tracing the movements of Lady Mamile, which was the same as tracing the movements of Queen Eleanor and therefore easy.

"I did meet her handmaid once," he said, "Lady Alix of Wanthwaite. The concubine of the late king."

My heart stopped, then raced, as Queen Isabella took up the theme. "John used to say I was the most beautiful creature alive, until he recalled this same Lady Alix. She must have been devastating—did you ever see her?"

"I heard of her," I said as if without interest, "but I never saw her."

Both the queen and her brother stared at me—did they suspect? Then, satisfied, they changed the subject.

"Aren't I fortunate to have such an attentive brother?" the queen simpered. "I get so lonely in this dank fortress!"

I assured her that she was indeed fortunate, though her life seemed easy to me and certainly she had all the company she wanted. Still, as an only child myself, I would have given much for such a sympathetic brother.

I saw Lord Peter with her every day for at least a week, though we didn't speak again until he said goodbye to me the day before he left to attend his estates close to Winchester. The queen's eyes looked as if she had been weeping.

His estates must have been in fine shape, for he was back in four days, hardly time to ride to Winchester and return. He and the queen spent every afternoon in the garden thereafter.

I knew I should avoid them—the mention of "Lady Alix" had been no accident, I feared—and succeeded. Then, one late afternoon, I barely missed stumbling over the brother's golden boots. I grabbed the lilac bush whence the boots were extended and waited. No one marked my presence. Heart still racing, I looked again: beside the golden boots were two bare feet, the queen's.

The situation was obvious. Even more obvious was my own danger! Had they seen me? Did they know I'd seen them? I must escape—I wanted no part in their deception, not when it was against King John! *Deus juva me!*

If the king ever believed I was in collusion with his queen—well, I need not ask my fate. I cursed her silently for threatening my real plan, which was dangerous enough.

I sought a bench just off the path at the far end of the garden. I wouldn't move farther until it was safe.

Queen Isabella approached so silently that I didn't hear her.

"Lady Marie-Françoise!"

I jumped.

"You're the very person I wanted to see. May I join you?"

Smelling strongly of love, she slid onto the bench beside me. She spoke with artificial gaity. I was amazed at her steely poise.

"You're a dear, Lady Marie-Françoise, not to nag me about your appointment with the king. Did you think I'd forgotten? Not at all, I assure you! No, on the contrary, I've been a busy bee on your behalf! I told him about your ruby and he's most interested!"

"Yes?" I stared into her beautiful, corrupt face.

"But, like all men, he needed nudging. I have an appointment with the king this very evening—soon, in fact—and I thought to nag him a bit then." She turned a hard face. "Of course, one favor begets another, does it not? You will assure me of your discretion."

"I assure you."

Our eyes held.

That same afternoon, she sent Lady Damiana with a message for me: I was to meet with the king in his office at the far end of the castle at sundown.

John Williams came to escort me to my appointment. By now I had my disguise completely in control and therefore trotted behind him with much more assurance than I'd had just a few weeks ago when I'd first come to Dover Castle. If he noticed, he made no sign. My only problem was that it was my time of the month; I hoped my cassis fragrance would confound Raoul.

John Williams walked briskly through the small rooms, through the Great Hall, and into the garden and a light rainfall. A sea storm was brewing; the sky was dark, the wind strong (though not cold), and I worried that the rain might wash away my moles. Though John Williams had no such concern, he ran to the doorway at the far end of the garden.

Both of us panted briefly in the dark before we began our climb. The narrow twist of stairs had footpads only on the wall side; though John Williams lacked the gallantry to offer me his hand, his heavy breathing showed me the way. At the top, four floors up, we entered a small anteroom where three knights lounged around a clerk turning pages in a large open book on his desk. John Williams muttered something to the secretary, then left without a glance at me.

As there was no place to sit, I leaned in a corner. A tall man in religious robes walked through the room without checking with the secretary and entered directly into the king's chamber. He spoke angrily in Latin; someone—the king? —replied. Then, for no reason that I could see, the secretary rose: "Is Lady Marie-Françoise here?"

I came forward.

"Follow me."

Together we entered the king's large office, where he was conducting business. He stood in the center, unmistakable in his scarlet robes (I realized with a start that this was the same robe Lord Peter de Joiny had worn). His short slender body, boyish face, shoulder-length blond waves, dark, arched brows over jewel-blue eyes with their thick, black fringe. He held a silver cup of wine in his hands. Yet there were differences from previous impressions: Despite the wine, he was not intoxicated; he listened intently and spoke little, and thus gained authority.

The prelate was still talking angrily. At last the king lost patience: "We thank you, Legate Pandulph, and we thoroughly understand the position of Pope Innocent. Please assure the pontiff that the barons' Magna Carta has not and will not be put into effect at any time during my reign; I am ever subservient to Holy Church. As for Stephen Langton, he is not in Canterbury. When he returns, we shall be ready."

The legate bowed, chattering effusively in Latin, and brushed past me as he left.

The king shifted his gaze from Pandulph to me. For a long moment, he looked directly into my eyes. Then he waved his hand toward a tier at the back of the room.

"Please wait until we finish, Lady Alix."

18

HAD THE KING SAID *LADY ALIX?* OH, *DEUS JUVA ME*, HOW HAD he guessed? He certainly hadn't seen me himself—who was his spy?

The queen, I thought; no, Lady Damiana; oh God, who? But then, what did it matter who? I was discovered—that was the point!

I crawled as high as I could on the tiers until I reached a shadowy area, though what did it matter now if the king saw me? It would make it more difficult to place a dagger, that's why! Despite hot tears, I chilled to my marrow, shook like a poplar leaf. I plucked nervously at an irritating mole, then another. My heart beat as painfully as it had in Fontevrault Wood, as if the years had just melted away. I fought against swooning—I had to stay alert. Though the tier faced a wall of windows open to the rising storm, the wind off the sea blew over our heads without entering the room. The storm was no more than a dramatic picture. No matter. *Lady Alix*, the king had said. *Lady Alix.*

Yet John didn't seem aware of my presence. He turned the pages of some bureaucratic reports of grain sales on the Continent. Since Wanthwaite was indirectly involved, I should have found it interesting and might have except for my terror. The sky darkened. King John bent close over the tome to see.

How long did I have to live? That darkening sky might be my last vision of earth.

Two pages carried pine torches on iron stands to tables piled with vellum. King John turned saffron in the light.

He spoke in Norman French to a tall man on the far side of the torches, "My lord duke, since you know the imports and exports from King's Lynn, suppose you tell us what you can about our sale of English corn to Scandinavia."

King's Lynn; the tall man must be the Duke of Norfolk, said by some to be richer than Lord Robert, second only to John himself.

Before the duke could reply, another man elbowed his way forward to answer; obviously displeased, John contradicted him sharply on every point he made. John prevailed, and not just because of his station; he knew his facts. His authority chilled me to the bone—this was the same authority with which he'd led his army to Wanthwaite. The king then asked the duke to confirm his contradiction, which the duke readily did. Because the duke also had authority? Was it his wealth? Listening, I didn't think so; both were masters of commerce. Who could have guessed that the killer King John was also a gifted bureaucrat? Probing, ruthless, and absolutely daunting in his knowledge of the smallest detail, he displayed unexpected skill in this chamber. Was this what Richard had meant when he'd warned never to underestimate his intelligence? No, I didn't think so. *Intelligence* meant penetration, such as knowing that I was Lady Alix. *Intelligence* meant *cunning*.

The king had moved to another table, another stack, this one about the wool trade. The king asked which breed of sheep produced the best wool (he himself provided the answer, the Oxford), the comparative number of lambs produced by different breeds, the maggots found at shearing time, the washing, the carding, and finally the distribution to markets overseas. Then how many finished woolen goods did we purchase from the Low Countries? How did the sale and purchase compare? Were these goods we bought made from English wool? If so, weren't we heading for a disaster? Our grazing lands were finite—and sheep cropped too close, thus ruining the fields—while making finished woolen goods right here would take little room, only skill, and give us a new item of export defined as English and of highest quality. Should we not consider even reversing the process buying wool abroad and manufacturing the finished product here? He had great faith in English skill.

"Ye'll ruin mony a guid herder!" a Scottish voice called. "Mayhap the londs below the oat line culd change, nocht us!"

He sounded like Enoch.

"Of course, those barren lands such as Scotland or much of northern England should continue to raise grazing animals; I speak of the west country and the south," the king replied.

"We be muckle prosperous wi'out fancy new markets!" the Scot rejoined.

Suddenly the king became angry. "Ignorant oaf! You think that your silly grazing lands produce your wealth? You are prosperous because England is enjoying an inflation! Are you even aware that every ingot of silver in England has been stamped into livres angevins?"

I had no idea whether inflation was connected to prosperity, yet I was impressed.

He finally moved on to the important subject of the day, the approaching war with France. Pages unrolled a huge map across two tables; knights and navy officers clustered close. The map billowed in the rising wind, at last entering the windows, and pages weighted it down at the corners. The king took a short pointer to indicate where ships approached our shores from Boulogne and Calais, along the usual lines of underwater plates, though the prevailing winds had changed since his spies had informed him. Though I bent forward, I couldn't see, so I listened instead.

"Look at this curved line: We have twenty-five warships in a semicircle around Dover port. The ships are camouflaged with brown paint, and each carries a catapult and Greek fire. No one can get past them, I assure you."

"The storm?" the Duke of Norfolk asked.

"Ah yes, the storm." The king walked to the windows. "So far, it's nothing serious. If it grows, we'll adjust." He picked up the pointer again. "Even with a storm, we have superior strength. Cogs from Portsmouth should be in port even now. I repeat that our strength, gentlemen, will stand against any invading fleet."

"Suppose they attack on land instead of by sea."

"Do you take me for a fool?" the king barked, then regained his equanimity—because it was again the Duke of Norfolk? Outside, the clouds had settled into a solid iron lid; fireflashes forked low to the ground; thunder rumbled and the whole room cooled. The king continued: "I would welcome a land war; three hundred seasoned Brabantian routiers have probably already landed. I have contracts with them, paid in advance."

"When did they leave Europe?" an officer asked.

"Yesterday."

"Who will lead them?"

The king exploded. "God's feet, who do you think? I'll lead, of course! This is an invasion of my country!"

The officer stepped back.

King John tried to recover. "No matter which approach the French use, I'm ready."

After a long silent moment, a priest raised his hands in dimissal, but didn't pray.

The officers walked to the stairs without further comment. The chamber was empty of all officials.

The king, now alone by the windows, stared at the sky. "Dover is noted for such weather, especially at sundown. But dangerous?"

The danger was not from the weather; the barons were riding toward Dover to welcome the French.

Pages removed the vellum and tables. As the sky darkened, the torches threw eerie circles of light in the room. Had the king forgotten my presence? I remained very still, deciding that I would withdraw quietly if I possibly could. Such retirement would end my plan for King John, but staying here might well end my life.

The king sighed deeply.

"A dramatic show," he said.

Was he speaking to me? To himself?

"Lady Alix, if you're still there, please answer." He shaded his eyes.

When had he turned toward me?

"*Oc*, Your Majesty, most diverting," I choked, cleared my throat.

"You need this." He walked toward me with a silver goblet of wine outstretched.

It was the best Bordeaux I'd tasted since I'd been with King Richard.

The king leaned forward and picked a mole off my face.

I sputtered wine all over my chemise.

"Sorry if I hurt you; it was better pasted than I expected, Lady Alix." He smiled.

"I'm—I'm—Marie-Françoise—"

"Oh, come now. Do you think I don't know who served Lady Mamile in my mother's court? Do you suppose that John Williams didn't recognize you the very first day you arrived? Or Baldwin of Béthune? Or that they didn't tell me?"

So why had he waited? What did he plan to do?

He stood a few feet in front of me. "If you've come to kill me, be warned that there are two guards just outside the door. You'll not leave alive."

I didn't speak.

"If you're worried that I'll kill you, you're probably right. I would like some information first, however."

"I came only to sell you a jewel! Didn't the queen tell you?"

"Are you working for the queen? Are you conspiring together?"

"Of course not!"

But it was a good question—had she betrayed me?

He kneaded my stuffed bosom until he could pull out the linen! "Where's your dagger?"

I pushed him away. "I have no dagger!"

His hand trembled and sweat formed on his brow. "Don't play games, if it please you! Of course you have a weapon!"

Then, abruptly, he went to refill his goblet.

"I've never killed anyone!" I shouted. Which was true— my dagger was in my braies.

He was back. "Please, let's not prevaricate. What else were you doing on Dere Street when that Scottish oaf pointed an arrow at my heart? Wasn't that not an attempt?"

"I had no weapon! And Enoch didn't shoot, did he? And besides, that was someone else's scheme, which you well know."

"The usual lie. Were you holding Richard's brat?"

"No." My heart squeezed. "That was Enoch's child, a girl."

"Enoch's?"

"By another woman. He married while I was in France."

"And you care for the child?"

"For the time being, yes."

"Why?"

My head throbbed. "Enoch and I live as brother and sister until we can get our differences resolved. He wants Wanthwaite—I claim it's mine. Neither of us will leave it."

"But Wanthwaite's burned." He sat beside me. "And you're dead. Heard it from Sancho, who did the deed—you and the Scot, both, skewered like roast pigs, he said."

I shook violently. "Thorketil and Edwina. But why?"

"Who?"

I explained.

"Too bad for all of us. You both deserved to die—you tried to assassinate me! And what about that dastardly Magna Carta? Weren't you skulking behind a bush?"

"Why did you betray it?"

"I obeyed for fifteen days. Never again."

On that we were agreed.

"So you and your husband are sister and brother. Sounds familiar."

I was afraid to speak—I saw his drift, saw the danger.

"Of course, you and your brother, Enoch, are both wrong: Wanthwaite is mine; it's my fief, and you rent it for a fee—which, incidentally, you haven't paid."

Then he put a finger under my chin. "Once again, Alix, and be careful, are you and the queen conspirators?"

"I told you we're not. She hasn't even seen my jewel, I assure you, and . . ."

"Did you blackmail the queen?"

"What? I don't know what you mean."

"God's feet, Alix, let's be honest at least. You came to kill me—the queen made the appointment. Am I a fool?"

No, but I was. I opened my palm. "I really do have a ruby to sell you."

He plucked three more moles off my face, including the one I was most proud of, which had hair "growing" in the center. He had to dig it out with his nail. "You look awful. I can't reach inside your mouth—you'll have to remove the padding."

Turning my head away, I did so.

"The wig?"

I removed that as well.

"The brown teeth?"

With the kerchief of my tunic, I rubbed away the tree bark.

"The most beautiful lady in Christendom. Even including my perfidious wife."

"The queen is indeed beautiful."

"Yes, corruption has its charms. How do you like her brother?"

For the first time, I heard his hurt.

"Her brother who is more than a brother, like you and your Scot."

"Enoch doesn't . . . !" I stopped myself.

"Fuck you?"

"No, he doesn't." Except to conceive Leith.

"Peter de Joiny fucks Isabella. Has for years. Interesting case. So do I fuck her, or I used to. Which of us do you think has fathered her four children?"

He didn't seem to want an answer, *Deo gratias.*

"I've heard that the offspring of incest were idiots. Do you think my son Henry an idiot?"

I'd seen Henry only from a distance, so I had no opinion.

"More?" He poured another cup for each of us. "Of course, as she reminds me daily, Peter and Isabella are only half brother and half sister. What a family! Have you met her mother?"

"No."

"Then don't." He shuddered. "Of course, you're not a king—she fancies kings."

"So do many people." I was thinking of his own reputation among women.

He was sharp. "Are you referring to my fucking the whey-faced wives of my barons? I plead both guilt and martyrdom. That's one of the burdens of being king, my dear, to reassure my lords that their political choices are viable as women; I also make a number of wives happy."

"That's not how the barons see it."

"Of course not. They play the game of outrage—I assure you that's not what they say privately. Back to the queen—have you seen her in action?"

"Yes, Your Majesty."

"I thought so—she's become careless." He settled beside me. "I have several choices: I could kill her; I could kill him. Then the children? What happened to Richard's brat, by the way?"

"He died."

"Pity—I might have made him my heir."

This so startled me that I spilled my wine again.

"You know, when my father put Eleanor in prison, it broke my heart. I was only a little fellow, but I swore to myself that I would never treat a wife of mine so. Isabella hasn't given me the political reasons that Henry claimed my mother did—but incest!" He shuddered violently.

"If you took my jewel to the light . . ."

"Still harping on rubies? You must think that Scottish oaf will succeed in his claim to Wanthwaite."

"Aye, I do." Now I shuddered.

"I could have him killed for you."

I tried to rise—he held me down.

"Perhaps he was taking orders, as you claim, but he did accept his assignment. I have every reason to have him dead.

Helping you is just one more." He suddenly laughed. "After all, we're practically brother and sister!" He giggled helplessly, now more like the John at Fontevrault.

I tried to change his mood. "No, don't! I mean, I appreciate that you're trying to help me, but . . ."

"Afraid his bastard will claim your estate? I could have her killed as well!"

My teeth chattered so that I couldn't speak.

He sighed. "I'm glad you escaped in Fontevrault, Alix, or we couldn't be having this little conversation." He bent over with his face in his hands. "God knows Henry wouldn't be the first bastard on the throne."

I glanced at the door to the stairs—could I escape?

Water was now splattering through the windows—could I distract John? Ask him to close the shutters? Then run?

"Your office is getting wet, Your Highness."

He didn't care.

"You were a marriage prize once. You could be again— we could both profit." His damp forefinger traced my chin. "After you've spent a few years in my bed."

"What?"

"You heard me. We have unfinished business, darling. You remember, Raoul remembers. You were my enemy once, but I always coveted you—you have to admit."

"Aye," I mollified him, "only not this night. I'm bleeding."

"I know—or rather, Raoul knows. I can smell your cassis, but he . . . remember Raoul? God's feet, how I do love you!" His eyes glazed. "However, I have to ride to Winchester this very night."

Winchester? Like the queen's brother? Had he been lying about meeting the French?

"But my jewel, Your Majesty."

"Why are you harping on your silly piece of glass? We've got much to settle!"

I set my jaw.

"God's feet, let me see it then!"

He took my stone to one of the pine-torch circles.

I waited so long for him to comment that I grew chill. "I realize it's very small. And somewhat pale in color."

He walked to the other pine torch.

"I'm sorry I bothered you with it. If you'd like . . ."

"Where did you find this?" he asked.

"Bonel, the Jew. Rouen. Why? Isn't it real?"

"Come over here."

Still with heavy padding about my hips, I waddled over to him.

"There now, a ruby, you say?"

Suddenly, I had doubts. This was a very evil man, to be sure, but he was no fool. And the stone, though brilliant, suddenly appeared small and pale, almost a chip.

"I studied gemstones for more than a year," I said slowly. "I'm certain . . ."

"And I've never studied at all, but apparently I know more than you do."

I trembled. "I'm sorry, Your Majesty; I'll take it back."

"It's a pink diamond," he said.

"A what?" Diamonds are colorless! "There is no such thing!"

"Rare, I grant you; I've seen only one before, on my

grandmother's coronation gown, the centerpiece of my treasure. Did you say you have more?"

I couldn't remember what I'd said. The diamond glowed
like a living thing. "Aye, one, its twin." Two fancies.

"Two pink diamonds!" His hand closed. "Do you love
me, Lady Alix?"

The question confounded me. "What, Your Majesty?"

"I'm asking if you will gift me with this stone. If you do
love me, you will."

Aye, the way he collected treasure from all his subjects, if
they did "love" him. I had no choice.

"I need money, Your Highness. If I lose my estate . . ."

"You won't lose it." His voice lowered to a whisper.
"God's feet, your eyes in this light. Gray diamonds."

"I lard to disguise," I admitted.

"I do love you, Alix." His own eyes glittered in the hissing
light. The torch also illuminated his features as I'd not seen
them before. The years had not been kind; still well shaped
and excellently groomed, his face was ravaged. Perhaps a soothsayer could read his lines; what I saw was self-indulgence,
cruelty, debauchery, murder. I grew confused—to be loved
by a werewolf! Or did he say this to everyone?

"And I want you. Not Raoul, but me, John. I've always
wanted you since that first time in Le Mans—remember?"

"Aye." When he'd come to see Richard.

"I know you think me a killer, and I am, a womanizer, and
I am, a king, but the least successful ruler in a family of kings.
Perhaps love is always incestuous—you bedded with my
brother. My mother loved you—she said so—and I love you,
too. We all love you."

Now he looked very young; he sounded sincere. What did he want? *Never underestimate his intelligence.* But this didn't seem intelligence; it seemed feeling. Again, I trembled.

"*Calme-te!* I want your diamond. Is it mine?"

Didn't he hold it in his palm? Of course, it was his!

"And when may I have the other?"

"If you want it, you must pay for it!"

He laughed softly. "With my body? Oh, I will, I will. You'll bring it to our assignation—is that what you're saying?"

"You speak of assignations and love, but that implies a place and time. You travel, and you have many castles."

"In fact, all the castles in Britain!" He laughed again. "I'll meet you in King's Lynn the first week in October."

"Where?"

"The port town in Norfolk we mentioned earlier, in the Broads just south of Lincoln, where I go each year to be feted at the Guildhall."

"The Guildhall? Do you stay there?"

"Not this year. I have a date with the bishop of Lincoln Cathedral, but the distance is too great to travel in one day from King's Lynn, though I will cross the Wash to make haste. By late afternoon, I shall be in Swineshead, a village north of King's Lynn, in Lincolnshire. The town has only one inn, but it's a very sweet place. You'll meet with me there." His voice thickened.

I knew not whether to make love or to die; the two were the same in this man's mind.

"And you'll show me your grandmother's pink diamond?"

"What a memory!" He pressed his hot forehead to mine. "You remind me of her."

"Was she a queen?"

"She should have been, but no, this diamond was on her coronation gown when she became empress of the Holy Roman Empire. I learned everything I know about rule from her."

"What did she say?" What I meant was, was she a killer?

"About the barons. They're like young eaglets, she said. When you train a predatory bird, you offer him bits of flesh; when he reaches, you cuff him hard and take back the flesh, then offer it again. That way they learn to associate you with largesses and punishment; they fear you."

Yet this king asked for love. Or did he?

I shuddered. "What's the Wash? Can I cross it?"

"Of course. A tidal inlet from the sea that makes King's Lynn rich, for seafaring cogs can dock there. You'll see."

"Tidal inlet—is it dangerous?"

"There have been a few accidents—water is always dangerous. They have excellent guides who know the tides, the quicksands, the shifts. Perhaps you can attach yourself to my train and cross with me."

"Perhaps, or perhaps I'll take another route to Swineshead." I was only beginning to see a plan.

He kneaded my cheeks. "God's feet, Alix! I've had dozens of women, but always you . . ."

"It's dark," I reminded him.

"You want to bed now? I don't mind a little blood if you don't—I could put out these torches."

"I was thinking of Winchester."

"Winchester? God's feet, yes!" Yet he fumbled under his robes.

"And the French are attacking."

"Winchester. So I said. To chop off a few hands and feet!" He laughed joyfully. "Oh, Alix! Swineshead—I can't wait!"

Before I could stop him, he clutched my cheeks in his two hands and kissed me on the mouth. His lips were soft as vair, seductive as Satan.

I lingered at the top of the stairs until I heard him ride out of the castle, then ran quickly down to the well. Behind a whipping bush, I shed my oversized tunic and my padding, and dropped them down the well. I now wore my familiar nun's habit. With my wimple pulled low, I walked out of the first and second gates without incident.

Enoch wasn't in our room at the church inn of St. Martin-le-Grand at the top of the hill, though I could see that he'd been sleeping on my mat, whereas he usually used the floor. At my insistence, Father Rupert told me that my brother had walked out on the breakwater to watch the waves in the wind, very much against his advice, for no one ventured on the breakwater in a storm. Yet I knew Enoch's purpose—he was watching for the French. Leaning against the blow, I followed his footsteps.

I was afraid of what I might see, afraid of what I'd just left, and apprehensive about King's Lynn, yet foremost in all the turmoil whirling in my fantastick cell was the fact that I'd just been kissed. I had no illusions about John's intentions now or in the future, but the fact remained: I had been kissed. It was hardly flattering, considering the hordes of women who'd been kissed by the same lips, and yet—I had been kissed. How long had it been? Richard? No, Bonel. Another life. Illusion it might always be, but a kiss puts one in a different universe, the world of love. Did I so crave to bed with a man that I could dream on a snake's embrace? Perhaps, for it was all I had. I forgave myself: everyone must feel so.

Mayhap the breakwater had served the Romans well when it was new, but now, a thousand years later, the sea overwhelmed the barricade. Familiar carrious gums foamed high and I trembled—the *Drage* foundered once again. Then I saw him, on the outermost stretch of the cement hook, waving and cursing at the sea.

"Enoch!"

My voice was swallowed by the furies.

"Enoch! Take care!"

He couldn't hear me.

Using my hands for balance, I crept over the slippery rocks to the breakwater. I must reach him! I became drenched within two steps onto the slippery cement.

Enoch was now staring in my direction—he'd seen me. He called something I couldn't hear, then pointed to the horizon. Watching him, I fell! Not into the pounding tide, but onto the concrete. For a moment, I just lay there, too surprised to move. Then, dragging a trail of blood where I'd skinned my leg, I sidled forward. I lay on my stomach, clutched the slippery cement edge. Enoch pulled me upright. "Cum, ye mun see!"

He cavorted like a fish on its tail down the breakwater to the corner, then along the parallel strip that disappeared at every wave.

"Can't you tell me what you see?"

He pointed to the French fleet in the distance. Blue ships in full sail stretched across the horizon as far as the eye could see, like so many clouds blowing along the surface.

"Where are the English?" I shouted aloud.

"Quhar be the king?"

I didn't answer, for I was following his finger. At our feet on the rocks piled around the breakwater, dead bodies were pounded by the waves. Young boys, many hideously wounded, all drowned—the Brabantian routiers John had paid in advance. What good would money do them now? All had open eyes fast losing color, all wore the red tunics of England, none was armed. But it was their mouths that fascinated me. Open, hardly one set of teeth among them, lips puffed and fast turning blue, they looked like blowfish. Yet those same lips had once been soft as vair. Had they kissed other lips goodbye?

"Quhar's the king?" Enoch repeated.

I told him. "It looks as if he'll lose."

"He ha'e lost befar ond cum back lak a cat. Did ye ha'e success wi' yer plan?"

"Aye, come back to the inn; I'll tell you."

By the time we reached solid land, the Roman lighthouse burned steadily. We climbed our hill slowly in the pouring rain. Father Rupert greeted me suspiciously because of my habit, but I paid no heed. Our room was tiny, pitch dark, and it had no windows.

"Ich mad a bit o' haggis yif ye're hungry."

"No, thank you."

I sat on the mat as he ate. "Enoch, we must save Leith!"

He choked. I told him what John had said.

"He doesna want her to inherit Wanthwaite?"

"It's a long story. Just tell me what we should do."

In short order, he'd summoned a runner to go to Wanthwaite. Gruoth and Dugan were ordered to take Leith to Scotland at once.

To Inverness, he told me, in the Highlands, far from the border. Though I felt sick because I would never see her again, I was also relieved. I didn't want another Theo.

"Now you, Enoch. He has orders out for your head because of the assassination attempt. I couldn't talk him out of it."

"He won't catch me. Tal me yer plan."

Though I knew he might challenge me about having rubies in my possession, I told him the truth: Bonel had gifted me with two rubies (no point confiding my whole cache) that turned out to be pink diamonds. I had a rendezvous with John in King's Lynn.

"Quhar?"

I explained. "The key is the Wash, Enoch. Just what Lord Robert demanded, a natural disaster."

"Waesucks."

The plan needed much refining, I warned, as I had only a sketchy notion of the layout.

"I'll go first. By the time you come, everything will be settled."

"A month," he said slowly. "Mayhap I con gae to Scotland mysel'."

"Aye. Do it."

He touched my shoulder. "Quhat aboot ye, Alix? Be yer lif in daunger?"

"Yes, he plans to kill me," I said. "Only he wants to bed me first."

19

SOMEONE PULLED MY TUNIC. "I HA'E A BOW-WOW!" A SMALL BOY announced.

"He manes *dog*," a woman lying on the wet sand scolded.

"Aye! His nam be Blackie!"

"He be yallow," the woman said.

"Here he cums now!"

An emaciated yellow hound loped around our fire.

I remembered Wolfbane. "There's no friend like a dog."

"Dogs mun eat," the woman pointed out.

"Boot not princes!" A small girl now tugged on my tunic.

"That be my sister," the boy explained scornfully. "She doesna know nofink. She's a babby."

"She be four," the mother said, "and he be six."

They both appeared to be about two, so emaciated were they. I wondered how old the mother was.

"A prince doesn't eat." I smiled at the girl. "Princes live on love. Nevertheless, I have a few morsels of bread in my sack that we can all share."

The dog almost snapped my hand off; the brother, sister, and mother were too hungry to eat. Then, to my horror, the little girl put her hand down her neck and presented a spotted yellow toad with three red lines between his eyes.

"May I hold your prince?" I asked. The toad hopped from my hand. "Oh, sorry, he got away!"

The toad disappeared in the weeds surrounding our island; the little girl burst into tears.

"Hush ye, Mary-Tilda, there be many mar whar he cum from," the mother said weakly. "They live in the marsh." She closed her eyes.

"Your mother's sleeping," I said gently.

"No, she be daid," the boy replied.

The little girl burst into tears, and I reprimanded the boy for frightening his sister so—but he was right! The woman was dead! Didn't breathe! Did she need water? A wrap?

"She's daid, dearie." Lonabee took my shoulder. "Naught fer ye to do—we'll take care."

"But the children!"

"Oh, they willlna mind."

Indeed, the little boy was petting his dog while the little girl dug in the sand.

I was aghast. Would Theo have behaved so if our fates had been reversed? Would Leith?

Lonabee turned me toward her. "That be their third m'am, yif I count rightly. Their real mother died whan little Mary-Tilda war born."

She then explained that our work of sifting sea salt from the sand gave us a short life expectancy; therefore, the women had formed their own guild for orphaned children. No child was ever left motherless.

At one level, I was dumbfounded at their generosity; at another, I wasn't surprised, for everyone belonged to guilds in this strange city, and the guilds were dedicated for the most part to workers. The largest group, the seaman's guild, owned the Guildhall where King John would dine shortly.

Still, no matter what the custom, the salt guild was the only organization owned and run entirely by women, at least that I'd ever heard of. And it didn't just look after orphans; women set the price for our sea salt, which was much prized overseas, set their own wages, looked after the sick and feeble among them, functioned in fact as a family is supposed to. I had found the work the very first day I'd arrived in King's Lynn, and I was fast getting rich.

Rich, and so far healthy. Generous as our guild might be, the fact was that we had so many deaths that it was hard to keep sufficient workers. At this moment, the next "mother" of the little boy and his sister was already leading them away. The dog followed.

I went back to sifting sand.

It had been easy to find work in King's Lynn precisely because the death rate was so high among women. Oh, I daresay that men suffered as well—many perished in the Wash or at sea—but I was witness to the women's woes.

Old-timers called King's Lynn simply Lynn, which in Celtic ("lin") meant island. Actually, the present city lay on the east side of the Ouse River and was made up of three islands, not one. Before it became King's Lynn (King John had given it a charter that spared it of taxes), it had been known as Bishop's Lynn and was owned by the Church. Under both auspices, it was really a seaport. The "three" islands were only one island at a time. Sea storms comparable to what I'd experienced on the *Drage* inundated the city almost daily. Not only did the sea bring storms, but the whole area was inundated with fresh water, which also engendered moisture. Natives might say that King's Lynn lay on the banks of the River Ouse (sometimes called the Purfleet), and indeed that was correct; great flat boats brought flax and iron for export. The rivers Nar and Gay also joined the Wash; these three rivers brought grain from the interior to send overseas.

By some strange coincidence, the three islands that made up the town were hit by storms in sequence, never all at the same time. Therefore, we women would go to a corner meeting place to learn which island was the most dry that day. We then worked on the "dry" island, where brine oozed at every step; this created the lucrative trade of gathering sea salt.

Going from one island to another as gales shifted the sea, we put "dry" sand into small jars—large jars were too heavy to lift—and waited for the brine to rise to the top. We then skimmed off the bubbles and heaved white scum into a kettle over a flame. Everyone liked to stir the kettle, for the fire was warm; we took turns. Once the water had boiled away, we put the dross on a screen to sift for the salt. We had two wagons to transport our salt to waiting ships, where the women bargained with rough foreigners. The women, kind as puppies to one another, were tough bargainers with the seamen. We owned our own salt, had organized our own guild, and wouldn't sell our labor cheap. Furthermore, the women divided their profits absolutely evenly. We might appear poor, might succumb to the climate, but we took care of ourselves as best we could.

So, it wasn't lack of money that drove me to the Guildhall this rainy night.

The handsome Guildhall, built of solid flint laid in cunning patterns, was located on High Street; a friend called Mistress Huldabert took me to meet with Master Whitfrock there, a friend of hers. She pushed the large door open without rapping and led me through the dim wooden dining area that smelled of spices, and had one taper burning at the far end beside a closed door. Mistress Huldabert pushed through this door as well and signaled that I should follow.

I paused to wring my wet shawl, then followed her into a brilliant, noisy kitchen. Young boys sprawled against the walls, jugbitten as mice. Two scullery maids were collapsed on a pile of grease, and I hoped they were jugbitten as well. What else could excuse their open bodices? Grown men in the center of the chamber, definitely jugbitten, pissed on the floor and argued loudly about a pastry. In the center of this group, a massive man with a red face and protruding gut shouted above all the others. Mistress Huldabert pulled on his smeared apron.

"Master Whitfrock, I brung ye the Frenchie I tald ye about!"

After several attempts, she dragged the bibulous cook to my side. He rubbed his eyes.

"If it please you, sire, I need extra coins. And it looks as if you could use another scullery maid."

He pinched my cheek. "Are you from Aquitaine?" he asked in thick langue d'oc.

Yes, Marie-Françoise from Poitiers.

He blinked bleary eyes several times.

"Ye be a lady!" he declared in French.

"Yes, Lady Marie-Françoise from Poitiers, though my title means naught in England; in Poitiers, I worked as specialty consultant to Queen Eleanor's kitchen."

"In the kitchen?" His eyes rolled. "How many ovens?"

"Eighteen."

He fell to his knees and grasped my hand. "You want to work for me?" He seemed on the point of weeping with gratitude.

"Yes, milord, if you have . . ."

"Have you worked with lampreys?" He pointed to giant wooden tubs.

"Aye," I lied brightly, though my stomach chilled when I heard the lampreys thrash against the wooden sides.

"And sharks?"

"Aye." Another tub rocked as the sharks turned.

"King John is said to enjoy sharks' fins."

"King John?"

"Yes, oh yes, the king is coming and he . . . do you know him? Queen Eleanor's son?"

Unfortunately, I did not.

Outside again, I thanked Mistress Huldabert profusely for her help, which she dismissed as nothing, and indeed it was nothing in King's Lynn. The people here were much punished by the heavens, but that didn't stop them from being the most loyal and kind populace on the earth.

I climbed slowly in the dark to the attic I'd rented. The house rocked in tonight's gale; *we'll not work tomorrow*, I thought. Rain entered the slats of my ceiling, and, though I was soaked through, I was looking forward to my pile of furs in the center where it was driest and a crust of bread I'd hidden in a tin against the rats. Groping in the dark, my hand was grasped by another's. Enoch had arrived.

"Waesuucks, ye're lak ice!"

He rubbed sticks and produced a spark on top of a flat rock; in a short time, I was eating hot haggis. Then a methier of whiskey. I began to feel human.

"Be werry quiet," he whispered. "Lord Robert be sleepin'—he's that weary."

I choked on the haggis, and he had to pound my back.

"What's he doing here?"

"'Twas his idea—ha'e ye forgot?"

His idea? Lord Robert was too frail for this climate. No point in arguing tonight, however. When I was sufficiently warmed, Enoch and I began to whisper. Aye, I had a plan, two in fact, for King John was like a witch's cat, full of lives; aye, there was a role for Enoch and I supposed Lord Robert in both.

"I'll show you the layout tomorrow. I won't be working."

"Nay, 'tis Sunday."

I'd forgotten—now I hoped for clement weather. I swallowed a lump. "How is Leith?"

"She be happy ond safe." He hesitated. "She seems to knaw she's hame—she is a Scot, ye knaw."

Yes, I knew. I was glad that she was happy and safe.

"She misses ye," Enoch said.

"Not so much as I miss her." We were silent. "We'll talk more in the morning, when Lord Robert awakes."

Sunday was sunny. Bells rang all over King's Lynn as if marking the miracle of the weather. Lord Robert, now completely rested, he claimed, greeted me most kindly. Indeed, we were all in festive disposition.

"Quick! Before it rains! You must get to know the area."

The two men, dressed in green like professional hunters, and carrying bows and quivers, followed me down Market Street. Enoch looked convincing, but Lord Robert still seemed aristocratic. He smiled at my appraisal and lifted his feathered cap to reveal a streak of white in his hair.

"Do I pass?"

"How strong are you, Lord Robert?"

"Strong enough."

In a short time, we stood on a small hillock overlooking the Ouse.

"That's called the Broads." I waved my hand toward a flat area before us. "You can see that it's broad, all right, and you can also see that it's almost submerged with water leets and rivers."

"That luiks to be a canal."

"You're right—they've begun to dig waterways for boats. This is a marine economy."

Lord Robert cocked his head at the many sour bells. "Or a papal economy? The Church still seems active."

"Yes, I'm taking you to St. Margaret's where we can ascend the bell tower, the highest in the area."

I led slowly. A strong breeze blew from the Channel; it was a miracle that it wasn't raining.

Enoch stooped by a tiny stream with his hand out.

"No!" I held his hair until a toad jumped away. "That was the golden leopard-prince, though he's misnamed. He's deadly poison."

"Sames a guid nam to me," Enoch said dryly.

I ignored him. "There are many in the Broads, so be careful."

"What do you call those?" Lord Robert pointed at another small stream.

At first I saw nothing except dead leaves, then what looked like a tangle of snakes.

"Those are the famous lamprey eels," I said. "King's Lynn io known for them ambrooia for kingo."

Enoch dipped his hand.

"Careful! They bite!"

He licked his finger. "Saline, the water be mixed wi' the sea. That be quhat eels lak." He peered more intently. "Boot they be nocht eels."

"Aye, lamprey eels. King Henry I is supposed . . ."

"To ha'e died fram eatin' them, Ich knaw."

"Then why did you say they're not lampreys? Everyone says so. Don't you trust me?"

"That be twa questions." He waited, but I said nothing. "Aye, everich one elsit be wrang. Luik at them fat round lips, them thick bodies. Lampreys they may be, boot nocht eels. Them be leeches."

Enoch shot an arrow into the black huddle and pulled out a dead eel. Black blood pooled on the thirsty sand.

"Auld King Henry micht ha'e died fram this beastie richt enow, fer humans doona digest blood."

We stared at each other.

We continued to walk. Lord Robert was obviously tired but didn't complain.

Enoch stopped. "This be turrible country. Na wonder folk fish fer lampreys ond sift sand."

"Economically, it's wonderful country!"

"No grass fer kine, no soil fer oats!"

"There are other criteria, Enoch!"

"Ond ye're contrary yif ye claim udderwise."

I pulled a reed. "See this? Perfect thatch! They not only farm it, they export it! And see those ducks? You can eat their eggs, eat the ducks themselves, use their feathers for stuffing or for writing, their tallow for candles! Ducks are the main animal here! Both domestic and wild!"

"Ye sound lak a native!" He grinned.

I was flattered.

St. Margaret's was a huge edifice with two high towers, the largest in King's Lynn. Though only a church—not a bish-opric, as was the cathedral in Hereford—it was a great church, similar in style to St. Paul's, that is, the new Gothic. Even Enoch fell silent when we entered the nave, a vast empty space even on Sunday. I led the men quickly past pointed arches and triple columns to the back right-hand corner, where I opened a small door.

"Who goes there?" a thin breathy voice called.

"Marie-Françoise, Father Anselmo. You told me I could take my friends up to see the view."

The thin priest coughed into view. He gazed at Lord Robert. "The stairs are steep and treacherous. Are you sure . . . ?"

"Positive," the lord replied.

The steps were indeed difficult, like going up a ladder, except that the stairs curved in tight circles. There were no rails, no ropes to cling to. Enoch went last, as if to catch us when we fell; though I objected to the intimacy, I was grateful for his strong hands on my rump. Lord Robert, who was first, stopped often to catch his breath.

"Here?" he called when we reached a platform.

"There's a higher one if you can . . ."

"I can."

Then Enoch began to curse.

"What's wrong?" I said softly.

"That haly faddir be followin' us."

"Yes, I'm here!" Father Anselmo's high, husky voice confirmed.

Well, his presence would prohibit any speculation, but I could still point out the path of the Wash.

We stopped on a highest platform, buffeted by a wind we hadn't felt below. Lord Robert's face drippd heavily. Father Anselmo, also breathless, stood at the back in the shadow.

"Qhar be the Wash, Marie-Françoise?" Enoch asked.

"There, the tide's coming in, see? That bubbling clay-colored stream of water rushing inland." The roar identified it more than my words.

"That's a new path—it changes frequently," Father

Anselmo added. He pushed forward. "It's changed course completely three times since I've been here and caught sixteen innocent children at play."

"Sixteen?" I challenged. "I heard six."

"How long have you been here?"

"That sun is difficult!" Lord Robert shaded his eyes.

Indeed it was: the watery land below now looked like a giant mirror.

"You're looking at a lake," Father Anselmo said. "The town is built on a lake."

I'd never seen the lake myself.

"St. Margaret's of Antioch is built on the Ouse, which you can see if you look straight down."

Only Enoch bent forward.

"The original town was built between the Millfleet and the Purfleet." Old names for the rivers, I knew.

I went back to the Wash. "It's a dangerous phenomenon, though it doesn't appear so from here. There is seductive soft sand at the bottom, I am told."

"We ha'e mony swich tidal waters in Scotland, anely we call them tarns."

"Yet I am told that wagon trains cross your Wash, even when the tide is in," Lord Robert mused.

We stared quietly. Blinding sun forced us to look away.

"Are you considering some event with King John?" Father Anselmo asked pleasantly.

We all started! Lord Robert signaled to Enoch and me to stay quiet—he would answer. "You mean at the Guildhall? Not unless the cook wants fresh game, which we might supply. When is the king expected?"

"You tell me, Lord Robert."

A shocked silence followed. Was the priest a soothsayer? A spy? Again Lord Robert signaled Enoch and me to remain silent. The lord didn't argue his identity. "It would seem that the king has many enemies. What is your complaint?"

The priest was quiet so long that I suspected I was right; he was a spy. "My obvious complaint is professional; St. Margaret's lost a huge tax base when the king bought King's Lynn." He paused. "We make up a little with our Saturday market, but only a little. Our bishop managed to keep St. Nicholas a Benedictine priory, which gives us some advantage when it comes to weddings and funerals. There are also personal issues, which I would rather keep private."

"I understand," Lord Robert said, thinking, no doubt, of Lady Gunnora and his daughter. Some priests still married—had Father Anselmo lost his wife to John?

"What more can you tell us about the Wash?" I asked.

It was highly unstable; the greatest danger was quicksand, which didn't show when the tide was out, so it couldn't be charted.

"Do you think King John will use it?" I asked.

He sighed. "Who can tell? He has before."

"Personally?" Lord Robert pressed.

"I'm not certain. Memory says *no*, only to transport his treasure, but I could be wrong."

Lord Robert's eyes narrowed.

"Would the king change his mind?" Enoch asked.

Oh yes, everyone did if the tide was out or even low; merchants frequently crossed at low tide. The Wash cut more than forty miles from the trip to Boston, in Lincolnshire, another trading center. The few natives who had specialized in leading tradesmen across the Wash made excellent money.

The two men looked at each other, then back at the scene.

"King's Lynn is built on rubble, you know," the priest informed us. "That's one reason it's so unstable."

"Is that Swineshead?" Lord Robert pointed to a spire above distant trees.

"No. It's much closer, a village called Wisbech, I believe. Another watershed."

We soon descended; we had no more questions.

When we reached the foot of the stairs, Lord Robert took the priest's arm. "Are you a spy?"

"No, Lord Robert, I am not. Are you?"

"If I am, I doubt not you will send me to hell in your prayers. If you are, I will send you to the same place with a knife at your throat. Do we understand each other?"

"Yes. I would add only that I would like to be part of your plan. I want to help."

Back in our garret, we drank grog. The expected storm was now raging.

"We hae muckle werk to do," Enoch said heavily.

"Father Anselmo seemed an angry man—do you think he's trustworthy?"

Lord Robert nodded. "I do, though it hardly matters. He has no proof that we're plotting, nor could he do anything if he did. What think you of the Wash, Enoch?"

"Con ye swim?"

Lord Robert laughed. "Like a lamprey!"

"Do you plan to lead merchants?" I asked. "I'm told it's hard employment to get, and . . ."

"I'm too old? Ah yes, but I'm a baron, my dear; I know the Duke of Norfolk."

"I con git it," Enoch said, "ond I con swim." He drank more grog.

Lord Robert stood. "Lady Alix, may I speak to you privately outside?"

I glanced at Enoch. "Would you excuse us?"

He waved his hand.

"Lady Alix," Lord Robert whispered. "Are you content?"

Was he referring to my dangerous job? "Yes. Why?"

"I feel guilty, you see, for imposing on your intimate time with your husband just before . . . I'm certain I could find other accommodations . . ."

"I doubt it, Lord Robert. And we need to be together, all three of us." We stared deeply at one another

"Thank you." He shrugged. "If you're certain. I'm grateful, Alix, for your sacrifice, but I admit I'm . . . you're a wonderful person—Enoch is lucky." I waited—he wasn't finished. "Enoch is very discreet about personal matters and . . . but I know he loves you. Anyway, thank you."

"Shall we go back?"

The next day, both Enoch and Lord Robert applied to be guides across the Wash, and within a week both were accepted, though neither would be assigned at once, for the work required great skill as well as strength, and they had to learn the topography of the tidal wash, the shifting sands, the sea patterns, and I know not what. Both men claimed to be strong swimmers, which Enoch was; both claimed to understand tides, and both did; both claimed expertise with horses, though Enoch was the only one who had worked with mules. In fact, Enoch learned his work as a guide much more easily than Lord Robert, though both men studied charts by rushlight at night, for, very simply, he was younger. Yet Enoch, too, was vulnerable. I was reminded in melancholy fashion of the Crusade, the *enfants perdus*, the men deliberately sacrificed so the heroes could seek glory. Be as it may, he learned the Wash as well as is possible in a few days and with such shifting patterns.

Meantime, I drained salt from the sand and worked in the evenings at the Guildhall. I conferred with the two men about my own plans, in which they also wanted to partake.

20

I worried about Lord Robert, I worried about what Enoch might be saying to him without telling me, but I worried most of all about Master Whitfrock.

The cook at the Guildhall was a skilled man, no doubt. Like most masters in his craft, he hailed from Aquitaine and he frequently spoke to me in that tongue. Then he began to make comments about my person, that I was *belle* and *délicate*. Then I became talented beyond belief, born with a gift from God in the art of cuisine. Though I had been hired as a scullery maid, he insisted on teaching me how to cook.

At first I was grateful, for I came to the Guildhall weary from sifting salt, and cooking was less onerous physically than scrubbing grease off floors. The lampreys were still my assignment, but we weren't ready yet to prepare them. Eels or leeches, it hardly mattered, for they were a nasty beast whatever their name. Aggressive, strong, deadly; everyone made a wide swath around their tubs. Even the sharks seemed benign in comparison; at least they were both stupid and limited by their solid bodies.

But I soon wearied of stirring sauces, though I did learn much from Master Whitfrock. I related my adventures to Lord Robert and Enoch at night, embellishing only slightly to amuse them. Enoch claimed that all men coveted me and at least I was learning something useful from this one; Lord Robert was more cynical, for he warned me that the man would use me for his own advancement.

On October 13, all of King's Lynn began to prepare for the king's arrival. Boys and girls in wooden clogs shoveled and swept the High Street, where he would ride; inside, on hands and knees, we scrubbed the surface off the floors, then waxed them to a high shine. Even the salt sifters put aside the finest salt they could make for his table; then we decided who would sit above or below the most excellent salt. Master Whitfrock kept me in the kitchen to personally prepare such delicacies as could be made ahead.

Our greatest dishes were from the sea, of course, for that was our reputation and, of the many fish dishes, the lamprey eel was the pièce de résistance, but we also prepared meats, vegetables, and desserts. Master Whitfrock taught me *fruytes ryal rice*, artichokes with blueberry rice, for example; or *roseye*, fried loach with roses and almonds, a most delicious dessert.

My principal assignment, however, was to care for the lampreys, a flattering job on the one hand, but also danger-ous. King John, like other kings, considered the lamprey fit only for a royal palate, partly because of their rarity, and partly, I suspect, because of their bloody flavor. Which led to the conclusion that—like him—they were killers. We now had four large wooden tubs filled with the beasts. Their stench filled the Guildhall, a bloody and fishy aroma com-bined, and they thrashed without cease, trying to leap from their tubs. Though shaped like snakes, their black, thick bod-ies were short, topped by large heads with bulging, scummy eyes. Their peculiar faces had neither nose nor mouth, just a round sucker where a mouth should be. Under the sucker with its thick "lip" was another hole lined with inset teeth like a comb. The sucking lips and teeth worked on a victim together: The sucker attached to the victim and sucked, while the teeth released a poison comparable to the hemlock, which both paralyzed the victim and thinned its blood so it was more readily available. Add to that a dangerous, aggressive disposition, and you have the lamprey. With the help of a boy namd Lewey, I managed to flop one of these foul creatures from his tub, and he lay thrashing on the floor. I beat him with a board until he stopped moving, then—with the same board—scooped him onto the cutting table. I chopped his head off at once to be sure he wouldn't fasten on me in his death throes, and black blood spilled over the tiles. The odor made me faint, but I persevered.

The day before the king arrived, we prepared six lamprey eels, as his first course was to be served cold. I crushed two pieces of coarse brown bread to start, added a cup of red wine, a teaspoon of cinnamon, a dash of pepper and salt, and boiling water containing skinned and cut-up lampreys, which we then placed in a pie shell to cook. On the morning of the sixteenth, we added a syrup of wine, ginger, and two more slices of bread crumbs. We cooked it at dawn, then put it aside to cool.

Master Whitfrock insisted that I serve the king myself.

"His own men serve him!" I protested. "Or his taster! Never a female!"

"I want he should know what elegance we have here in King's Lynn."

It was true that I wore my silver tunic for my assignation

with the king and that Lord Robert and Enoch had both remarked upon my beauty that morning, but I had no intention
of the king seeing me emerge from the kitchen! I convinced
Master Whitfrock that there was no way to force me, but I
lost valuable time.

I lost even more time when Enoch and Lord Robert suddenly appeared in their Wash garb. Father Anselmo hovered
behind them on the pretext that he must bless the food! They
told Master Whitfrock solemnly that they'd come to see their
sister prepare food for the great monarch. All three men gazed
at the lampreys, though none, *Deo gratias*, asked to taste the
mess. Then Enoch suddenly took my cheeks and kissed me on
the lips, farewell to his beloved sister in case he foundered in
the dangerous Wash. Lord Robert hastily did the same. The
priest spared me.

At least those kisses wiped the memory of John's lips
from my mind. On the other hand, Enoch's evoked such
memories that I swallowed hard to prevent tears.

When the king's horns bleated on the High Street, our
kitchen emptied, for every scullery boy and girl rushed to see
the magnificent train—three hundred men, I was told. And
the king! Had anyone ever beheld such magnificence? Like a
god! Clad in scarlet trimmed in miniver, a gold chain at his
neck, but most of all his face! So noble, so handsome, so condescending!

When he entered the Guildhall, his sweet woodruff
battled with the fish smell of lampreys. My little darlings,
still about ten of them alive, lashed viciously in their tubs,
wanting to suck the royal blood before he got them first, no
doubt. Casting me a scornful look, Master Whitfrock sent a

boy out with the lampreys, followed by a spiced red wine to clear the palate. But no, the king so loved his eels that he asked for more. He ate the entire pie.

I hastily prepared a jug of hypocras to clear his palate.

We then began his bird courses: lark in strawberry sauce, duck in honey-cream sauce, chicken in prune sauce. The ducks and chicken were relatively fresh, but the lark benefited greatly from the strawberries. The king then asked for more lampreys and was told there would be some delay, as we would have to prepare them. While I quickly smashed the heads of two more, emptied their thick bodies of blood, and sliced them on a board, Master Whitfrock stirred a sauce of pine nuts and parsley, for there was no time for a pie.

I marveled at the king's appetite, for he ate all day long. Between courses, he drank red wine. His laughter grew louder; he banged on the table in pleasure. If King's Lynn loved John, John certainly returned the admiration. At long last we began the dessert courses: plum and current tarts, pear with carob cream, a tricolored fig confection. The sun was low by the time he left the Guildhall.

Managing to evade Master Whitfrock, I sneaked out the back door. I threw a hooded cape over my finery—for there was now a chill in the air—and mounted a mare at the end of the king's train. Though the reports had said he had three hundred people in his train, that wasn't true. He did, however, have a vast number of animals, mules mostly, loaded with heavy packets—his treasure?—and it needed only one man to handle two beasts. We began a slow march through King's Lynn.

We continued to walk after we'd passed through the city

gate; the path was well defined, the earth—though a little damp—was hard-packed sand. Suddenly, we stopped. No one at the back could say why. Then we began to march again, this time for a shorter time before we again stopped. At last the reason reached us: The king had diarrhea, probably because he'd overeaten, as always.

The next time we stopped, however, the Wash appeared beside us, empty of water, a dry, harmless gulch. The king had decided to cross to save time. Now there was muttering: It was too late in the day, the tide was due, the king shouldn't attempt such a dangerous route when he was having difficulties. I had brief glimpses of Enoch and Lord Robert with their wooden staffs. Then the word came back that guides were going to take the treasure across the Wash; the king would spend the night in nearby Wisbech and join with his train on the morrow.

The guides joined the king's men to lead the mules; Enoch and Lord Robert worked steadily, though with strained faces. It was not our plan that they die in place of King John. And this was a late afternoon in October; the twilight would be short, the sun would set soon. Experienced guides grumbled in loud voices that the Wash had been dry since before the king had arrived—it was time for the tide. Didn't they have tables? Enoch glanced briefly at me—he'd claimed the tables were mostly guesswork. So why did he, too, look worried?

Enoch and Lord Robert milled somewhere in the middle of about twenty other guides. All the men bound themselves together with long ropes, and each carried a flat board, presumably to use as a float. Enoch turned once, but he didn't see me behind a large mule.

It took a long time for the treasure train to enter the Wash. The steep sides were treacherous—one mule went to his knees—and the bottom was less stable than it looked. Of course, the mules carried heavy loads, but even the men's feet sank ankle-deep. Finally, however, the last mule was in the Wash and on its way.

Our much-diminished train moved slowly forward toward Wisbech. Though the king made no sign, I knew he'd seen me. We stopped frequently, and word came back that the king was suffering most terribly from indigestion. Indeed, as we passed places where he'd relieved himself, the foul odor of lamprey made everyone choke.

We didn't enter the actual town of Wisbech after all. Lord Reginald of Lincoln had offered his castle, which lay between King's Lynn and Wisbech for the king's comfort. We were waved past the usual guarded gate in the wall to face a fortress pocked with arrow slits and not much more. We all recognized that the fortress was not more comfortable than Wisbech, simply closer. By this time the king couldn't control his agonized cries; his litter disappeared through the front entrance. The rest of us were led to the side ramp to accommodate our horses. Just as my mare reached the ramp, I heard the roar.

The Wash!

Everyone heard it. The silence in our ranks spoke louder than words: The train couldn't possibly have gotten across in this short time. Then everyone stood back. Supported on two sides, John walked into the yard. He couldn't see the Wash, but he must know. The king's pale profile glistened with sweat; he couldn't stand erect even with support. His valets lifted him in their arms to retreat to the castle.

The rest of us listened. Then a small group of knights galloped in the direction of the Wash. The roar grew. The knights returned after nightfall, their voices stilled. Yet one told us that never had the water been so deep, never so roilsome. The king's entire train had disappeared. I couldn't breathe, couldn't think. Oh, *Deus juva me*, Enoch. Lord Robert. Dangerous, yes, but not this! Not death!

I followed the knights back to our ramp. I huddled in a dark corner and wept through the night. Though I was the only woman, no one paid me any heed. I was not the only person, however, who knew men who had crossed the Wash. One knight still sobbed at dawn.

When we left the castle before sunrise, John lay flat and silent on his litter.

The distance to Swineshead was said to be short, but a sorry train makes slow progress. Some knights wept for their king, who was obviously in bad condition; others wept for the lost train of beloved friends and servants. Perhaps a few wept for the treasure. I felt a desolation beyond death.

It was midafternoon by the time we entered the tiny village of Swineshead. The inn, as John had promised, was a sweet dwelling with two large maples with bright red leaves in front, though I doubt if the king noticed them as he was carried inside. The host had put out fresh cheese pies and ale, but the melancholy company ate and drank nothing. Again, though I was the only woman in the tavern, no one paid me any heed.

Then a stable boy ran into the room, panting and trying to speak in vain. Finally, he blurted it out: a few guides had survived the disaster!

Had any treasure been saved?

He didn't know.

Shortly thereafter, two burly men appeared to tell us more: the *guides*—all but two—had managed to survive. Most of the king's men and all of his mules had been sucked down by the treacherous sands and no one could rescue them, though many had tried. While the company wailed about the lost men and the lost treasure, I rose to see the men who were straggling into the inn.

Lord Robert touched my arm; Enoch stood behind him.

Both men wept as they told their tale. The mules had foundered, the crates had sunk, and many of the king's men had thrashed through the muddy water in an effort to save something!

Six more guides stumbled in during their recital. Others, they said, had returned to their families at King's Lynn. Enoch and Lord Robert huddled close to me, their bodies shaking. Neither could eat.

Now the company fell into profound melancholy for the king's condition. A physician came from Lincoln, then priests. The king was very sick—should he be told of his loss?

Yes, he should.

One of his Norman routiers came back from his room:

The king had taken his loss—all except his grandmother's coronation gown—with surprising equanimity.

"Because there was no treasure," Lord Robert whispered. "He spent it all."

The routier continued that the king was praying for his soul, for he knew he was dying.

"Quhat soul?" Enoch whispered. "Be he prayin' to auld Clootie?"

Since the king was so ill, a covered litter was fashioned to remove him to the bishop of Lincoln, who resided in Newark. When he was carried down the stairs, only about half the knights were still in the tavern.

"He's a sinking ship," whispered Lord Robert.

I stepped forward and touched John's shoulder. He opened brilliant blue eyes.

"Alix," he whispered. "Where were you?"

"I came here, Your Majesty, as you instructed me."

He shook his head in vexation. "I meant in King's Lynn. The *lampreys.*"

"You ate too many."

"Oh yes, I ate too many. Well, never mind, I was going to do the same to you."

"Do what?"

"Love you, of course." A pain shook his body. "Will you kiss me?"

A request, not an order. I did so.

"Give me your hand."

Again I did so; his were cold as ice. He continued to watch as I opened my palm; inside lay my pink diamond.

"But why . . . ?"

He smiled. "Because I do love you." A spasm shook him. "I love England! You are England," he whispered. "A wand of birch in the wind, silver reed in the . . ."

They carried him away.

Lord Robert, Enoch, and I rode out as soon as he left, though in a different direction.

"Weil, Ich be sorry fer the villain, no matter quhat," Enoch said. " 'Tis a turrible death."

"Not so horrible as burning alive on a spit," Lord Robert retorted. He grabbed my rein to put me on a narrow path. "This way to Dere Street." We rode in single file. "At least his death was natural!" He suddenly laughed. "Natural! Damn bad luck that he caught the flux, though." He shuddered. "That water in the Wash was cold."

"What happened to the priest?" I asked.

"What priest? I saw no priest, did you, Enoch?"

Enoch didn't answer. I let it pass.

"So, are we under French rule now?" I called to Lord Robert's back. "What happened in Dover after I left? Did Prince Louis land safely?"

Lord Robert raised his hand. "King for ten heartbeats! The barons recognized—they decided—that they prefer England for the English! Enough of foreign rule!"

"Did they knw of your plan?"

"What plan?" He laughed. "However, the Duke of York joined the French. Eustace might have as well if he'd been alive, but maybe not. His biggest estate was in Normandy, you know, though he died fighting for the Scottish king.

I heard you believed he'd gone over to John, Enoch. Not true."

"Ich knowed he couldna follow John. I wish he war alive to see England governed by Magna Carta. He wuld ha'e bin vindicated."

"Magna Carta was a failure," I reminded him.

"Under King John, yes," Lord Robert agreed. "We'll push it through again, though, and this time without time limitations."

"Aye," Enoch nodded.

They would have to find a new scribe, for I would have "disappeared" in London.

We rode silently for a time.

Lord Robert pulled his steed level with Enoch's. "King John had a young prince, Henry by name."

I recalled the pale child at Dover who might not be John's blood son.

"He'll need a regent; we'll press for the regent to sign."

"Aye." Enoch agreed.

We rode quietly again for a time.

Lord Robert slowed his steed. "John is dead." He laughed again. "Think of it! We designed Magna Carta, the pope killed it, and now—with Henry—we can bring it back as a royal manifesto with an underage king!"

I thought of Theo.

His horse snorted. "This has been a good day for England." His voice choked. "I can't believe it."

Aye, though for me, personally, John's death was also a loss. Of Enoch. Of Wanthwaite.

Lord Robert reined his horse to a halt. "See that ridge

yonder? It goes directly to what there is left of Dunmow, so if you'll forgive me . . . Farewell, my friends. I must ride on that ridge to reach my bride!"

"Bride?"

"Lady Nicola." He touched my chin. "Not so beautiful as you, my dear, but I do love her! And she loves me! Do you mind?" He laughed at my confusion. "She is your friend, after all!"

And a baby! He was an old man!

"Oh, I know I'm too old, but life is short and . . ." His voice shook.

We watched him disappear into the hills.

"He's richt; he be followin' his heart."

"Is Wanthwaite closer by the ridge? Should you take it?"

"Dere Street be safer."

He'd caught that *you* instead of *we* and emphasized his words. "We'll pick up Dere Street yet today."

"Aye, that seems reasonable." Where he would turn north and I would go south.

Enoch and England.

Yet London was also England, wasn't it? Hundreds of people must love it or they wouldn't live there. And there were good people: Master Peterfee, my new employers in the jewelry trade. It was the people that counted after all; look at King's Lynn. And there were all those greens we'd seen from the Thames boat.

And yet, how I did love Wanthwaite! The tall elms and maples against the endless English sky, salmon leaping in the Wanthwaite River, my parents, now Theo. Leith. And Enoch. I wished he hadn't kissed me in the kitchen. A lump formed.

Yet I was still in the countryside, wasn't I? Catch the moment! The deep sky slanted and birds were silent; they'd flown south. But wait, there was an English hare on his hind legs, brown with a white tail, nose twitching. He hopped away.

"Did ye see the rabbit?" Enoch asked.

"Aye."

"Quhy did it lape away?"

I turned my head. "We should stop—'tis Haute Tierce."

"Aye."

We bent over a running stream to drink, then filled our methiers with bones Enoch supplied to purify the water, and let our horses drink. Enoch had taken two cheese pies from the inn in Swineshead. We both slept a short time, then remounted. Now, I thought, I must speak now.

He rode ahead of me except where our path widened, and then he rode beside me. I could sense his thoughts racing with mine: John was dead, and with him, this farce of pretending to be brother and sister. We'd made an agreement. I must tell him that I'd paid for our annulment, but I didn't, not yet.

With the bones clinking in our methiers, we again slaked our thirst. I pretended to choke on a bone to cover my anguish.

We rode on slowly, still without speaking. In the distance, we heard singing: male travelers on Dere Street. We were almost there. Cows huddled for the night under an oak ahead, but sheep still grazed on a steep, dark green hill. Farewell, England.

"Enoch, do you remember when you accused me of going to the Church after we made our agreement?"

"Quhy do a hare hop?" he asked.

I started—had he gone totty? Or deaf?

"In Dunsmere, when the ecclesiastical court visited from Durham, remember?"

"Thar be sum law we doona knaw yit. Hares hop, people walk on twa legs, horses on four. 'Tis in each natures to move so. Natural law. Ond it applies to feelin's."

"Enoch, I beg you, don't tease, not now. This is serious."

"Dome fortes deme."

And I stopped arguing, for we were saying the same thing: fate, fortune's wheel.

"Aye, Enoch, that's it! I was fated to return after you married! If you'd known I was alive . . . in any case, canon law grants you the annulment because that's the law for female infidelity, and I paid for it." I waited till I regained my voice. "It was very expensive—two gold pieces—but I did it!"

He seemed not to have heard. "Quhat did John gi'e ye?"

"A pink diamond, very valuable. Bonel gave it to me first." I handed it to him.

He seemed confused. "Did ye luv John becas he war Richard's brudder?"

"Of course not! He murdered Theo!"

Murder. John, too, had been murdered. The murder of King John. Did "of" refer to Theo or to John himself?

"The diamond be mine," Enoch said for the second time.

"Aye."

"Waesucks!" He held it to the light. "Bonel ga'e it?"

"Aye, to put me in business in case . . ."

"Ah." He turned away, then turned back. "Did Bonel tal ye?"

"Tell me what?"

"Quhat I sayed that day?"

The second night, when Bonel had been late. "No."

"He war angry becas I raped ye ond made Leith."

"And you did! Leith is proof!"

"Aye, that we mad houghmagandy. Boot Ich tald Bonel hu ye asked me to, begged me."

I stopped my horse. What did he mean?

"Ich tald him hu ye sayed, *Enoch ond England, Enoch ond England,* ond ye sayed it agin ond agin as yif we war riding ond . . . I did it, Alix! Ich couldna help myself! 'Tis my nature—Ich canna live wi'out ye, ond . . ."

I stared at him wildly. Was it possible? *Enoch and England*—how else would he know?

And Bonel knew! He'd heard me say it and . . . that was why . . .

Enoch's red-gold hair stood in a point like a beacon, his blue eyes were steady. Something inside me burst, and I began to scream.

"Waesucks, stop!" He put his arms around me.

"Wanthwaite?" I whimpered.

"Ich ha'e drawed plans; mayhap we con mak a country estate instead of a motte."

"Aye. Oh, Enoch!"

His face came close—his lips—I was home! With Enoch, in England.

Much later, in the dark, he asked, "Ye sayed as hu the annulment cost twa gold pieces? Do ye think the priest would gi' me the gold back again?"

He should—it took us three days to reach Dere Street.

NOTES ON THE RESEARCH

MAGNA CARTA

I assume that most Americans share the scant knowledge of the Magna Carta that I had when I started this book. I had seen a copy in the British Museum; I had visited Runnymede; and I had a vague idea that it was somehow similar to our Declaration of Independence.

After years of research, I know that my assumptions were wrong. The experts (most of them English) give it short shrift: It had virtually no effect in its own time; the barons' motives were highly suspect. There seem to be two basic approaches in discussing it: the historical, which recounts its influence over politics, and the legal, which does the same in terms of its influence on law.

Yet despite a general disparagement among scholars, the myth of the Magna Carta continued to grow. Why is that? Let me suggest that the idea of people taking the reins of their own destiny is one of the most appealing notions in the entire world. The concept of one-man rule, sustained by naked force, crumbled on several occasions. One occasion was when the Magna Carta was forced on King John, and another was when the American colonists forced the same idea on King George. Yet a brief scan of the two documents reveals their fundamental difference: Magna Carta was intended to free the baronial class from the king's injustices, and it was based on the law of precedent; the Declaration of Independence asserts that *all* men are created equal. What happened between the two documents was the writings of John Locke (and some say Thomas Hobbes); Locke inadvertently gave ammunition to French Philosophes, thus creating the French and American Revolutions (and perhaps the Russian). As a bit of a joke, I have made Enoch discover natural law in terms of the attraction between a man and a woman.

CHARACTER OF KING JOHN

John, like many medieval characters, has gone through a recent revision: He wasn't as bad as everyone (including Shakespeare) says; he behaved exactly as his father, Henry II, and his brother, Richard I, had when they were kings. I suppose your opinion of John depends on your nationality, your former reading, and whether you're looking for a subject to revise. My evidence suggests that he was very bad indeed. Years before he was king, he behaved like a monster, and getting absolute power simply gave him the license to behave even worse.

His preying on women comes down as "gossip" (no monk writing in his cell was going to record any item that would end his life); the murder of Arthur of Brittany is likewise gossip, though generally believed. The sad tale of the de Braose (also spelled de Briouze) family has been substantiated. One discrepancy: The religious stone with the description of

Arthur's death was found in Ireland, not Wales, and dictated by Lord William de Braose, not his wife.

John's death is also a mystery. Revisionist historians writing today give him a natural death, even noble insofar as he took it with such equanimity. Yet there has always been a suspicion that he was murdered: Shakespeare gives the deed to an unknown priest. When I visited King's Lynn, the people I talked to had no doubt that he was murdered, pretty much as I have told it.

ISABELLA OF ANGOULÊME

This unknown queen and King John must have had a most troubled marriage. She was rumored to have had love affairs with her own half brother Peter and with John's half brother, William Longsword. She was also rumored to have been extraordinarily beautiful.

John allowed her almost no freedom during their marriage and was exceedingly close with money. He put her in a prison tower, presumably one of great comfort, and after he died, she rushed to Winchester to pick up her daughter, Joanna, who was betrothed to Hugh IX of Lusignan, the son of the man to whom she'd been betrothed when John married her. Now, upon seeing the son, Isabella married him— there's no record of what happened to the daughter.

Isabella may have seen her son, King Henry III, when he visited Poitou (though there is no record of it), but she never saw any of her English children again. She bore nine children to Hugh of Lusignan and became a rich woman.

Nonetheless, she always called herself queen of England,

and when she died, thirty years after John, she had herself buried beside Eleanor of Aquitaine at Fontevrault, where she wears the English crown.

THE BARONS

They existed pretty much as I have indicated. Lord Robert fitzWalter and Lord Eustace de Vesci were exiled to Normandy because of their aborted assassination attempt. The informers were also as I indicated. The barons' complaints against King John can be deduced from the charter itself, but there are other records. One can also take a larger historical view and claim that the barons were simply expressing the "wind" that was blowing through Europe. Kings largely fought, and nobles had become weary of constant warfare.

ARCHBISHOP STEPHEN LANGTON

I have accurately described the biographical facts of this man of the Church and then deliberately left his connection to the Magna Carta somewhat murky. Though he seems to have backed the charter (he gave a stirring sermon at St. Paul's on its behalf), he was loyal to Pope Innocent, who did not back it. The medieval period can be defined as the partnership of kings and popes, never an entirely happy relationship since both believed in absolutism and couldn't agree on who was absolute. I have read both sides of the arguments about Langton's involvement and prefer to leave the conclusion up to the reader.

MAGNA CARTA

TRANSLATED BY HARRY ROTHWELL, M.S., PH.D.,

PROFESSOR OF HISTORY, UNIVERSITY OF SOUTHAMPTON

There is no "original" of the Charter of Liberties of 1215. Four copies sent out from the royal chancery shortly after the meeting at Runnymede on June 15 survive; two are in the British Museum, one at Lincoln Cathedral, and one at Salisbury Cathedral. Each consists of a single sheet of parchment measuring approximately fifteen by twenty inches. The punctuation, division into paragraphs, and numeration of them in the translation that follows are in accordance with the practice of modern editors.

There has been no full-scale commentary on the charter since W. S. McKecknie, Magna Carta. The second edition of this (Glasgow, 1914) was much revised from the first. Its interpretations of John's government and the baronial purpose need much further revision in the light of modern knowledge, but its elucidations of the technicalities of the charter can be read with much profit.

THE CHARTER OF LIBERTIES OF 1215

John, by the grace of God, king of England, lord of Ireland, duke of Normandy and Aquitaine, and count of Anjou, to the archbishops, bishops, abbots, earls, barons, justiciars, foresters, sheriffs, stewards, servants, and to all his bailiffs and faithful subjects, greeting. Know that we, out of reverence for God and for the salvation of our soul and those of all our ancestors and heirs, for the honor of God and the advancement of holy Church, and for the reform of our realm, on the advice of our venerable fathers, Stephen, archbishop of Canterbury, primate of all England and cardinal of the holy Roman

Church, Henry, archbishop of Dublin, William of Longer, Peter of Winchester, Jocelyn of Bath and Glastonbury, Hugh of Lincoln, Walter of Worcester, William of Coventry and Benedict of Rochester, bishop of Master Pandulf, subdeacon and member of the household of the lord pope, of brother Aymeric, master of the Knights of the Temple in England, and of the noble men William, earl of Warenne, William, earl of Arundel, Alan of Galloway, constable of Scotland, Warin, son of Gerold, Peter, son of Herbert, Hubert de Burgh, seneschal of Poitou, Hugh de Neville, Matthew, son of Herbert, Thomas Basset, Alan Bassett, Philip d'Aubigny, Robert of Ropsley, John Marshal, John, son of Hugh, and others, our faithful subjects:

[*1*] In the first place have granted to God, and by this our present charter confirmed for us and our heirs forever, that the English church shall be free, and shall have its rights undiminished and its liberties unimpaired; and it is our will that it be thus observed; which is evident from the fact that, before the quarrel between us and our barons began, we willingly and spontaneously granted and by our charter confirmed the freedom of elections which is reckoned most important and very essential to the English church, and obtained confirmation of it from the lord pope Innocent III; which we will observe and we wish our heirs to observe it in good faith for-ever. We have also granted to all freemen of our kingdom, for ourselves and our heirs forever, all the liberties written below, to be had and held by them and their heirs of us and our heirs.

[*2*] If any of our earls or barons or others holding of us in chief by knight service dies, and at his death his heir be of age and owe relief he shall have his inheritance on payment of the old relief, namely, the heir or heirs of an earl £100 for a whole earl's barony, the heir or heirs of a baron £100 for a whole barony; the heir or heirs of a knight 100s., at most, for a whole knight's fee; and he who owes less let him give less according to the ancient custom of fiefs.

[*3*] If, however, the heir of any such be underage and a ward,

he shall have his inheritance when he comes of age without paying relief and without making a fine.

[4] The guardian of the land of such an heir who is underage shall take from the land of the heir no more than reasonable sums, reasonable customary dues, and reasonable services, and that without destruction and waste of men or goods; and if we commit the wardship of the land of any such to a sheriff, or to any other who is answerable to us for its revenues, and he destroys or wastes what he has wardship of, we will take compensation from him and the land shall be committed to two lawful and discreet men of that fief, who shall be responsible for the revenues to us or to him to whom we shall assign them; and if we give or sell to anyone the wardship of any such land and he causes destruction or waste therein, he shall lose that wardship, and it shall be transferred to two lawful and discreet men of that fief, who shall similarly be responsible to us as is aforesaid.

[5] Moreover, so long as he has the wardship of the land, the guardian shall keep in repair the houses, parks, preserves, ponds, mills, and other things pertaining to the land out of the revenues from it; and he shall restore to the heir when he comes of age his land fully [totam] stocked with plows and the means of husbandry [waynagüs] according to what the season of husbandry requires, and what the revenues of the land can reasonably bear.

[6] Heirs shall be married without disparagement, yet so that before the marriage is contracted those nearest in blood to the heir shall have notice.

[7] A widow shall have her marriage portion and inheritance forthwith and without difficulty after the death of her husband; nor shall she pay anything to have her dower or her marriage portion or the inheritance that she and her husband held on the day of her husband's death; and she may remain in her husband's house for forty days after his death, within which time her dower shall be assigned to her.

[*8*] No widow shall be forced to marry so long as she wishes to live without a husband, provided that she gives security not to marry without our consent if she holds of us, or without the consent of the lord of whom she holds, if she holds of another.

[*9*] Neither we nor our bailiffs will seize for any debt any land or rent, so long as the chattels of the debtor are sufficient to repay the debt; nor will those who have gone surety for the debtor be distrained so long as the principal debtor is himself able to pay the debt; and if the principal debtor fails to pay the debt, having nothing wherewith to pay it, then shall the sureties answer for the debt; and they shall, if they wish, have the lands and rents of the debtor until they are reimbursed for the debt that they have paid for him, unless the principal debtor can show that he has discharged his obligation in the matter to the said sureties.

[*10*] If anyone who had borrowed from the Jews any sum, great or small, dies before it is repaid, the debt shall not bear interest while the heir is underage, whosoever tenant he may be; and if the debt falls into our hands, we will not take anything except the principal mentioned in the bond.

[*11*] And if anyone dies indebted to the Jews, his wife shall have her dower and pay nothing of that debt; and if the dead man leaves children who are underage, they shall be provided with necessaries befitting the holding of the deceased; and the debt shall be paid out of the residue, reserving, however, service due to lords of the land; debts owing to others than Jews shall be dealt with in like manner.

[*12*] No scutage or aid shall be imposed in our kingdom unless by common counsel of our kingdom, except for ransoming our person, for making our eldest son a knight, and for once marrying our eldest daughter; and for these only a reasonable aid shall be levied. Be it done in like manner concerning aids from the city of London.

[*13*] And the city of London shall have all its ancient liberties

and free customs as well by land as by water. Furthermore, we will and grant that all other cities, boroughs, towns, and ports shall have all their liberties and free customs.

[*14*] And to obtain the common counsel of the kingdom about the assessing of an aid (except in the three cases aforesaid) or of a scutage, we will cause to be summoned the archbishops, bishops, abbots, earls, and greater barons, individually by our letters—and, in addition, we will cause to be summoned generally through our sheriffs and bailiffs all those holding of us in chief—for a fixed date, namely, after the expiry of at least forty days, and to a fixed place; and in all letters of such summons we will specify the reason for the summons. And when the summons has thus been made, the business shall proceed on the day appointed, according to the counsel of those present, although not all have come who were summoned.

[*15*] We will not in future grant anyone the right to take an aid from his own freemen, except for ransoming his person, for making his eldest son a knight and for once marrying his eldest daughter; and for these only a reasonable aid shall be levied.

[*16*] No one shall be compelled to do greater service for a knight's fee or for any other freeholding than is due from it.

[*17*] Common pleas shall not follow our court, but shall be held in some fixed place.

[*18*] Inquests of *novel disseisin,* or *mort d'ancestor,* and of *darrein presentment,* shall not be held elsewhere than in the court of the county to which they relate [*in suis comitatibus*] and in this manner—we, or, if we should be out of the realm, our chief justiciar, will send two justices through each county four times a year, who, with four knights of each county chosen by the county, shall hold the said inquests [*assisas*] in the county court, on the day and in the place of meeting of the county court.

[*19*] And if [all] the said inquests [*assisas*] cannot be held on the day of the county court, there shall stay behind as many of the knights and freeholders who were present at the county court on that

day as are necessary for the sufficient making of judgments, according to the amount of the business.

[20] A freeman shall not be amerced for a slight offense except in accordance with the degree of the offense, and for a grave offense he shall be amerced in accordance with its gravity, yet saving his way of living [*contenementum*]; and a merchant in the same way, saving his stock-in-trade [*mercandisa*]; and a villein shall be amerced in the same way, saving his means of livelihood [*waynagium*]—if they have fallen into our mercy; and none of the aforesaid amercements shall be imposed except by the oath of upright men of the neighborhood.

[21] Earls and barons shall not be amerced except by their peers, and only in accordance with the degree of the offense.

[22] No clerk shall be amerced in respect of his lay holding except after the manner of the others aforesaid and not in accordance with the amount of his ecclesiastical benefice.

[23] No community or individual [*nec villa nec homo*] shall be compelled to make bridges at riverbanks, except those who from of old are legally bound to do so.

[24] No sheriff, constable, coroners, or other of our bailiffs shall try [*teneant*] pleas of our Crown.

[25] All counties, hundreds, wapentakes, and tithings shall be at the old rents without any additional payment, except our demesne manors.

[26] If any one holding a lay fief of us dies and our sheriff or bailiff shows our letters patent of summons for a debt that the deceased owed us, it shall be lawful for our sheriff or bailiff to attach and inventory chattels of the deceased found upon the lay fief to the value of that debt under the supervision of law-worthy men, provided that none of the chattels shall be removed until the debt that is manifest [*clarum*] has been paid to us in full; and the residue shall be left to the executors for carrying out the will of the deceased. And if nothing is owing to us from him, all the chattels shall

go to the deceased, saving to his wife and children their reasonable shares.

[27] If any freeman dies without leaving a will, his chattels shall be distributed by his nearest kinsfolk and friends under the supervision of the Church, saving to everyone of the debts that the deceased owed him.

[28] No constable or other bailiff of ours shall take anyone's corn or other chattels unless he pays spot cash for them or can delay payment by arrangement with the seller.

[29] No constable shall compel any knight to give money instead of castle-guard if he is willing to do the guard himself or through another good man, if for some good reason he cannot do it himself; and if we lead or send him on military service, he shall be exempt from guard in proportion to the time that because of us he has been on service.

[30] No sheriff or bailiff of ours, or anyone else [aliquis alius], shall take the horses or carts of any freeman for transport work save with the agreement of that freeman.

[31] Neither we nor our bailiffs will take other people's timber for castles or other works of ours except with the agreement of him whose timber it is.

[32] We will not hold for more than a year and a day the lands of those convicted of felony, and then the lands shall be handed over to the lords of the fiefs.

[33] Henceforth all fish traps shall be cleared completely from the Thames and the Medway and throughout all England, except along the seacoast.

[34] The writ called *Praecipe* shall not in future be issued to anyone in respect of any holding whereby a freeman may lose his court.

[35] Let there be one measure for wine throughout our kingdom, and one measure for ale, and one measure for corn, namely, "the London quarter"; and one width for cloths whether dyed,

russet or halberget, namely, two ells within the selvedges. Let it be the same with weights as with measures.

[36] Nothing shall be given or taken in future for the writ of inquiry concerning life or limbs, but it shall be granted free of charge and not withheld.

[37] If anyone holds of us by fee farm, by socage, or by burgage, and holds land of another by knight service, we will not, by reason of that fee farm, socage, or burgage, have the wardship of his heir or of his land that is of the fief of the other; nor will we have wardship of the fee farm, socage, or burgage, unless such fee farm owes knight service. We will not have the wardship of anyone's heir or land that he holds of another by knight service by reason of any petty sergeanty that he holds of us by the service of rendering to us knives or arrows or the like.

[38] No bailiff shall in future put anyone to trial upon his own unsupported testimony, without reliable witnesses brought for this purpose.

[39] No freeman shall be arrested or imprisoned or disseised or outlawed or exiled or in any way destroyed, neither will we set forth against him or send against him, except by the lawful judgment of his peers and [vel] by the law of the land.

[40] To no one will we sell, to no one will we refuse or delay right or justice.

[41] All merchants shall have safe and secure exit from and entry into England, and dwelling and travel in England as well by land as by water, for buying and selling by the ancient and right customs, free of all evil tolls, except in time of war and if they are of the land that is at war with us. And if such are found in our lands at the beginning of a war, they shall be taken and kept in custody [attachientur], without injury to their persons or goods, until we, or our chief justiciar, know how merchants of our land are treated who were found in the land at war with us when war broke out [tunc], and if ours are safe there, the others shall be safe in our land.

[*42*] Without prejudicing the allegiance due to us, it shall be lawful in future for anyone to leave our kingdom and return safely and securely by land and water, save, in the public interest, for a short period in time of war—except for those imprisoned or outlawed in accordance with the law of the kingdom and natives of a land that is at war with us and merchants (who shall be treated as aforesaid).

[*43*] If anyone who holds of some escheat such as the honor of Wallingford, Nottingham, Boulogne, Lancaster, or of other escheats that are in our hands and the baronies dies, his heir shall give no other relief and do no other service to us than he would have done to the baron, if that barony had been in the baron's hands; and we will hold it in the same manner in which the baron held it.

[*44*] Men who live outside the forest need not henceforth come before our justices of the forest upon a general summons, unless they are impleaded or are sureties for any person or persons who are attached for forest offenses.

[*45*] We will not make justices, constables, sheriffs, or bailiffs save of such as know the law of the kingdom and mean to observe it well.

[*46*] All barons who have founded abbeys, in respect of which they have charters of the kings of England or of which they have had long tenure, shall have custody of them in a vacancy, as they ought to have.

[*47*] All forests that have been made forest in our time shall be immediately disafforested; and so be it done with riverbanks that have been made preserves by us in our time.

[*48*] All evil customs connected with forests and warrens, foresters and warreners, sheriffs and their officials, river-banks and their wardens shall immediately be inquired into in each county by twelve sworn knights of the same county who are to be chosen by good men of the same county, and with forty days of the comple-

tion of the inquiry shall be utterly abolished so as never to be restored, provided that we, or our justiciar if we are not in England, have previous intimation thereof.

[49] We will immediately return all hostages and charters given to us by Englishmen, as security for peace or faithful service.

[50] We will entirely remove from their bailiwicks the relations of Gerard d'Athée so that in future they shall have no bailiwick in England, namely, Engelard de Cigogné, Peter and Guy and Andrew de Chanceaux, Guy de Cigogné, Geoffrey de Martigny and his brothers, Philip Marc and his brothers and his nephew Geoffrey, and all their following.

[51] As soon as peace is restored, we will remove from the kingdom all foreign knights, crossbowmen, sergeants, and mercenaries who have come with horses and arms to the detriment of the kingdom.

[52] If anyone has been dispossessed or removed by us without the legal judgment of his peers from his lands, castles, franchises or his right, we will immediately restore them to him; and if a dispute arises over this, then let it be decided by the judgment of the twenty-five barons who are mentioned below in the clause [61] for securing the peace: for all the things, however, from which anyone has been dispossessed or removed without the lawful judgment of his peers by King Henry, our father, or by King Richard, our brother, which we have in our hand or are held by others, to whom we are bound to warrant them, we will have the usual period of respite of crusaders, excepting those things about which a plea was started or an inquest made by our command before we took the cross; when, however, we return from our pilgrimage, or if by any chance we do not go on it, we will at once do full justice therein.

[53] We will have the same respite, and in the same manner, in the doing of justice in the matter of the deafforestation or retention of the forests that Henry, our father, or Richard, our brother, afforested [cf. clause 47], and in the matter of the wardship of lands

that are of the fief of another, wardships of which sort we have hitherto had by reason of a fief that anyone held of us by knight service [*cf. clause* 37], and in the matter of abbeys founded on the fief of another, not on a fief of our own, in which the lord of the fief claims he has a right [*cf. clause* 46]; and when we have returned, or if we do not set out on our pilgrimage, we will at once do full justice to all who complain of these things.

[*54*] No one shall be arrested or imprisoned upon the appeal of a woman, for the death of anyone except her husband.

[*55*] All fines made with us unjustly and against the law of the land, and all amercements imposed unjustly and against the law of the land, shall be entirely remitted, or else let them be settled by the judgment of the twenty-five barons who are mentioned below in the clause [61] for securing the peace, or by the judgment of the majority of the same, along with the aforesaid Stephen, archbishop of Canterbury, if he can be present, and such others as he may wish to association with himself for this purpose, and if he cannot be present the business shall nevertheless proceed without him, provided that if any one or more of the aforesaid twenty-five barons are in a like suit, they shall be removed from the judgment of the case in question, and others chosen, sworn, and put in their place by the rest of the same twenty-five for this case only.

[*56*] If we have dispossessed or removed Welshmen from lands or liberties or other things without the legal judgment of their peers in England or in Wales, they shall be immediately restored to them; and if a dispute arises over this, then let it be decided in the March by the judgment of their peers—for holdings in England according to the law of England, for holdings in Wales according to the law of Wales, and for holdings in the March according to the law of the March. Welshmen shall do the same to us and ours.

[*57*] For all the things, however, from which any Welshman has been dispossessed or removed without the lawful judgment of his peers by King Henry, our father, or Richard, our brother, which

we have in our hand or which are held by others, to whom we are bound to warrant them, we will have the usual period of respite of crusaders, excepting those things about which a plea was started or an inquest made by our command before we took the cross; when, however, we return, or if by chance we do not set out on our pilgrimage, we will at once do full justice in accordance with the laws of the Welsh and the foresaid regions.

[58] We will give up at once the son of Llywelyn and all the hostages from Wales and the charters that were handed over to us as security for peace.

[59] We will act towards Alexander, king of the Scots, concerning the return of his sisters and hostages and concerning his franchises and his right in the same manner in which we act toward our other barons of England, unless it turns out to be otherwise according to the charters that we have from William, his father, formerly king of the Scots, and this shall be according to the judgment of his peers in our court.

[60] Moreover, all these aforesaid customs and liberties that we have granted shall be observed in our kingdom as far as it pertains to us toward our men, all of our kingdom, clerks as well as laymen, shall observe as far as it pertains to them toward their men.

[61] Since, moreover, for God and the amendment of our kingdom and for the better allaying of the discord that has arisen between us and our barons we have granted all these things aforesaid, wishing them to enjoy the use of them unimpaired and unshaken forever, we give and grant them the underwritten security, namely, that the barons shall choose any twenty-five barons of the kingdom they wish, who must with all their might observe, hold, and cause to be observed the peace and liberties that we have granted and confirmed to them by this present charter of ours, so that if we, or our justiciar, or our bailiffs, or anyone of our servants offend in any way against anyone or transgress any of the articles of the peace or the security and the offense be notified to

four of the aforesaid twenty-five barons, those four barons shall come to us, or to our justiciar if we are out of the kingdom, and, laying the transgression before us, shall petition us to have that transgression corrected without delay. And if we do not correct the transgression, or if we are out of the kingdom, if our justiciar does not correct it, within forty days, reckoning from the time it was brought to our notice or to that of our justiciar if we were out of the kingdom, the aforesaid four barons shall refer that case to the rest of the twenty-five barons, and those twenty-five barons to-gether with the community of the whole land shall distrain and distress us in every way they can, namely, by seizing castles, lands, possessions, and in such other ways as they can, saving our person and the persons of our queen and our children, until, in their opin-ion, amends have been made; and when amends have been made, they shall obey us as they did before. And let anyone in the country who wishes to do so take an oath to obey the orders of the said twenty-five barons for the execution of all the aforesaid matters, and with them to distress us as much as he can, and we publicly and freely give anyone leave to take the oath who wishes to take it, and we will never prohibit anyone from taking it. Indeed, all those in the land who are unwilling of themselves and of their own ac-cord to take an oath to the twenty-five barons to help them to dis-train and distress us, we will make them take the oath as aforesaid at our command. And if any of the twenty-five barons shall choose as they think fit another one in his place, he shall take the oath like the rest. In all matters the execution of which is committed to these twenty-five barons, if it should happen that these twenty-five are present yet disagree among themselves about anything, or if some of those summoned will not or cannot be present, that shall be held as fixed and established which the majority of those pres-ent ordained or commanded, exactly as if all the twenty-five had consented to it; and the said twenty-five shall swear that they will faithfully observe all the things aforesaid and will do all they can to get them observed. And we will procure nothing from anyone, either personally or through anyone else, whereby any of these concessions and liberties might be revoked or diminished; and if any such thing be procured, let it be void and null, and we will never use it either personally or through another. And we have fully remitted and pardoned to everyone all the ill-will, anger, and rancor that have arisen between us and our men, clergy and laity, from the time of the quarrel. Furthermore, we have fully remitted to all, clergy and laity, and as far as pertains to us have completely forgiven all trespasses occasioned by the same quarrel between Easter in the sixteenth year of our reign and the restoration of peace. And, besides, we have caused to be made for them letters testimonial patent of the lord Stephen, archbishop of Canterbury, of the lord Henry, archbishop of Dublin, and of the aforementioned bishops and of Master Pandulf about this security and the aforementioned concessions. Wherefore we wish and firmly enjoin that the English church shall be free, and that the men in our kingdom shall have and hold all the aforesaid liberties, rights, and concessions well and peacefully, freely and quietly, fully and completely for themselves and their heirs from us and our heirs, in all matters and in all places forever, as is aforesaid. An oath, moreover, has been taken, as well as on our part as on the part of the barons, that all these things aforesaid shall be observed in good faith and without evil disposition. Witness the above mentioned and many others. Given by our hand in the meadow that is called Runnymede between Windsor and Staines on the fifteenth day of June, in the seventeenth year of our reign.

ACKNOWLEDGMENTS

To my agent, Julia Lord, and her office (Riley Kellogg, and Adam, specifically). Julia and her staff are dedicated readers with excellent critical eyes and honesty. Add to that that they believe in fiction in this bleak, nonreading world, and you have a perfect office.

To my new editor, Allison McCabe, who has been receptive to my requests during the transformation of manuscript into books.

They say that writers write from their own experience. Perhaps. In my case, it was just the opposite: Alix lost her baby son at the same time that I lost my own Theo. Thus, the dedication. My son was not a prince of any realm and he was not murdered (unless you consider a brain tumor murderous), but he had the sweet imperious manner I've used in my fiction.

To my secretary, Barbara Nelson, who has faithfully typed two long historical tomes for me. *The Prince of Poison* was recorded under difficult circumstances as I sent pages from Illinois to California, but Barbara ignored gaffs and repetitions to do her job. The book couldn't have been written without her.

To my remaining son, Bruce Coy, who cared for his brother. Bruce, a first-rate historian, read the manuscript for errors.

To my late husband, Charles Kaufman, novelist and screenwriter, whose advice and criticism still reverberate in my mind.

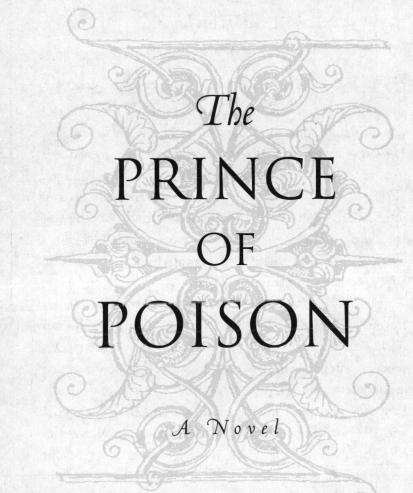

The
PRINCE
OF
POISON

A Novel

PAMELA KAUFMAN

About This Guide

For decades, Pamela Kaufman has entertained a loyal readership with the mesmerizing and often hilarious adventures of Alix of Wanthwaite, madcap medieval beauty. In *Shield of Three Lions*, the unflappable Alix braved the crusades dressed as a man to spar with the king of England over her birthright. *Banners of Gold* saw her taken hostage, drawn into a web of international politics, and entangled in the heartstrings of three different men. Now, *The Prince of Poison* finds Alix homeward bound at last, with a half-royal child in tow and an angry monarch on her trail.

Set amidst the pomp and savagery of twelfth-century Europe, the Alix of Wanthwaite trilogy renders a glorious mishmash of ruffians, peasants, troubadours, murderers, pretenders, barons, princesses, and popes in charming and disarming detail. Alix's bawdy, free-wheeling narration wickedly lampoons historical notables like Richard the Lion Heart and Eleanor of Aquitaine, spinning the historical novel in a fresh direction. This guide is designed to enhance your group's discussion of Alix's escapades in *The Prince of Poison*.

Questions for Discussion

1. Much of the action in the novel occurs at the intersection of humor and violence. The attempted rape in the novel's opening pages is dotted with puns, for example, and the horror of the shipwreck on page 85 is mitigated by the comedy of Alix resuscitating ducks. How does this affect your reading of the many tragedies in the novel, from Bok's decapitation to the murder of the pregnant woman at the gates of La Rochelle to the rape of various barons' wives and daughters? What point is the author making with this juxtaposition?

2. Of her infant son, Alix states, "I was deliriously happy to be loved without ulterior motive" (page 42). What ulterior motives drive Enoch, Bonel, and John in loving (or thinking they love) her?

3. Who leaks the news of Alix's presence in Rouen? Why does Queen Eleanor have a vested interest in helping Alix and Theo escape? Given their complex history, why does Alix trust Eleanor this time?

4. What is the symbolic significance of the poison frog that Alix nearly strokes on her way home to Wanthwaite? Why does the image recur when Alix arrives in King's Lynn? Why does Alix initially pretend to lose the little girl's frog rather

than tell her the truth about its dangers? What does this tragic scene on the beach signify?

5. How does Lord Robert convince the Pope that the assassination attempt on John was not only innocent and thus pardonable, but in fact laudable?

6. What does Cardinal Langton stand to gain by assisting the barons? What argument does he present against the writing of a charter? How does he sabotage the Magna Carta they so painstakingly compile?

7. Why has Bonel's ardor cooled by his second night at Wanthwaite? Why does he refuse Alix's offer of private acreage on Wanthwaite as a safe haven?

8. What bargaining chip does Alix gain over Queen Isabella? What weakness does it expose in John?

9. What does Bonel mean when he tells the assembly of barons: "I mean no disparagement when I say that we are all Jews together" (page 250). How does his comment affect Enoch?

ABOUT THE AUTHOR

PAMELA KAUFMAN, PH.D., created the Communications Department at Santa Monica College. She is the author of *The Book of Eleanor*, as well as *Shield of Three Lions* and *Banners of Gold*, books one and two of the bestselling Alix of Wanthwaite trilogy. She lives in Los Angeles.

ALSO BY PAMELA KAUFMAN

One of history's greatest women, celebrated by her contemporaries, descendants, and biographers, comes to life in this mesmerizing novel.

The Book of Eleanor
$ 13.95 / 0-609-80809-5

The enchanting Alix of Wanthwaite returns in a suspenseful and richly textured adventure in which nothing less than the future of England is at stake.

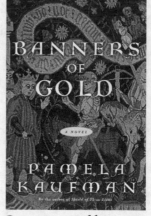

Banners of Gold
$ 13.95 / 0-609-80947-4

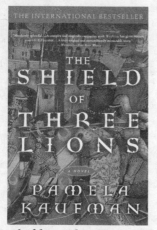

The first thrilling tale in the Alix of Wanthwaite saga.

"Superbly written . . . The richness of the characters, the historical details, and the story as a whole make this novel a memorable reading experience."

—CHICAGO SUN-TIMES

Shield of Three Lions
$ 10.95 / 0-609-80946-6